The Box of Words

Nancy Veldman

NANCY VELDMAN
with Paris Milla

ISBN: 1-4392-3952-5
ISBN-13: 9781439239520

Visit www.booksurge.com to order additional copies.

The Box of Words

Also by Nancy Veldman

To

My husband, Richard, who stood by me even though he could not hear the words being whispered in my ear from a place we cannot see. And to Trudy, my steadfast friend who also understands the purpose that permeates my life and drives me to achieve things that I otherwise would only dream about.

Prologue

Yesterday was the day Sam died. On what appeared to be a normal day in the spring, with the curtains blowing in the light breeze coming off the ocean across the way, Kate lost her soul mate of thirty years. It happened so fast that she was unable to get her breath and even think of what to say to him. He was just gone. She could feel his spirit leave the room… and suddenly, even though he was still lying there, she felt very alone. There was a quietness that she had never heard before. Silence.

The doctors had tried to prepare her for the end, but nothing really does that. All the Internet sites she had researched and all the books she had read on cancer did not prepare her for the end. He was so brave. Oh, he was brave. Sam never complained and was there for her until the end. The funeral was planned out and his place at the cemetery was ready. They had prayed together three days ago, and Sam was ready to go, to meet God face to face. He had gone over every single issue of their life that she would now have to deal with, and had laid it all out for her. Every step. But she felt so alone, so scared. With her elbows on the kitchen table, holding her head in her hands, a thought crossed Kate's mind; *I'm at a crossroads in my life.* She rubbed here eyes. *I'm fifty years old and never thought I would be alone this early in my life.*

She got up from the table and poured another cup of coffee. Sam's cup was sitting there empty. She reached over and touched the handle and smiled. A tear came rolling down her cheek as she realized again that he would never drink coffee with her in the mornings. She would never smell his cologne, kiss his lips, or touch his face with her fingers, tracing over all the lines that years of work outside had placed on his face. He was such a handsome man and they had fit so well together. A rare thing she knew only too well, for her best friends had not been so fortunate in their choices of husbands.

Kate moved away from the edge of the counter and rubbed her shoulders. It was an empty day, with no edges, wide open. An abyss to swallow her up. If she did not move, or do something, she would stop breathing.

Chapter 1

On a Saturday afternoon in June, when the smell of cut grass was in the air, and a slight breeze was coming across the trees from the ocean, Kate found herself driving around Martin City looking for a house. Her window was down, and she could smell the salty air and feel the heat of the morning sun as it was beaming down on her arm. The roads in Martin City were winding and many trees lined the streets, creating lovely shadows that danced as the wind blew. It was one of the clearest days Kate had ever seen; as the sky was bluer than her own eyes, and she had a feeling that today she might find the house that would help her go forward in her life.

Just yesterday Ella and Seth were talking to her about leaving for a month or two and going abroad for a trip that they had wanted to make since the end of their high school days. Kate was *for* the trip, because they had worked hard at the University and needed a summer break from all the cramming of exams. She encouraged them to go, knowing she would be left alone to sort out her feelings that remained from Sam's death. The children had taken it pretty well, because he had suffered quite a while; but children seem to recover quickly from tragedies. *It's the older ones like me,* she thought, *that hold on too long to the closeness that they once had.* Kate had missed Sam even before he was gone. He had been her soul mate for life, and neither had known that his life would be cut so short with an illness so debilitating. Kate brushed her hair out of her face, and smiled. *I know this is right, the children going off,* she thought. *I need this time to find a new place to live and today seems like the perfect day to do it.*

As she drove through the neighborhoods and looked at the houses listed for sale, her mind was racing through all the events that had taken place since Sam had died. It was enough to make her head spin. He had been a good man, and took care of most things about the house. The finances were not in the best of shape when he got the sickest, and she was so busy taking care of him that she couldn't even get to the bank to work it all out. All she could think about was keeping him alive, and the other things that really needed taking care of just had to be set aside. After he died, she had to face them alone, and it was not an easy task to say the least. He had made investments and some of them needed to be changed. Kate contacted a friend of the family who was with a brokerage firm and he gave her a lot of sound advice. However, after paying taxes and winding up loose ends, Kate had enough to live on and even though she could have kept the house, she felt like it might be better for her to sell it and move into a different home to facilitate a fresh start. The kids were going to be leaving soon, and she would be on her own.

Turning down Madison Avenue, Kate slowed down, as there were several homes for sale on this street. It had been one of her favorite streets growing up because there were great oaks causing a canopy over the road, and the houses were on spacious lots that somehow did not remove the feeling of warmth that she had always felt as a child. The homes were older and larger, almost like she were stepping back in time. The same street lights were lined up along the edge of the sidewalk, separated by dogwoods.

A sign was in front of Old Tom Winson's home. *I guess Old Tom finally passed away*, thought Kate, as she passed in front of the old towering antebellum home. It must have been there for over one hundred years, but was kept to perfection by Mr. Tom and his family. An iron fence covered with jasmine surrounded the yard, both front and back, giving it a feeling of privacy. Kate pulled over to the curb and sat looking at the house, enjoying the memories of years past and thinking ahead to what her needs were now. Just as she was about to get out of the car and stroll up to the house, Jim was walking by with his huge Great Dane. "Well, how could I be so lucky," he said, with a big smile and a wink.

"Hey, Jim," Kate said quickly, wishing there was a way out of this awkward situation. She was not ready to be charmed off her feet, and he was a known lady's man in the neighborhood. All the women loved him and he was a very kind-hearted soul. But not anything like Sam. Her Sam.

"What brings you to this neighborhood, lady?" Jim asked with a raised eyebrow.

"Oh I'm just window shopping for something to do," said Kate, "and I've always loved this neighborhood. It holds lots of memories for me."

Jim talked and talked, holding her there much longer than she really wanted, and she kept looking at her watch to find a way of escape. Finally, an old friend of Jim's pulled up in a Mercedes convertible, and Kate bowed out of the conversation with a "thank you, Jim, it was nice seeing you again" and hurried back to her car. She pulled out and hurried down the street, leaving a trail of smoke behind her. Jim made a mental note to call her soon for dinner.

Turning the corner to head back home, Kate spotted another home for sale on Madison Avenue. She hadn't noticed this house before. *Surely it wasn't a new home, right in the middle of this ancient neighborhood?* It was set back under trees and difficult to see from the street. Something about the house drew her, and she parked the car and walked up the long path lined in violets to the front door. There was ample landscaping in the front; blooming azaleas, iris, and her favorite, gardenias. The lawn was crisply cut and the front door was massive and stuck back into an archway, making the entrance a bit intriguing. She knocked on the door and there was no answer. Kate was disappointed, but made a note to call the owner for an appointment. There were children playing in the yards of the homes nearby, and she enjoyed for a moment the sounds of their laughter. The moment was short-lived when her phone rang. Her morning plans were over. Maria, one of her patients, was having a bad day. *I guess my house hunting will be delayed one more day*, thought Kate. She loved her job as a psychiatrist, but it was tough being on call all the time. Maria could be a pain in the neck, but she had no family to turn to.

Kate walked back to her car a little reluctantly, headed to the office, and as she pulled away from the house, she turned to look one more time.

Chapter 2

Walking in the front door with her arms full of groceries, Kate hurried to set them down on the counter, and out of the corner of her eye she caught a note lying on the table. It was from Ella. Her scribbled handwriting said that she and Seth had their travel plans underway and would be leaving in a week for Europe. She smiled knowing they must be excited, as this was their first trip that would take them so far away from home. *I wonder if I should've volunteered to go with them*, Kate mused. And then she shook her head, knowing Ella would roll her eyes on that thought. *They need to get away just as much as I do*, thought Kate. Just as she was picking up the phone to call Ella, it rang.

"Hey Katie," said this male voice she quickly recognized as Jim. *He hadn't wasted any time in calling her*, she thought. *Isn't that just like a man.*

"Hello Jim." She sighed with a raised eyebrow. Her stomach was in a knot as she knew what he was about to say, and she just wasn't ready. Two years should be long enough, and for some women it was. However, she was just not going to allow another man in yet.

"It was so good to see you today, and I thought, hey, maybe we could run out and get a bite to eat, and catch up with each other," he said with such enthusiasm.

"Well," she paused, "I really need to do some things here, Jim. I had to work this afternoon and it was a rather complicated case. Could we make it another evening?" Kate answered with less enthusiasm than she should have had.

"Oh, sure," said Jim, "I know it's spur of the moment, but I just thought I would try, since you popped up today in my world."

Kate smiled at the comment, but knew she was doing the right thing. "Thanks, Jim. I appreciate the offer, but I have so much on my plate right now."

Kate could not hang up fast enough. He was a nice guy, but at this point her life needed to be as simple as possible.

She climbed the stairs to Ella's room, pulled out a large suitcase from the closet and set it out on the bed. She stood and looked around the room which was full of girlie things that were favorites of Ella's from high school years. Kate felt a pull on her heart as she stood in her daughter's room. *One day soon I'll have an empty nest here; it is almost that way now. They both are at school,* she thought. *Really they've already moved out.* She shrugged and turned to walk away. A folded note caught her eye as she was headed toward the door. She bent over, picked up the note and unfolded it. She could tell it was a letter written to Ella from a boy she had dated last year. She almost read the words but thought better of it. She carefully placed the note on the dresser and walked out of the room. *Trust. Respect. Hard to do when you are a mother.* But she trusted Ella, and felt good about most of the guys she dated. *One of these days it was going to happen; she was going to fall in love,* she thought as she left the room.

Next she went into Seth's room. There was a faint smell in the room that reminded her of his football days. *Why did a guy's room always smell? It was hard to get rid of the odor, even after he graduated high school. Oh well, one day I'll wish I could smell it!* She reached into the closet and pulled down the huge suitcase and dusted it off. Seth hadn't been anywhere in so long the suitcase was practically new. She laid the suitcase on the bed and opened it to make sure it was not full of trash from Seth's last trip with friends to the beach. As she lifted the straps to check out the inside of the top of the suitcase, her hand hit a corner of an envelope that was tucked into a sleeve. *What is this,* she chuckled to herself; *my day to find secret notes?* She pulled out the envelope and was surprised to see that it was a note addressed to Sam. *He must have used this suitcase on one of his hunting trips,* she thought. Her hand was shaking as she held the letter, but she lifted the flap of the envelope and slid out the letter. It was a short note, handwritten in a woman's handwriting. Her throat closed up and she sat down on the bed, her heart racing in her chest. *What had Sam done?*

Her eyes scanned the note. It was very short, but intimate.

Sam,

I'm sorry I missed you this weekend. Will catch you on your next trip to the lodge.

Yours, Alison

Kate was afraid to move, afraid to breathe. *What did this mean? Oh please, don't let this mean Sam was having an affair! How could that be? How did I not know this?*

She sat up straight and held the letter, thinking about the past few years and how much they had done together. *How could he have had time to have an affair? Did this woman always meet him at the hunting lodge? How long had this been going on?* Her mind was racing. There was no address on this envelope, and no way to know who this woman was. Kate stood and picked up the envelope, tucked the note back inside and walked downstairs into her bedroom. Her eyes filled with tears as she sat down on her bed, their bed, and lay back on her pillow.

So this was how the end of his life with me will end. Kate was sure he had no idea she would ever find out. He had been good to her until the very end, so there was no reason ever to think he was being unfaithful. She closed her eyes, with tears running down her face and thought of all the years they'd had together. Her heart was beating wildly in her chest and she knew she needed to calm down. *Why would Sam ever have felt like he needed to have an affair? How could I have missed this? Surely I'm wrong and there is a good explanation for this note.*

She had to find a way to work through this without totally losing her mind. This note had thrown her for a loop to say the least. It was the last thing she thought she would ever find in Seth's suitcase. She walked downstairs and headed for the kitchen. It had been a long day and even though she was a not hungry, she prepared a quick hot meal and sat down to watch the news to get her mind off the note. She couldn't focus on anything because her mind kept wandering back to the note and Sam. *Talk about something coming right out of the blue! This has totally hit me blind-sided. I would never have thought Sam would have an affair. I don't want to over react, but this does not look good. How can I find out the truth? I don't even know where to begin looking. . . .*

Kate tried to get her mind off the note and ate some of her dinner. It still felt weird in a way to be eating alone, although she should have been used to that by now. She laid her plate on the end table, unfinished, and leaned back to rest her head on the back of Sam's favorite chair. *He always enjoyed sitting in this chair,* she remembered. She slowly closed her eyes wanting to escape the thoughts she was having of Sam being unfaithful to her, and drifted into a fitful sleep. She woke suddenly, almost like a noise had disturbed her, and went upstairs, leaving her plate on the end table. She lay back on her bed and without taking her clothes off; she finally fell into a deep sleep. The note lay beside her on the bed.

Chapter 3

The sun was coming through the thin curtains in the bedroom, stirring up the dust in the room, and causing the sunbeams to show up across the bed. Kate stretched and sat up. She had been asleep all night in her clothes. She rubbed her eyes and looked at the clock beside the bed; it said nine o'clock. Her head was foggy, but suddenly it all came back to her. She looked down and there was the envelope lying on her pillow where she'd left it. She put her hand on her forehead and felt dizzy for a moment. *What am I supposed to do with this note?*

She reached down beside the bed and put her slippers on, grabbed the note, and walked down the stairs. On the way to the kitchen, she passed photograph after photograph of Sam, the children, and herself on the walls. She teared up for a second, and then went to the kitchen to make some coffee. Her mind was racing through all the years with Sam, trying to think of any time that she might have missed that would have given her a clue. She could think of nothing, but it was there, somewhere. She poured a cup of coffee, sat down at the table and reached for the phone. She needed a woman to talk to, and Susan was the perfect friend to call. They'd been friends since childhood, and even though their lives were different, they understood each other to the core.

The phone rang a few times before Susan answered.

Kate hesitated a moment and said, "Hi Susan. It's Kate. Do you have some time this morning? We need to have a talk."

There was a silence on the other end, and then Susan cheerfully said, "Of course, Kate. Is everything okay? Are you having a bad day again?"

Kate paused, thinking of what to say next. "Oh, it's a bad day, alright. I'll wait for you to get here to say anymore. What time can you come?"

"I'll be there in about twenty minutes. I can give you about two hours, but that's all today. Hang in there. I'll be there soon."

Kate stood up and walked to the window. The sun was shining so bright and it was such a clear summer day. Nothing had changed in her world except for the note. The kids were happy about their trip, and she loved her job and even was excited about looking for a new place to live. But the note was so unexpected and what it might represent was so shocking. She had a sick feeling in her stomach that probably wouldn't go away for a while. *Susan will be good for me,* thought Kate. *She'll be able to be more objective and will help me sort this out quickly. It's been two years since Sam died, and none of this should darken my memory of him.*

Waiting for Susan, Kate walked into her office at the house and looked over the stack of mail. *What a pain to go through all of this today,* she thought. Most of the mail was junk mail and she dumped it immediately into the trash. The bills were light and she stacked them on the check book. She lifted the laptop open and began checking her emails. As she sat down, she scanned the last few weeks and saw that most of her mail was junk mail with the occasional client emailing her of a new problem that had arisen. She had decided early on to allow her patients to email her about things so that it saved some time in the office. She kept all the information in their files so she could refer back to it, and it seemed to actually calm most of them down to know they had access to her between visits.

Suddenly she had an idea. *What if Sam had corresponded online with this Alison?* She went back into emails and checked to see if any were still there from two years ago. She found a few but nothing seemed out of character. Then she looked under sent mail. There were a lot more emails saved in this file, and her heart started beating faster for fear that she would come up on something. There was one email Sam had sent to a business, and she opened it up. This looked interesting, and Kate began reading the email. It didn't say much, except after talking about his day, he simply said, "see you soon. Love Sam." Kate felt anger rising up in her. *Was he that stupid to think she wouldn't find this at some point?* Then she had to laugh, for it had been over two years and she hadn't even thought to look. The email didn't have a name on it. It was a company email. So she didn't know if this was Alison or not.

The door opened and in bounced Susan, with her new Shitz Tzu puppy, Lola, and a bag of fresh donuts. "Hey, girl!" said Susan. Kate jumped up and hugged her, and for a minute didn't want to let go.

They parted and Kate said, "Please, let's go into the kitchen at the table and have some coffee and hit those wonderful donuts I smell." Kate grabbed the laptop and they headed into the kitchen.

Seated at the table, Susan got right to the point. "So what's so important this morning? I thought you'd be at work by now," she said with a raised eyebrow.

Kate poured her a cup of coffee and sat down, putting her elbows on the table and resting her chin on them. "Well, you won't believe what I'm going to tell you, my dear friend," Kate said quite slowly. "I know you're in a hurry this morning, so I'm going to get right to the point. I was upstairs getting suitcases down for Ella and Seth, and found an envelope in Seth's suitcase that was for Sam. He had left it there by mistake when he returned from his last hunting trip," She brushed her blonde hair off her face and looked straight at her friend.

Susan looked back at Kate warily and said, "Uh oh. You don't look too happy. You might as well tell me what it says."

Kate moved her chair back a little and took the envelope and laid it in front of Susan. "You open it. See for yourself."

Susan took the envelope and pulled out the note. She read it quietly and showed no emotion on her face. She looked up at Kate and said, "Who in the heck is Alison? Where did she come from? And how long had this been going on?"

Kate looked down, and then back at her friend. "I have no idea, and I had no clue that Sam was even seeing anyone. I found something else this morning on my laptop, as I was checking my emails. I went into the *sent mail* and found one email to a business that I didn't recognize, but opened it to find this." Kate pushed the laptop towards Susan and let her read the simple email. "There was no name, nothing. So you see, I've been mourning Sam, and now I discover he was possibly involved with someone else. I can't help but be angry, Susan!"

Susan was thoughtful for a moment and then pushed her chair back a little. She looked at Kate and smiled. "We don't know much about this whole thing right now. We may be jumping to conclusions here. Let's not build a case against Sam until we know more facts. What if this was legit? What if there was another reason for this note?" Kate saw her point and mustered a smile. She had never mistrusted Sam, not even once in all the years they were married. Surely there would be an explanation here that would erase all her doubt.

"You're right. I'm still a little fragile because I'm missing Sam so much. And you know, it really doesn't matter now. He's gone, and I may have no way of ever finding out about Alison." The two women began catching up on the last few months and made an agreement to meet for lunch soon. The donuts were left on the table, and the two friends strolled arm in arm to the front door.

"Hey, Katie, don't let this eat at you. You mentioned you were going to look for a house, right? Well get on with it. Don't let anything stop you from going forward in your life. I know this hurts, but Sam did love you, and you need to remember the good things so that you can move on, right?" Susan hugged Kate and they looked at each other.

Kate smiled and agreed. "Yes, we did have a good marriage and maybe I'm freaking out over nothing. I'll put it aside for now, at least. And I'll keep you posted on any house that I fall in love with!" Kate walked her best friend to the door and thanked her for coming by on such a short notice. As she closed the door, she took a deep sigh and put her hands on her face. *I guess I'd better get to work*, she thought, and walked back into the kitchen. The sight of the envelope on the table made her feel weak again, but she picked it up so that the kids would not see it if they stopped by today.

As Kate walked upstairs to her bedroom to get a shower, she again saw the photos on the wall of her family. *Do we ever really know someone*, she pondered, staring into Sam's face. "I thought I did," she whispered. "I thought I knew you, Sam."

Chapter 4

The Westley Medical Building was an old masterpiece in the center of town. Kate loved her office. It was on the fourth floor and had a wall of windows looking out over the town. There were great oaks stretching across Main Street in town and the sidewalks were lined in crepe myrtles all in bloom. She sat at her desk waiting for her first patient of the day. Her head was clearer and she felt better being at work where she could focus on solutions to problems that were not her own.

On her computer she was searching houses for sale in Martin City. She'd already looked at the morning paper after Susan left, but sometimes there were more listed on the internet than in the paper. She had no pre-conditions on the type of house she was looking for; she just knew when she saw it that it would be the right one for her. As she was browsing the sites available, a knock on her door interrupted her day dreaming. It was John, her first patient of the day.

She pulled his file and began looking through it as he was getting comfortable on the sofa. She was reminded of the fact that he had had a terrible childhood, physical abuse, and both parents were alcoholics. She dove into the hour and lost herself in the words of pain and struggle. As she moved through her patients for the day, one by one, she was unaware of the time and did not even think about the envelope for the rest of the day. She had one phone call from Laney, another schoolteacher friend, who wanted to have dinner with her after work. She made a mental note to call her back between clients. *It would be refreshing to get out tonight* .

"Hey Laney," Kate said laughing. "I've missed you so much, and I cannot wait to see you tonight."

"Me too, Kate, It will be fun to have a quiet dinner somewhere and catch up on the last few weeks," said Laney. "I've had a busy week and could use the company."

"I agree. And I have a lot to share with you. So let's meet at 6:30 at Rondell's, if that's okay with you?" Kate could already smell the delicious aroma of Rondell's. It was a *fine dining* restaurant but had a middle of the road price. That made it perfect for a good evening with a friend. She knew the chef there and he always did something special for her when she showed up with a friend. It used to be her and Sam's favorite place to go. She did need to watch her money until she decided about the house and where to move, but she also needed this time with her friend.

"See you at 6:30, Kate," said Laney.

After seeing patients it was about time to wrap up the day. She made notes while things were still fresh in her mind. So many people hurting. It could be overwhelming if she had not learned to let things go when she walked out of the office. She was the only psychiatrist in the building, and she was busy every day with more than her share of patients. It helped tremendously having her work to depend on after Sam died. Even through his illness, she was able to focus on her patients. Now it was even more important that she had this work to occupy her mind. If she didn't watch it, that one envelope that was now hidden in one of her dresser drawers could ruin everything in her life.

The restaurant was full, and she was seated in one of the side booths, where they could have some privacy. She had arrived first, before Laney. It gave her time to get her thoughts together and decide what to say and what not to say. *Laney is a good friend, but I'm not sure whether to bring up the envelope or not,* thought Kate. *I think I will play it by ear.*

Laney came on time and Kate scooted out of her seat and hugged her. "What a wonderful idea you had tonight!" Kate said with a broad smile.

Laney hugged her back and took her place at the table. "Well, I knew if we didn't make a date, this would get put off for another week or two. So I took a chance that you might be free, and it worked."

Kate passed her a menu, and sat back in the seat. "Well, Ella and Seth are going to Europe for a couple of months. They just broke the news to me recently and I really think it's a great idea. They need to get away, and it'll give me time to regroup and make some badly needed decisions in my life," Kate explained.

"Wow!" Laney exploded. "That's absolutely fabulous. I'm so proud of them, and I know you are too! When are they leaving?"

"I'm not sure, but they mentioned in about a week." said Kate, casually. She was at peace with them going, so there was no tension in her voice about this trip.

"I'm very proud of my kids and it's a chance of a lifetime that they get to take this trip. Soon their lives will be full of responsibility and stress and I want them to have this time to see what the world is about."

"I agree," said Laney with a big smile. "I wish I could've had children, but I've watched you with yours and know you're very proud of them. So what's new, Kate, other than this fabulous trip?"

Kate chose her meal on the list of rich entrees, and gave her menu to the waiter. Normally the wait staff here were men, but this was a young woman maybe in her thirties and she was very quiet. Laney placed her order and then they were left alone again to finish catching up.

"Well, Laney. I know it's been two years since Sam died, but I still deal with issues about his leaving me and am not ready to get into a relationship yet. In my line of work, I know this can take time. It's different for every person and how they deal with a loss, but I had no idea I would still feel like it happened yesterday." Kate hesitated, and then added, "I'm looking for a new house; something that's different and that helps catapult me into a new life. I've been looking over in the area of Madison Avenue, because I grew up near there and it has a lot of good memories for me. You know how that neighborhood feels? The trees are massive and there are so many well kept older homes there."

"I do. I love that neighborhood. Have you found many homes for sale in there?" Laney asked, surprised that Kate could move out of the home she raised her kids in.

"Oh yes, there are several great homes for sale, and I'm going over there soon to check some of them out. I'm impressed by the way the neighborhood has remained so well kept and I do see young families living there. That brings such life to an area. I don't want a bunch of old fogies living there who aren't outdoors much. I love to hear children playing." Kate laughed.

"I might call you and see if you want to go with me to see the inside of some of the homes, and also get your feel of the area. What do you think about that?" *It might feel good to have someone with me,* Kate thought. *This is a big step and I don't want to be entirely emotional about my decision.*

"That would be fun, Katie. Just call me and I'll run over and check it out with you. I have the summer off and this could be a fun adventure. I'm making a few trips while I'm off, but James and I also want to do some work around the house, so I'm sure I can find the time to go with you."

13

The two friends enjoyed their meal together and soon Kate was pulling into her driveway, ready to relax and get her mind wrapped around moving and the change it would bring into her life. As she walked into the house, the face of the waitress came into her mind, and she stopped in her tracks. She remembered something that had happened during dinner. After she had ordered, the waitress had taken her menu, and said "Thank you, Mrs. Morrison." She had not even paid any attention to it when she ordered, because she and Laney were talking so much. But now it occurred to her that this waitress knew who she was. *She knew my name. . . Did the owner of the restaurant recognize me and share this information with the waitress? There was no name tag on her blouse. Who was she? Do I know her, and not recognize her? Oh well,* Kate thought. *It probably is nothing to even think about. I know am tired,* she thought. *Maybe I am overreacting a little about this. But, it still bothers me that the waitress knew my name.*

When Kate lay down on her bed, turning out the lights, she closed her eyes and the face of the waitress smiling at her was what she saw. Her sleep was restless and unfulfilling. She wrote it off as stress from worrying about the note, and her desire to move out of a home she had been in for many years; most of her adult life.

The waitress went home and could not sleep at all. Her stomach was in a knot, and tears were streaming down her face.

Chapter 5

Kate woke to the sound of Ella and Seth arguing in the kitchen. For a moment she felt like she had slipped back in time, when the children were younger and always fighting. She sat up and stretched, knowing she had a full day ahead of her. She put on her robe, brushed her hair, looked in the mirror at herself long and hard, and frowned. *All of this stress is getting to me,* she thought. *Maybe I need some time away; a weekend away with the girls to get my mind clear and then I'll be ready to make a decision on a house.*

She slipped downstairs quietly and peeked around the corner into the kitchen. Her grown son and daughter were sitting there, one at the table, one sitting on the countertop, talking about their trip and laying out their game plan. Seth wanted to go to England first and Ella wanted Paris. Back and forth they went until they suddenly realized that they were being watched.

"Oh for heavens sake, you two. Are you still at it, after all these years?" laughed Kate. "I'm enjoying this, so early in the morning. What are you fighting about?" She aimed her question at Seth, as he was the eldest of the two. Seth stretched out his long legs and looked at his mother. *She is a lovely woman,* he thought. *I know that she misses Dad, and she has to be lonely. Here we are leaving her.*

"Mother, Ella's being her stubborn self again! She always wants her way. Paris is fine, but England has history, castles, so much that I want to see first. We have some friends who would meet us there and then continue on our trip with us. It'll be more fun if we travel as a group and stay together," Seth said stubbornly.

Ella jumped down from the countertop and said angrily, "Seth you're driving me nuts. I don't want a lot of people around. Oh Mother, do something with him, will you?" Ella stomped out of the room and Seth looked at his mother and smiled sarcastically.

"See Mom? She hasn't changed one single bit since high school. What do I do with her? She has never been to Europe and we have friends that have been several times and know all the places to go. I'm going to stick with this plan, and she's just going to have to adjust. Don't you think, Mom?" He looked at her with such frustration that she could not help but laugh.

"I think you are very wise, Mr. Seth" Kate said, and leaned over and gave him a kiss on the cheek. "Be sure and leave me your itinerary so I can keep up with where you are. What are your flight plans? And do you need me to take you to the airport?" She was so excited about this trip for them. "I know you're going to have a ball, and I'm thrilled you both have this wonderful opportunity before finishing college and hitting the real world!!"

Kate walked over to the window and looked out at the sky. "You know, Seth, I've been looking at houses lately, and I haven't talked about it much with you and Ella. I hope you're okay with this, as I really feel it's something that'll help me move on in my life. You know I miss your father terribly, but everything in this house reminds me of him so much that it's nearly impossible for me to go forward in my emotions. Do you understand any of that?" Kate looked at her son. It was incredible how he looked like Sam. Strong features, very masculine, dark hair, dark eyes. It was hard to look at him this morning, for some reason.

"Mom, I totally get it. Just relax and do what you have to do, okay? Don't even think of me and Ella. We are cool with it." Seth got up, walked toward his mom, and reached over and hugged her.

"You better get breakfast and get ready for work. Did you see what time it is?" Kate looked at the clock on the wall and laughed. She had overslept by an hour.

"Seth, please look at me. We're both in such a hurry every time we see each other; I need to know you're okay inside. That you feel grounded and have a direction in your life." Kate pulled him to her. Just as she was about to say more to Seth, Ella popped her head around the corner.

"Mom! Why are you selling the house? Why do you feel like you have to move? I love this house. It's all I know. It holds all the memories of this family. If you move we will have no history in that new house." Ella was already near tears because of her fight with Seth, and now this just added to her stress.

"I know it'll be hard," said Kate, going towards her to give her a hug. "Just know I need this so that I can move forward. I'm not rushing into anything. Just looking. You and Seth go have fun and when you get back, maybe I will have found something that I feel comfortable with." Kate felt tightness in her chest, but did not let on.

"Okay you two. I'm going to head upstairs and get ready for work. I probably have a full slate of patients coming in today. Have a great day and get this thing settled between you so you can have a good trip." She waved them on, and went upstairs to shower and dress. The phone rang as she entered her bedroom and she grabbed it.

"Hey Kate, This is Jim. I know you are busy, but couldn't we have dinner tonight? I'm still remembering how nice you looked the other day, and I sure would love to take you to dinner." Kate caught her breath. *Will this guy ever give it up? She really didn't want to go, but how could she keep turning him down without being just outright ugly to him?* She ran her fingers through her hair and laughed. *It's becoming a joke, really.*

"Ok, Jim, you win. I'll go to dinner with you. I should be off around 5:30 so I'll see you here at 6:30?" There was a slight pause on the other end, and then Jim jumped in.

"Of course, that is perfect. I'll pick you up at 6:30 prompt. I hope you have a terrific day." Jim breathed a sigh of relief and sat back in his chair grinning.

Kate sat down on the bed and rubbed her head. *What had she done just then? She really didn't want to go. Oh well, I guess one date won't hurt anything,* she muttered under her breath. She showered, dressed, checked herself in the mirror and hurried downstairs to get her coffee and rush to work. She hated being late more than anything.

Kate had a pile of mail to go through when she got to work and emails to answer. She checked her schedule and noticed appointments in the morning, but the afternoon was completely open. That meant she would have time this afternoon to sneak off and do some house hunting.

With that energy, her first patient walked in, and Kate was ready to solve some problems. She had done some serious research about some new drugs that were out on the market. She also wanted this patient to consider aggressive exercise methods to encourage her endorphins to give her a feeling of well being. She tended to be a lazy person, and this added to her depression. In the back of Kate's mind was the dinner date she had agreed to, reluctantly. Hoping she hadn't made a bad move, she let the thought go and focused on her patient.

This woman had struggled for years with deep depression, and the whole family was tired of it. She had threatened suicide many times and her husband's nerves were shot. So the research was promising on these new drugs and she was excited to share this with her client. *Changing lives is what this office is all about,* Kate thought. *Not just writing prescriptions.* But this has been a very difficult case. Complicated to say the least. Depression is a confusing illness, and there's no quick fix. It was her plan to start this woman on a road to healing, and they were about to delve into many issues that might cause the woman much stress.

"Goodmorning, Judy. Please sit down." Kate could already see the tension on her patient's face.

"Goodmorning. Although I rarely have good mornings anymore. I almost cancelled this appointment because I don't ever see myself getting any better."

"Well, I see it another way, Judy. I've seen huge strides on your part in trying to open up more about your past. It's going to be a long slow road to healing. But you are making efforts, even if you do feel you take two steps back every time you make any headway."

"I'm still so angry at my father and mother that I don't know how I can ever come to grips with how all this was allowed to happen. I mean, we were all under the same roof, you know? She knew it was happening to me. She had to know."

"Did you ever talk to her about it? Was she able to hear what you were trying to tell her, as a child?"

"No, Dr. Kate. She raised her hands up and said she didn't want to ever hear me speak of this again. Do you know what that does to a child? I lived this hell all alone. No one wanted a part of it."

"I know that had to be devastating, Judy. After she made that statement to you, did you ever go back to her as you were growing older, to try to bring it up again?"

"No. I basically shut down toward her and anyone else in the family. I felt like I was nothing to them; that my life did not matter, much less my feelings about the filth of what was happening."

"There is a lot of abuse in families that remains hidden, and it is not uncommon for the other parent to deny it for years and years. When they finally do face the situation squarely, it takes years for them to deal with all of the emotions that they tucked away for so long."

Kate listened as Judy poured out her heart again about the destruction and abuse she suffered. At one point she tried to steer the conversation towards the present and Judy's future.

"I want you to work on something Judy. I'm going to ask you to make a list of your dreams for your future and what you would like to change about the present. Be relaxed when you write these things down, as there are no incorrect answers. And Judy, I'm proud of how far you have come. Don't be so hard on yourself, okay? You're a very intelligent, productive woman and I feel confident that you'll get past this portion of your path to healing inside."

Judy left the office with a slight smile at the corners of her mouth. *It had been a year and they were still talking about the first few years of abuse,* she thought. *But maybe, just maybe she might make it through this window of struggle and have a good life after all.*

Before Kate knew it, it was one o'clock and her patient list was all checked off. She stood up and stretched. A lot of emotional garbage had been shoveled through today. She felt good about what had been accomplished and grabbed her purse to run out the door, before the phone could ring and ruin this opportunity to house shop. She stood looking out the window of her office for a moment, watching the crowd. People were walking in all directions with such a purpose. Suddenly, she spotted a woman standing still in the middle of the sidewalk and she was looking up at Kate's building. Kate watched her for a few minutes but couldn't tell who it was, or even if it was anyone she knew. The girl stood for a few more seconds, seeming to wipe her eyes, and then walked away, losing herself in the crowd of people going to lunch.

That was strange, thought Kate as she hit the elevators to go down to her car. *I wonder what that girl was looking at?* It could've been anything. She let the thought go and hurried to her car so she could enjoy the afternoon. Even though the summer was heating up already for June, there was a nice breeze blowing off the ocean. Kate just realized again that she never took the time to walk on the beach, and made a promise to herself that she would go and walk on the beach very soon.

There's something about the ocean that calls you, she pondered. *It's so deep and unending. It might help me relax,* she measured. She turned at the light and headed to her favorite place in all the world; Madison Avenue.

Chapter 6

This was where she met the man of her dreams. Walking home from school one day, she felt someone coming up behind her, and it was Sam. He smiled his charming little smile and asked her if he could walk her home. He'd been trying to get the nerve to ask her for weeks and finally just decided to take a risk. She was floored, as she'd had a crush on him all through high school, and here in her senior year, he was making a pass at her! Kate blushed as she remembered that treasured day with Sam. He was so young then.

As they grew up and dated in college, Sam walked her back down Madison Avenue to propose. So for her to end up on this street after his death would be like coming home. The kids just didn't understand that, and she couldn't expect them to. It was something between her and Sam, and she would keep it that way. *I know he's smiling at me now*, she thought. She turned the car up into the driveway of Old Tom Winsons' home, and walked up to the door. There was an agent there on duty, so Kate walked right in and asked if she could walk through the home.

"Of course you can look around. I'm Mary Hughes and I'll be more than happy to answer any questions you might have."

Kate smiled and shook her hand. "Oh, I've been here before. I used to have a girl friend that lived here. This house belonged to her grandfather and then passed on to her father. I spent the night here several times."

Mary was surprised and told Kate to take her time and look around. She went back to her desk near the front door and Kate walked back into the kitchen.

It was almost like stepping down memory lane as she meandered around the house. A lot had been done to change the face of the house inside. New hardwood floors, new banister on the stairway, new kitchen appliances. But it still had a feel of the past floating through the halls and rooms. She could almost hear the voices of the family that had lived there when she was young. The house was too big for her, but she just had to take the opportunity to look one more time. She went into the family room which was called the den back then, and there was a baby grand piano in the corner. She walked over and tinkled the keys. *Oh well*, thought Kate. *At least I can say that I came back to this old house. Susan would remember this house I'm sure.* She smiled to herself as she walked back to the front door and thanked Mary for the tour.

"Have a great day, Kate" said Mary sweetly. Hope you find the house you're looking for."

Kate pulled out of the driveway and drove down the street further, to the house she was really curious about. It was the one tucked back off the street. It looked like someone was there because a car was parked in the driveway when she pulled in. She walked up the path to the door and knocked. A male voice answered "Come in, please."

Kate walked in and introduced herself to the sales agent.. "My name is Kate Morrison and I'm interested in looking at this house. I've been by one other time and the house was locked. I'm so glad you're here today so that I can finally look inside."

The gentleman walked up to her and held out his hand. "I'm Stephen Jones, and this is my parents' home. They passed away last year, and I've finally reached a point where I can sell their house."

"I'm sorry, Stephen. I know it must be difficult to part with a home that holds so many memories for you. Actually, that's exactly what I'm doing. Our house that we raised our children in is up for sale." He was a handsome man, and she noticed that he did not have a ring on his finger. Her mind ran away with her as she looked around the room.

"I'm fond of this house, but if I can find just the right person to sell it to, my mind will be at ease. After all, we'll always have our memories, right?"

Kate smiled and nodded. She drifted into the front room and noticed that the ceiling was vaulted and with a large chandelier. It was massive and would light up the whole front living space. As she looked to her left there was a stairway that wound around and ended at the next floor with a wrought iron banister. The floors were a rich wood and the house smelled clean and fresh. The house sat at the end of a cul-de-sac where there were more trees. Two streets over was a winding road that ran along the ocean, so in the evening or early morning when it was still quiet, the ocean could be heard. Kate loved the ocean, so this was a plus for her in choosing this as her own home. She entered the main living room and noticed huge windows at the back of the room that faced the back yard. To the left of the living room was the master bedroom, and then to the right was the kitchen.

Kate walked through each room, and pulled out a notebook to jot down things she loved about the house. It was a little large for her, but the layout was perfect. She felt at home in the house immediately. Somehow she knew this house was for her. In the hearth room Kate whispered "Sam, do you think this is a good thing? It feels so good being here... I know you would love to live on Madison Avenue with me." She teared up for a moment, but kept on moving through the house, knowing the more she saw, the more she would feel like it was right for her.

Stephen found her walking through the laundry room and asked her some questions.

"Kate, would there be more than just you living in this house?"

Kate turned smiled. "No, it's just me right now. My children are in college and are about to leave for a long trip to Europe before they graduate from college. So I would be the only one here if I bought the house. It does feel nice to me, and I somehow feel very comfortable here. Its odd how we can suddenly feel like something belongs to us or that we were meant to be in a certain place at a certain time in our lives. That's how I feel about this house. Hope that doesn't sound strange to you!"

Stephen smiled. "I know that feeling well, because I spent many years in this house, so near the beach. My parents had moved here before I was born, and my whole life was in this house." Stephen stared at her for a moment. It almost made Kate uncomfortable for his eyes seemed to look right through her.

"It's funny how we can attach ourselves to a place when we are young, and we want things to remain the same as we grow older. It never does. Nothing ever stays the same. I know that only too well." Kate headed for the front of the house.

"Feel free to come back and look anytime, to help make up your mind. Here's my card. Call me, and I'll open the house up again anytime."

Kate thanked him and walked back to the front door.

"The house is lovely, Stephen. I'm going to give this some serious thought in the next few days, as I would hate for you to sell it before I make up my mind."

"Somehow I get the feeling that you just might be the one who needs to live here. You already seem to have an innate feel for the house. Forgive me if I'm sounding a bit weird about it."

Kate turned to look at him face to face and said "No, not at all. I appreciate your honesty. You'll be hearing from me very soon. I promised to bring one of my friends house shopping with me, and I want her to see this house. It can't be an emotional purchase for me, and she is good about speaking her mind." Stephen laughed and held out is hand.

"Thank you for stopping by, and I hope you come back very soon." He held her hand for a moment, looking straight into her eyes. Then he dropped it and stepped back. Kate walked out the door a little moved, not only by how comfortable she felt in the house, but also the feelings she had when Stephen held her hand.

Stephen looked out the window as Kate walked away. His wife had died suddenly ten years ago with cancer. He had turned to stone when she left. Somehow that stone was cracking a little, and Stephen smiled to himself. She was beautiful.

Kate started the car and drove home slowly, treasuring the warm feelings she'd had in that house. *Yes, I do believe this is the one. It happened so quickly that it almost seems too good to be true. But sometimes things do happen fast, don't they?* Kate rubbed her eyes and pulled into her driveway. She sat there moment thinking about her day; the patients she had worked with, the young woman she saw staring up at her building. The talk with Seth this morning. Ella being upset about her selling the house.

This has been quite a day, Kate thought as she walked into the house. The kitchen was a mess from the kids being there this morning. Their cereal bowls were in the sink, a knife was out on the counter near the toaster, and glasses were still sitting on the table. A note was there, written by Seth in his scrawling writing:

Mom, we figured it all out. We are going to England first and Ella has agreed that the other friends being along is a good thing. Can you believe she gave in? It ain't right mom. But I won't argue that point anymore. Lol. Thanks for the talk this morning. We love you and will get the itinerary to you in a couple of days. Hope today was good, Mom.

Love, Seth

What a nice note, thought Kate as she cleaned up the kitchen. *I sure love those kids.* She wandered upstairs to change clothes. Her date would be here soon. Regretfully so. But she would at least get a good meal, and right now she was starving!

Chapter 7

In the middle of town, in an apartment building full of people, there was a young woman who was alone. Lying in her bed, she cried herself to sleep. Her life had come to a crossroads and she did not know which way to turn. There was no one she could talk to, and she didn't feel safe telling her parents. Her best friend wouldn't like what she was going to tell her, so she spared her the mess.

Her room was full of lovely things, and she had a closet full of clothes. She had travelled many places and she had eaten at the best of restaurants. But all of it had been hidden, and now she was at a place where she thought she would never be. She had heard all her life that making decisions that hurt others was never a wise move. You would be found out one day.

Before she lay down, she pulled out a letter that was written three years ago. She had unfolded it so many times that the edges were fringed and worn:

Sweet angel,

I know you are having a hard time knowing how to deal with things. I am here for you. I am only trying to make your life better, and I despise having to do this all in secret. I know you understand why I can never speak about you to anyone. It would destroy my family. Even though, I know you are part of me, I have to remain hidden when I see you. I love you with all my heart, and want you to keep your chin up. Somehow we will make it through this.

Don't ever forget my love for you. No matter what happens.

Love, Sam

The letter was lying on the bed beside her as she fell asleep. Tears were running down her cheeks and wetting the pillow. Her heart had turned to stone. And it was nearly impossible to breathe without him. He was all she had. And now he was gone.

Chapter 8

Jim walked up to the door and waited just a second before he rang the door-bell. He was sure she didn't want to go. He didn't know why she did not like him, and he was sure he had done nothing to repel her. But he could feel it every time he saw her out somewhere. She was so lovely and he couldn't help wanting to get to know her better. She just seemed so illusive.

He stepped up and rang the bell. Inside he heard someone hurrying to the door. It opened and there was Kate.

"Hey, Jim, how are you? I'm almost ready, so please step in for a second and let me get my purse." Kate ran upstairs and got her purse and checked again in the mirror. Her hair was a little frizzy from the dampness of the air. She adjusted her skirt and put some lip gloss over her lipstick to tone it down; she was as ready as she would ever be. She looked at herself in the mirror and shook her head. "I have no idea why I agreed to go tonight," she whispered to the image in the mirror. "But I'll make the best of it for one night."

Walking down the stairs, she saw Jim looking up at her. He was overwhelmed with her grace. He took her hand and walked her to the door. She got her keys out and turned and locked it as they went out. "So tell me about your day, Kate. How many patients do you see in a day? And do you ever get overloaded with their problems?"

"I never get tired of listening to my patients. But I do run out of time at the end of the day. I can usually see about eight or ten people a day, depending on how long they need. I've done this for so long that it's second nature to me, and yet, it hasn't lost the satisfaction I feel when I have helped someone over a hurdle in their life."

He listened contentedly. "I can relate to that. I love being a photographer, and even though it carries its own stress with trying to please everyone involved, I still get joy out of the finished product.. I've always wanted to do it, and had toyed around for years taking photos everywhere I went. I've spent a lot of money on cameras and equipment, and now have a great set up at home where I can do portraits and family shots. I often go to the ocean to take photos of people and children."

It didn't really add up to Kate, as she listened, for he was such an extrovert and so talkative. But somehow there was a creative side to him that he had found later in life.

"I would never have dreamed you are doing this, Jim" said Kate, smoothing her hair out. "I'm amazed at how late in life you found this new talent."

Jim laughed and said, "I thought you might be surprised. There is a lot you don't know about me, Kate."

"I know all the women love you. It's just that photography is such a settled career, and it doesn't seem to fit your personality somehow. Anyway, I'm so happy you enjoy it and I look forward to seeing your work. Now where are we eating tonight?"

"I heard from someone that your favorite place to eat was at Rondell's, so I made a reservation for two, if that's okay with you?"

Kate was taken aback and wondered who he had spoken with. *Was it Laney?* Anyway, she tried to relax and appear unphased. "Of course, Jim, that's wonderful. I'm hungry and they have the best food around, in my opinion." So she sat back and enjoyed the drive along the beach to the restaurant.

When they entered the restaurant, the maitre d' took Jim's name and found the reservation. He then took Kate on his arm and Jim followed to a corner seat near the back of the restaurant, where they would have more privacy. Kate raised her eyebrow at this, but was not too worried. Jim seemed pretty calm tonight, and she was determined to be nice. Jim pulled her chair out for her, and as she seated herself, he touched her arm and then sat down across from her. Kate remembered the waitress and looked around the room to see if she saw her. She was no where in sight.

The evening went quickly with all of the conversation; Jim wasn't one for a pause and jumped from subject to subject, entertaining her through the whole dinner. She was a little more at ease with him than she anticipated. The food, the low lighting, and her tiredness helped her relax around him a little.

"Jim, I might want you to take Seth and Ella's photos soon. I haven't taken many since they have grown into young adults, and it would be wonderful to have some professional photos of them. Is that possible after they return from their trip to Europe?"

"I would be happy to take their photographs. Just let me know when you expect them to return, and I'll set aside time to do some work for you. I wouldn't mind shooting some of you, also. I'm sure the children would appreciate some new photos of you to keep for later."

Kate smiled and thanked him. *He is a lot nicer than I had expected. When I saw him out on the street he seemed like such a cad.* She laughed at herself, thinking such things while she was sitting here eating with him. *Laney would die if she knew; but maybe she did know.*

They ordered dessert, her favorite was crème brulee. Rondell's had the best crème brulee in the world and her mouth was watering just thinking about it. Jim ordered lemon pie.

"Kate, please take a bite of mine. I'm sure I'll want to taste that crème brulee." Kate laughed. She shared desserts with Sam every single time they ate out. *When would she stop remembering it all?* She put her fork into his pie and took a small bite. It was good, but not as good as what she could make at home. Jim tasted her crème brulee and rolled his eyes.

"Oh my," he said. "That's way too good."

As they were walking out to the car, Kate remembered that she had promised herself that she would walk on the beach, and it was still light out.

"Jim let's take a short walk on the beach before it's completely dark. Are you up for that?" Jim grinned and pinched himself. *Was she kidding?*

"Of course! Tonight I would take you to the moon if you asked." They both laughed, and Jim pulled the car around and headed for the beach road. He parked the car on the ledge off the road, and they both got out. They would have to hurry because darkness was creeping over the horizon very quickly. Kate left her shoes in the car, and got out. She grabbed Jim's hand and they ran toward the beach enjoying the warm sand under their feet. The waves were crashing in to shore with such a force that if they stood there too long, they would have knocked them down. Kate was amazed at the surf.

"We shouldn't walk out in the water, Jim. There probably is a terrible undertow right now." Jim agreed, and they decided to just stay on the sand. They studied a sandcastle someone had left near the shore for a minute. Kate thought it was sad that the tide coming in would destroy such a masterpiece.

Walking slowly, she bent over and picked up some shells that had washed up in the heavy surf. She walked ahead of Jim, who was enjoying just standing ankle deep in the foam looking out to sea.

I wonder where everyone is tonight, thought Kate. The beach was nearly empty except for some people miles down the beach. When she looked back, Jim was a small dot standing in the water. She had walked farther than she thought. She stopped, looking out to sea where she was standing. Suddenly her eye stopped on something in the water. It looked like a white fluffy shirt floating in the water.

She tried to motion for Jim to come, and she yelled, "Hey Jim, come here! Something's in the water." She waved wildly at him until finally he saw her and came running.

When he reached her, he said "Are you okay? What in the world did you see?"

Kate walked out into the water a little. "I saw a white floating shirt, or what looked like a shirt, right out there." She pointed out a little just past where the waves were rising.

Jim saw the shirt and rolled up his pants in a failed attempt to keep his pants dry. He stepped out farther into the water and Kate started to panic.

"Don't go out there! You might get caught up in the rip tide!" But Jim was already headed toward the white floating shirt and reached it without too much of a problem. When he got there, out of breath, for the water was now up to his chest and the waves were pounding, he realized it was a person. He tried several times to grab hold of the body, but the waves were fighting him so hard.

"I think it's a person," he yelled. Kate was panicked. *Who would be out here in this surf?*

"Be careful. Please don't get sucked under." Kate looked frantically around the beach for someone to call out to. No one else was around. Jim finally grabbed hold of the white shirt and pulled as hard as he could. He was able to lift and pull the body up and over where the waves kept breaking. He was swallowing water and grimaced at how salty it was. He had forgotten the amount of salt in the ocean and it was almost overwhelming. He pulled and dragged the body until he had it on shore. Kate was standing there shaking, worried about Jim, and for some reason she felt cold. Very cold.

"Can you tell if it's a man or woman? Can you tell who it is?" Jim pulled the body to shore and dropped it. He went to his knees beside the body and caught his breath. It had not been smart to go out that far. He could've drowned like this person had.

"Kate, it's a woman," Jim said. "You may not want to come too close. It's very upsetting to see this."

Kate walked slowly over to Jim, and leaned over the body. Long dark hair flowed over the face. She pulled the hair away and nearly fainted. She screamed out. "I know who this is!"

THE BOX OF WORDS

Jim thought she was just overwhelmed by what had just happened. "Now Kate, calm down. You couldn't *possibly* know this woman. Get your cell phone out and let's call the police. She has family somewhere, and we need to report this."

Jim was still out of breath and getting chilly himself. In fact he was about to lose the supper he had just eaten. Kate fell back and nearly fainted. She was pretty sure it was the waitress at Rondell's. She felt sick inside. *Why did this girl drown? Was this suicide or did someone drown her?*

"Kate, *listen to me*, we need to call the police and report this now." Jim grabbed the phone and dialed 911. In minutes they heard sirens and soon police cars and emergency vehicles were all over the beach. Jim wrapped Kate up in a blanket that a paramedic offered. She was upset and crying, and Jim was cold and damp. The police had questions and wanted to know how they found the body. Did they know who it was? So many questions unanswered, even though Kate and Jim gave as many details as they could to the officer. The body was taken in an ambulance to the hospital. Kate and Jim walked back to his car. Kate could hardly breathe. Jim was worn out from fighting the surf, but glad that he had gotten the woman out of the water. It really looked like she had not been in the water all that long.

"Jim, I know who that person is. I saw her at Rondell's when I ate there with Laney. I'm sure it's her." Kate was so shaken. Jim tried to console her.

"You can't be that sure right now. Let's go back to your house and then we can have some coffee, warm up, and talk about this." Jim started the car and took off down the road. This had turned into a horrific night they would never forget. And all he had wanted was a nice dinner with Kate.

When they pulled into Kate's driveway, Kate took time to gather her wits about her.

"Please, you don't have to come in. I'll be okay. It's just unnerving. I'm pretty sure this woman was the waitress I met the other night. I don't know her name, though. She didn't have a name tag on."

Jim interrupted, "Now Kate, I'm going to take you inside and that's all there is to it. I want to be sure you are okay before I leave."

Kate didn't argue the point. She was suddenly exhausted and a cup of hot coffee sounded fabulous to her. She unlocked the door and let them both in. The smell of her house was great comfort to her.

"Sit down and I'll make some coffee for both of us." Jim reached over and took the filter out of the pot and told her he could make the best coffee in the world.

"Just show me where things are, Kate, and I'll do it. You need to relax and try to get yourself together. This has been a horrible night and I know you're upset. I just hate this happened on our first date."

The police had taken down both their numbers and addresses for more questions. Kate had shared with them about Rondell's, so she was sure they would be asking the restaurant owner a lot of questions.

"So that's why I didn't see her tonight when we were eating," She said to Jim as he walked to the door.

Jim leaned down and kissed her forehead. "If you need anything, anything at all, please call me. I'll be here in a flash. Will you?"

Jim looked at her in the most sincere way she had ever seen. "Thank you, Jim. You basically risked your life to get that woman out of the water. I'm proud of you, even though you scared me to death."

They said goodnight, and Kate leaned against the doorway as Jim drove off. It was almost too much to handle. She didn't know what to do next. But she had a deep, sinking feeling that this was not over yet.

Chapter 9

Seth dropped by early on Tuesday to leave the itinerary for their trip. He could tell his mother had not gotten up yet because the coffee wasn't made. He quickly made a pot and carried a mug upstairs. When he entered her room, Kate was stirring. At first she didn't remember the night before. She didn't even think about the body that had washed to shore. But as she woke up, it hit her hard. Seth quickly said hello so as not to scare her.

"Hey Mom. Just dropped by the itinerary for you and left it on the kitchen table. I brought you a hot cup of coffee fixed your way, to help wake you up. "

Kate forced a grin for her son and responded sleepily. "Oh my goodness. Thanks Seth. You could spoil your mother very quickly. You on your way out the door?"

Seth shuffled his feet and said "Yeah, I have a lot of errands to run before this long trip."

"Well, go have a great day, and if you need me for anything, I'll be at work for a while and then back home. Thanks so much for the coffee. It really helps."

Seth disappeared and Kate sat back on her pillows for a few minutes to think things through. *This woman was driving her crazy. Who was she? What was she doing in the ocean? Did someone drown her?* Kate's mind was going so fast trying to sort through every angle. The problem was there was no angle. She was unnerved about the whole situation. Too many unanswered questions...

I'm sure the police will tear this up one side and down the other, Kate thought. But it bothered her that this woman looked sort of like the woman who had stared up at her building the other day. Getting out of bed slowly, she headed toward the shower. She still needed to phone Laney about dinner last night, and also to see if she wanted to check out the house she was looking at. She had Stephen's card in her purse, and could set up an appointment once she knew when Laney was free.

Out of the shower, she opened her underwear drawer, and saw the envelope sitting there. She opened it again and re-read it. *Will I ever know who this woman is?* She asked herself. She was sort of relieved that she hadn't found it while Sam was alive. At least their last days together were wonderful and they were able to tie up all the loose ends without any strain between them. *I know he would have freaked out if he knew I had run up on this stupid envelope in Seth's suitcase,* she thought, frowning.

Still buttoning her blouse, she grabbed her purse and shoes and headed downstairs. She unplugged her cell phone, checked for messages, and put it in her purse. On the counter in a bag were the donuts the kids had brought. She grabbed the bag and her coffee and headed out the door. It would be nice to be early for a change. She preferred that actually so that she could have time to go over the charts before the patients came in.

She found herself in early rush traffic but her mind was busy with thoughts about her day; the house; talking to Laney about Jim, and so many other things. When she got to her office, there were messages to return, and mail sitting on her desk. She poured through the emails and tossed out any junk mail. There were bills, credit card offers, magazines, and just as she was about to toss out everything but the bills, a small envelope fell to the floor. She picked it up and looked at the handwriting. There was no return address. It could possibly be from one of her patients, since one of them would write to her from time to time. She usually would just make notes about it, and stick the notes in their file for later reference. She wanted to call Laney before she got busy, so she picked up the phone and dialed her number.

Laney picked up, and Kate smiled. "Hey girlfriend. You busy today?"

Laney laughed. "I'm headed to school for another meeting but will be out in about three hours."

"Well we have a lot to talk about! So give me a ring when you are free, and I'll pick you up for a look at the house I have my eye on. How does that sound?" Kate was so excited every time she thought about the house and it was a great distraction from all of the other things that have been happening lately.

Laney jumped right in. She was always game for a fun day of shopping or anything that Kate could dream up. "I'll be ready, Kate. I can't wait to see what you have found. What else is going on? "

Kate smiled again. "Nothing much. Just a date with Jim Peterson, that's all." There was silence on the other end of the line.

"What?" shouted Laney. "Are you telling me you actually had a date?" Kate laughed out loud.

"Oh relax. I just had dinner with him. He kept on pressing me, so I thought what would one little date hurt?"

"I can't wait to hear all the details! I'll call you as soon as I am free."

Kate had already looked at her schedule and found a way to re-schedule a few appointments so that she could get out when Laney called.. *This is going to be a great day,* she thought. But the image of that woman's body was stuck in the back of her mind and she was having a difficult time getting rid of it.

She placed the letter in her purse to read later, just as her first patient of the day came in. Her mind got pre-occupied with the problems that were in front of her, and the hours slipped by very quickly. When Laney called, she was ready to go. She grabbed her purse, told her secretary to hold all calls for the afternoon, and out she went.

Kate felt a bit guilty for re-arranging some of her patients' sessions so that she could go house hunting, but for some reason she was driven to get back to that house. *Stephen said I was the perfect one to buy the house,* she thought. *Stephen!* She hadn't even thought about him lately. She needed to call quickly and make an appointment or Laney and she would be sitting in the driveway of a locked house.

"Hello, Stephen. This is Kate Morrison. I was there the other day looking at your parents' home. Do you remember me?" she asked.

"Oh yes, Kate. Good to hear from you again. Do you want another look at the house?" Stephen asked, noticing his heart beating a little faster.

"I certainly do! But I feel terrible about calling you on the spur of the moment like this! I would like to see it as soon as possible. I'm picking up a friend to come by and see the house with me now. Is that pushing you too much for time?" Kate asked with a slight pout.

"Heavens no!" Stephen said without hesitation. "You can see that house any time night or day. Just give me a buzz and I'll meet you there." He was so thrilled that she seemed to love the house almost as much as he did. *I know nothing about her,* he thought. *All I know is that she is looking for a house. I don't know why I am acting like this. It's ridiculous at my age. But she is so beautiful....*

"Okay, Stephen. Let's say about three thirty this afternoon. Would that be okay? "Kate was getting very excited now, and she could not wait to show Laney.

"That's fine. See you then. "Stephen hung up the phone and whistled. *I get to see her at least one more time.*

Kate pulled up at Laney's house and honked the horn. Laney must have been sitting there waiting because she came out of the door immediately. In the car, the two women couldn't stop talking.

"So what do you mean you just went out with Jim for dinner?" Laney jumped in and asked.

"Well, you know how pushy he is. He was a complete gentleman though, and we had a great dinner. But someone told him I loved Rondell's. Could that have been you, dear Laney?" Kate tilted her head back and laughed.

"Well, I did run into Jim at the grocery store the other day and told him about our dinner there . . . and I may have mentioned that you really loved their menu." Laney looked at Kate with raised eyebrows.

They both broke into laughter.

"Well, we had a good time." Kate shared with her friend. "But something terrible happened, Laney, after dinner." Kate almost teared up for a second but caught herself before her eyes got too watery.

"We have a few minutes before we have to meet Stephen at the house, so let's stop and get something to drink at this café on the side of the road." Kate pulled over and they got out and went inside. They ordered cold drinks and shared a stale pastry at a table in a corner of the room.

"I had a great idea to go to the beach last night, after we finished our desserts, and Jim was all for it. It was already dusk and we did not have long before it would've been too dark, so we rushed out to the car and hurried to the beach." Kate's throat was getting tight. She paused and took a sip of her Coke.

Laney was sitting on the edge of her seat and leaned forward to listen, as she could tell Kate was upset.

"We got to the beach, left our shoes in the car, and we started walking. Jim was enjoying standing in the powerful surf huge waves were rolling in. So I walked down the beach a ways, picking up some shells along the way." Kate paused, remembering all the broken shells that had washed to shore. Laney kept silent. because she could tell Kate was growing more upset.

"Well, I was down a ways from Jim and turned to look at the water. Suddenly, I thought I saw what looked like a white shirt floating in the water. I yelled at Jim, and waved my arms frantically, and finally he caught sight of me. I don't know what in the heck he thought had happened, but at least he came running." Kate took a deep breath and another sip of Coke. Her heart was beating fast, but it was important that she be able to tell this to Laney. She needed help in sorting all of this out.

Laney sat back in her chair and waited for Kate to finish her story. It was obviously leading to something terrible. Laney felt her stomach tighten just looking at Kate's face.

"Jim walked right into the high surf and reached for the shirt. He pulled and pulled and it nearly dragged him under, but he finally got a good grasp on the shirt and yanked it up over the next wave. Slowly he was able to pull the body into shore and then he just sank down in the sand, exhausted. I ran over to him and he begged me not to look. But I had to, Laney. I had to look. I pushed back the long dark hair, and Laney, it was the waitress you and I had at Rondell's". Kate stopped and put her head in her hands. She thought she was going to be sick. She was almost afraid to look at Laney.

"Oh my gosh!" Laney gasped. "That's eerie! How did she drown?" She looked at Kate straight in the eyes. "You have to be upset by all of this."

"I have no idea how she ended up in the ocean," said Kate. "Nothing adds up here." The two women looked at each other and shook their heads.

"Laney, I'm sick about this poor girl. I have lost sleep over this whole situation. But I forgot to tell you something else. There was a young woman standing outside my office staring up at the building the other day. I was taking a break between patients and looked outside my window. I saw her standing there and then suddenly she walked into the crowd and I lost sight of her." Kate rubbed her eyes in fatigue and slowed down as they were near the house on Madison Avenue.

Laney shook her head in disbelief. "Do you think she's the same woman?" she asked Kate with hesitation.

"Yes, I'm pretty sure it was. But I have no idea what she was doing in front of my office building. And I don't know why she would end up in the ocean, drowned."

They finished their drinks and walked to the car. Laney put her hand on Kate's hand, and looked at her. She touched Kate's hair and brushed it away from her face. "You've been through something very traumatic. Are you sure you want to go ahead with looking at this house? We can do this another day, don't you think? "

Kate shook her head, and said "No. Maybe this is just what I need right now. To get my mind off things. This has really taken a toll on my emotions, and if I could relax with you for an hour while we check out this house, it would be wonderful."

Kate drove to the house and pulled into the driveway. Stephen was already at the door of the house waiting.

I hope I don't look too anxious, he laughed to himself. *If I'm honest with myself, I haven't stopped thinking about this woman since I saw her the other day. I haven't felt this way about another woman in a long time. It sort of scares me.* It set him back for a minute, as he saw them coming up the walkway to the front door.

"Hey ladies!" Stephen said as he snapped his mind out of a daydream. "Come on in and let me show you this wonderful house." He shook Laney's hand, and then looked at Kate.

She caught the look in his eye, and smiled. "Hello Stephen. So good to see you again." He shook her hand and didn't want to let it go. But he dropped it and stepped aside, so the two friends could walk around and check out the house without feeling like they were being hovered over.

He watched Kate walk away, and his heart flipped in his chest. *Don't be a child. You don't even know this woman. Get a grip man.* Stephen laughed at himself, and sat down at a table to look at the morning paper. *If there was such a thing as a cupid, he certainly has shot an arrow into my heart,* he thought, smiling.

Chapter 10

Detective Brandon Mills sat at his desk, jotting down notes on a pad that was in the middle of the messiest desk in town. He was probably the most disorganized policeman in the whole unit. But he had a knack for solving cases, so his issues were tolerated to a point. He was in the middle of a case where a young woman had drowned, and this was a first for Martin City. Nobody had drowned in over ten years on his watch, and he was puzzled as to why this woman ended up in the ocean.

He had a few leads, but needed to go talk with one of the servers at Rondell's. She seems to know this woman and may have something to tell him that would reveal why she drowned. The other lead was downtown. Someone had seen a woman walking on the beach that late afternoon by herself. The surf was dangerous and it occurred to them that she was really too close to the water. There were no lifeguards out that day, and there were red flags everywhere on the beach. He checked his watch, logged out at the station, and got in his car to drive to Rondell's. For some reason this felt like a better lead. It would be a miracle if he solved this case so quickly. He also wanted to talk to the couple who found the body, again. The woman seemed so upset, that he decided to wait and catch her after she had a day or two to get over the shock of finding a body in the ocean.

He pulled out all the phone numbers and changed his mind. He decided to try Kate first. He rang her cell, hoping to catch her while she was in between patients. He had taken note that she was a psychiatrist. Her cell rang and rang, and suddenly, on the last ring, she picked up.

"Hello," Kate said. She was balancing the phone on her shoulder while looking at the cabinets in the kitchen of the house.

"Ma'am, I'm sorry to disturb you. This is Detective Mills at the police station; I just want to ask you a few more questions about the drowning victim. Could you tell me when it would be convenient to meet with you?"

Kate punched Laney in the side and whispered that it was a detective on the phone. "I can be free to meet with you at around five thirty this evening, Detective Mills." Her stomach was churning. *Just when I had gotten my mind off of this terrible thing, I get a call from the police.* She put her hand over her forehead and leaned up against the counter.

"Kate, we can go now. You can look at this house another time," Laney said.

"No, Laney. I came to see the house with you and that is exactly what I'm going to do. That detective can wait for a little while. I don't have to see him until five thirty and that gives us plenty of time to check out this house."

Stephen peeked around the corner and asked if they needed anything. "Is there any kleenex in the house, Stephen?"

He found one on his desk and brought it to her. She dabbed at her eyes and then smiled. He seemed like such a nice guy.

"I do love this house, Stephen. Why don't you show us the rest of the house."

Kate and Laney followed him through the house, making comments on the molding, the faux finish on the walls, and the high ceilings. Kate especially loved the light fixtures and fans. Stephen led them into the master bedroom, and showed them the closets that you could sleep in, they were so large. Then the bathroom, which was roomy, held a large stand-in shower and oversized whirl-pool tub. Through the master bath there was a dressing table with a large mirror on the wall to do hair and makeup. Then walking through this small area, he led them into the woman's closet. It was huge and had a window facing the front of the house. There were walnut stained plantation shutters on the window which warmed the closet up.

They walked through all the bedrooms, an office, and laundry room then up the stairs to the other three bedrooms. *What in the world am I going to do with all of this room?* thought Kate. She smiled. She turned and looked at Laney. "So what do you think, Missy?" They both laughed.

"Of course I'm in love with it, Kate," Laney shot back. "Anyone would love to have this house. It's warm and inviting, and I love the way the house is laid out."

Kate lingered in the master bedroom. *Sam would have loved this room,* she thought. *But that part of my life is gone now. I'm starting over.* It had been over two years, and it was time for her to move on with her life. As she was walking out into the main room, Laney was talking to Stephen about the house. Kate could hear them talking about his parents and how much they loved the place. He opened up the French doors on the side of the house, and they could hear the ocean clearly. There was a slight breeze that was refreshing. Kate could picture sitting outside and just listening to the sea.

Stephen walked them to the door. It was time to go, but Kate really could have stayed longer. Laney thanked Stephen and walked out to the car. Kate shook his hand again and smiled.

"Stephen, I'll be calling you soon. You know my home is for sale, and that has to happen first before I can buy this one. I hope you don't sell it before I have a chance to buy it!"

Stephen held her hand again and reassured her that it would be here for her. He took a risk and said "and Kate, would you allow me to take you to dinner one night very soon? I would love to talk to you more about the house and the memories here. A lot has happened in this house, and I'm sure you would find it interesting."

For some wonderful reason she warmed at his touch. It was a new feeling to her, and she drew her hand back for a moment. *Was it too soon? Was she betraying Sam? Sure she had gone out with Jim, but it was strictly out of obligation. This was different because she was actually feeling something inside that she thought would not happen again...* "I would love dinner with you Stephen. Just give me a call, and we'll set a date. Thanks so much for walking us through this lovely home. Somehow I do feel like I'm supposed to be here. I really can't tell you why." Kate walked away, and headed toward the car. Stephen stood in the doorway way too long, watching her go. As the car pulled away, he bowed his head down and stood there a moment.

He tucked her card into his pocket and went over to the desk to look at his calendar. He wouldn't put off calling her for dinner. He was afraid something would come up to change her mind. He was a little overwhelmed by the feelings he was having since they had met. *What was it about her that was drawing him to her?* He had adjusted to living alone, and hadn't sought out female companionship for a while. Kate was different somehow. He wanted to find out why.

Kate dropped Laney off at her house and headed home to get ready for the detective's visit. Laney was nothing but enthusiastic about the house. Kate was thrilled but now she had to face this police officer and talk about the drowning. What a change of pace here. *I will be so glad when this is all over with,* she thought as she walked up to her door. She went inside and sat her purse down, and checked the phone messages. There were none. She went upstairs to freshen up, wash her hands, and change her shoes. Then she went back downstairs and made a fresh cup of coffee. *Now is when I wish Sam was here,* she thought, as she sipped on the coffee. Steam was rising up out of the cup. She felt lonely all of a sudden, and a little overwhelmed about seeing this detective. In an hour it would all be over, and she could climb in bed and watch TV, and let it all go.

She reached into her purse to get some lipstick out, and her hand touched the small envelope inside. She had forgotten to read that note. She set it out on the table, propped up against the salt shaker, so that she would not forget. The doorbell rang, and Kate ran to let Detective Mills in. He came into the kitchen and sat down, getting his notes out so he could talk to Kate about the incident of the drowning. She picked up the afternoon paper and brought it inside, sitting it on top of the table. The envelope fell, and slid down inside the newspaper.

Now began a conversation that she would not forget.

Chapter 11

A light was turned on over the kitchen table, casting shadows across the floor. Kate was hungry and ready to get this interview over with. Detective Mills placed a clean pad of paper and a freshly sharpened pencil on the table. He was fumbling through his briefcase, looking for something, seemingly preoccupied. Kate got up and poured another cup of coffee, and offered him one. He agreed, so she gave him Sam's mug. She sat back down and Detective Mills began sharing with her and asking questions about the night she and Jim were walking on the beach.

Kate talked about the beach, how empty it was at that time of evening, and how she suddenly saw something white in the water that looked like a shirt. She shared how Jim had waded in against the strong surf and pulled the body to shore. She was shaking just thinking about that night. *It was a nightmare. Something you read about in a book. Not something that happened in your own life, on an innocent walk on the beach.*

"Kate, I know you're tired and this isn't pleasant for either one of us. Let's go over what we know for that night. You and Jim were walking on a fairly deserted beach. Did you see anyone that could remotely have been connected to this woman, or anyone running away?" He was jotting down things she was saying, and rubbing his white beard. He was a friendly officer and seemed to know his job.

Kate rubbed her head and tried to think back on that night.

"I really don't remember anyone running at all. Not even a jogger. The beach was empty except for families that were way down the beach."

"Well, it looks like suicide here, unless we can gather a motive for someone who would want to kill her. I'm going to Rondell's shortly, to talk to some of the servers there. We got a tip that she worked there." At that remark, Kate stood up and walked to the window. *It was her. I knew it was her.*

"There's something I need to tell you then," she said quickly. "I had dinner with a friend there the other night and this woman waited on us. When I saw the body, I mentioned to Jim that I thought it might be her. I was pretty sure of it."

Detective Mills shook his head. "I'm hoping I'll dig up something, like who she was dating, who her friends were. There has to be some reason that her body ended up in the ocean. I don't like this happening on my watch."

Kate leaned forward and looked him straight in the eye. "Officer, I have a reason for saying this. I was up in my office the other day on the top floor, looking out on the crowd of people walking around. I was suddenly aware of this one woman standing still in a crowd of moving people, staring up at my window. It was from a distance, so I can't be absolutely sure. But it occurred to me on the beach that it might be the same woman I saw that day in the street."

Detective Mills pushed away from the table and thought a minute. "Kate, do you know the name of the server who waited on you at Rondell's?"

Kate looked him right in the eye. "She had no name tag on the night I was there."

"If I tell you her supposed name, will you tell me if you have ever heard of her before? I need you to be honest because everything we can dig up on this woman will help us to solve the problem." He sipped his coffee and waited for her to answer.

"I doubt I know the woman, but I'll be glad to tell you if I do." Kate answered, feeling a little queasy.

"Well, we believe her name to be Alison Stratford."

Kate couldn't breathe. She couldn't even move. Her face froze into a mask, and she felt her stomach churning. The thought was dizzying. *What did he say? It couldn't be true. Surely this wasn't the woman who wrote the note to Sam.* Kate's mind was going at the speed of light. *What do I say? I'm not ready to admit that I have this note.*

"Officer, I don't recognize that name, but I'll certainly keep it in mind if something comes up." Kate exhaled quietly and stood up. She thanked Detective Mills for coming by, and asked him if there was anything else.

"Kate, I know this is tough. If you think of anything else, please call me. Here's my card with all of my numbers. If anything at all comes up, I'm asking you to let me know. I appreciate your help, and Jim's help, in recovering the body. Now we have the terrible task of finding out who took her life, or why she took her own life."

Kate walked the officer to the door and watched the lights as the car pulled out of the driveway. *God, I hope he didn't feel my tension. I pray he didn't sense anything,* she thought, shivering. She was afraid and her emotions were running wild. She wanted to go upstairs and burn the letter. No one would even know it was ever written. Sam was gone. No one else knew. Her heart was racing. *How could she handle all of this alone?*

Kate managed to walk up the stairs to her bedroom. Before she headed out of the kitchen, she grabbed her coffee and the newspaper lying on the table. She didn't see the envelope that was tucked just inside the folded paper. Walking upstairs, she was thinking only about the note in the dresser drawer. *Who was this woman? Was Sam really having an affair? All arrows pointed to that. So if that is true, why did the woman kill herself?* So many questions flooded her mind, with no answers coming back.

She was no longer hungry and sat down on her bed and turned on the television for something to distract her. Suddenly the phone rang. The ring jarred her out of her thoughts and she jumped up and grabbed the phone.

"Kate? It's Jim. I'm calling to check on you. I know you're upset about what we found on the beach, and I'm here to tell you, it's a night we both will never forget." Jim paused. He could hear Kate breathing heavily.

"Kate, are you okay? Is something wrong?"

"I just had a visit from the detective about the body we found. He said she might be the waitress at Rondell's that I mentioned to you on the beach, when you found the body. My stomach is sick, and my head is spinning. I think I need to just go to bed and sleep this off." Kate sighed, feeling the tension in her shoulders. Across the room, in the drawer, was the note that the police would love to have. But she just couldn't bear to let it be known. In keeping it hidden, she knew she was breaking the law.

"I wish I could've been there with you when the detective was there. That had to be nerve wracking. I know you're exhausted; maybe it wouldn't hurt if you took something to help you sleep. If you need anything, and I mean anything, please call me." Jim felt her fear and worry. He was feeling pretty helpless sitting on the other end of the phone.

"The detective may come and see you, too, so I want you to be ready."

"I'll wait for his call. Don't worry about anything. Just rest and maybe tomorrow you'll feel better about all of this."

Kate said goodnight and leaned back on the pillow. She had to call Susan. She was the only other person who knows the note exists. She jumped up and got her cell and dialed the number.

The phone rang and rang. Kate hung up the phone. So weary and frustrated, she cried out to Sam. "How could you leave me like this? What do you expect me to do now?" She finally started crying and laid her face in a pillow in total despair. Her heart could not take any more, and she fell asleep, again, in her clothes, thinking about Sam.

In the middle of the night, groggy and still sick, Kate sat up in bed. She wiped her eyes, which were sore from crying so hard, and got up and went to the bathroom. When she came back, she realized that she had lain on top of the newspaper. She bent to pick it up. The white envelope fell to the floor. *Almost like an answer from Sam,* she thought.

She sat down on the bed and her hands were shaking as she slipped her nail under the flap and tore it open in a thin straight line. She almost didn't want to take out the note. *What could it possibly say?* She tugged hard and two notes came out of the envelope. One that was written on crisp paper and one that had ragged edges. She opened the crumpled one first, and nearly died inside when she saw Sam's handwriting. *Oh my God,* she thought. *What now?*

Kate began reading the note, with tears streaming down her face.

Sweet angel,

I know you are having a hard time knowing how to deal with things. I'm here for you. I am only trying to make your life better, and I despise having to do this all in secret. I know you understand why I can never speak about you to anyone. It would destroy my family. And even though I know you are part of me, I have to remain hidden when I see you. I love you with all my heart, and want you to keep your chin up.

Don't ever forget my love for you. No matter what happens.

Love, Sam

Kate's hands were shaking. *What did this mean?* She tore open the second note with tears streaming down her face. Through the blurring tears she read:

Kate,

I have waited a long time to write this letter to you. As you see, I have enclosed a letter from Sam for you to read so that you can understand that what I am about to tell you is the **absolute truth**.

I know you have been hurting for a long time. Sam's death had to be devastating for you, as it was for me. But I have something to tell you, and I have chosen to not be there when you finally find out the truth.

I'm Sam's daughter, Kate. I was born in South Carolina. My mother was from there and met Sam by sheer accident on one of his hunting trips. They only were together once, and she got pregnant with me. Somehow she tracked Sam down, and allowed him to be aware of her pregnancy. He has taken care of me all these years beautifully, but didn't want to disclose the truth and we had to *honor* that wish.

I know this comes at a great shock to you. It's been very hard on me, not being able to come out in the open with this information. Near his death, I moved here to Martin City to be close to him, as I loved my father very much. I know you'll understand this, as you are a good mother yourself. I know all about you, Kate. But you know nothing about me.

By the time you read this, *I'll be gone*, as I can no longer live like this, hidden, and tucked away. Sam was my whole life. He encouraged me to become who I am today, and I cannot bear to live without him. I've had my share of problems, but have done pretty well for myself. I'm sorry you had to hear about this in a note. I waited on you at the restaurant and somehow knew it was you. *You are so lovely*. I called you Mrs. Morrison without even thinking.

Have a good life, Kate. I'm sorry I'll never get the opportunity to know who you are. Your step-daughter, Alison

Kate sat there holding the note, her hand shaking. She looked up and screamed Sam's name. *Why did you betray me like this? What made you seek someone else? Why did I not know something was wrong?* She put her head in her hands. *I know he loved me;* she went over the situation in her mind. *This is not fair Sam. The poor child had to handle this all on her own. For so many years. This was not what I had expected at all. I thought Alison was Sam's lover, not his child. Now I finally know he did have an affair, even if for one night, and this is the result. How sad can you get? A life was gone, all because of a secret.*

She looked at the clock. It was four o'clock in the morning. Susan was up early, but not this early. Kate made a note to call her as soon as the sun was up. She needed her friend more now than she ever had before. Maybe this was a good time to get away. To take a break. She just didn't know how much more she could take. Kate decided to get up and put on her shorts and a hoodie and go out walking. The fresh early morning air would do her good, clear her mind. Her heart was so heavy she didn't know if she could walk. But she knew she could not stay in the house one second more. Sam had let her down in a way she would've never dreamed in a million years...

As she walked down the streets, one right after the other, she found herself walking down Madison Avenue. *How odd. Like coming home.* That's how that house felt. She walked right up to it and peeked in. Then she walked around back and climbed over a fence to the backyard. She went up to the back of the house and sat down on a porch swing. She could hear the ocean. The same ocean that swallowed up Alison.

Chapter 12

Stephen was an uncomplicated human being. He was also brilliant. Sometimes his brilliance got in the way of his ability to express emotion. But he could love deeply. His wife had died early in their marriage and he had been so broken about it that he wouldn't let anyone else in. He was an only child of parents who were both of Mensa intellect. His father was an inventor who had developed one of the first prosthesis that could be used for a child. He worked closely with doctors to develop the cutting edge technology that would change the lives of people who had suffered great losses. His mother was an artist and had showed her work in many galleries across the United States. Stephen followed in his dad's footsteps in a way; he became a research physician. He worked in a lab developing the newest technologies for curing cancer and other top killers. He was an introspective, deep thinker. What might be considered a flaw; his quiet, steady personality, actually turned out to be a great virtue. For once he loved, he loved forever.

Stephen opened up the house again this morning, as always, loving the smell when he first walked in. For some reason, even when the house was cleaned out, and painters had come and painted all the rooms, the smell that he remembered as a child in this house remained. He loved that about a house. It seemed to almost be alive. He had seen how fast an abandoned house took on the look of death.

He walked through each room, making sure everything was okay, and then went back to his desk to check his emails and make a few calls to his office. He had arranged his schedule so that he could spend some time trying to sell his parents home. He didn't want to give it to a real estate agent, because then he would have no say in who purchased the house. And he really wanted to like the person who moved into this place he knew as home. *Kate just might be that person,* he mused. *She has something about her that I can't put my finger on. Grace, yes, but something more. Her heart is powerful and she has great compassion for others.*

Stephen was getting older and he didn't ever dream he would marry again. Kate was just someone he was drawn to and he really didn't know why. His mind didn't allow him to go any farther. But he was drawn to her beauty inside and out. He wanted to know more about her. Making a date with her was his first goal. The rest would take care of itself.

He looked out the window at a van that pulled up. It was too early for a house hunter. It looked like a family with a dog and small children. He went to the door and greeted the family. They came in like the wind and walked through the house. It was a large home, and it would fit them nicely. But the price was too high for them. They left fairly quickly and he was back at his desk, again, going over messages. His mind kept wandering back to when he was married to Betsy. She was a tall, lithe woman, with a smile that would kill any man's heart. She loved the theatre and the arts. He really could've cared less, but went along to please her. When she got sick, their lives changed rapidly. From travelling and going on cruises, operas, theatre, musicals, dinners on the town, to hospitals and doctor's offices from one day to the next. Her health deteriorated so fast. He still couldn't believe how fast she was gone. But he enjoyed all the years he had with her. He really had resigned himself to living alone for the rest of his life. His work kept him very busy, and he loved to read, so at night he filled his time with reading and being inventive.

They had no children. He'd regretted it, but Betsy couldn't have children and for some reason didn't want to adopt. This hurt Stephen at first. He really had wanted to have a son or daughter. But he did not push her and now was sorry he didn't. He would have children to love and take care of, and with her being gone, it would've made his life richer.

He went out back to check on the irrigation, and something caught his eye on the patio. It looked like someone was laying in the swing. He went cautiously toward the swing, and there, to his surprise, was Kate. He watched her for a few minutes. She was so peaceful that he hated to awaken her. He noticed that she was in her shorts and a hoodie. *Wonder how long she has been there?* He walked over to her and touched her hair. He didn't want to scare her. He sat at the other end of the swing and slowly pushed it with his feet. He began to hum and she stirred.

Slowly she woke up and sat up straight, looking at him with a puzzled look on her face. She was shocked to see where she was.

"Oh my gosh, Stephen. I had no idea I had fallen asleep here on the swing. I'm so embarrassed." She got up quickly and straightened her clothes.

Stephen smiled. "Kate, relax. I was coming outside to check on the irrigation and saw you laying here. No one has seen you but me. I did have one family stop in to see the house, but apparently they never made it to the backyard. If they had, their kids would have awakened you for sure!"

Kate smiled and walked toward the gate. "I was having a bad night and needed some fresh air. This seemed like the perfect place to sit and listen to the ocean. I guess I had better get back home. I need to shower and get ready for work."

Stephen jumped up and said "Wait Kate. I'll get the car and drive you home. Hold on a minute." She really didn't feel like walking home. She was mentally exhausted and just wanted to crawl back into her bed and never leave. But she had a full day of work ahead of her. She had taken a lot of time off, and needed to see some of the patients she had re-scheduled.

Stephen pulled up into her driveway and was going to hop out to open her door. She beat him to it and jumped out.

She peeked into the car and said "Thank you, Stephen. You have no idea how badly I needed that rest."

Stephen quickly said "Hey Kate? Will you go out with me tonight? We can make it an early dinner and maybe take a walk on the beach?" He was so nervous he could hardly breathe.

She rolled her eyes, hoping he didn't see.

"Oh, I would love dinner with you. But I don't know about that walk on the beach. Give me a call, and we can set a time. Thank you again for the drive home".

Kate went into her house and immediately fixed some hot coffee. It tasted so good as she climbed the stairs to her bedroom. She almost hated to go into the bedroom. The notes would be lying on the bed where she'd left them last night. She reached for them as soon as she got into the room, and tucked them back into the envelope. Then she put it in her purse for later, when she met with Susan. She had already decided not to tell the police about the letters, even though she knew she was lying to them. Withholding information. She was pretty convinced that Alison's parents would not say one word about Sam. So she was going to let it slide. No good would come out of the world knowing this information. It was true that she didn't know Alison but if the police found out about her being Sam's daughter . . .

Kate stood in the shower, letting the hot water slowly take the tension out of her body, staying in as long as she could. *My life has turned into a nightmare. I thought I had dealt with Sam's death and had closure for the most part. Now I find out about a daughter he had, and she drowns. It is a wonder that I haven't lost it trying to hold things together. And now I am withholding information. Have I lost my mind?*

She stepped out of the shower and dressed for work, still in shock. There was so much to do and that helped her to get her mind focused again. *It had been good to see Stephen again, and now a night with him could be just the thing I need right now if I can focus long enough and relax. I have no idea what he does for a living, or anything else about him,* thought Kate. *But somehow I do trust him and I think it will do me good to get out of the house.*

The day was starting out smooth, considering what Kate had discovered. She tried hard to hold it together. Friday the kids would leave for Europe. She knew she needed to call them and check to see if they needed anything. Ella was being so quiet lately, that it was worrying Kate. *I need to spend more time with her but she is so illusive to me. No matter what I say it always seems to be the wrong thing.* She got out of the car and hurried into her office. Once there, she could not help but look out the big window behind her chair, and remember the girl she saw standing still in the street, looking up at her building. Now she knew why. It was very hard to believe that Sam had another child. *I bet I would've loved her but now I'll never know.*

Hours into her day, Kate got a message that Susan called. She found a moment between patients and dialed her number from her cell.

"Susan, it's Kate. I'm returning your call. Actually I wanted to talk to you myself," Kate said with a little shudder. Susan had no idea what had happened, and Kate needed someone to talk to desperately.

"Hey Katie. I'm so glad that you called back. I've been wondering about you, and how things are going. When can we catch up?" Susan could sense tension on the other end of the line.

"I have a date tonight. With a man who is selling a house on Madison Avenue. . ."

Susan giggled and Kate jumped in fast. "No, it's not what you think. He is really a nice man and well, we just need to talk. I have so much to share with you and I am about to lose my mind if I don't talk this out to somebody."

"Well, dear one, let's pick a time. I'm wide open for the next two days. How about tomorrow at lunch? Can you swing that?"

"My kids are leaving on Friday for Europe. But I will make the time for you and me at lunch. I'll meet you at the café down from my office. It's on the corner. Do you remember that one?"

"Yes, I know exactly which one that is. I'll meet you there at noon."

"Great. See you then. Thanks so much, Susan. I can't wait to see you."

Back at work, Kate addressed the patients one by one, but her mind was not on her work. Now she was thinking about the conversation she was going to have with Susan. *Could anything else happen in my life? What in the heck has happened to my safe little life? All I wanted to do was find a new home and move,* thought Kate. *My kids are going to Europe for a wonderful trip and I wanted to be so happy for them. Now I'm thinking I wish they were going to be home. I want to gather the family I have left around me and feel safe and familiar.*

Kate's desk was a mess by the time her day was over, and she took some time to resort files and get rid of things she didn't need. It took a few minutes, but once it was done, she began to feel a little more organized. At least one area of her life was organized!

She picked up her purse, turned out the lights in her office and said goodbye to her secretary. This dinner with Stephen should be relaxing and enjoyable. *He is such a thoughtful person,* she thought as she was driving home, *and I wasn't looking for someone to be with at all. Jim is a nice guy, but I just have never been that attracted to him.* She smiled. All these thoughts were new to her. This dating scene. She hated it actually. But she did not want to live the rest of her life alone either. An age old dilemma.

Pulling into her driveway, she parked in the garage and lowered the door. For just a moment, in that quiet darkness, she thought she could feel Sam. She closed her eyes and just breathed him in. *Sam, I wish I could've known this was your daughter. I wish I could've spent some time with her and introduced her to the kids.* Kate sighed. *Oh Sam, don't you see it wasn't wise to hide this? It's too late now. She has taken her life. But it was a death that should've never happened. I know I would've loved her, Sam. Because she was a part of you.* Kate put her head in her hands and cried. She cried for Sam. For Alison. And for her children who would live the rest of their lives without their father.

When she opened her eyes, she felt very alone. She got out of her car, walked into the house, set her purse and keys on the table and walked upstairs slowly, looking again at the family photos that had come to mean so much; moments caught on film like time that was stopped for a second. She ran her hand over the photo of Sam. When she looked into his eyes, he was not looking back at her. He was gone.

Chapter 13

Ella sat pensively looking out the window of her apartment. She was so excited about leaving for Europe, but had a lot of loose ends to tie up. She loved her job at the café down the street, and they were so good about her hours. But her boyfriend, James, had different hours than she did, and it was getting harder and harder to catch each other free. She really wished he could go with her to Europe. *Working and going to school is tough. It stinks. But I know Dad would be proud of me,* she thought, as she sauntered over to a full length mirror to look at herself.

She had not mentioned James to her mother, yet. In fact, she hadn't mentioned anything to her mother. She seemed different since her dad died. Ella felt like she didn't know her anymore. She knew her mom was lonely and working too hard, but she still felt her mom didn't make time for her. And with Dad gone, Ella and Seth didn't go home as much. It just didn't seem like home. Ella suddenly felt sad and alone. She needed her mother in a different way now, and it just didn't seem to be there.

Her phone rang. It was James. "What's up?" James said, smiling.

"Oh, nothin' much really. Just thinkin' about packing and getting things sorted out before Friday." Ella answered. She loved this guy so much. If her mother only knew.

"Can I see you tonight, Ella?" he asked with his southern voice.

"I would love to see you, but come here first. I have a lot to do today." They hung up and she lay on her back on the bed with her legs dangling off the edge.

I think I'm going to write Mom a letter, Ella said to herself. *I have some things I need to say, and it's hard now to talk to her.* She got her pad and began the letter to her mom that she knew was going to hurt a little and also surprise her. She decided to mail it to her until just before she left for the trip. That would give her mother time to digest the contents of this note until they could talk about it together.

Mom. I know when you get this note I'll be on the plane headed to Europe. I thought it was better this way, as I need to be able to say some things to you that you may need time to think about.

Since Dad died, you haven't been the same. I don't feel as close to you as I used to, and I don't know what to do about it. You are always busy, and now you are going to sell the house I grew up in. All my memories are in this house, Mom. And you didn't even ask me how I would feel about it.

I'm in love, Mom. I've found a special guy that you have not met, who I really love. His name is James Simpson and he's a senior at the university. He's working for his father at the Ford dealership in town. We get along so well. He makes me laugh. He may not meet your approval, but for now, this is who I want in my life.

I'm glad about going on this trip, Mom. But Seth is meeting his girlfriend over there and I'll be all alone. I know you aren't aware of that, but that's why I was in such a bad mood at the house the other day. It's cool. I'll work it all out. I'll take lots of photos so you can see what we did on our trip.

Mom, when I get home, could we have lunch sometime? Can we sit up and watch a movie like we used to when I was a kid?

Take care, mom. I do love you. But I feel like I am no where in your life.

Your daughter,

Ella

Ella re-read the note and then she folded it up and tucked it into a large envelope. She didn't tell her mother that she had tried drugs. She didn't mention that she was struggling in school and didn't know what to do with her life. And she didn't say that she missed her father more than breathing. He left so fast that she hadn't had time to adjust to his being ill. Two years had passed, and Ella still thought she would see him walking down the street or coming into her apartment with his booming voice. She missed him grabbing her up in his arms.

She wiped her tears and smiled. He was such a good dad. She went over to the window and looked up toward the sky.

"Dad," she said. "You don't know how much I miss you here. But I hope you are happy in heaven. I hope you can see us down here, and that somehow you let me know you are okay." She went to her desk and pulled out a pheasant feather from one of his hunting trips. He told her that angel's wings were made of feathers finer than this one. She ran the feather across her face and tears came

NANCY VELDMAN *with Paris Milla*

down her cheeks. She set the feather down, grabbed her purse, her list that she had made of things she needed for the trip, and headed out the door.

When she shut the door, the feather floated off the desk and fell into her open suitcase that she was packing for her trip.

Outside the window, there was a large bird sitting on the windowsill.

Chapter 14

Seth was walking through the park to get to the office where he worked for the summer. Only one more day, and it would be time for their trip. It was hard to believe he and Ella were going so far away. It was going to be cool in Europe, and he was thrilled that he was going to meet up with Lila in Paris. How could they have timed things so well? It was meant to be. He hadn't told his mom about Lila coming to Paris. But he was on his own now, and he didn't have to report back to her about everything. She was so busy having a new life now that she really didn't even try to keep up with them anymore.

She seems quite different since Dad died. I know she is lonely. She has to be. He looked around the park at all of the joggers. He breathed in the fresh air and jogged a little the rest of the way to work. He really missed running, and after today, seeing all the joggers, it made him want to do it again.

He was working in a CPA office, getting some on-the-job training. He loved numbers, and it seemed like the perfect fit for him to be a CPA. He was very athletic, but also loved math. So he was torn for a while about which way to go with his career. He had a scholarship in basketball, for he was tall like his Dad. But he really thought he would get bored with a career in sports. The accounting felt more natural for him, and this was a great way to try it on. There were a few girls in the office that thought Seth was the cutest thing they had ever seen, but he brushed them off. He had his eye on Lila, and she was certainly wrapped up in him. *I can't believe that I actually have found someone who gets me;* he smiled and sat down at his desk. Her photo was sitting on the desk top, and she was smiling back at him. It was going to be a great evening.

Outside there were fire trucks going by. He didn't pay much attention, but went right to work on a job he was working on. More sirens and police cars.

Seth was in another world of numbers and figures. He never looked up, nor did he see which direction the trucks were going.

"Hey bud," his boss said as he walked by Seth's desk. "How's it going?"

"Great, Mr. Warden." Seth was nervous around this guy. He felt like Mr. Warden was always checking up on him. "I'm working on the Johnson return right now. I'll bring them to you as soon as I am finished, if that's okay."

"Sounds great to me, Seth. Just be accurate. We have no room for error here. We are obligated to do our best and take a huge hit financially if we make a mistake."

"Oh, I totally get that," said Seth. Sweat was forming on his brow. "I assure you that it will be accurate."

Mr. Warden walked away smirking, and Seth relaxed a little. *Gosh, don't put any pressure on me, or anything, will you? Thank heavens this job is temporary,* Seth sighed. He planned to join a big firm when he graduated and make some good money. *And I'm hoping I won't have some heavyweight walking by my cubicle every ten minutes to see what I'm doing.* He laughed to himself, and went back to work. He needed to finish this before he left on Friday. He was working this night shift because he had gotten behind on this job. Pressure. Always pressure.

* * *

Stephen had picked Kate up for dinner, and they were on their way to the restaurant when they heard fire sirens going by.

Kate looked at Stephen, and said, "Where are those fire engines headed?"

Stephen looked in the rearview mirror and said, "They're headed toward Madison Avenue. We better see what's going on, Kate." He turned the car around, speeding up to see if he could catch the fire trucks. He didn't have to go far, because they were stopping right in front of Old Tom Winson's house. The house was in flames.

"This could be a mess. Are you sure you want to watch this?" Stephen whispered to Kate.

"I grew up around this area, Stephen, so it means a lot to me. I just went in that house recently, before I saw your parents' home for sale." Kate was flabbergasted. She couldn't believe her eyes.

"It's an old old home, Stephen. Could the wiring be that bad?"

"At this point, who knows what it could be." Stephen rolled down his window, hoping to catch a police officer walking by. The place was swarming with police cars and fire trucks. The home was all wood, so it was already in flames from front to back. The wind was blowing, which did not help, and the firefighters were spraying everywhere. Neighbors were outside their houses, worrying about the wind and the chance of the fire spreading. This wasn't a normal night for anyone living in Martin City, but especially on Madison Avenue. This neighborhood had withstood all kinds of storms and the homes on this street had been around for nearly a hundred years. A fire could take these homes down in minutes.

Kate and Stephen watched as the old home succumbed to the flames. It was devastating to see, and especially when Kate had known the owners of the house for all of her young life.

"Does anything last in this life?" Kate asked with a little more sadness in her tone than she intended. She really was thinking out loud. Hearing despair in her voice, Stephen put his arm around her.

"Hey, sweet woman, let's get out of here. There's nothing we can do now. We need to stay out of these guys' way and let them do their job. Come on; let's get something to eat." Stephen started the car and took off down the road, while smoke billowed into the evening sky behind them. It was staying light longer, and the sun was casting odd colors against the smoke. Kate knew he was right, but it was tough leaving the scene of this huge fire. Her heart sank in her chest, for this was a memory that she loved so much. And now it was gone, like Sam. So fast. Without any warning.

The restaurant was busy when they pulled up. Couples were walking arm in arm, and laughing. Kate had lost the lightness of the night, and felt weary from watching the fire destroy one of her favorite houses. Stephen took her arm and they walked in. The maitre d' seated them after finding their reservations, and laid the white napkin in Kate's lap.

After he walked away, Stephen took her hand and said "Katie, just relax now. We're going to have a wonderful meal, a good glass of wine, and some conversation with each other. How does that sound?" he asked with an adorable look on his face. Kate noticed that his eyes had a twinkle in them. He was being so nice to her.

"I think I can handle that, Stephen," she said. She shrugged her shoulders to get the tension out of them, and looked around the restaurant. It was a lovely place, full of fresh green trees and plants everywhere. The rooms were stately, and were fitted with round tables with white tablecloths. The carpet was a light blue and made her feel like she was walking on air. The aroma coming from the kitchen was irresistible and the servers were friendly. It felt refreshing inside and as she looked around she noticed people were laughing and having a good time. She had heard that there was an award-winning chef here and couldn't wait to see the menu.

"It does feel good to just sit here with you and relax. I have to admit it's been quite some time since I've been able to really relax. Obviously, on the swing outside your parents' home was one of them!" They both laughed and she relaxed even more. *What a nice evening this is*, thought Kate. She took a moment to look at Stephen as he was looking at the menu. He really was a very handsome man, calm, cool, and collected. But he did have a sense of humor that charmed her. She had such a wall up around her that usually nothing could penetrate. *But he feels so comfortable to be around*, she thought. *I am going to sit back and enjoy this night for once.*

Kate picked up the menu and began reading all the choices for entrees. Stephen took his turn at watching her. He absolutely was in heaven sitting here with her. Two weeks ago he was alone and not allowing anyone in. And here he was, drooling, looking at one of the most beautiful women he had ever met. He was glad to see her relax. She deserved a nice evening. *I'd like to give her more than just one nice evening*, he smiled to himself. *But I'm getting way ahead of myself here. This is our first date. What am I thinking?*

The waiter came and took their orders, and brought some of the house wine. It was delightful. Kate sat back and sipped her glass of wine and enjoyed the music that was playing. There was a gentleman in the next room sitting at a baby grand piano, playing wonderful music that floated in the air. It was perfect for this night with Stephen. She really was glad she had agreed to come. There was quite a difference between Stephen and Jim. *Oh my.* She laughed out loud, and Stephen looked up and raised an eyebrow.

"Have I missed something?" He inquired, smiling.

"Oh no" Kate answered, tucking her head down for a minute to control herself. "I was just thinking about something. This wine is fabulous. Are you familiar with it?" she asked.

"No, I'm unfortunately not. I usually don't drink at all. But I felt like a glass of wine was appropriate for us both tonight. With the stress of the fire, I thought we both could use one." He picked up his glass and tipped hers.

"Here's to our first date," he said. She smiled at him, and tipped his glass.

The waiter brought their salads and bread, and they both ate quietly for a moment. Kate's phone vibrated in her purse, and she picked it up and saw it was Seth. She excused herself with Stephen and took the call.

"Seth, are you okay?" she asked, worried.

"Sure Mom, I'm fine. I'm working late. But I had turned on my radio at my desk and heard that there was a fire on Madison Avenue. That was the Old Winson's Place that burned down." Seth sounded wired and anxious. He knew his mom would be upset at the news.

"Oh Seth, you're so sweet to call. Stephen and I were on our way to dinner and we passed by the fire on the way to the restaurant. It was devastating and made me very sad seeing that old familiar home burn down. I'm beginning to believe that nothing stays the same in this life." She said with a crack in her voice.

"Mom, I know it was hard for you to see that. I just wanted to make sure you knew about it. Just enjoy your meal with Stephen, and I'll catch up with you tomorrow. Love you, Mom."

Kate excused herself from the table and went to the ladies room to wipe her eyes. When she returned to the table, Stephen looked at her with a question in his eyes. "Are you okay?"

"Yes. That was my son, Seth. He was just letting me know about the fire."

She smiled and took another bite of her salad. She was determined to enjoy her meal and not take any more calls tonight. As the night went on, the conversation turned to what they had done in their lives and how they planned to live out the rest of it. Two hours passed before they realized how long they had been sitting there. Kate was learning more and more about Stephen and his work as a research physician. She was very impressed with his research and knew that he'd helped a lot of people. She was sad that he'd never had any children, because he would've been a great father.

"I know how you feel in a way, Kate, about Sam dying so fast. My wife, Betsy, was gone so fast that we didn't really get to enjoy each other very long. It's very difficult to start over after you lose someone you love like that, especially to an illness. I'm grateful it wasn't a slow death for her. But it's harder on the one who remains. I sort of made a decision that I wouldn't remarry because I didn't want to take the chance of loving someone and then losing them. It's an awful feeling. I'm not completely over it yet, and it's been ten years since Betsy died. Actually I put myself so deeply into my work, that I've tried not to keep up with how many years it's been." Stephen pushed away from the table and headed towards the men's room.

Kate sat there with the information he just gave her floating around in her mind. She had wondered about his wife, and had no idea she passed away so soon into their marriage. No children. No parents. *He's an only child. He has no one to lean on, no one to talk to. Why, I would go nuts if I had to live like that. I have my two children, my friends. I guess it's different for a man,* she pondered. *But for me, I need to have someone to share my life with.*

When Stephen returned, he asked her a question. "How long were you and Sam married before he died?" Kate looked down for a minute and then smiled.

"We were married about thirty years. We married very young. But all I've known is Sam. I fell for him early in high school, and there just never was any room for anyone else. We hit it off so young, and it just kept us together through all these years. I thought we would grow old together."

"Well, it sounds like you did have a great marriage, and two wonderful children. A lot to be thankful for." Stephen paid the bill and pushed back his chair. "Let's go for a drive. I know of a lovely lake outside of town I would like you to see. Are you game?"

Kate stood up and grabbed her purse. "That sounds like a great idea! Is this a favorite fishing spot?"

"No" he said, smiling. "It's a place I go when I need to sort things out. Our conversation made me think of sharing it with you. You're going through a lot and need a place that is quiet so that you can get restored in your heart."

Kate was taken aback by the depth and sincerity of his words. She smiled sweetly and leaned over and kissed his cheek.

He took her arm, and they walked out of the restaurant together, talking.

Chapter 15

The moon was out by the time they arrived at the lake. There was no direct access to the lake from the road, so Stephen parked on the road's shoulder, and said they could take a footpath the rest of the way. Kate had a hard time walking in her heels through the tall grass and brush.

Stephen, a few steps ahead of her called back, "It's not much farther."

When they came around a small bend of the path, Kate's breath was taken away. "Stephen, it was well worth the trouble walking this far. Look at this magnificent lake with the moon shining directly in front of the pier. What a lovely sight. The reflection of the moon's rays in the water is absolutely mesmerizing." She was speechless for quite some time, and just stood there looking. She was unaware that Stephen had stepped away from her and was walking toward the pier.

She finally focused on where she was, and saw that he was already leaning against the rail, looking out at the water. She followed his steps and walked slowly to him. He turned and put his arms around her and held her tight. She let herself feel the warmth of him holding her, and she fought to hold back the tears. He was so loving, so tall, and so warm, that it was almost too much for Kate.

He nuzzled into her ear. "Things are going to be okay. I promise." Kate relaxed in his arms and just stood there with her eyes closed. "Nothing happens to us by coincidence. I'm sure we were meant to meet each other, if for no other reason than to come here tonight and stand on this pier."

Kate looked up at him and allowed a smile to bend the corners of her mouth.

"Maybe, just maybe, I can let you into my life as a friend, Stephen. You've been so good to me tonight, and it does feel good to get my mind off work and all the other stress I have. I have forgotten what it feels like to be on a date!"

Stephen hugged her tightly and then pulled away so that he could see her face.

"You are good for me. I don't know why, but I feel it in my bones. I feel so comfortable around you that I would love for us to become close friends. I don't know where this is going, but can we just take it one day at a time?" Stephen lifted her face and kissed her once.

"It's difficult for me to allow another man into my life. I've told you how close Sam and I were. I know it's time for me to open up a little, and you've been so kind to me, so loving. It feels so good to be this close to you; I didn't realize how much I was missing the arms of a man around me."

"I understand completely. I wasn't looking for anyone when you walked into my life. I'm a very organized person and I had my life in order. In a place where I could handle it. So you've thrown me for a loop, and that's why we need to go slow. I would never want to make you feel rushed or compromise you in any way."

"My heart is hurting so much right now, and I didn't realize how Sam's death would affect me. I guess no one ever does. I have to make a new life for myself and completely start over. I do have my children and I adore them. But they are grown and have lives of their own, which they should, of course. I have loved this night with you and hope that we can spend more time together to really get to know each other." Kate stood on her tiptoes and kissed his cheek again.

"I went through the same thing when Betsy died, Kate. It ripped my world apart. I had no idea I was even ready to commit myself into another relationship. I know things happen for a reason, and I'm grateful I've found you now. Let's just give it time and be open with each other. How does that sound?"

"I think that's the only way right now, Stephen. It feels good to be near you and I love that we can talk about anything. I want to know more about what you do and what your desires are for the rest of your life."

They turned and walked back to the car, hand in hand. His hand was so big and warm. Unlike Sam, Stephen had a larger frame and was much bigger than Sam. She felt very safe tonight. After what had happened with the fire, she really didn't think it was going to be a good night. But Stephen had proved her wrong. He was so steady and this had a very calming affect on her. *I'm amazed at how charming he is with me. It's so refreshing to be around such a gentleman. Kate smiled in the darkness of the car.*

They drove back to Kate's house and Stephen turned off the car. He took her hand and thanked her for such a wonderful night. He got out of the car, came around to her side and opened the door and they walked to her front door.

"I won't ask to come in tonight, Kate. I know it is late for you, and you have to work tomorrow. Thank you so much for spending this night with me. It was probably one of the best nights I have had in years."

Kate stepped up to the door and turned. He caught her then, and kissed her lips quickly. It certainly caught her by surprise but she smiled and thanked him for such a wonderful night, and turned to go in. Stephen called after her.

"Kate."

She turned to look at him.

"Thanks for a wonderful evening. I really mean it." Stephen turned and walked back to the car. As Kate entered her house, she thought she heard him whistling.

Kate closed the door and leaned against it, thinking. *I've had a lot to face since Sam died. Things I never dreamed I would have to deal with. My heart is still broken about his having an affair, and my not having the opportunity to know Sam's daughter. And to make matters worse, she is gone. I'll never know her. It's still tough to swallow the fact that he hid all this from me for so long a time.*

Kate walked into the living room and sat down on the sofa, leaning her head back and closing her eyes. It had been a long but meaningful night .*Stephen is so much more than I thought he would be,* she smiled. *In spite of all that I'm going through inside, somehow I'm able to have feelings for him. He has stirred up emotions that I thought were hidden beneath piles of leaves in my heart. Perhaps we feel safer holding on to the memories of the one we lost. It is frightening to step out and tread new ground.*

She got up and walked up the stairs to her bedroom, deciding to take a long shower before she went to bed. She needed one corner of her life to be stable and nourished; she had her job, but she had missed the closeness a relationship\ brings. It felt so good to be in Stephen's arms. She stepped into her pajamas and climbed into bed. The warmth she had felt carried her into a deep, relaxing sleep.

Chapter 16

The real estate agent was putting up a large sign in her front yard, when Kate came down for coffee. She had awakened to the sound of hammering, and could not for the life of her figure out where it was coming from. She opened the door and waved.

"Good morning," she yelled to the woman in her yard. "Thank you so much, I'm hoping this house sells fast."

The agent walked up the driveway. "Hi, Kate." she said, smiling. "I'm sure we'll have no problem selling your house. It's in perfect shape and there are no other homes in this neighborhood for sale. That's in your favor, Mrs. Morrison."

Kate nodded and said, "Well Jane, I think I've already found the house I want over on Madison Avenue."

Jane raised her eyebrows in amazement.. "Wow. So fast? Well we'll do the best we can to sell your house for you." She walked back to her car, checking the sign one more time, and then got in her car and drove away.

Kate closed the door, leaned against it, breathing a sigh of relief. Her house was officially up for sale. It felt really good for some odd reason. She had lived here for nearly thirty years with the man she loved, and now she was willing to walk away from it so easily. She thought about this for a moment, and then walked upstairs to get showered and dressed. This was going to be a full day of patients, because she had taken off so much. She opened the dresser drawer again to get her underwear out, and she touched the envelope again with the notes from Alison. She didn't know what to do with them now, but she knew she was not ready to throw them away. Her heart was stuck in her throat as she stood there with her hand on the dresser drawer. *Would this ever get any easier?* She put her hand on her forehead and felt overwhelmed for a moment. "Sam. Why did you do this to us?" she asked to the air.

* * *

The shower felt good as she stood rinsing off the shampoo in her hair. She let the water just run down her for a few minutes, trying to shake off the mood she was in. It wasn't all bad in her world. What a special night she had had last night with Stephen. What a perfect gentleman he was. But so much was going on that it overwhelmed her. So many different emotions. Anger. Frustration. Unbelief. If only Sam had been honest when he was alive. They could have worked through all of it together. *I don't know how I'll ever get over this hurt he has caused me. it runs deeper because he is gone. I can't talk to him or work things out. It's just me dealing with it all alone. I hate this!*

She realized that she had lingered too long and hurried out of the shower. She heard the phone ringing as she stepped out and wrapped a towel around herself.

"Hey Kate! It's Jim. I've been thinking about you for the last couple of days. Are you okay? I've thought about that night on the beach over and over." Jim was really missing Kate, but didn't want to push her right now.

"Good to hear from you." Kate rolled her eyes. "Yes, I've had a tough time dealing with that night on the beach. Thanks for calling me. I've not heard anymore from the police and I'm grateful," she paused. She realized she didn't sound too enthusiastic to hear his voice.

"Well, I was wondering if you wanted to do lunch. I really enjoyed being with you, in spite of the traumatic experience we both had."

Kate winced when he said that. "I really am slammed today, Jim. Can I have a rain check on that lunch?"

Jim frowned. "I guess we can. I was just hoping to spend more time with you. I'd like to change your memories of a night out on the town turned nightmare, to a nice pleasant lunch at a café."

Kate smiled. "I know you would, but it just can't happen today. I'll give you a call after things settle down a bit. Ella and Seth are headed to Europe today, and I'm up to my neck in patients. I wanted to see them off, and I'm still going to try to figure a way to do that."

Jim understood now. "Okay, no pressure. You have a lot going on in your world, and I'll wait for things to settle down. But I will not forget this rain check, okay?"

Kate smiled. "That sounds great, Jim. Hold me to it."

She hung up and shook her head. *He really is a nice guy. Why am I not attracted to him? He has a great sense of humor, and is a go-getter. But I'm drawn to Stephen more and am finding myself thinking of him way too often. I'll have to let Jim down easy.* Kate dried her hair, and picked out something different to wear to work. She tended to get in a rut with her clothes, so today she was going to wear red. Sam always told her she looked pretty in red, so she pulled a flowing scarlet dress out of her closet, even though it was not her favorite color. It matched her invigorated, bold mood.

At her office, things were getting hectic. The phone was ringing on all lines, and the secretary looked up at her and raised her one free hand up in the air.

"Laura. I'll get one of the lines for you," said Kate as she rushed into her office. She sat down and took the first line lit.

"Good morning. How can I help you?"

"Hi Mom. It's Ella." There was a pause and Kate jumped in.

"Hey Sweetie. Are you ready to go? Are you excited?"

Ella rolled her eyes. "Yes, Mom, I'm excited. But I really don't like leaving my friends behind. One particular friend. Are you coming to the airport to see us off?"

Kate hesitated. She really did want to come, and was trying to work it out. *Why am I so busy today, of all days? I should've planned my schedule around the kids' departure, instead of getting caught like this with a full day ahead of me. What was I thinking? Am I that distracted that I couldn't be there for my children? That's so unlike me to be so preoccupied with my own life.*

"I'm going to try my best, Ella. I'm stacked up here all day with patients, but I'm going to do my best to find a way to run to the airport and see you off. I love you so much Ella and I want you to have a wonderful time. If for some reason I don't make it, please tell Seth for me that I want you guys to have a ball."

Ella sighed. *Here we go. She's not going to make it to see us off. Just too busy.*

"Okay, Mom. Whatever you can do is fine. Just wanted to say goodbye." Kate grimaced at the slight in Ella's voice, and hung up the phone feeling like a jerk. Her daughter really needed her to be there, and she was going to have to make time and reschedule things. She also picked up the phone and called Susan to cancel their lunch date. No answer. She left a short message and greeted her first patient.

The first patient was late, and that usually threw her whole day off. But Kate made a point of cutting their visit short so that she was on time for the next patient. She saw four people before ten thirty and her head was aching. *I need some coffee,* she thought to herself. She ran out to her secretary to see if there was anyway to sneak out for an hour sometime around one o'clock. Laura just looked at her with a blank face.

"Are you joking, Kate? Do you realize how many people are coming this afternoon? And these are some of your patients that you already had to re-schedule." Kate sighed. What in the world was she supposed to do? She walked back into her office, ordered lunch in, and asked for the next patient. From that point on she cut them short on their visit by about ten minutes. They did not seem to notice, and it just might give her time to sneak away. The clock was sitting on one o'clock, and her phone rang again to her private line. She picked it up to hear Ella screaming into the phone.

"Mother, are you not coming to see us off? Are you really not coming?" They had checked their bags and were waiting to go through security. Their flight was leaving in less than an hour, and Ella was freaking out.

"Ella, I'm trying my best to get there. I'll leave here in about ten minutes. Please understand my predicament."

Ella sighed and hung up the phone. She turned to Seth and commented in a low tone. "I knew she wasn't coming."

Seth looked at his sister, and then uncharacteristically hugged her.

"Come on, Ella. Get a grip. Mom is busy. Don't be so hard on her. She'll try to get here. Give her a break, will you?" Ella shrugged and walked to her seat, picked up the paperback she was reading and sipped her Coke.

* * *

Kate ran through the airport, looking for the right gate. Finally she saw Seth standing at a window watching planes take off.

"Seth!" Kate called out.

He turned and smiled. "Mom! You made it. I can't believe it." He ran to her and gave her a big hug. He loved his mother so much, and didn't want to put any pres-sure on her. He was a bit protective of her, and knew she was under a lot of stress. "Where is Ella?"

"I think she is over there", Seth said, pointing to the waiting area. Kate walked over to Ella and tapped her on the shoulder. Ella looked up and saw her mother, and started crying.

"Oh Mother, I can't believe you made it. I really didn't believe you were coming. I just wanted to say goodbye. That's all I wanted. Just to say goodbye." Kate wrapped her arms around Ella and hugged her a long time.

They both were quiet and then Kate said "Ella, you know how much you mean to me? I'm sorry we have been apart for a while. I don't know what you are thinking half the time. You must be going through the same stress I am over losing your father and I know it's hard on all of us. I may not have handled everything like I should have, but that doesn't mean I don't love you or care about your life. I'm so sorry." Ella wiped her eyes. They were calling the flight numbers out and Ella heard their flight number.

"Mom, this is it. We have to board the plane. You almost missed us." Kate hugged her again.

"I know, Ella. But I made it. That's all that matters. I want you guys to have a ball. Please call me or I'll try your cell phones. I'll pray for you. Be careful and stay close to each other." Seth walked up to hug his mom goodbye.

"Mom, take care of yourself. Don't do anything I wouldn't do!"

Kate smiled. "Seth, watch your sister, will you? Take care of each other. And keep in touch with me. You're going to be gone a long time and I need to know where you are. I love you, Seth." She kissed Seth and waived to Ella. They ran to their gate looking back at her before disappearing in the crowd.

Kate watched as long as she could, then turned and walked out of the airport. She suddenly had a funny feeling in her stomach. She brushed it off as nerves about them going overseas. *This was a big trip for them to do all alone. I'm so glad that their friends are going to meet up with them later on the trip. The more the merrier, and in this case, the safer.*

She raced back to work and finished her lineup of patients. Laura was annoyed that Kate had left. Some of the patients were sitting in the waiting room for an hour. Kate really tried to keep that to a minimum, for she didn't like to wait in a doctor's office herself. When she had seen the last patient and was working on some paperwork before heading home, she turned on the small radio on her desk to listen to the local news. There was a news break that mentioned that a plane had crashed into the ocean just outside of Martin City. As Kate was hearing this she thought, *there's no way it could have been their plane! This is crazy. Maybe I need to call and check.*

Her hands were shaking when she dialed the number to the airport. "Can you tell me please what flight crashed today? I just heard the news on the radio."

"Yes, ma'am. It was flight 745. Did you have someone on that flight? Kate dropped the phone and screamed.

Chapter 17

Stephen's cell was ringing. He ran through the house to grab it and just missed the call. A voice mail was left. He punched the play button, and heard Kate saying she had to talk to him. She was screaming.

He was at Kate's office in less than five minutes. Kate sounded pretty upset. Even though she hadn't explained what it was, he knew it was something pretty bad, or she wouldn't have sounded like that.. He went up the elevator to the top floor and got off. He almost wished he didn't have to go through the door to her office, for he didn't know what he would find on the other side. After brief hesitation, he pushed the door open.

Inside her office, he saw no one. He stepped further into the room and saw Kate sitting on the floor with her legs pulled up, hugging them. She was crying and rocking back and forth.

Oh my God. Stephen's heart was racing. *What in the world has happened to this woman?* He rushed to her.

"Kate, Kate! Talk to me. What happened?"

She made no notice that she even heard him.

"Kate, listen to me! **Look at me!**" She did not respond at all. So Stephen picked her up and put her on the sofa and held her. She screamed into his shoulder and cried hard, shaking, and sobbing. He reached for some tissue on the end table and gave it to her. He held her tight. He smoothed her hair, and talked to her in a low voice. She slowly got control of herself and moved away for a minute to blow her nose and wipe her face off. Her mascara had run down her face.

"Kate, talk to me. Tell me what's going on. Did Ella and Seth get off okay to Europe? Is that what you're upset about?"

Kate looked at him with hollow eyes. She could hardly speak. She didn't want to repeat what she heard on the phone, because that would make it truer. She was hoping they were wrong.

"Stephen, I saw them load on the plane. I just saw them a few hours ago."

Stephen held her shoulder and lifted her face up to his. He kissed her forehead and held her.

Kate shuddered. "They said there was a plane crash. The plane went down in the ocean. They were headed to JFK to change planes, and then on to Europe. They are searching for survivors." Barely getting the sentences out, Kate slid down the sofa to the floor. She didn't know if she wanted to live, she was so worried about her children. *How could this have happened so quickly? There is no way I can live without my children. I feel like I'm losing my mind wondering where they are. God please let them still be alive.* Kate wiped her eyes slowly and covered her face with her hands.

Stephen sat down on the floor with her and held her the best he could. He couldn't believe what he just heard come out of her mouth. How did a plane just go down? After a few moments, Kate calmed down long enough to talk to Stephen a little more.

"I need to go to the airport. Since they are looking for survivors I want to be around when they announce anything. I really don't know what to do, Stephen."

Stephen picked up the phone and called the airport. He spoke with two or three people before he got someone who would help him. "I suggest that she go home and try to get some rest. The police, Coast Guard, search and rescue and the National Transportation Safety Board are doing all they can to rescue any survivors and to bring to shore any bodies they have found. Mrs. Morrison can call this phone number to see who the survivors are. I am sure there will be a list here. The number is 765-2345."

Stephen hung up and sat down on the sofa next to Kate. She looked at him with questioning eyes.

"Did they tell me what I need to do?" She looked at him with a numbed, emotionless face.

"They want you to go home. To wait and see what they find. They are attacking this with all the forces they can, to get the survivors out of that water." Stephen kissed her face.

"Come on, baby, let's get you home. I'll stay with you until we find something out."

Kate grabbed her purse and walked to the door with Stephen. She left a note on Laura's desk saying she would not be in on Monday and that there had been a plane crash. She would call Laura later and explain. In fact, right now, she didn't know if she could ever come back. If she made it home, she wouldn't want to leave.

Her mind could not wrap around what had happened. *My children were on that plane. I can't live without them. I have already lost a husband. Now this? No.* She would not take this sitting down. Her strength came back a little and she got her keys out and gave them to Stephen. He reminded her that he had his own car in the parking lot.

"Let's take mine and leave yours here. We'll come back and get it later."

She didn't fight him. She got in his car and he shut the door. When he got in, she was crying again. So he turned on the radio and talked to her, until they got to her house.

"Kate, let's go in and make some strong coffee. I'll order in some food that might sit easy on your stomach. You need to eat something, and I'm hungry too. Let's get settled down and wait this thing out."

Kate was so thankful that Stephen was here to help her; she didn't know what she would've done if he hadn't been there. *He seemed to take over effortlessly and get everything done that needed doing,* she reflected as she took a mug of hot coffee from him. He brought in some steaming chicken soup from the corner café. He also had purchased some muffins to go with the soup. The aroma was enticing to Kate, since she had not eaten all day. Her nerves were pretty much shot.

"Stephen, this is perfect. This is all I need right now. Something light. Thank you so much. I don't know what I'd do without you," Kate said in a very quiet voice.

"You do very well for yourself, and I'm thankful to be a part of your life right now. I'm glad to be here; I care about you." He sat down beside her and sipped on the soup with her. The muffins were fresh and it perked him up a little to get some food in his stomach.

Kate went upstairs and changed into her pajamas and robe, and brought pillows downstairs and a blanket. She lay down on the sofa, and gave Stephen a pillow to use. He turned on the television and they watched the news together, knowing the plane crash would be one of the big stories of the night. They were correct in their assumption. It was all over the news, on all stations. They were finding bodies but not many survivors yet. There were no names posted yet because they were still looking. Everything was spread out over a wide section of the ocean, and it would take some time to find the survivors and also collect all the bodies. Kate watched with a fervor that only a mother knows. She didn't want to turn off the television, but Stephen finally grabbed the remote and turned it off.

"Kate, we have to sleep. We're going to need plenty of energy tomorrow morning. Do you have something I can give to you to help you sleep? If you do, I may take it too."

Stephen knelt down beside her and caressed her head. "You poor thing," he said.

Kate cried again, and laid her head against his. "I just can't believe this has happened, Stephen. These are my children. Surely they survived. They have to have survived."

"I don't know, Kate. We can pray they did. We need to pray hard that they survived. Let's say a prayer now, that God will protect them and that He will bring them safely home to you." Stephen closed his eyes and prayed a very serious prayer to God. It may have been the most sincere prayer he had ever prayed, except when Betsy was diagnosed with cancer.

It soothed Kate to hear him praying, and she closed her eyes. When Stephen was through, she told him where the sleeping pills were, and he went upstairs to get them. He passed by the hallway of photos and a lump was in his throat as he looked at Sam, Ella, and then Seth. A beautiful family. *What happens to families that so disrupts their lives?* He ran to the bathroom to get the pills and came back down quickly. He didn't totally trust Kate by herself just yet. She was still in shock and might be for a day or two.

He gave her the pills, took two himself, and they lay back on the sofa and were quiet, both lost in their own thoughts about the events that had happened. Stephen was thinking about his own life. *I have no children. I don't know what it would be like to be ripped apart because your child, your flesh and blood, might be dead.* Kate was so deeply sunken in sorrow and fear, that she could hardly think at all. Her mind was going in so many directions. If her children were in that water, then she couldn't bear to think of what they were going through. She wanted to go there and get them out. She could almost hear Ella screaming for her. Seth would make it. He was strong. But Ella, her Ella, how would she *make* it in that water.

* * *

Morning came fast. Stephen woke first with a terrible crick in his neck. He got up from the sofa and stretched hard, looking around. Kate was in a ball on the floor with the covers over her head. He left her there and went to the kitchen to make some coffee, turning on the television to see if there was any news about the crash, or any more survivors being found. He heard a noise but couldn't find where it was coming from. It sounded like a buzz. He searched and searched and then realized it was a cell phone buzzing on vibrate. It must be Kate's phone.

He looked for her purse and opened it up. *Yes! That was it.* Her phone was ringing but she had forgotten to take it off vibrate when she left her office. He answered it, and nearly dropped the phone. It was Seth.

"Seth! Oh my God. Is that you, Seth?" Stephen was beside himself. He walked quickly over to Kate and bent down to wake her up.

"Kate! Wake Up! "Seth's on the phone." He shook her and she jolted and sat up too fast and felt dizzy.

"Here, Kate. Take your phone. It's Seth." Stephen handed her the phone and Kate absolutely lost it. She began crying and screaming and trying to talk all at the same time.

"Mom, Mom! It's me. I'm okay." Seth couldn't bear to hear his mother so upset.

Kate calmed down long enough to hear her son say he was okay. She tried to breathe deeply and get a grip on her emotions so that she could talk to her son.

"Seth! Oh my God, I'm so thankful you're okay. I've been sick all night with worry about you and Ella. Where are you? Where is your sister?"

"Mom, they've taken me to a hospital just outside of Martin City. I'll call you when they are through questioning me. You can come here if you like. I know they wouldn't mind. I think other people's families are here." Seth paused. "Mom I don't know where Ella is yet."

Kate gave Stephen the phone to get the directions and ran upstairs to clean up. Stephen got a pen and wrote down where Seth was, the room number, and told Seth not to leave. Not to go anywhere without calling her first. Seth promised he wouldn't and they hung up.

The trip to Jason Memorial Hospital seemed to take forever. It was the longest drive Kate could remember in her whole life. Kate quickly dialed Laney. "Laney, I can't talk long. Have you head about the plane crash? My children were on that plane! I am on the way to the hospital to see Seth. He sounds like he is alright, but they haven't found Ella yet."

"Oh my God Kate! Do you need me? I can try to get off work; I'm sure they would see this as an emergency situation."

"No, don't do that. Stephen is with me, Laney. But I just wanted to hear your voice. I tried to call Susan, but I guess they are out for the evening. I know she mentioned that they might be going out of town, but I don't remember when. Watch the news, and I'll call you later to catch you up on any news about Ella."

"I'll be thinking of you, Kate. *Be strong.* I'm sure they will find her."

They found Seth's room quickly and ran in the door. He was sitting up on his bed in a hospital gown, with a needle in his arm connected to a bag of saline solution. He didn't seem to be hurt at all, just a few scratches on his face and arms. Kate ran up to him and hugged him tightly.

"Oh Seth, I thought I'd lost you. I nearly went crazy when I heard the plane had crashed."

Seth looked at his mom as tears rolled down his face.

"Mom, **we all thought we were going to die.** It happened so fast that we really didn't know what was going on. The next thing I knew there was a huge explosion and we were in the water. I hit the water so hard, with such force, that it nearly knocked me out. But I grabbed a piece of a seat that was floating near me and it kept me above water until I got my senses. I never saw Ella, mom. I screamed for her over and over. *I never saw her.*"

Kate stood up and wiped her eyes. She was so overwhelmed with seeing Seth that she could hardly hold herself up. But the thought of Ella still being out there was just more than she could take.

"Stephen, could you take me to where the plane went down? Can you get me closer to where they are searching for survivors?

Stephen walked over to Seth and shook his hand and patted him on the back. "Seth, I'm Stephen. I am proud of you for keeping your head. It may have saved your life. Did you see many people alive, while you were in the water?"

Seth thought a moment and wiped his face off with a towel that was around his neck. "I remember hearing people crying, and yelling. But there was an awful lot of smoke and it was hard to see anything. I was scared of what was in the water below me."

Seth looked at his mom. "They won't let you get anywhere close to the crash site. Even on shore they have it roped off. We have to wait for them to find all the people. That's is the only way for us to know if Ella is alive or not."

Kate walked to the window and looked out on the street. Life was going on as usual. No one knew what she was going through. Ella, her girl, her precious daughter, might be in that deep water. She may be drowned. Kate wanted to curl up in a ball again and sit in the corner of this hospital room. But instead, she tried to get a grip on her emotions, and asked Seth if she could get him anything.

"Mom, they brought me food, and they asked me what I wanted. They have been so nice to me and the others who came out of the water first. I'm fine now, just a little beat up. I think they're going to let me go home tomorrow morning. Maybe I'll come and stay at your house until we know about Ella. And I need to contact our friends to let them know we aren't coming to meet them."

Kate was numb. She was amazed at how brave her son was. She sat in one of the chairs in the room, near the window, and just looked at Seth. Stephen went out to get some coffee for them both, and Seth lay back on the pillow and closed eyes. He was absolutely worn out from treading water and trying to keep himself where someone could find him. He would never ever forget that vision of floating out in the ocean surrounded by smoke, with only the flames lighting the water. He had read stories of what happened to people who were lost in the ocean, and he didn't want to be food for some *giant shark*. He was so very thankful to be alive. His thoughts were running rampant in his head, from one moment to the next.

Kate looked up and noticed Seth had fallen asleep. She went to him and touched his forehead and leaned over and kissed it. *My son. Thank God he is alive. . . . Sam, I wish you were here. You wouldn't believe what is happening to our family. Who would have ever believed that I would lose you, and maybe Ella and Seth?* Kate was so overwhelmed with grief that she couldn't think clearly anymore.

Stephen brought coffee and led Kate out into the waiting area where there were sofas. He asked the nurses for a couple of pillows and a blanket for Kate. He sat beside her and let her lean on his shoulder. There was a small television in the corner of the room with news on about the crash. He watched it for a while and then dozed off, with Kate leaning against him.

On the hospital sofa, Kate was trying to find her daughter all night long in her sleep.

Somewhere in the darkness of the water, there was a girl lying on top of a piece of the plane, stretched out, with blood everywhere, crying for her mother. She had floated out away from the crash. The water was calm, but smoke was still blocking the view for rescuers. She cried out for help every time she thought she heard someone. She could not raise her head to see anything at all. So she just laid there and prayed for God to save her.

Above her, there was a helicopter searching with a strobe light, and it made a few passes near her. But the light kept missing her body. The workers were having a difficult time lifting bodies out of the water. There was so much debris floating that it was hard to distinguish what was a body and what was debris.

Ella could hear men shouting orders to each other. She could hear the choppers overhead. But they couldn't hear her. And the one word she kept saying over and over was *Mother.*

Chapter 18

As they pulled up in Kate's driveway, Stephen decided to park his car in the driveway and pull Kate's up into the garage. They had stopped by Kate's office to pick up her car so that she would have it in case she needed it. The other side of the garage still had boxes of Sam's things that Kate hadn't been able to throw out yet, or he would have pulled his car into the garage beside hers. The neighbors didn't need something to talk about.

Inside, Kate checked her phone messages, shook her head and sat down at the kitchen table. She had come home to change her clothes and shower, knowing Seth was resting and coming home soon. *Another day without knowing about Ella. How long can she be in that water and still be alive?* She waited for Stephen to walk in, and asked him that question.

"How long can a person last in the water, Stephen? Let's say Ella *is* out there somewhere. How long can she last?"

Dreading this conversation, Stephen looked at Kate and sat down with her at the table. He put his hand over her hands, and smiled at her.

"Kate, sweet angel, I don't *know* how long Ella could last out there. We don't know the water conditions, and we don't know if she got hurt or not. All of that makes such a difference in the equation." He knew it was killing her to not know where Ella was. Sometimes it is a relief to find the body, than to wait and wait and hear nothing.

"I have hope still," said Kate, looking down, "but I'm not sure how long that hope will hold out. God did answer our prayers partially. I have Seth back. I'm so grateful for that. But I need to know about Ella. She is so young to die and not be able to live out her life. Have you heard anything about the body count or anymore survivors?"

Stephen got up and walked over to the television sitting on the kitchen counter. He turned it on the local station and they waited for the news to come on. Finally they heard the newscaster announce that fifty bodies had been recovered from the crash. The survivor count was at twenty-three right now, and they were still looking. Someone from the airlines came on and stated that basically it is not uncommon to find bodies days after the crash. He was encouraging families to not give up hope, that they had found someone alive early this morning floating on a seat cushion a mile away from the crash site. Helicopters were working around the clock, searching the area of the crash and then going out in all directions, hoping to spot people who have made it through the night.

Kate perked up and looked at Stephen.

"See, there might be hope. I don't know how strong Ella is, and if she is hurt that would weaken her a lot. But I am praying that they will find her soon. Stephen, they just have to find my child."

Stephen made a suggestion that Kate go upstairs and have a long shower, clean up and go with him to check on his parent's house. She shrugged and went up the stairs slowly. After she was gone, Stephen called the airlines and asked questions concerning the bodies that were found. The names were not released yet on some of the bodies, but they reassured him that they were working as quickly as possible to get the information out to the families who were waiting for news of their loved ones. Stephen thanked the gentleman and put his head in his hands. He was tired, his neck was sore, and he was so worried about Kate he didn't know what to do. She was a strong woman but this was pushing her too far. He hated to think what would happen if Ella wasn't found.

Kate's cell was ringing and Stephen answered it.

"Hey Stephen. Seth here. Just wanted Mom to know I can come home today. Think you guys could come and get me?"

"Of course, Seth. We'll come as soon as your mom gets ready. She's showering now. Are you okay, Seth?'

"Yeah, I'm great. I'm just worried sick about Ella. Any news yet on her?"

Stephen took a deep breath and said "Afraid not. But we are hoping they find her today. We'll be there soon, so hang loose, okay Seth?"

"Cool." Seth hung up and got his clothes ready. He was wearing the same thing that he landed in the water in. His luggage, of course was history. He picked up the hospital phone and called a couple of friends, and also his boss. This would come as a shock to his boss, but Seth knew they'd want to know.

* * *

Down from the crash site, about a mile away, Ella had passed out on the piece of the plane that she was floating on. Her wounds were drying up, which was a good thing, but she was getting dehydrated lying in the sun. The helicopters were flying all around her, but for some reason, couldn't see her on top of the plane debris. She began to stir and was whimpering. Sharks were gathering around the plane crash site, as the bodies that hadn't been found were floating up to the surface a few at a time. It was an ideal situation for sharks. Ella opened her eyes and tried to get her bearings. For a moment she didn't know where she was. Her legs were numb and one of her arms was broken. She tried hard to sit up, but was afraid she would fall off. If she fell, she would drown, and that put her in a panic.

She turned her head to access the situation. As far as she could see, there was debris scattered across the water. She didn't see anyone around her that was alive. She squinted and thought she saw some bodies floating in the distance, but she couldn't be sure.

"I'm not ready to die, God, "she said out loud. " I'm too young to die" Ella started to get angry and began to cry. "I need you to help me, God. No one can see me floating here. I can't move. My legs may be broken, and my arm is broken. What do you expect me to do? I want my mother; I want to know where Seth is."

Ella cried hard and fought the desire to roll off the piece of metal she was balancing on. She was so thirsty she thought she would die. She decided to scream really loud but her throat was parched. She tried several times to scream, but it wasn't loud enough. There was no one in her vision. So how could they hear her? In the distance she thought she saw a boat, and people moving around. But the sun and glare against the smoke was blinding her, and she couldn't be sure of anything. She raised her good arm and waved. She tried to make a noise, but sounded so hoarse that they probably couldn't tell what it was. She waved and waved and the piece of metal began to rock up and down. She panicked and tried to stop it from rocking too much, and it started to flip. She leaned to one side as best she could to compensate for the flip, but the metal was slippery and she couldn't get a grip.

In all her struggle to stay on the piece of plane, Ella slipped off into the water and went under. The piece of metal she had been on floated away in the current, and there was nothing but *complete silence*.

Chapter 19

Underwater, a diver was looking for dead bodies that had not yet come up to the surface. He saw a lot of plane debris in the ocean. He had only a little air left before he had to go back to the Coast Guard boat. Out of the corner of his eye something moved. At first he was afraid it was a shark, and his heart started racing. But he looked closer and saw it was a girl. He thought it was odd that she was going down now. *Where had she been?* He dove to get to her and was almost out of air when he grabbed her arm, which appeared to be broken, and pulled her up to the surface with him. He didn't know if she was already dead or not, but he was going to give it all he had to save her if she was still alive. He motioned to the men to come and pick him up and lifted her head out of the water. She didn't look good, and for some reason he felt like she had fallen from something, the way she was going down in the water. The Coast Guard came quickly and put out a rope he could grab hold of. The men on board pulled the young girl into the boat. They wrapped her in blankets and performed CPR on her. Water poured out of her mouth and nose. They were about to give up when she coughed. The diver held up a thumb and smiled. **She was alive.**

The diver looked out across the water and saw something floating on the surface where he had rescued the young woman. He swam closer to it and saw that it was a large feather. He picked it up and realized it was a feather from a bird that could not fly over the ocean. It was a pheasant feather. He grabbed it and swam back to the boat. They dropped a line for him and pulled him aboard. He was exhausted.

Ella opened her eyes and tried to speak, but couldn't get anything out. One of the rescuers leaned over her. "Stay calm and try to sip some of this water." She was very thirsty and hurting all over her body. But she was alive. *I almost died.*

I almost died. Ella could not quit saying that in her mind, over and over. She began to shake and threw up. The men calmed her down and gave her more water to drink. They tried to warm her up and talk to her to keep her mind off the near drowning. She heard one of the men radio in to shore that a live passenger had been found. She halfway smiled, because he was talking about her. *Mom will be so relieved,* thought Ella. *I've never wanted to see anyone more in my whole life, than I do my mother.*

"Young lady, we have a phone here on board. Is there anyone you would like us to call?"

* * *

Kate was in the car with Stephen, headed to the hospital to pick up Seth. She was talking to Laura to catch her up on Seth and Ella. Her phone beeped. She looked at the screen and it said she had another call coming in. She did not recognize the number, but thinking it could be a representative with the airline, she told Laura she would get back to her and rushed to take the call.

"MOM! MOM! It's Ella."

Kate screamed out loud. "Ella! Where are you? *Oh my God!* Where are you?" Kate was shocked to hear Ella's voice.

"Mom, I'm on a Coast Guard boat in the middle of the ocean." Silence.

"Ella! Ella! Are you there?"

"We're headed to shore...... Mom, they saved my life!"

Kate could tell Ella was very weak and hoarse. She turned her head and told Stephen. "It's Ella. **She's alive! My daughter is alive!**"

Stephen shouted "Thank heavens!" and watched Kate closely while she was talking to Ella.

"Tell me where they are taking you. We'll come to you." Kate waited anxiously for an answer.

"They are taking me to the nearest hospital to be checked. I think I've got a lot of broken bones. I can't feel my legs and I know one of my arms is broken." Kate could hear the shakiness in her daughter's voice.

"I know where they are taking you now. We are headed there to pick up Seth. I'll see you when you get there. I can't tell you how *relieved* I am to hear your voice. Take it easy, Ella. We will be there soon. Just try to get your breath and do what they tell you to do." Kate let out a sigh of relief.

"Mom, Mom!" Ella screamed.

Kate had almost hung up the phone. "What baby? What is it?" Kate asked.

"I love you, Mom. I love you." Ella said, and started to cry.

"Ella dear, you have no idea how sick and worried I've been. I can't wait to get my arms around you. We'll see you in a moment. I love you too, so much. I'm so thankful that you are okay. You just don't know the hell I've been through waiting to see if you were dead or alive." They hung up the phone and Kate began to sob uncontrollably. Stephen reached over and put his hand on her arm. This was a good cry for Kate. She had her daughter back. He silently thanked God for this miracle.

In the boat, the EMT worked on Ella, preparing her for entry into the hospital. He stabilized her legs and wrapped her wounds. She was in a lot of pain, but also in shock. She was incredibly tired and kept falling off to sleep, even while they were working on her. The diver sat and looked at Ella for a long time. He had almost swam away from her in the water, thinking she was a shark. His air was going so quickly that even two minutes more and he would have been in trouble. He touched her hair. He was so thankful that she was going to be alright. Her family must have been mad with worry, and now her mother could rest her heart, knowing her daughter was on the way to the hospital, instead of floating to rest on the bottom of the ocean floor. His other dives hadn't been so productive. At this point in the game, he really hadn't expected to find a live person in all this mess. *What a nightmare.* He touched Ella again on her arm, and then went to the front of the boat to get something to drink. He was worn out and needed a break. It had been a long day and not very many recoveries.

Ella slept until they were at the shoreline. They moved her carefully onto a stretcher and into an ambulance that had been summoned. There were two police cars flashing their lights and leading the ambulance out onto the highway. She thought she saw cameramen but her head was spinning. She laid her head down and rested. She was scared, tired, and wanted her mother. That was the only thing that she could think about.

Stephen and Kate drove way over the speed limit to get to the hospital. Kate was so excited and relieved that she was talking faster than Stephen had ever heard her. He patted her arm and tried to keep her calm. *Both of her children survived this horrible crash. What are the odds of that? I'm not a betting man,* he thought with a smile. *But I bet it is a million to one odds that both children would be alive after this kind of catastrophe.* He barely knew the kids but he was near tears from all the stress, and of watching Kate suffer so much. He might start gambling if life with Kate was going to be this stressful! He laughed out loud, and Kate looked at him with a raised eyebrow.

She had not stopped talking since she heard from Ella.

"Ok, Mr. Stephen. What was that laugh for, if I may ask?" Kate looked at him and smiled.

"Oh, nothing Kate. Just so relieved for you that both of your children are going to be okay." Stephen took her hand and held it for a minute. Kate laid her head back on the seat and took a deep breath. There was a bond that was forming with Stephen that felt sort of like her bond with Sam. Only different. No one would be like Sam. But maybe, just maybe, God had put Stephen in her life for a wonderful reason. And she was going to watch to see just what that reason was. He already had shown her so much compassion that she was overwhelmed. *I guess when things quiet down,* she thought, *I'll be able to know why this relationship feels so good.*

Chapter 20

The plane crash was big news on the front page. A lot of people had lost their lives and the passengers who were found alive had multiple injuries. Kate and Stephen discovered how fortunate Ella and Seth really were, after seeing some of the other passengers in the hospital. Another reason for being grateful.

Seth walked into Ella's room and sat on her bed. He hugged her and they cried. Neither of them remembered much about what happened, only the explosion when the plane hit the water. And then they found themselves in the ocean trying to survive. Seth was so proud of Ella for not panicking too badly. *She kept herself on that piece of metal for a long time.* Ella was so glad to know Seth was alive, and this experience created a bond between them that was unspoken

"I called our friends, Ella, and told them we wouldn't be meeting them in Europe. They heard about the plane going down but didn't know we were on it since I didn't tell them when we were arriving. It was scary for them to hear that you nearly drowned." Seth put his hand on her good arm. Ella was so thin, and frail. He was becoming more and more protective of her as he aged. They were so close in age that it was almost like they were twins. He was so thankful that she was alive.

"I need to call James," said Ella, grinning. "Mom doesn't know about him yet. But she will. I put a note in the mail to her before we left, and she should get it any day. I'm surprised she hasn't gotten it already. "Ella looked at her legs and grimaced. Both legs broken. But at least she would be able to walk again before too long. The doctors told her she would need a lot of therapy to walk normally again. But right now she was treasuring being in the hospital in a bed with blankets, food, water, and her family who she was beginning to treasure more and more. Frankly, just to be alive was awesome.

Kate walked in with Stephen and found Seth sitting on Ella's bed. She ran in and hugged them both and leaned over Ella and kissed her. "Ella, this is Stephen. He owns the house I am looking at on Madison Avenue. He has been so wonderful through all of this and I am glad you are finally able to meet him."

Stephen shook Ella's hand and smiled. "You are a very brave young lady, Ella. Your mother was just about at her wit's end waiting to hear if you were okay or not. Man, this has been a tough wait."

"Oh my God Ella! I've been sick worrying about you for the last two days. It's been more than I could handle. But you're here. You're okay," Kate kissed her again. The three sat on Ella's bed and talked and talked, and Stephen sat back in a chair near the bed and smiled. It was such a *relief* to have them all together again, that he wanted to savor the moment. He didn't feel left out at all; quite the contrary. They had made him feel like part of the family in such a short time. He and Kate had really only been on one date to speak of. Things were moving faster than he had ever dreamed.

A doctor walked in the door and saw what looked like a family reunion. He smiled and came straight up to the edge of Ella's bed.

"Well, this looks like a homecoming for sure!" as he opened her chart. "Ella, you're a very lucky young lady. You're going to be here for a few days, and then have a lot of therapy. We might be able to switch all of that over to your local hospital. I'm going to make a few calls, and see if I can get you transferred over to Martin City Hospital, so you can be closer to your family. I know that'll make your mother happy." The doctor checked Ella's few wounds and asked her if she was in much pain. She said no, and he walked out to make a few calls.

Things looked like they were going to settle down some and Kate was finally relaxing a little. She would never forget this time with her children for as long as she lived.

She left Seth and Ella for a moment and walked over to Stephen.

"I want you to know what you have meant to me these last couple of days. I've put you through hell and you just stayed right by me through this whole catastrophe." Kate leaned down and hugged him and kissed his cheek. He stood up and gave her a big hug and told her that he wouldn't want it any other way.

"I'm so glad I could be here for you, and that things turned out like they did. It's such a relief to know your children are both safe. This has been such a nightmare, Kate."

Kate turned around, and both kids were watching them. *At least they are smiling.* Stephen decided to go down and eat in the restaurant on the first floor and bring Kate back something good to eat. Seth was hungry too and Ella was asking for a hamburger. He jotted down their requests and went downstairs to fill their orders. Kate was left alone for the first time with her children, and she cherished the moment. She went over and sat with Ella and waited to see what Ella had to say about what she had been through.

"Ella, I don't want to overwhelm you, but how did you feel out there all alone in the ocean?"

"Well, Mom, let's put it this way. I thought I was going to die. And I told God I wasn't ready to die. I guess He heard me, because when I fell, that diver was right there to bring me back up. I heard the rescue team say that he was almost out of air when he found me. It's amazing. It's a miracle that he was there at just the right time." Kate shook her head and agreed. *She owed that diver her life.*

"When we hit the water, I don't remember much after that, Mom. After I came to, floating on that piece of metal, I was petrified that I was going to drown. It was the worst thing I've *ever* been through in my whole life. Like something you would see in a movie. Only it was happening to me in real life."

"We need to get that man's name and track him down. I would love to give him a hug," Kate said, smoothing back Ella's hair.

"He basically risked his life to save you, Ella," Kate added.

The *heaviness of the diver's sacrifice* hung in the air for a few minutes.

"I know we're thankful that you both survived this tragic event. So many did not."

Stephen returned with some hamburgers, fries, drinks and plenty of napkins. Everyone dug in and ate. Hamburgers never tasted so good. It was quiet in the room for the first time.

When they were through, Kate looked at her watch.

"Ella, I know you're worn out and you need to rest. Seth, I think you told me you were going to be able to come home today. Why don't we check into that and see what's going on with your release?" Kate said, as she walked out of the room toward the nurse's station. Ella was exhausted, but she was so happy to see her mother, and Seth, that she was not even thinking about her lack of sleep. Kate came back and said that the doctor was getting Ella transferred to Martin City Hospital, and that Seth was released and could leave with them now.

"I think it's a great idea, Seth said. "And maybe after you are settled in your new room in Martin City, we'll all come up and camp out with you!" Seth got up to get his things in his room.

Kate kissed Ella again.

"You're my precious angel. I'll see you later. Get some rest, baby. I know Stephen may need to go home, so we'll regroup. I'll get you a new cell phone so you can call me anytime, Ella. You have a lot of recovery ahead of you, and I'll get a room ready for you at home to make things easier during your recovery." Ella smiled and kissed her mother back.

"It's so good to be back in the world again, Mom. The ocean was so black and deep. I was so sure I was going to drown out there."

"I can't imagine what you were going through out there all alone. I know we were going crazy waiting for any news about you. I'm so proud of you for being so strong, Ella."

"It was the worst nightmare of my life, Mom. I wanted you so badly out there all alone. I have never felt so alone in my whole life. But I made it, and that's what matters now."

"We all are *so* relieved. You have no idea how much we prayed for you. I kept dreaming I was looking for you so that I could save you, Ella." Kate leaned over and kissed her daughter. "We'll be back shortly. Please rest some and I'll come back up as soon as I get things sorted out. Stephen needs a break, I'm sure."

"Okay, Mom. I'm pretty exhausted." Ella hugged Seth and they both teared up a little.

"Ella, you had me worried there for a while. I *never* lost hope that they would find you. But I have to admit I was getting worried."

"Thanks Seth. I'm so glad you weren't hurt. We both are pretty lucky, you know?"

"Yeah. So get some shut eye and we'll be back in a bit, okay?"

On the way home, it was pretty quiet in the car. Everyone was lost in their own thoughts about what had happened in the last couple of days, and how it all could have turned out much worse. Stephen took Kate's hand and held it on the way home. She had been through so much, and he was proud of her. And he was thankful things had turned out the way they had. Kate had her kids back, and maybe now her life would soon get back to normal.

When he got to her house, he helped Kate get into the house, and made sure that Seth didn't need anything.

"You two take care of each other tonight, Kate. I'm going to head on home so you can enjoy your son all by yourself." He leaned over and gave her a light kiss, and told her he would call her later. Kate stood up and walked over to him.

"Stephen, I wouldn't have made it through this without you. You were absolutely wonderful to me and I'll never forget this as long as I live." She reached up and kissed him on the mouth, lightly, and smiled. Their eyes met for a moment, and *something happened.* Somehow they both knew that life would not be the same as before. Stephen walked out of the house and got into his car. He was whistling again. Kate heard it inside the house. She smiled.

Stephen was smiling in the car. His life had been turned upside down since he met Kate. But he also acknowledged that he was falling in love with her fast. As he pulled out of the driveway he noticed the mailbox and realized that Kate had probably not gotten her mail in a couple of days. He pulled up to the box and pulled out the mail. There was quite a stack. He opened his door and jumped out and ran up to the door.

"Kate," he said as he opened the door. Here's your mail." She came running and took the mail.

"Thanks, Stephen. You're so thoughtful. Please go rest. And thank you again for all you've done."

Stephen closed the door and got back into his car and drove home, feeling relieved for Kate and her children. No one would believe it if he told them all the events that had taken place since he and Kate's lives had crossed paths. He had trouble believing it himself. And now he was in love with her.

Kate looked through the mail quickly and saw a letter from Ella. *How strange. She must have mailed it right before she left to get on the plane!*

Seth was upstairs getting a shower. She opened the note and read it, with tears streaming down her face. "*. . . . . .since dad died you haven't been the same. I don't feel close to you and I don't know what to do about it. You're always busy, and now you're going to sell the house I grew up in. All my memories are in that house, mom. And you didn't even ask me how I would feel about it.*"

Kate sat down in the kitchen and quickly read the rest of the note. There was a lump in her throat and a burning. *This was her baby writing this to her. . .the words were piercing. They had always been so close. Able to talk about anything. What happened?*

"*Mom, when I get home, can we have lunch sometime? Can we sit up and watch a movie like we used to when I was a kid?. . . . . . .*"She walked up the stairs to her bedroom, refolded the note and tucked it in the same drawer with the other notes. *I haven't been there for Ella in the way she needed me to be. Somehow I missed that while I was trying to save myself from drowning. She and Seth are too young to know how it affected me when Sam died. One day they will understand. Now I need to put myself aside and be there for them a little more.*

There was a lot of emotion in that dresser drawer. A lot of pain. She decided right then and there, that one day soon she would share with Ella and

Seth about Alison. But for now, she had to find a way to bring Ella back into her world.

Kate sat on the edge of her bed and cried. She had to find a way to pull her family together again, and it might come when she sold this house, and bought another one, thought Kate. Wiping her tears, she lay back on her pillows and listened to the shower and Seth singing. One day these times of struggle and pain would be a thing of the past. *A memory.* It was already beginning with Stephen.

She closed her eyes and fell fast asleep. She didn't hear Seth finish his shower and peek in to see if she was still awake. She had left the drawer open, and Seth came over to shut it. As he reached for the handle he saw envelopes in the drawer and picked them up. He turned his head to see if she was awake and watched her slow, steady breathing. He pulled out one of the envelopes and took the letter out. He read without stopping and then read the other note that was in the same envelope. His heart was beating fast. *So my mother never knew about Alison. Good gosh; I can't believe my dad hadn't ever told her!* Seth had gone on some hunting trips with his father, and one time there was a girl that showed up one day. She asked Seth where his father was, and Seth told her that he had gone into town. He asked her if she wanted to leave a message, and she said no, that she'd wait for him. So they sat down and talked and for some weird reason, they connected right off the bat. Alison decided to confide in Seth and tell him her story. But she made him promise not to tell anyone, especially his mother. *So Seth promised.* He didn't even tell his father that he knew the truth.

And now she knows. I know this had to come as a shock to her, he thought. *Poor Mom. She would've loved Alison if they could have just met. I wonder why Alison wrote this note to Mom. Maybe they did meet somewhere?* Walking out of her room, he went and checked his wet wallet. Everything was ruined in it. But he dug inside the wallet, underneath the flap, and there he pulled out a photo of a young girl. He laid it underneath the flap and smiled. It was Alison.

He had kept that secret for a while. This was not the time to tell his mom that he had known Dad's secret for years. *I don't know if I can ever tell her,* Seth thought as he went into his old bedroom. He leaned back on his bed, and closed his eyes. He fell fast asleep; a sleep that was desperately needed. He left his wallet out on the nightstand to dry.

Chapter 21

Kate's desk had so much stacked up on it, that she could hardly see her chair when she walked in the door. It had been a few days since she had been to work, and patients were calling wanting to make appointments. She went through her mail rapidly, throwing out all the junk mail, and checking on the statements that came in. There was a personal letter in a pile of bills and checks, and she laid it on her desk. She didn't recognize the return address, but knew she would read it in a few minutes. She swung her chair around and looked out the window. There were crowds of people going in all directions hurrying to work. She still recalled the woman standing still and it brought a chill up her spine.

Laura was out front at her desk taking appointments, when suddenly the door opened to Kate's office. Mr. Dawson walked in and walked straight up to her desk.

"Sir, I don't take walk-in appointments. You have to go back to the front desk and make an appointment with Laura." Kate stood up and walked around her desk.

"No. I've waited a long time to make an appointment with you, and I'm tired of waiting. You're here, so why can't I see you now?" He was standing right in front of Kate, glaring at her.

Kate thought a moment, looked at her calendar that Laura had brought in this morning, and agreed to see him, making a rare exception, but only for thirty minutes. He sat down, and waited for Kate to begin.

"So what is so urgent that you couldn't wait your turn, Mr. Dawson?" Kate tried hard not to sound too irritated at his barging in on her day.

"I had a horrible week and my meds have run out. I feel like I'm overwhelmed with my life and needed to talk to you immediately. I don't seem to be able to cope with stress at all, Dr. Kate. You have to give me something stronger. This isn't working."

"I can't give you anything else, as you've shown problems with addiction to drugs. I know you hate group therapy, but that's what you need Mr. Dawson. I'm sorry you had a difficult week. Why did you let your meds run out?"

"I was working late and somehow lost track of how many I had left in the bottle. My son is in jail for marijuana charges, and my youngest daughter is failing in school. My wife lost her job last week and that just pushed me over the edge. I mean, how much can one person stand?"

Kate had to fight off a smile. "Oh, I can relate, Mr. Dawson. We all have issues that come up in our lives that we're not fully prepared for. And sometimes they stack up on us. But you have to have more self control than what you are showing me today."

"I apologize for barging in, but I felt like if I didn't see you today I was going to lose it completely."

Kate worked for the full thirty minutes with him, trying to help him manage all of the issues he was having with his family. Keeping him on his meds seemed to be a huge issue. When he left, he appeared to have calmed down some, but she was concerned that he was going to balk about going to therapy twice a week.

The day went on, crazy, like it started. Her patients were upset, full of problems and wanting help immediately. She felt like they were all so demanding, and guessed it was par for the day. Her nerves were frazzled. She needed to check on Ella. She knew Seth was okay, because he was still at the house and didn't have a car to go anywhere. She rang the hospital and asked about Ella. She was told that Ella was in route to Martin City hospital, so Kate phoned Seth and gave him the news.

Kate left the office with paperwork still undone. She had placed the letter in her purse to read later. She still had no idea who it was from, but she would find out soon enough. She phoned Stephen and left a message on his cell phone that Ella was headed to the local hospital. Heading home, Kate took a deep breath and rubbed her face with one hand. She was exhausted, after the week she just had. *So many patients today and everyone was so angry.* She pulled into her driveway and parked the car. Something told her to read the letter now, before she went in, so she pulled it out of her purse and opened it. Immediately, Kate's stomach went up into her throat. There was a photo of a girl inside and it was Alison. The letter was from her parents and the last paragraph really tore at Kate.

Even though you didn't ever know our daughter, we want you to know she did love her father. Sam sent her money and saw her occasionally at the hunting lodge. She honestly adored him and wanted to spend more time with him because of his illness. That's why she moved to Martin City.

We're sorry for the shock this must have been to you, but Alison meant no harm in your lives. She didn't want to upset your family or cause mistrust between you and Sam. I'm just sad that you never got to know her. It might have saved her life.

Truly,

Martha and Dave Stratford

Kate put her head on the steering wheel; her emotions were locked up. She didn't think she had any tears left in her. *That poor child. Her death was a waste. All because Sam could not tell the truth. I know he thought he was doing the best thing, but this time he was wrong. If I had only known, Allison might be alive right now. In fact, I know she would. There is nothing I can do now, but I feel so much frustration inside.*

There was no way to talk to Sam now. All she had left was Ella and Seth. So she was determined to speak with them about Alison soon. She folded up the letter and put it back into her purse.

Inside, Seth was waiting on Kate to come home so they could go and spend time with Ella. Kate walked in, greeted Seth, and ran up the stairs to change into some jeans and a shirt. She grabbed a cup of coffee and a granola bar, and ran out the door. Seth grabbed a Sprite and was already in the car. They pulled out and headed towards the hospital.

* * *

Stephen had been at his desk at work when Kate's call came in. He was on the phone and couldn't take her call. It was time to head home anyway, so he checked his voicemail and headed straight to Martin City hospital. He'd been thinking about Kate all day, in between phone calls and paper work. He also was wondering how Ella was holding up with two broken legs. *That girl has been through so much. I hope this is over for the whole family.* Stephen did not have any family left alive, except for a few distant cousins. So he really respected this family and cherished the time he'd spent with them. *It felt too comfortable.* He was overwhelmed with how he was feeling. But he also realized that at his age, it didn't take long to figure out whether he loved someone or not. He was pretty sure Kate was at the same place.

Kate's cell phone rang and it was Jim. A voice she had not heard from in a while. "Hey Kate! How's my girl?" Jim was unaware of all had taken place and had a very aggressive tone in his voice.

"Well, Jim. We have had some pretty traumatic days since I last spoke with you. I know you remember that my two kids were going to Europe?"

"Yes I do remember you saying that."

"Well, their plane crashed into the ocean not too long after takeoff. Seth is fine, just a little shaken up with a few scratches. But Ella has two broken legs and a broken arm. She nearly drowned, Jim. A search diver saved her life."

Jim sat back in his chair and ran his fingers through his hair. Kate had been through a nightmare. *Why hadn't she called me?*

"I meant to call you, to let you know, but I've had my hands full just getting my kids to dry land and safe."

Jim responded quickly. "Hey Kate, do you need any help? I can be there in minutes if you need me."

Kate shook her head. "Oh no, we have it under control now. But that is sweet of you to offer. I'll catch you up on things soon. I promise." Kate hung up quickly so she didn't have to get into the part about Stephen being around.

I don't think I'm going to get any closer to Kate, Jim thought, shaking his head. *This event we shared does not seem to have made us any closer. In fact, it may be the knife that separates me from ever having a chance to get to know her better.*

Chapter 22

Stephen was pulling up in the parking lot about the same time as Kate. In fact he saw her car pass him in the next aisle. He parked the car and began walking in their direction and finally hooked up with them on their way into the building. He hugged Kate quickly and shook Seth's hand.

"Hey you two! How are things this afternoon?" Seth smiled. "I'm great, Stephen. Just worried about Ella right now. She has a lot of mending to do."

"I know, Seth. She's been a brave young woman." Stephen opened the doors to the main hospital and they walked up to the elevator. Kate had called ahead and asked for Ella's room number so they could go straight to her room.

"I can't wait to see her again," said Kate. "She's been so brave, like you said, Stephen, and she needs some extra TLC from her family."

They walked into Ella's room and there was a young man sitting on her bed. Ella was smiling and talking to him. She turned and saw her family coming in the door, and James stood up quickly.

"Mom, I didn't know you were coming so soon." Ella was blushing.

"Well, Ella, introduce us to your friend," said Kate, laughing.

"Mom, this is James Simpson, a friend of mine. Stephen, this is James." Stephen stepped up and shook his hand.

"Hey, dude!" James said smiling.

Kate came up and shook his hand. "How are you James? Nice to meet you." She looked at Ella and raised an eyebrow. Ella knew her mom was surprised. They'd had some long talks on the phone since that night, and she had never mentioned about James to her mother in those conversations. But she also knew things were cool, having James there. It felt so good to have him around, even just to hang out in the room with her. She had missed him so much.

Kate discerned that Ella needed some time with James alone. She winked at Seth and smiled. "Ella, are you hungry? We're all starving, and thought we'd run downstairs and get a bite to eat. Can we bring you something?" Kate walked to the bed and gave her daughter a huge hug. "James, can you keep her company while we run and eat?" James nodded, looking at Ella with a smile.

"Sure, I'll keep her company. That's cool."

Seth said he wanted to hang out with Ella and James, and asked his mom to bring him a burger and fries. Kate looked at Ella for any sign of disappointment but saw nothing, so she and Stephen left the kids and went downstairs to the cafeteria and to eat supper in peace. When they sat down at the table, it was the first moment alone that they'd had together since their date and the crash, to really sit and talk quietly. It felt so good to relax for a few minutes.

"How have you been, sweet one?" asked Stephen. "I know you had to have been swamped today at work."

Kate smiled. "You have no idea, Stephen. On top of which I've been think-ing about Ella all day. She's really taking this like a trooper, but I know it's still hard on her emotionally and physically. She has to be in a lot of pain. But I also had something else interesting happen today." she paused and ate a few bites. "There's a lot I haven't told you about these last few months. Maybe this is not the time to start, here in the hospital. I know we're going to be interrupted so maybe I will wait until we get back home." Stephen took her hand in his and smiled.

"We need that time alone to really get to know each other. I feel so close to you after this past week, but we have not had a lot of alone time."

They finished their meals and walked back upstairs to the kids, carrying burgers, tacos, fries and drinks for all three of them. They hung out in the room with Ella all night long, laughing, watching her favorite shows with her, and eating. She enjoyed herself so much, and was relieved to finally introduce James to the family. The doctor had come in while Kate and Stephen were eating and told Ella that she probably would be in the hospital for at least a week and then she could go home. The breaks were simple fractures and he thought she would mend just fine. After the casts came off, she would have a lot of rehab to do.

The night came to an end, and Stephen walked Kate and Seth to their car. They followed each other back to the house, tired from the emotional stress of knowing Ella was safe. Seth was ready to hit the sack and went straight upstairs to his room when they arrived home. Kate asked Stephen in.

"Kate, you've had a very long day, and maybe it would be better for us to see each other in a couple of days so that we can catch up on things."

"I know you're right. But I have some things we need to talk about. Please let's just go in for an hour or so. She leaned forward and kissed Stephen and they hugged.

"I've loved you being involved like you are. It really has been so much help and the kids feel so at ease with you around. You really are amazing, Stephen. You just go with the flow."

Stephen kissed her back. "Okay, Kate. I'll come in for an hour. But we don't need to over do it tonight."

They walked into the living room and Kate motioned for Stephen to sit down on the sofa next to her. "Stephen, I hardly know where to begin… so I'm going to just jump right in and tell you what's been going on. When I was helping Ella and Seth get packed for their trip, I ran across a note that was tucked into Seth's suitcase. It was a note that a women had written to Sam. At first I thought she was having an affair with Sam, and it shook me up pretty badly. However, I later found out she was his daughter. Stephen, Sam had a child with a woman he met while he was off on one of his hunting trips!"

"Oh my gosh Kate! Are you joking? This is unreal, what I'm hearing. How did you find out it was his daughter?"

"Well, it's a long story that I'll try to shorten for you. I went to dinner with one of my girlfriends and the server we had was a young woman. She had no name tag on, but for some reason when she gave me the check, she said my name. It puzzled me how she would know my name and later I found out why." Kate paused and sat back on the sofa looking at Stephen's reaction to all of this.

"Some time later I was at work and I stood up to look out my window and there was a girl standing in the crowd below looking up at my office building. I watched her for a few minutes and then she disappeared in the crowd. I wasn't sure then that it was the same girl that waited on us, but now I'm convinced it was. Stephen, she moved here to be near Sam when she found out he was dying. He had taken good care of her all her life and they were apparently very close. Sam had made an agreement with her that his family would never know about her, so she was alone in her secret. When he died, it was too much for her. She drowned in the ocean, and I found her when I was walking on the beach with Jim, an acquaintance I had dinner with. What are the odds of that, Stephen? That I would find her? Does any of this make sense to you?"

"No, Kate. I'm trying my best to keep up with you. It's quite a story and I can't imagine what you must have felt when you found all this out. How in the world did you ever cope with finding her in the water, Kate? That had to be a little freaky! Did you know it was her in the water when you found her?"

"No. Jim pulled her to shore and we called the police and an ambulance. They couldn't revive her. Later, a Detective came to my house and shared her name with me. It blew me away because the name was the same as the person who signed the note to Sam. *Alison Stratford.* To top things off, I have now received a letter from her parents saying how they wished I could've known their daughter, as she probably would be alive today if I had."

"Kate, please don't take on the responsibility for her death! She was obviously distraught and we don't know if you could've saved her or not. I know you wish you'd had an opportunity to know her. But that was not meant to be. Did the kids know about this?"

"At this point I don't think they know. I plan to have a talk with them at some point. I just have to find the right time after I get Ella home and settled. Anyway, I wanted to let you know what has been going on. I didn't mean to wait so long to share this, but it's not like we have had any time together to speak of, where we could really talk about things."

Stephen hugged her and laughed lightly. "There has been so much going on that it's a wonder we even know our own names. I don't know how you have processed all of this and are still able to hold down the fort at work. Do you need to go see someone and maybe get on some medication to help you through this time? You have to be struggling with the fact that your husband had an affair; he had another part of his life you knew nothing about."

"I'm coping. Granted I do feel overloaded and have been under tremendous stress for a while. It really sucks that Sam did this to his family. And to hide it makes it even worse to me. It's not just the fact that he had an affair, but he also had a child that he hid from us. I guess anyone in his situation would probably not have been able to tell their family. I thought Sam was different. It makes me feel kind of like I really didn't know him, you know? I am hoping when Ella comes home that things will settle down and we can get back to our lives. I don't know what normal is anymore."

"It might have been better if you hadn't found this out, Kate. But now that you know, you are going to have to somehow put this all behind you. I'm not saying it will be easy. But it is crucial for your mental health and for your children. I'm sorry you have to deal with all of this. I had no idea. But I'm here now if you need to air it out. You definitely need someone to talk to about all of this." He looked at his watch and stood up. "I need to get out of here so you can get some sleep. We've had a long day, Kate. I'm so glad that you shared all of this with me and now I just want you to take care of yourself. You have your daughter coming back under your roof for a time and she's going to have a long recovery. Promise me you'll take time to rest and not get worn down."

"I'll do that, Stephen. You are something else! I never dreamed things would move as quickly as they have between us. But I want to thank you for all you've done for me, and for us. The kids seem to just accept you as part of the scenery right now. I'm so grateful for that. However, I need to work on my relationship with Ella, and I'll be able to do that with her in my house for a while. I'm going to enjoy this time with her, and with Seth."

"You rest tonight, and we'll talk tomorrow. I want to do everything I can to make your life easier. I just wish I could do more. I feel helpless sometimes because I don't know exactly what to do to make things better. Time will make things easier to bear. Just know I'm always a phone call away from you." He kissed her lightly and held her close. For a moment she allowed herself to relax into his arms. He walked to the door and she said goodnight. She stood at the doorway and watched him pull away, suddenly very tired.

Kate plopped down on the sofa and went through her mail. She remembered the letter in her purse and got up and took it out, deciding to run it upstairs to the dresser drawer. She had decided to keep all her notes from now on in that dresser drawer. They were safe up there, and generally the children didn't look through her drawers. She would have to write the Stratford's back, and that was going to take some thought. It'd been a long day, and Kate turned down the lights in the house and headed upstairs to her bedroom. It felt good to have Seth there, but she knew this might be his last night. He was ready to get back to his apartment and his friends, and she didn't blame him at all. She looked into his room to check on him and walked over to see if he was asleep yet. On his nightstand was his wallet. She picked it up and the leather still felt wet. She decided to open it up and let it air dry better, and when she did, a photograph fell on the floor.

Kate bent over to get it and nearly fainted. It was a photograph of Alison. *How in the world did Seth get this photo? How did he know her? Oh my gosh! When will the secrets stop in this family? I could tell that Ella and James had been around each other a lot, as they were so comfortable with each other. So Ella had hidden that relationship until now, and probably would have still hidden it if she hadn't been in the hospital recovering from a plane crash. Part of that could've been my fault as our relationship had slipped while I was trying to get my life back. Now this photo pops up! Where in heck did he meet her? **Was I the only one who didn't know?***

She laid down Seth's wallet and looked at the photo in the hallway under better light. *She was such a lovely girl. I can't believe she's gone. This just doesn't seem real to me at all. It's like a bad dream.* She put the photo down on the night stand and walked into her room. She was tired and got into her most comfortable pajamas and climbed into bed. She turned the television on and listened to the news for a while. The anger and hurt that she felt began had given her a pounding headache. She closed her eyes and fell asleep, dreaming about Sam and the web he had weaved with that one secret. In her dream, she met Alison face to face.....

Chapter 23

Kate woke up to a phone ringing. She jumped up and grabbed it, looking at the clock. It was Saturday, and even though she didn't have patients on Saturday, she was going in to do some paperwork, undisturbed.

"Hello," Kate's voice sounding a bit hoarse.

"Kate, this is Jane, I have some good news!"

"Well, I could use some good news this morning!" Kate laughed.

"The first couple I showed your house to made an offer. Jane paused, and Kate gasped.

"Are you joking?" Kate asked. "I can't believe this. Was their offer very low?"

"No, actually, they offered $10,000 below our asking price, which is still above appraisal. I think we should take the offer, Kate, considering the soft market right now. How do you feel about that offer?"

Kate thought for a moment. She really was ready to buy Stephen's parents home. "I agree with you. I think it's a good offer. Let's split the closing costs with the buyer, and I'll be happy." *So it looks like it's a done deal,* thought Kate as she made her bed and hurried downstairs to start the coffee pot. *I know Ella's going to be upset, but just wait until she sees this other house. I can hardly wait to decorate it and make it a home. Stephen will be thrilled with this news!*

The phone rang again and this time it was Susan. "I just got back in town and heard about the plane crash! I have been dying to talk to you, Kate. Surely your children were not on that plane! I have been sick with worry. I had to wait until I knew you were awake to call."

"Susan, Thank God you're home. I'm sorry I haven't been able to get you on your cell. You wouldn't believe the hell we've been through the last few weeks. My children were on that plane that went down but they survived! It has been one of the worst times in my life. I sure wish you could have been here, Susan. I need to bring you up to date on things."

Susan was shocked. "You're kidding me, Kate," she said, shaking her head in disbelief. "I want to hear all about the children. I need to know how they survived al of this. You had to be going through hell, Kate. Can we have lunch today?" Kate thought a moment and decided that she could work it into her schedule.

"I would love to see you, Susan. Today would be wonderful."

"Okay. I'll meet you at the café near your house at about 11:30," Susan said, smiling. She was dying to hear about her kids. She had been so worried that something bad had happened and now Kate had confirmed her fears

.

Kate hopped in the shower and got dressed. She made a phone call to Stephen to let him know about the possible sale of her house. He didn't answer, so she left a message, and then she called the hospital to check on Ella. The phone rang and rang. Suddenly she picked up.

"Ella?" Kate asked, worried. "Are you okay?"

"Sure Mom! Just had to go to the bathroom and heard the phone ringing. They took the hard cast off my arm, and I'm now in a tight sling. It won't be long before I can go home, and then I know there'll be lots of rehab. James is here with me now. He says I'm doing really well."

"I'm very proud of you, Ella. And I know you're so ready to get out of the hospital. I'm assuming you are coming here, right?" Kate had already gotten her room ready for her, and made adjustments in the room since she would be in a wheel chair for a while.

"Yes, Mom. But I want James to be able to come over a lot to visit and help me with my rehab and stuff." Ella was hoping her mom would not object.

"That's fine, Ella. I look forward to having James around, so I can get to know him better. Just let me know when they're going to let you out. I'm having lunch with Susan at 11:30 but I want to see you after that. Stephen may want to come with me to pick you up."

"Okay Mom. I'll call you the minute I know I'm released. I love you."

Kate hung up and tapped her chin. *I wonder where this relationship with James is headed?* She really wanted Ella to finish school before she got so serious with someone. But Kate knew that's not always how things happened. She fell in love with Sam right off the bat and wanted to spend all her time with him. So she should understand how Ella felt about James.

She went over to her dresser drawer to put up some laundry and saw her notes had been moved. She had them underneath some camisoles and now they were lying on top of a stack of underwear. In fact, one of the notes was coming out of the envelope. *Who had been in my drawer? It had to be Seth! What made him look and when did he find the opportunity? How would he know to even look for anything?* She was puzzled and didn't know quite how she would approach her son. *I guess it's time to have a discussion with both the children about Alison and their father. She decided to do it when Ella came back home.* She also remembered suddenly that she had not written Alison's parents back.

Kate went to her desk and pulled out some paper and a pen while she was thinking about it and sat down to write a short letter to a Martha and Dave Stratford. It was succinct, but kind.

Dear Martha and Dave,

You were so kind to write to me and thank me recently. I want you to know I'll never forget that night on the beach, and thank God that I was there to find Alison.

I was unaware of the fact that Sam had a daughter, but I assure you I would have loved knowing Alison.

My deepest sympathy to your family.

Kate

Kate folded the letter and put it inside an envelope. She addressed it and put it in her purse to mail on her next trip out. She laid the letter from Martha and Dave in the drawer with the other notes. She reminded herself that she had to talk to the kids soon about all of this. The note stack was getting larger and larger.

She was about to leave the room and noticed that Sam's ball cap had fallen on the floor. She leaned down to pick it up and happened to look underneath the cap as she picked it up. There was a white folded sheet of paper, not very large, tucked inside the cap. Kate was amazed that she had not seen it before. But she probably had not picked up that hat since Sam died. She unfolded the note and read it;

I love you, Kate. Sam

Her eyes brimmed with tears. She and Sam had for years written little notes for each other to find. Amazingly she found this one after Sam was gone. *Oh Sam. It feels like you were here today and left that for me to see.* She took the note and put it in the dresser drawer with the others. Her heart was heavy with the weight of his deceit. *What else would she find to put in that drawer? This was a little much for one morning.*

She walked downstairs to get more coffee and sat down at the table to think about the last few weeks. Who would have dreamed her life would have turned out like this? She and Sam were supposed to grow old together, and sit outside in rockers with the grandchildren. *I don't know what my future holds,* thought Kate pensively. *I'm slowly learning that even though things do not always turn out like I want them to, I don't always know what is best for me. . .* She thought about Alison's parents, Ella and Seth, and her own future. There was a lump in her throat that didn't want to go down. This month had been more than she could bear. And without Stephen being there, she probably would have collapsed.

Chapter 24

Susan was waiting at the quaint café. She was tired, although the trip to Africa had been worth it. It was something she had always wanted to do but never thought she would actually get to go. Her husband had been asked to give his services to one of the poorer hospitals in Ethiopia. It was a very dangerous and rewarding trip and they both were amazed at how it had affected their lives.

Leaning over the bar, Jim was trying to eat a quick lunch before heading back to work. He was doing some great photo shots this afternoon of a young woman who wanted to do some modeling. She needed a good portfolio to send to the modeling agencies, and he was excited about this opportunity. He glanced around the café before he paid his bill, and saw Susan sitting at a nearby table. He slipped over and sat down.

"Hey Sue! How are you?" He winked at her. She was a lovely woman, but she was married.

"Hi Jim, how are you? I didn't see you sitting over there." Susan replied with a smile.

"So where in the world is Kate these days? Has she disappeared from the face of earth?" Jim asked. "We spent some time together while you were in Africa and boy did we have a traumatic experience. Has she told you anything yet?"

Susan looked at Jim with a frown and said "No, she hasn't. What happened, Jim?"

Jim looked around the café, and then leaned forward. "We had a great dinner at Rondell's. Laney told me that Kate really enjoyed that place. We had a fabulous time, and she really seemed to be having a nice evening." Jim was getting excited.

"Okay, Jim. Take it easy. I'm all ears, but you better hurry because Kate is going to show up in a few minutes." Susan looked at her watch, surprised that Kate was this late.

"Well, after dinner we went for a great walk on the beach, and I was just standing in the water looking out to sea , as Kate walked farther down the beach picking up shells. All of a sudden she started yelling and waving at me. I came running and asked her what was wrong. She pointed to a white shirt floating way out in the water. I jumped in and went after it, fearing it was a person. I got a hold of the shirt and pulled and sure enough it was a body. The water was very rough, and it took a lot out of me pulling that body to shore, but I made it. I begged Kate not to look, but she did anyway. When she came over, she brushed the hair away from the girls face, looked at her, and screamed out. She said it looked like the waitress at Rondell's that she and Laney had."

Susan was so intent in listening to Jim that she didn't even see Kate walk up to the table. Suddenly Kate interrupted Jim.

"Hey you! Can I tell my own story?" They all laughed and Kate sat down. She didn't want to say too much while Jim was at the table, so she went along with his story.

"Yes, it was quite a night to remember. The ambulance came and took the body away and later a detective came by my house to ask some questions about that night." Kate looked at Susan and rolled her eyes.

"Jim, I meant to call you, but I've had my hands full for a few weeks. I'll get back to you soon, as I still want some photos taken of Ella and Seth. Is that okay with you?"

Jim got up and shook Susan's hand, and hugged Kate. "Sure,Kate. I also remember a rain check that you promised." He stood there smiling at her.

Kate looked down and then said "I do remember saying I wanted you to take some photos of my children. I'll give you a call and set up an appointment for that."

Jim looked at her with hurt eyes, and said, "Well that's not exactly what I had in mind, but I know you're busy. I've been so worried about you." He reached out and hugged her hard and kissed her cheek.

"Please call me soon and let's get together." Kate nodded and Jim turned and walked away. Somehow he didn't quite believe that Kate would ever call him back.

Susan was about to have a heart attack. "What in the world was that all about? You and I have so much to talk about and I know you don't know where to start."

Kate smiled and sat down. She spent the next hour and a half talking to Susan about Alison, Sam's betrayal, and the notes she had gotten from Alison and her parents. She also told her about Seth having the photo of Alison. Susan was overwhelmed by all of it.

"Kate, no other woman would be able to handle this. How did you swallow that fact that Sam had a child with someone else?"

Kate thought a minute. "I've never been so shocked in my entire life, Susan. You could have pushed me over with a feather! Sam and I had a perfect life. Or at least I thought so. To find out that he slept with someone even once and had a child with her that he hid for years, was just way over the top of what I could imagine. I thought I would die inside. I saw Alison at Rondell's, only at the time I didn't know it was her. And she was also the woman outside my office looking up at my window. I think she really wanted to know me, but she was afraid of my reaction. And I can so understand why. Sam had made her promise not to ever tell anyone."

"I don't know if Seth had met Alison or not, but he had her photo in his wallet. That makes me think he knew her, and that makes the fact that Sam did not share it with me even more difficult to handle."

"I have more to tell you Susan. This is not the main thing I want to talk about, but I wanted to mention that the old house on Madison Avenue, Old Tom Winson's place, burned down while you were gone. I was out with Stephen and we drove over there when it was already engulfed in flames. It was a sad sight to see. It scared me when I heard the sirens, as I was afraid it might be the house I wanted to buy from Stephen!"

"I remember that house, Kate. We always loved that house as kids. How sad."

Kate nodded. "The major thing I want to share with you that I mentioned the other day on the phone, is that my two children were in the plane crash that you read about! There is no quick way to tell you what I have been through."

Susan looked completely shocked. "I was so shocked when you said that the other day. It made me feel panicked, Kate. What in the world happened? I want to hear about this. Are you just about to lose your mind?"

"You just don't know what I've been through, Susan! Seth was thrown out of the plane when it hit the water and miraculously attached himself to a floating seat. After being in the water for a while they rescued him with no problems. He was basically unharmed but shaken up. Ella's experience in the crash was a nightmare! She landed on top of a floating piece of airplane in the middle of the ocean, with no one around her, and she was there overnight in the water alone. Can you imagine her terror, Susan? Both legs were broken, one of her arms, and she was very dehydrated and afraid. The piece she was floating on became unstable in the waves and she fell off, basically drowning, when suddenly a diver from out of nowhere lifted her up to the surface. He saved her life."

"Kate, hold on. You're going too fast for me to keep up with you! This is almost too much for me to take in. What happened next?"

"We later heard that his air was running out and he risked his life to save her. The timing of that was unreal. It had to be a miracle... She saw him coming and it was like an angel saving her from drowning. She wants to meet the man now and thank him. I'm going to try to arrange that soon." Kate paused, thinking of how she would arrange this meeting,

"I know I have condensed this, but it was hell, Susan. And if it hadn't been for Stephen, I would not have made it. We haven't even known each other all that long, but this tragic event has caused us to become close very quickly. It has been the roughest time in my life, actually, and you were away." Kate reached over and grabbed Susan's hand. Susan looked back at her with tears in her eyes.

"This is so hard to take in, Kate. You have lived this out and I'm hearing it for the first time today. I love you dearly and it breaks my heart that you had to suffer like this over your children. You nearly lost your children, Kate!"

Kate looked at Susan with a sober face. "You have no idea what I went through while Ella was out on the water alone! My emotions were running rampant. They kept searching for bodies and survivors, but they didn't find her. I was about to accept the fact that she was gone when we got the call from Ella, when she was still on the rescue boat, that they'd found her. When I heard about this diver, I lost control and broke down."

"No one will ever know how hard this was for you. It could've been a total catastrophe, Kate. Thank God your children are safe, and Ella just has to go through rehab. You had to be in total shock while all of this was going on. Was Stephen there for you?"

"Totally. He was like a rock, Susan. All I had to do was pick up the phone no matter what time it was and he was there. I couldn't have survived this without him."

Susan looked at her watch, and apologized that she had to run. "Kate, we need more time. I had no idea there was so much going on in your life. Promise me that we can get together again. I have a lot to share with you too."

The two friends stood up and hugged each other tightly. "Call me if anything else happens. I want to know. If you sell your house, call me. You can stay with me if you have to close before you are through with the purchase of the other house. Whatever you need, I'll be here for you."

NANCY VELDMAN *with Paris Milla*

"Thank you so much, Susan. I'm sorry we had to hurry the conversation. And I want to hear all about your trip. Let's not wait so long to get together. Maybe next week we can catch a lunch. I love you." Kate kissed her goodbye and made it home in time to catch the phone ringing. It was Stephen.

Chapter 25

Ella was going home at last. She was so excited! The hospital had been wonderful to her, and she'd had photographers all over the place taking pictures of her recovery. It was going to be on the news and in the papers, along with other survivors. The attention helped some to get her past the panic attacks she'd begun to have in the hospital, remembering when she was lying on the piece of metal in the middle of an ocean. She was so panicked about what was under the water. It made her quiver just thinking about it.

James had been terrific. He was there every day after school and at night. It seemed her mother came and went, each time missing James. He really seemed to care about her, and this made her feel safe. She hadn't heard from him this morning and he knew she was being released. She had phoned his cell and he hadn't responded. So she went for a short outing on her floor, getting used to maneuvering around in her wheelchair, to see if any of the other survivors were around. She had gotten close to some of them and wanted to say goodbye.

✳ ✳ ✳

Across the city, a young man was sitting on his sofa thinking about Ella. Michael had been a rescue diver for several years and really enjoyed his job. He had done it on the side while he was in his early years of college and now he was about to graduate. His major was in physical education with an emphasis on physical therapy. He would enter physical therapy school next fall. He was busy and his life was full, but right now he couldn't get a young woman off of his mind. No one quite understood why he felt this way about her, but he couldn't get her off his mind. She just floated down *out of nowhere* and it kept hitting him that if he had not been there at that one single moment, she would've drowned. There was a bond forming between him and this woman, even though she knew nothing about it. It was kind of odd, and after talking about it to several other divers on the rescue team, he realized that it was rare to feel this way, since they saved so many people in a year.

Michael decided this morning, without the encouragement of his peers, to call the hospital and ask about this young woman. He knew her name was Ella, but that was all. He was hoping it wouldn't be too difficult to find her since she was one of the survivors of this recent plane crash that had been all over the news. He picked up the phone and called the information desk at the hospital in Martin City and spoke with the operator.

"Ma'am, I don't know this person's last name, but her first name was Ella and she was one of the survivors of the recent plane crash." There was a silence on the phone as the receptionist looked at the list of survivors. The hospital had so many calls that she was told to keep a list on her desk of all the names of the people who had survived the crash that lived in Martin City or the surrounding area. Families in the beginning were calling the hospital every day to check on a loved one already being treated for injuries from the crash, or to check and see if a loved one had been admitted to the hospital. Finally, she saw the name of Ella Morrison, and asked the gentleman if that sounded familiar. He guessed that it had to be her, and asked for her room number. The receptionist gave him her room number, 422, and he thanked her and hung up.

It was going to take some nerve on his part to go visit this girl. He was not even sure what he wanted to say. She would barely remember his face as she was so upset when he brought her to the boat. She was cold, scared, and hurting. She'd just been through the worst experience of her life and she probably won't remember much from that day at all.

His drive over the hospital was torture of the worst kind, because he was having feelings he didn't understand about Ella, and he knew she would see him as a stranger. Sure he saved her from drowning, but that would be all she thought of him. He had to be very careful what he said to her, and how he said it. He didn't want to freak her out in any way, but there was something about her he couldn't get out of his mind. Maybe it was just the unusual way he found her. It was so weird that she would come floating down like that. Most people he found underwater had been there a while before he got there, or they were up on top of the water struggling. She obviously was falling, it was clear that she wasn't going to make it unless someone got there. The odds of that were a billion to one, if not more. *I can't help but think in the back of my mind that there was a reason that I found her.* He wiped the sweat off his face and swallowed. He took a long drink of his coffee and took a deep breath. He couldn't remember ever feeling this nervous except for when he made his first dive rescue.

Ella had just wheeled back into her room and was about to try to get herself back onto her bed, when there was a knock at her door. She thought it was James being silly.

"Oh come on in dude! Like I don't know it's you." She laughed and waited. The door opened slowly and in came a young man who at first she did not recognize.

"Ella good morning! I'm Michael Hayes, the diver that pulled you out of the water." Michael swallowed hard and kept going. "I've wanted to find you and see how you are, and just couldn't stop thinking about it. So I took a chance this morning and drove to the hospital."

Ella was so shocked and excited that she could hardly speak. "Oh my gosh! I can't believe it's you! I just told my mom that I wanted to meet you. I can't believe you just walked through the door." Ella teared up. She wanted to run up and hug him but she couldn't move.

Michael saw her teary eyes and walked over to her. He squatted down and hugged her right there in the wheel chair. "So do you want me to help you get back in the bed?" he asked, smiling. Ella nodded, and wiped her tears away. She was shaking and did not know why.

"Michael, you don't know what this means to me, you coming here today. I have wanted to say thank you so badly and didn't know how to go about finding you."

Michael sat down on the edge of the bed and looked at Ella. His heart was about to burst and he didn't know why. All of the emotions he felt when he pulled her up to the surface came rushing back in. There was an unusual sense that he knew her, and maybe that was normal for this situation.

"Ella, I have thought about this time, too, of meeting you. I just didn't want to scare you or bother you while were healing. Look at you! Two broken legs and an arm in a sling. And you look wonderful! How are you feeling? And has this been difficult for you to handle? I know it would be for anyone who nearly drowned!"

Ella looked straight at Michael. She wanted to know this man who God must have put in the water to save her. There was something different about him, and she couldn't put her finger on it.

"It's been horrible. I've been having nightmares every night about falling off that piece of metal. I felt so helpless with one good arm knowing there was no way I could even try to swim. I really felt like I was going to die. I didn't see you down there."

He put his hand on her good arm and patted it. "I know this is hard for you. I didn't see you either. I saw something out of the corner of my eye going down past me. I grabbed hold of what I saw and realized it was a girl floating downward. I couldn't understand where you had come from!"

Ella laughed and so did Michael. It was funny now, but also traumatic to remember. "I didn't ever think I would be saved, because I could hear the search boat and voices but they seemed far away. I didn't think I had a chance in a million to make it back to the surface."

Michael looked at Ella and shook his head. "This kind of thing doesn't happen every day, you know? I feel a bond with you and I know we don't know each other. Do you feel that?" He was almost afraid to say it, but he felt this was his only chance.

"Yes, Michael, I do feel a bond with you. It is beautiful. I can't tell you enough how much it means to me that you came by today. I'm leaving soon. In fact I'm waiting for Mother to come and get me.

"I want to give you my phone number. Any time you need or just want to talk, would you feel okay about calling me? I mean, I don't want to push it or anything. But I really think I would like to know who you are. I have a funny feeling, and I may be wrong, but I feel like we were meant to meet. Granted, it is a strange way for us to meet, but I haven't been able to stop thinking about you since the rescue."

Ella was amazed and smiled, blushing. "That is the sweetest thing anyone has ever said to me. Of course I'll call you. And I'll give you my cell number. Do you have a pen?"

Michael pulled a pen out of his pocket and grabbed a sheet of paper from her nightstand. "Okay, shoot." Ella gave him her number and they both hugged. Michael sat back and looked at her again.

"You're a very *beautiful* woman. I look forward to getting to know you. Please don't worry about your nightmares. They're very normal and may disappear soon. I just don't want you to feel like you are crazy for dreaming them. After enough time passes, it'll have less of an effect on you."

Ella smiled and touched his hand. "You're such a gentleman... Just like I thought you would be. Please let's talk soon. I'll get in touch with you when I get to my mom's. You can come over for a visit."

Michael got up and gave her another hug. Then he walked to the door and smiled at Ella. "Get well. I'll be talking to you soon." And he was gone.

Ella just sat there and wondered how in the world this all had happened. Her cell rang and it was James. "Hey babe. Is your mom there yet? I meant to call earlier but got delayed." They chatted about her nightmares and then Ella said goodbye so she could get ready to leave.

Ella was alone in her thoughts of Michael. *How nice of him to come by and see me. Gosh, I was hoping I would get to meet him and I had no idea he wanted to see me. He was so sweet, so caring. His eyes showed so much emotion in them. Mom will be so glad.* She was taken aback at the difference between James and Michael. Of course she barely knew Michael. But the difference was pretty loud. James was more immature and Michael was more polished. Sure of himself. He knew what he wanted to do with his life.

She looked around the room and it all seemed so surreal. The whole thing was so hard to comprehend. She had come so close to death, closer than most people, and somehow she was saved by the nicest guy in the world. *How cool was that?* She laughed out loud.

She picked up her phone and called her mother. "Mom hey! I'm ready to come home. Are you about ready to leave yet? I know I sound over eager, but I guess I'm excited about coming home and spending time with you while I get some rehab. But guess what?"

Kate, wondering what it could be, said "What baby? Do you have good news about your rehab?"

"Mother, you'll never believe who came to see me today." Ella sounded so happy that Kate was surprised.

"Who, Ella? I'm sitting on pins and needles here." Kate smiled.

"It was Michael, the rescue diver! Mom, he actually drove over here to the hospital to see me!" Ella was ecstatic and bubbling over about the visit.

"Oh my goodness," said Kate. "I know how much you wanted to meet him, and he just walked into your room?"

"Yes, Mom. It's totally turned my world upside down. You wouldn't believe how sweet he is. How caring. He was so nice to me. We exchanged phone numbers and he wants to get together soon and talk. He said he feels some sort of bond with me. Is that sweet or what?"

"Ella, that's fabulous. I'm so glad that he took the time to come and see you. That visit had to be wonderful for you both." Kate smiled and thought, *Good thing James wasn't there.*

It was almost like Ella could read her mind. "And Mom, let's not say anything to James just yet. I don't want him to freak out or anything, you know?"

"It's not my place to say anything to James, Ella. I will be there shortly to pick you up. Stephen will see us later."

"Is my room ready, Mom?"

"Yes, Ella. I've had it ready for a while now. So just relax and I'll be there in a few minutes to bring you home. I know it will feel good to get outside and breathe the fresh air again."

Ella hung up the phone and just sat there thinking.

On the road, Michael was smiling to himself. *She was so cute. Maybe beautiful is a better word. And there may even be a chance that we might see each other again. That would be just too weird. No one would believe it*

He opened his glove compartment and pulled out a long feather he had found floating on the water when he rescued Ella. He thought it was so weird that a feather of this type would be floating in the ocean. He had shown it to the other guys on the boat and they laughed at him. He reached over and put the feather back inside the compartment. *Maybe Ella would not think it was so funny.*

Chapter 26

Kate made a phone call to her realtor to see if the couple that had wanted her house had accepted her counter offer. She was so ready to make a change in her life, and even though Ella was going to be upset, Kate really thought it was a good move.

"Hello, Kate. I was going to call you today! "Jane had just pulled Kate's number out and laid it on her desk. The contract was ready to be signed and all she needed was to go over it one more time with Kate.

"I have good news. They did agree to pay half the closing costs and were wondering if the drapes were going to be sold with the house." Kate laughed. "Well, sure. That is no problem at all. My drapes won't fit in the other house anyway. When do they want to close?"

"Kate this is a cash sale. They need no financing, so the closing can happen as soon as thirty days from now, if that is acceptable to you."

Kate sat back and put her hand on her forehead. That was pretty fast for a closing. She thought she would have about three months to get the kids adjusted to the fact. And she hadn't even bought the other home yet.

"To be honest, Jane, could we make it forty-five days? That would give me time to address the purchase of this other house, arrange for the move, and get my kids thinking in that direction. We didn't think it would happen so quickly."

She hung up with Jane and sat there in shock. Her house was actually sold. Now she could move on with her life, and she was having mixed emotions. She knew she was doing the right thing, but all of a sudden things were going too fast.

Stephen had come over the other night and was so sweet and honest about his feelings. I'm feeling the same way about him, she thought. *But I'm scared we are moving too fast for the children. I know we are older, and it doesn't take that long to figure out if you love someone, but the kids may need time to adjust. However, they are not showing any signs that this relationship bothers them in the least.*

Kate dialed Stephen's number and when he picked up she said "Stephen, you won't believe this! My house is sold. So I guess we need to talk numbers here, and get things rolling on your parents' house. I'm going to have to move in forty-five days. Do you think that's possible?"

Stephen was thrilled. "Just relax. You can move your things over here anytime you would like. Since it's my parents' home, I'll allow you to move in before the closing. At least the furniture you aren't using now. It would make your move easier, since the timeframe is narrow."

Stephen was so glad that this was actually going to happen. He was worried that Kate might change her mind, but apparently she was getting comfortable with the idea after all. . He was hoping that she would move so that he wouldn't have to always be in the house where Sam had been. That might be a little fast-forward for Kate.

"Stephen, that's so nice of you. You sure have been good to me, "Kate said. "I want to come over and look again in the house to see where I'll put things. Is that ok with you?"

"Yes, I can understand why you would. I need to bring you a key so you can have it when you want to come here. I'll run over tonight and give you your own key. How does that sound?"

"That would be great! Why don't you have supper with us? Ella is coming home tonight, and I know she would love to see you. Seth is back in his own apartment so I'll call and see if he can come too."

Kate and Ella came rolling in the door an hour later. James was behind them with her few things that were at the hospital. She was smiling ear to ear, and so glad to be out of the hospital.

"I know you're happy to be here. James, take her on back to the bedroom on this floor. Ella, I have turned this room into your room because of the wheelchair. I knew you couldn't make it up those stairs!"

Seth was coming over with Lila, and Kate was happy that all of them would be together for a night. She left Ella and James to get her settled into her room and walked up to the front of the house to fix some fresh coffee. Dinner was ready and in the oven. She made some ice tea and sat down for a break. She was going to love the new house because there was a lovely spacious porch out back where she could sit and think, or read. It was very peaceful there and the sound of the ocean was so relaxing. She would miss this house, but she could carry all the memories with her into the new home.

It was not long before Stephen knocked on the door. Kate opened up the door and let him in, with his arms full of fresh bread, flowers, and a dessert that looked decadent. Kate took the flowers and put them in a vase she had in the cabinet, and set them on the table. Then she took the dessert and put it on the counter and smelled it. It was a chocolate cake with mousse and whipped crème. *Oh me,* she thought. *So much for watching my waist line!*

Soon the family was around the table, even Ella in her wheel chair at the end of the table. Grace was said by Stephen, and every one dug in. Kate sat there listening to the chatter, warmed by all the love in the room. *Sam would love this gathering,* she thought. *Even Stephen. Yes, she was convinced that Sam would like that man. Oddly, they would've had a lot in common.*

Later, after dinner and dessert, Kate and Stephen went into the living room and sat down on the sofa. He put his arm around her and snuggled her a minute.

"You're so lovely, Kate. I think of you during the day, and just smile. It's such a great feeling to love someone like I've grown to love you. I know it's happened fast, but when it feels so right, it's hard to hold it all back."

"I love you too, Stephen. I feel so comfortable around you. And you've been with me through so much lately. The way you handle things so easily takes such a load off of me. Don't think for one minute that I don't notice all that you do. It means so much

"Kate, I'm so excited about your buying the house. You're going to love being there, and it's a comfortable home that you can spend the rest of your life in. Don't you think?"

"It already feels like my home, even though I haven't bought it yet."

"Kate, please look at me. Just for a moment. I want to tell you something; I never thought I would ever want to love someone again. Until you walked into my life, I was perfectly happy being alone. Now things are so different. I wake up each day thinking of you and how I can make your life better. I look forward to our time together so much, and I've grown to love Seth and Ella. You really do have two wonderful children; and I didn't have that opportunity, you know."

"I know, sweet angel. You didn't get to be a father, and what a father you would've been. I know my kids miss Sam so much, and it feels good to have a man around. They've been so good about accepting you in my life. I am amazed at how easy this has been with them. I was worried. I don't mind telling you that now. I was really worried that they would balk and get upset about my dating again. Actually you and I haven't dated that much. We just jumped in with both feet. Because of all that's happened we have spent a lot of time together and it has made us closer, I think, than actual dating would have."

"I couldn't agree more, Kate. I know we need to have respect for the kids, and I'll take it as slow as you want me to. They are getting older now, and have their own lives. Remember that Kate." He moved closer to her and kissed her softly on the lips. "I just want you to know I'm here, and I'm willing to be here forever."

Kate *really* was falling in love with Stephen. He was so open and easy to talk to that it was hard not to just want to get married right away. But she had decided to wait until she moved into the house and gave herself time to adjust to being away from this house and all the memories of Sam. Then she would be ready to have a life with Stephen.

"I love how you talk to me. They are both healing and encouraging. I never thought I would feel this way again. Let me get the move over with, Stephen. Then we can talk about where this relationship is going. I know that I want you to be in my life. There is no question about that."

It was getting late and Stephen had some important work to do in the morning. So he stood up and Kate walked him to the door. He told her to hold on a minute, and he walked back to Ella's room. When he walked through door he saw Seth, his girlfriend Lila, James and Ella all piled on Ella's bed. They all turned around, smiling, and said hello. Stephen walked up to them, and patted Seth on the back.

"You kids are something else. I'm so glad you're home Ella. I know it feels terrific to be here with your mom, and friends. You're quite a girl, Ella. I'm so proud of you for being so brave." Ella rolled her eyes and smiled.

"I know you're tired of hearing that, but it's true. Seth, I'm glad you're healing fast, and it's nice to meet you, Lila. "He hit James' hand that was up in the air. "See you, James."

Then he was out the door, with Kate blowing a kiss. As she closed the door, Kate leaned against it and breathed a sigh of relief. Her life has been a whirlwind since Sam died. *I can't believe how much has happened and is happening, and sometimes I just wish I could step off for a moment and take a breath*, she thought to herself, making a face. *Things will slow down after I move. They have to! At least I have my children and I'm grateful for that.. To think how this all could have turned out....*

She sat down at the table and drank the rest of her coffee and just for a moment, let the world pass her by.

Chapter 27

Walking around the house was heaven for Kate. Stephen had given her a key and now she could come and go as she pleased. She just stood there and breathed in the smell of the house. It was the layout that drew her in, and the feeling that the house had character. A life of its own. She moved into the kitchen and looked through all the cabinets, the refrigerator, the oven, the microwave. The countertops were granite, and the floor was tiled. She walked into the hearth room and there were windows lining the left side of the house. It let so much light in. Kate decided right then that those windows would remain open.

In the kitchen there were windows also looking out, and she was never going to hide that view with drapes. The living room also had three huge windows that were arched, and those would remain open also. She had always wanted a piano in the house, even though she had not played for years, but it would be so wonderful to have a black piano in front of those windows. Her mind went on and on, as this house slowly became hers.

When she left, she had gone over every single room and thought through how her things would fit in. She would have to get rid of some of her furniture, and then buy pieces that would better suit the rooms. But that was the fun part. Her head was swimming, thinking of packing and moving after 30 years in a house. That is a lot of living in one single place, and her children had many memories that they would have to take with them in their lives.

I'm about to start a new life of my own, she thought.

Seth was walking out of Ella's room, when Kate got back to the house. She had a thought that this might be a perfect time to have a discussion with them about *Alison*. Her stomach went up into her throat again, but this needed to be said. She grabbed Seth and went back into Ella's room. Ella was on her phone with James, but hung up when she saw Kate and Seth coming into her room.

"Okay, guys. We need to have a family meeting. There are a couple of things we need to talk about and I want you to feel free to comment anytime. First, I know it is painful for you, Ella, to even think that we are selling this house you grew up in. But it's time for me to move forward. I need to let you and Seth know that this house has sold."

Ella immediately began to cry. Seth came over and put his arm around his mother.

"That's great news, Mom," he said in his deep voice. "I know you're ready to have a life and I think you've done so well these last two years in trying to piece your life back together."

Ella dried her tears on her sleeve, and sat up straighter. "Mom, I'm sorry. I don't know why this hits me so hard. I'm not even living here anymore. I guess kids always want to be able to come back home. And if you move, it won't be home anymore."

"I understand totally, Ella. It was hard at first for me to come to a place where I would even consider selling the house. But now, I feel very happy inside and know Sam would want me to do this." Kate explained that she'd been over to the new house today and that she walked through all the rooms to see where all the furniture would go.

"It's a lovely house and it's already beginning to feel like home. You'll get used to it, Ella. I want you to come to see it soon to get a feel for it."

"There's something else a lot more important I want us to talk about, kids." Kate sat down in the corner in a chair across from the bed. She folded her hands in her lap and looked at her children. They were so beautiful to her.

"Well, there's no easy way to say this." She paused for a moment. "I wanted you to know that your father made a mistake years ago, and got a woman pregnant. She gave birth to a girl whose name was Alison." Seth began to fidget a little, and this did not go unnoticed by Kate.

"She grew up knowing your father, as he asked her often to come to the hunting lodge when he took his weekend trips. He gave her money to help get the things she needed, and loved her very much. He made a decision not to share this with us, but I've found out in a terrible way that Alison was his daughter."

Kate then spent an hour talking to the kids about the date with Jim, and walk on the beach, and the body floating in the water. The kids were shocked, and Seth was visibly upset. Ella was freaking out, but was also taking in what her mother was saying.

"This has been a very difficult time for me, Ella and Seth. I had to look at Alison laying there on the beach, not breathing. And I thought she was only the waitress at Rondell's. Later I learned from notes that I've found and one that Alison wrote to me, that Sam was her father. Since then I've heard from her parents, who have thanked me for finding her that night."

Ella interrupted Kate saying, "Mom, how in the world did you handle this news after losing Dad?"

"It was hard, Ella. It hurt bad that your father did not want to share this with me. I know he was worried about you, Seth and me getting hurt. But I would've loved to have known Alison, and I wished she could've known you."

She turned to Seth and said, "Seth, I'm afraid you might have something to share with us too. Am I right?"

Seth came and sat at the foot of the bed and looked at his mother. His eyes teared up, but he tried to be strong. *She knows that I know,* he thought nervously.

"Mom, I *did* know Alison. I met her by accident on one of those hunting trips. Apparently Dad didn't know she was coming that day, and she walked right into the cabin where I was sitting. We talked very openly, and she was easy to like. He gave me her photograph to keep in my wallet, and I know I should've shared it with you, Ella, but I was afraid Mom would find out and be upset. I couldn't understand then why Dad did not tell you, Mom. I'm so sorry."

Kate walked over and hugged Seth. He was taller than her, and so much like Sam.

"I know your heart. I realize it was hard on you to have to keep that secret. I saw the photo when you came home from the hospital. It was in your wet wallet, and I pulled out things to dry. I'm not upset at you, Seth. That was a tough thing for you to have in your heart, to carry that secret around for so long. I am upset with your father because he didn't share this with me before he died. I suppose he was pretty sure I would never find this out."

Kate sat back down in the chair. She looked at Ella and asked her if she wanted to say anything.

"I guess I just want to know how it happened, Mom. How did Dad make that kind of mistake? And why did he not tell you about Alison. Now she is dead and we'll never get to know her. "Ella teared up and Seth tried to stop her. Kate walked over and sat down with the kids and they all hugged each other and cried.

The talk went very well, thought Kate. And they reacted just like I thought they would.

"We don't have to talk about this again, but I just wanted you to know I'm alright with it. I regret not having a chance to love her. But this is a lesson to us all, that we do not keep *secrets* in this family. We stay open and agree that no matter what happens in our lives, we talk about it with each other." The kids agreed and Kate left the room.

Ella looked at Seth. "How could you *not* tell me, Seth? I'm your sister."

Seth looked at her square in the face. "Alison made me promise that I wouldn't tell anyone! She knew how Dad felt, and she was told she had to honor that. So I felt like I was trapped between her and Dad."

Ella laid back and tried to sort through all of it. She could not believe her mother found Alison dead, floating in the ocean. How in the world do you deal with that sort of thing? *I would have nightmares for the rest of my life,* she thought. *So Dad had an affair.... And a daughter I never knew. Poor Mom. I know this hurts her. . . How could he do that to her? To us? I am so confused.*

Kate left the children to their conversation and went out for a walk. She needed some fresh air. *Well,* she thought. *I feel so much better getting all of this out in the open. And Seth has to feel so much better inside. How in the heck he kept that a secret all these years is beyond me. I feel so ignorant that I didn't pick up on anything. I guess if it was a one time thing it would be tough to recognize there was an issue. But how did Sam reconcile this in his own heart? How did he live all those years with such an enormous secret? I feel betrayed and so left out of the loop with all of this. I need to talk to Ella again after she heals. She has been through enough trauma without having to deal with the death of a step sister she knew nothing about.*

Kate breathed in some fresh air and tried to shake off all of the negative feelings she was carrying in her heart. *I have a chance to start over, regardless of the past. So I need to focus all of my energy on the children and this new relationship I have with Stephen.. Sam was a good man. But he was not perfect. I had him on a pedestal and he has fallen off royally.* She smiled faintly.

All that is remaining for me to do is buy this house and move. Then maybe my life will settle down and be calmer and more serene. She walked for twenty minutes and turned to head back home. She made supper for the three of them and ate with Seth and Ella sitting on Ella's bed. The children were laughing and talking about memories of their mother finding odd things in their rooms. *Under their beds.* It was good to laugh after such a serious conversation.

The phone rang and Stephen asked her to go have ice cream after supper. She accepted with only a little guilt about eating ice cream and hung up the phone. She walked upstairs to change her shoes and freshen up and she passed the photograph of Sam and looked him in the eye.

"Sam, I know you thought you were doing the right thing. But this has been hard on us. I love you, Sam. I miss you more than life. I didn't think I could breathe without you. But God has shown me another way to breathe. You are missed. You are loved. And us leaving this house does not mean you won't be remembered. For you shot an arrow into my heart and you will always be my first love, Sam. But you have hurt me to the core. I know I will forgive you, because I know you loved me all of our marriage. *You were nothing but giving to me.* It will take time, Sam. I have to say I'm disappointed in you. Mostly because you felt like you could not confide in me, your one true love." For a moment, she almost thought his eyes teared.

She kissed the photo and walked down the stairs. Stephen was waiting downstairs.

Chapter 28

Seth was at work sitting at his desk, working hard on a project. He was near graduating from school, and was planning on applying at a CPA firm down the street; Barton, Smith and Harrington. He knew one of the men who worked there, and used him as a reference on his resume. He was nervous but needed this job to seal his future. The job with Mr. Warden wasn't going to cut it. He raised his head as the boss walked by, nodding. Mr. Warden probably liked Seth but was miserable in his own life, so he took it out on everyone else. Seth had never seen him smile, not once. How miserable it must be to live like that. One reason more for Seth to move on. Lila and he were getting closer. He loved her. But he wanted to be secure in a good job before he asked her to marry him.

His mother might freak out if she knew how close they were. He had not talked too much about Lila to his mom. She had been through so much lately that there was really not much time. He was doing great in his classes. Numbers were his thing. He loved math. He drove himself crazy thinking about numbers. This was a chance in a million to get this job and he was going to do all he could do to become a part of this firm. His dad had advised him about this company; that it took a lot to get in, but once you did, you were there for life. Seth could be a company man, if that is what it took. He really was a loner, but he knew how to be flexible.

Lila was a quiet girl, but she had a heart as big as a lion. She was involved with a salon down the street, and had been through cosmetology and also esthetician schools. She was trained in laser and other anti-aging technologies. He wanted her to open her own aesthetician clinic. But that took money and he wanted to achieve his goals that so that they both could do what they loved. She deserved this. Her life at home had not been the best, and she was a smart girl. Her dad was an alcoholic and her mother was ill. She basically raised herself and decided that she was going to be different than her family.

Seth was working overtime now, completing tax extensions, so there was a lot to do. But he was getting better and better and even Mr. Warden was leaving him alone now. It made him feel better, but he still wanted to leave. After work, he drove over to pick up Lila. They were going out to dinner to celebrate their two year anniversary. She picked out the restaurant, Spaghetti Warehouse, and he went along with it. It really did not matter to him. He got a flat tire on the way, and that slowed him down for a while. But he hurried and made it there nearly on time. She was dressed to the nines.

"Hey baby," Seth said. "Man you look good tonight." He hugged her and gave her a kiss.

"Hey Seth. Did you have trouble getting away from work tonight?" Lila was dressed in light blue, and with her long black hair she looked fabulous. Her eyes were black and seemed to look right through him.

"Come on angel. I had a stupid flat. I'm sorry I'm so late; let's get going. I want to enjoy this night with you."

* * *

Ella was home in her wheelchair, and had rolled herself up to the front of the house to get something in the kitchen. Kate had gone over to see Stephen, and Ella was on her own for supper. She made something light to eat and was rolling back into her room when her cell rang. She rushed down the hall to get it and caught it on the last ring.

"Hello Ella! How are you?"

It was Michael. Her heart flipped in her chest. "Hi Michael! I'm doing better. How are you?"

Michael was excited to hear her voice again. "I thought I would drop by tonight if that was ok with you. I wanted to bring you something."

"Oh great Michael! I need to tell you where my mom lives. I look awful, with these casts on my legs; I can't take a shower yet. Can you forgive me?"

Michael laughed. "Okay, Ella. I can get past the casts as long as you don't smell!"

She laughed.

Ella gave him directions and hurried with her supper so she could brush her hair, put on a little makeup and freshen up. She had not told James about Michael. And James was not coming over tonight. She looked in the mirror and suddenly wished she was out of the casts. It would be so wonderful if she could walk and put on cute dresses. Sitting in the wheelchair just did not get it for her. She did what she could to freshen up and put on some lipstick and mascara. She didn't look too bad. *But she could look better,* she thought, smiling at her reflection. It wasn't too long before she heard a knock at the door. She was in the living room, and wheeled up to the door and opened it. Michael walked in with pink roses, and a gift that was wrapped, and he had a big smile.

"Hey beautiful!" he said with a smile. "How is the bravest girl in the world?"

"I'm doing wonderful, but can't wait to get these casts off so I can stand up!" Ella said. "What do you have in your hands? Those flowers are so lovely."

He handed them to her and asked if she had a vase to put them in. She rolled over to the cabinets and pointed to a vase for him to use. Michael got the vase down, put water in it, and arranged the flowers the best he could. "Where do you want them?"

Ella decided that she wanted them in her bedroom so they went back down the hall and Michael set them on her dresser. Then they went back into the living room so they could talk.

"So how have you been doing, Ella? When do you get those casts off?"

"It'll be soon. Then I start rehab vigorously. I'm ready, boy am I ready." Ella smirked and then laughed at herself. The doctors had treated her so well and made this as easy on her as possible, but it was really a pain not to be able to do much of anything for herself.

"Ella, I want to go into physical therapy and I would love to help you get better when you get those casts off. Would that be okay with you?" Michael held his breath. He could think of nothing better than to help this sweet girl get back on her feet, after nearly losing her life.

"Sure Michael. My gosh, how could I turn that down? I would love for you to work with me, but I know you have a job and are in school. How will you fit all that in?"

Michael ran his fingers through his blonde hair.

"Oh, don't worry about that. I'll find plenty of time to work with you!"

He stood up to leave, and took a chance and leaned over and gave Ella a kiss on her cheek. She blushed and tucked her head for a minute. Then she looked up and smiled.

"You've been so sweet to me, on top of saving my life. It's almost overwhelming, Michael. I can't do anything for you yet, because I can't get out of this chair. But when I can walk, I'll do something wonderful for you to show you how very thankful I am for what you have done for me."

"Ella, I would be lying if I didn't say I was drawn to you. I haven't been able to get you off my mind since that day I saw you in the water. I hope I'm not being pushy, but I don't want you to get away from me. I'm sorry if I'm coming on too strong, Ella. I feel such a closeness to you and it may be unfounded. Please tell me and I'll back off."

Ella rolled back a minute and looked at Michael. She could not believe what she was hearing from him. *What a wonderful heart he has.* She was so touched that she was almost speechless.

"Michael, I'm not turned off by your attention. I'm overwhelmed by them. I guess we have to take our time and get to know each other. I would love for you to work with me when my casts come off, and get me to walking again. We'll spend enough time together and get to know each other very well. Then we can see what'll happen between us. I'm cool with that. You know I'm dating James. And until you came along, I was pretty content with him. He has been good to me and was there for me through this whole thing. But then you walked into my life and everything has a different color now."

Michael walked to the door and looked back. "Ok, Ella. We'll take it slow. I respect that you are seeing James. I wouldn't do anything to interfere with that if you are serious with him. But I want to see more of you. I'm being honest on the front end. So you'll have to tell me no; otherwise, I'm going to be calling you and wanting to take you out."

Ella had tears in her eyes. She didn't know what to say. It was all happening so fast, but she knew it was good. It felt right.

"Michael, just know I do care about you and am so grateful. I want to know more about you, too. If we can take it slow at first, I'm all for us getting to know each other. You are such a gentleman with me and so open with your feelings. I'm not used to that, but that doesn't mean I don't like it. So we can work on this, and you can call me if you like. I know we'll have a great time."

Michael walked over and lifted her face up, and kissed her gently. Then he turned and walked out the door.

Ella couldn't move for a while. She was confused and also elated. And James was calling her on her cell phone. She looked over at the sofa and realized she hadn't opened the gift that he brought her. She rolled over to it, letting her phone go to voice mail, and opened the box with the beautiful pink ribbon. She lifted the lid, and pushed away the tissue. Inside, lying on velvet was a pheasant feather. *Oh my Gosh.* Ella nearly fainted. *This couldn't possibly be the same feather that my father gave to me! There's no way that that could happen.* She thought back to when she was packing for the trip. The feather was sitting on her desk and right below it was her suitcase. *Oh my gosh, there's no way that feather could've gotten inside of her suitcase!*

And it would've had to come out of the suitcase during the crash. How did he find it? It's just too much to even grasp.

Michael hadn't said a word about the feather. Actually he had forgotten about it, because he got so caught up in talking to Ella. He rang her cell quickly. Ella had picked her phone up to call James and heard the call coming in. She took the call and it was Michael, laughing.

"Hey sweet girl. I gave you a gift and I forgot to let you to open it. Have you yet?"

Ella smiled. "Yes, I just did. But I'm in shock. Tell me where you got this feather?"

"I saw it on the surface after I brought you to the boat. They were lifting you into the boat and I saw something floating on top of the water. I swam over and it was a pheasant feather. I didn't know how that type feather was doing out in open water like that, but I thought it was lovely and decided to give it to you."

Ella was crying hard by now. "Michael! This is the feather my *father* gave to me, from one of his hunting trips. It must have ended up in my suitcase, which got blown apart on the plane. What are the odds of that feather coming to the surface? And what are the odds of you finding it?" Ella couldn't speak for a moment. She was overtaken with grief for her father, and love for Michael. This was just too much.

Michael waited a minute and said, "Ella, This is what I'm talking about. You and I are meant to get to know each other. I can't believe what you're telling me. But it just confirms what I've been feeling all along. I hope you'll give me that chance." Michael was in shock about the feather story. *Could it really be the same feather her father gave to her? It had to be! The odds of a feather like that being out in the ocean are zero to none. It had to be the same feather!*

"Promise me you'll call, Ella!"

"I promise, Michael. Thank you for making my night!"

Ella rolled back into the bedroom and laid the feather on her pillow. She got herself in bed with a struggle, lay down and thought for a long time about what had just happened. *I would've never dreamed in a lifetime that Michael would feel this way about me. In a way I can understand, because rescuing someone is very emotional for both parties involved. But he feels so drawn to me. I really do care about James, but this is different. I don't know why exactly, but it is so so different. I need to go slow. Even though he's very aggressive about us belonging together, I need to go a little slow. I feel confused. . . sort of funky inside, because we really don't know each other. Yet I do feel close to him in a lovely way. . . . .*

She dozed off with the feather on her pillow. James would have to wait until tomorrow.

Chapter 29

The moving truck pulled up to the house on Madison Avenue, and backed into the driveway. Kate drove up behind it and jumped out to open the door. She led the movers into the house and guided them in placing the furniture in the right rooms. She had only packed the furniture that was not being used at home. It felt good, for this was the beginning of a new life for Kate, and as soon as her house closed, she would close on this house. It was going to happen now. No more dreaming about it. She had thought about it for enough hours in the middle of the night, and worried so much about the children adjusting to all the new events that were taking place. Stephen had stepped into her life smoothly, almost like changing partners at a dance. It was nearly seamless, and he was amazing at adjusting to the environment of the moment. *I hardly know he's in the room when I'm visiting my children, but when I need him to come forward, he does with such strength*, Kate pondered.

Today, Ella was going to come and see the house. Michael was bringing her. Kate was excited about her coming and really hoped it would feel warm and inviting. *Maybe it'll help to have some of our things in the house. Ella can be tough on me*, she mused as she directed the movers. There wasn't that much furniture, but it did help warm up a couple of rooms. She thanked the men, paid them a tip and then she was alone for a moment. She walked through the house slowly, getting a feel again for where to put her things, and also to take in the aura of the house. Stephen had told her recently that his parents had rented out the house to a family for years after they moved out; this house that held many memories. She loved to hear Stephen's memories of when he was young and had Christmas in the house. He really enjoyed living here. *I wonder how the other family felt over the years. Of course, they had only rented and didn't own the house, but still, they made many family memories here.*

She was coming into the living room when she looked up and saw Ella with Michael behind the wheel chair. Ella would be getting her casts off soon.

Ella smiled and waved. "Hey Mom! Finally made it here!" She had Michael move her into the living room so she could see out the windows.

"Quite a view, Mom. I want to see the rest of the house." So Michael strolled Ella through the house, with Kate giving a commentary on each room and what she was going to do with the space. Kate could see Ella softening in her feelings about the move. *It might have something to do with all the attention she is getting from Michael,* Kate thought. She had a feeling this might be the one that Ella settled down with. *Just a hunch.*

Ella went off with Michael and rolled through the rest of the house. They were talking and laughing and Kate was enjoying hearing their voices float in the air. One day soon this would be her house. She could not wait. She stayed a little while after they left to pick up paper and trash that had been left by the movers, not wanting to leave, but knowing she had promised Stephen some time together.

When she got home, Ella and Michael were already there fixing something to eat. She went upstairs and got ready for her dinner date with Stephen. *It will feel good to just relax and talk,* Kate said to herself, as she pulled the sweater over her head. *So much has happened so quickly. It feels like a wheel is turning and there is no way to stop it.* Tonight she was going to talk to Stephen about how to slow things down. She was so busy at work; so much going on in everyone's life. *We must find a way to enjoy all the moments, or our lives will just pass us by.*

On her way down the stairway, her hand briefly touched the photo of Sam without thinking.

* * *

Stephen was waiting at the restaurant for Kate. He had asked her to meet him there, so he could light some candles and get ready for what he wanted to talk to her about. He was sitting at the table with his head in his hands when Kate walked up.

"Stephen, what a lovely table!"

Stephen jumped up. "Kate! I didn't see you come in. How was your day? Did you get things moved ok?"

"Yes I did, sweetheart. I'm exhausted. But it was a good day in spite of all the work. Ella came to see the house and ended up loving it!"

Stephen pulled her chair out and Kate sat down, putting her napkin in her lap. "Relax. I know you have had a long tiring day. This night is supposed to be just you and me, and the world can go away for a bit."

"That sounds good to me. I love the lit candles and the flowers. Thank you, Stephen." Kate was looking over the menu, trying to choose something different. She decided to pick the pecan crusted grouper and asparagus, while Stephen chose Filet Mignon and Potato with spinach casserole. The waiter left the table, and Stephen picked up his glass of wine.

"Kate, darling, here's to better months ahead for your family. New beginnings for both children, and you and me"

Kate smiled and toasted his glass. "What a nice evening, Stephen."

"I have waited to tell you this exciting news! As you know, I've spent years developing new cancer treatments. Now I've been in on something so powerful that it could change the world. Cancer causes so many deaths in the world and billions have been spent in research to find a cure. I want you to know we have found bark from a tree in the rain forest that seems to cure cancer, shrink tumors, and attack the cancer cell itself. It seems too good to be true, but we are testing on animals, and so far we are seeing huge promise in this natural substance."

Kate was very surprised by this news, as she had no idea Stephen's work would carry him into this direction in research. "I'm amazed at you. What a wonderful experience to have discovered something so powerful."

"This is the most exciting thing I could be involved in right now, so I'm sitting on cloud nine with this new discovery."

Their meals were brought to the table, and they sat and chatted about many things, while they enjoyed their dinner. The restaurant was full, but Kate didn't notice. She was drinking in this quiet time with Stephen, and let all the stress that had built up over the last year fall away for a while. She wanted to know more about this man who had come into her life. As he talked, she was watching his eyes, his mannerisms, watching how he interacted with her and how he took care of things in his life. He just seemed to pull things off seamlessly and without strain. That was a rare characteristic. She was so proud of him with his work, and also how well he fit into her family. He was an only child, and a lot of times people who didn't have a large family are uncomfortable with so many people around all the time.

Stephen was watching Kate, too. He was looking at her eyes, listening to her words and wanting to know her heart. He had come into her life at the point when she was under the most stress, and had watched her handle very difficult situations very well. Her work had in a way trained her not to overreact in tough situations, and whether she realized it or not, she had learned an incredible lesson in *grace* under stress.

"Stephen, I admire your mind, and the compelling nature you have to discover new things. That's rare and you are also using that ability for the good of mankind." She reached across the table and took his hand. They looked at each other and the chemical attraction added to the genuine love for each other took over and caused them both to blush. He squeezed her hand and winked.

"Let's get out of here, girl. It's time for me to spend some quality time with you. Did you enjoy your dinner?"

"Yes, Stephen. It was a beautiful night and I so needed this quiet time with you to come down. I can't keep up this level of stress for much longer. I'm thinking that things are going to settle down after I get this move over with. Can you and I get this contract going so I can make it legal?"

Stephen laughed. "Of course! We can do that this weekend. I'll get on it right away and have the contract drawn up. We can close immediately and the house can be yours!"

Kate took a deep breath. The sound of that just rang in her heart; a home on Madison Avenue. Almost like a dream but this time she was living it out. Sam wouldn't believe she was going to be on the street where he proposed to her. She felt a little guilty thinking about Sam while she was out with Stephen. She wiped the corner of her eye, hoping Stephen did not notice.

The rest of the evening, Stephen held Kate in his arms. And they ended up outside her home-to-be on Madison Avenue, on the porch swing, listening to the ocean come in and go out.

Chapter 30

It was a windy evening and waves were crashing to shore; the moon was beginning to come up in the sky and the movers had put the last box in the living room. Kate had turned on every single light in the house and was sitting on the sofa in the hearth room just staring out the window. She was exhausted and glad to be finished with the moving. Putting everything up would be a daunting task, but this was her new beginning; a fresh start with new memories. She felt sad in a way, and so tired. There had been so much emotion taken from her in the last six months that she could hardly wrap her mind around all of it. Her family had been through so much, yet somehow they had pulled through it all. She was so proud of her children and felt good about where they were in their lives now. But this one step she had made, to move into a new home, separated all of the family from a home that held years of memories. Especially their memories of Sam; the yard he kept, the house he remodeled, the Christmases they'd shared there, and the hundreds of nights together at the kitchen table sharing their day with each other.

There was a knock on the door, and before Kate could get there to open it, in walked her two children with Michael and Lila. They were carrying flowers, a houseplant, and food! It was hard for Kate to get used to seeing Ella up and around with no wheelchair. What a relief that had to be to finally be able to walk again. Good thing she had the cane, though. Kate could tell she was still struggling a little to get around.

"Hey Mom. Just wanted to give you a welcome in your new house!" Seth said, hugging Kate hard. "You know we didn't want you to be alone the first night in your new house!"

"Yeah, Mom! Come on. Let's all sit down at the table and enjoy some Chinese food and I'll get a vase for the flowers." Ella laughed, as she went to the kitchen to find a vase or large glass in all the boxes stacked everywhere. Ella had a glow to her since Michael had come into her life. She was not the same girl who had gotten on that airplane, all feisty and moody. Gosh had she been moody! But now, she always had a smile on her face and was ready to chip in and help. She and Seth were getting along famously so Kate was all for this relationship with Michael.

"Ok, guys. You've made my night, here. What lovely flowers. I'm starved and can't believe you've walked in with food like this. It couldn't be more perfect for our first dinner together here in the house."

Just as they sat down, another knock on the door. This time, Stephen strolled in, wanting to surprise everyone.

"Hey guys. You beat me to it!" He also had flowers and food from the local Thai Restaurant around the corner. He had another small gift wrapped with a red bow, for Kate. He was going to wait to give it to her later. Something small but significant.

"Come on in, Stephen," Seth chimed in. Good to see you, man." They shook hands and Stephen walked over to Ella.

"My, Ella, you look a lot better than the last time I saw you. I know you're loving being out of those casts. How is the rehab going?" He smiled at Michael and winked.

"Oh, the rehab is going terrific, but may take a little more time than we'd originally thought," laughed Michael. "But we're enjoying every moment of it, aren't we, Ella?"

"Oh sure. I adore being told what to do and treated like I'm in the Marines or something!"

"Ok, guys. Let's sit back down and tackle eating all of this lovely food. Stephen, come and sit at the head of the table and let's say grace before we eat." The family all held hands and bowed their heads. A lot to be thankful for...

The night passed with much laughter and conversation. Just what Kate had wanted for her first night in the house. Boxes were opened that were full of books and accessories that would make the house feel like it belonged to someone. Kate was grateful to have the help. At the end of the night, when everyone left but Stephen, he walked over to her and pulled her close to him. "I want you to know how much I love you and how happy I am that you are finally living in your new home." He hugged her and they both laughed.

"I know this house holds a lot of history, and I want you to sit down soon and tell me about some of the families that have lived in this house. Thank you for being so kind tonight, for the flowers and the food. The conversation went well with the kids and you always make everyone laugh with your dry humor!" Kate was tired and sat down on the sofa.

"Well, I always love being around your kids, lady." Stephen sat down beside her and pulled out a small box for her to open. "Now, don't fuss or say a word about this small gift. It is special to me, and I wanted to give you something to remember this first night."

Kate opened the box slowly and found a beautiful gold bracelet with the words *As deep as the sea my love is for you. Stephen.* Kate's eyes filled with tears; her first gift from Stephen, and in her new home. She was overwhelmed. She hadn't allowed herself to focus totally on all the emotions that were in her heart. She turned and wrapped her arms around this new man in her life. He was always there, always the same, for her and her family ever since he walked into her life. It felt so right.

"Thank you so much for this lovely gift. You didn't have to do this! But I adore you for doing it. I do love gold and this is so feminine and simple."

"Well, when I saw this bracelet, it felt like you, Kate. I want to be a part of your life. Now I want to address our relationship." Stephen hugged her close and kissed her mouth. Kate melted into his arms and allowed herself to at last feel the love that she had hidden in her heart, tucked away, for this man.

It was getting cold outside, and they decided to light a fire in the fireplace, and found the stereo system and plugged it in, so they could have some music. They unpacked the things she would need for her first night in the house and then it was time to just sit back and relax and share the night together. Kate had so many thoughts running through her head, as she looked around the room. The hearth room would be one of her favorite places, because of the warmth and coziness. The fire made everything in the room glow and created a feeling of safety, and as she sat there with Stephen, it almost felt like this was forever. Like she had known him for a very long time.

"Stephen, I know there is a plan in our lives, but I also know we have to be willing to walk it out. I have been somewhat afraid to allow myself to feel anything close to love for you, because of what I've been through with Sam. I know you understand all this, but it's time that I allow myself to feel what has been in my heart for quite some time. I do love you, Stephen. I adore how you are with me and my children. You never say the wrong thing; you are intelligent and always read the situation correctly. You know how to diffuse anger and frustration in Ella. It's unreal how you get along with Seth. He was so close to his father. I'm amazed even now they both have allowed you into our family so easily." Kate laid her head back on the sofa and smiled. *It just feels so good being on Madison Avenue, in this house, with Stephen in this moment in time.*

"Kate, you and I've been through some pretty difficult situations in the months that we have known each other. I want to laugh with you, to walk on the beach with you, and to know what is in your heart. I realize this may be strange for a man to talk this way, but I really do enjoy hearing what you have to say, and how you feel about life, politics, and everything else we talk about."

The night moved forward in the old house on Madison Avenue, as Kate and Stephen stretched their legs out on an ottoman in front of the sofa. Kate was so exhausted that she fell asleep listening to the music, feeling the warmth of the fire, and having Stephen right next to her. Stephen sat there awhile watching the fire and feeling so at home with her. He finally found a blanket and covered her up, and gently closed the front door, letting her enjoy her first night in her house, lost in her dreams. He walked to his car smiling, for Kate had said she loved him, and those words would never leave his heart. *One day soon, I'll make her my wife*, he thought as he got into his car and drove home.

The leaves stirred up off the street in swirls as he drove by, settling back down in piles along the edge of the curb. In the rear view mirror, he could see the smoke rising up from her fireplace into the night. *His Kate.*

Chapter 31

On her way to work on Monday morning, Kate was smiling from ear to ear. This was her first week in the house and she was loving it already. The kids had come by several times, and she could tell that Ella was really adjusting to this house quickly. *There was something about the house that just draws you in,* thought Kate. *Hard to put her finger on it, but it was there.*

Her day was going to be busy, but there was a window of time for her to have lunch with Susan. She had phoned her and couldn't wait for them to be able to catch up. She got to her desk, scanned her mail, jotted down any phone calls she needed to make, and pulled the files for the first few patients she would see for the morning. Her first patient came in and he was a gentleman who had a drinking problem. She was sending him to a psychologist because he needed to work through some issues, but at least she had diagnosed his ADHD and OCD issues, and had gotten him on the right meds. He was very intelligent but very addictive. She felt like the psychologist she had chosen for him would be perfect for his problems. He seemed open to the suggestion and took the card from her with the appointment on it. She moved down the line pretty quickly, and it felt good to be addressing these patients and finding solutions.

She had a buzz from her secretary saying she had visitors. They didn't have an appointment, but they were insistent on seeing her now. Kate got up and opened her door. In came a couple she had never seen before and as she asked them to be seated, she introduced herself, and asked their names.

The man stood up and said, "Kate, we're Alison's parents, Martha and Dave Stratford". Kate's jaw dropped as she tried to think of what to say. This was a total shock to her, and caught her off guard.

"It's so good to meet you, Dave and Martha." Kate shook their hands. "I got your note you sent to me, and hope you received my letter back to you?"

"Yes, we did, Kate, but we really have wanted to stop by and see you in person. We just had to thank you again for finding our daughter. You don't know what that has meant to us. Otherwise, we would've never known what happened to her, you know? We are talking about peace of mind, here." Dave was sitting on the edge of his chair, and slid back to allow Martha a chance to speak. Kate did not fail to note Martha's natural beauty.

"Kate, this is awkward for me, to say the least. I know you didn't know anything about Sam and I meeting each other long ago. It was a moment in time, and meant nothing. "Sounds pretty weak for an excuse but it wasn't a love affair. I just had to meet you face to face and say I'm sorry for what happened back then, and I've paid a price for what I did. Over the years I've regretted what we did, as I'm sure Sam did also. I never dreamed I would have to bury my daughter. She was suffering inside so much from her father's death and I was totally unaware of her pain. She kept up a front that only showed how happy she was. I never knew she was so attached to Sam."

Kate swallowed, and came around her desk. This was a tough situation. She wanted to handle it smoothly, and try not to get over emotional. "I do understand now that Sam just made a mistake with you, but he did at least honor his daughter and take care of her; meet her needs. That is something I want you to reassure me of, for it would really upset me if he had not." Kate took Martha's hand in hers.

"I know this is awkward, but it's something that we can overcome because I did love Sam with all my heart and believed in him. I know I would've loved Alison if I had met her when she was young. I'm sorry you both felt like it had to be kept a secret from me, but I do understand why you might have felt that way." There was no point in her sharing any other feelings with Martha and Dave. This happened so long ago, and now there was nothing any of them could do to change things.

"Actually, it was Sam's insistence that you not know anything about Alison. He just couldn't bear to hurt you, Kate. He loved you and it was very obvious that our one night stand was a huge mistake." Martha dropped Kate's hand and straightened her dress. She cleared her throat and looked up at Kate.

"I'm not upset now, Martha. I know this is hard for you, coming here to meet me. I know it must have been hell to bury your own daughter. That's every parent's nightmare. I've prayed for you both so many times and I know it'll take a long time to get over such a thing. I've recently been through a nightmare of my own with Ella and Seth, my two children. They were in a terrible plane crash and I didn't know for a while if Ella was alive or dead. I can truly understand what you have been through with the loss of Alison."

Dave stood up and pulled Martha to her feet. "We are very thankful you did not lose your two children, Kate. I am sure you have been through enough. We don't want to take anymore of your time. I appreciate you being so nice about this; we just wanted to see you face to face. I know that night was hard on you, and finding out about Alison. She was a wonderful girl and the tragedy is that she won't have the joy of living out her life. I hope she is in heaven with Sam, for she *lived* for him. I knew that a long time ago. I loved her as best I could, but she adored her father. I couldn't even try to take his place; didn't want to try."

They headed towards the door, and Kate thanked them again for coming by. As the door shut, she sat down at her desk, her legs feeling weak, and she wiped the tears from her eyes. Her next appointment was waiting and she had to pull herself together. *I knew one day they might come,* thought Kate. *I just didn't know it would be today....*

Sam, she thought. *You have no idea how this has affected all of us. It might have been better just to tell me the truth.* Kate put lotion on her hands, looked out the window of her office and took a deep, long breath. It was almost time to meet Susan at the café, and she was more than ready now for a long talk with her friend. Her last appointment was easy and ended on a good note. Kate grabbed her purse and headed out the door. Stephen had called, but it wasn't urgent. She would call him back after lunch. It seemed she could not get there fast enough. She hadn't talked to Susan in a few weeks, and there were so many things to share.

Susan was waiting at the café, sipping some coffee, and looking over the menu. In walked Kate all flustered and wind blown. She came over to the table and hugged Susan and sat down with a loud sigh. "Susan, you'll never guess who I just talked to."

"Girl, I'm all ears. We haven't talked in way too long, and I want to know what all is going on in your life. You look wonderful, Kate, but a little frazzled!" Susan laughed. She could tell Kate had a lot on her mind.

The girls spent the next two hours talking, catching up on everything Kate had been doing; about the children, her move, Stephen, and last but not least, the visit from Martha and Dave. Susan was blown away at all Kate was telling her. They were nibbling on their lunches and had sipped a glass of cheap wine and two hours quickly. After the stress of the day, Kate decided that she wanted a dessert and split it with Susan. They laughed after all the stressful conversation and hugged each other. What else could happen in their lives! Kate felt relieved that she had finally had an opportunity to share all of this with Susan, and went back to work with a lighter step. Things didn't seem quite as huge now that she'd gotten things off her chest.

As soon as she got back to work, before her next patient, she phoned Stephen back. He was busy in his lab, but told her he would see her after work. Things were going very well with the experiment and he was excited to share it with her later. She looked down and touched the gold bracelet she had on. The words hung in her mind as she pulled the next file out.

Stephen had worked his way into her life without a strain. It was so smooth it was hard to believe. Yet it was there, invisible, yet stronger than anything she could remember since Sam. *Am I saying goodbye, Sam?* She thought with a shudder. *Am I letting you go for good?* Kate swallowed what felt like a boulder in her throat. *How long would it take before the pain left when she thought of Sam? She almost felt like she was cheating on him, but she knew it wasn't true.* The smell of him was slowly floating away. The sea was taking it all away, like the sand at the edge of the beach. She kept trying to bring it back, but it wasn't that simple anymore.

She bit her lip as Mrs. Garth walked in and took a seat. Just a few more and she could go home.

Chapter 32

Before Stephen got to her house, Kate had changed clothes, lit a fire, and was walking around the rooms, still putting things away. *So much to do in this house, but it was shaping up nicely,* she thought. She ran up the flight of stairs nearest the kitchen, and saw a door heading to the attic. It occurred to her that she had never really looked in the attic before. It was nice to find that they had floored the attic, so it really gave her a lot of extra storage room. Kate walked around a little, seeing a menagerie of things that were strewn about in the attic that had never been thrown out. One of the items was an old clothes line rack. It was leaning against the brick of the chimney, with spider webs and old insulation on the bottom of it. There were a few lampshades, a bag of old cloths, a few toys scattered about, and an old doll carriage. At the end of the attic, in the darkest part was a blanket piled up. She was afraid to pick it up, for fear of spiders, but laughed out loud at herself. She lifted the blanket and there was a medium size box underneath. It was covered with dust and cob webs, in spite of being under the blanket. She reached for it and a crocheted doll fell behind it. She grabbed the doll and the box and lifted the lid slowly. Inside, Kate could see a stack of papers, so she closed the box and decided to take it downstairs with her.

When she got into a well-lit room, she lifted the box lid again. It smelled very musty, and she could see words written in pencil and pen on the papers. Some looked like a small child's writing. She decided to wipe the box off and take it back to her room and put it down on her large nightstand near the bed, making a promise to herself to read the notes inside later.

Stephen arrived, bringing dinner and roses again, and Kate told him about her trip into the attic. "It was like stepping back in time, she said, smiling. "I was stumbling around over pieces of wood, and left over toys strewn around.

I thought I was going to trip, but I just wanted to see what was up there, and also how much storage room I had. I found a wonderful box up there that was filled with papers. Some of the writing was like a child had written it, but I didn't read anything yet. Can you tell me anything about the people who lived here after you moved out?"

Stephen smiled at her little adventure in the attic and said, "I really don't know that much about the family that rented our house after we moved out. The house sat empty for a while, and then my father decided that he would like to rent it so that I could have the option of keeping it for myself, later, or selling it. It was a small family, with two children; a boy and a girl. My mother has told me that the little girl was very shy and that she kept to herself and played alone in her room or in the attic. I really don't know how long they lived here as I was busy living my own life and dating Betsy. It'll be interesting to see what is written on those papers that are inside the box you found today! Let me know, will you?"

Kate sat back in her chair. *A little girl,* she thought. *Did she write the words in the box or could it have been her mother?* "I will, Stephen. What did the father do for a living, do you know?"

"Well, I think he was a carpenter. Mother always said he was a big man, and kind of quiet. The wife stayed home during the day and kept the children. Actually the whole family was very 'to themselves', if you know what I mean, but my parents didn't care, because they took good care of the house and kept the yard in shape. It was nice to have someone in the house so it didn't just sit empty, you know?" Stephen got up and walked over to the window to look out on the backyard.

"It's never good to leave a house empty for long. I'll read the notes in the box soon. It looked like quite a bit, but some of them were folded, so it's hard to say. I'm just glad to be here at last." Kate smiled and felt so peaceful. She looked at Stephen standing in the window, and thought what a handsome man he was; how strong and self assured. She needed that calmness in her life right now, as things had been so hectic since Sam died. She would've never dreamed life could be so complicated.

"Kate, let's bundle up and go sit outside on the swing!" said Stephen. He had grown to enjoy sitting out there with Kate.

"Sure! Why don't we light the outdoor fireplace? Wouldn't that be cozier?" Kate got up and put on a jacket with a hood and took a throw off of the sofa to put across her knees. Stephen put on his coat and opened the door. There was a slight breeze, and it would feel great to have a fire going outside. It was a gas fireplace, and had been put in after Stephen was out of college. Hopefully it still worked.

After the fire was lit, and they were settled in the swing, Kate brought up the interesting visitors she had during her morning. "Stephen, you'll never believe who walked into my office today!" Kate smiled now, but it was not a bit funny this morning.

"I can't imagine, Kate", laughed Stephen. He was hoping it was a good thing.

"I was about to see my last patient and my secretary buzzes me and tells me that a couple was outside wanting to see me. They were adamant about it, so I told her that I would see them. I opened my door and in walked a couple I did not recognize. I introduced myself and they sat down. The gentleman then said to me "Hello, Kate, we are Alison's parents, Martha and Dave Stratford."

"You could've knocked me over with a feather" laughed Kate. But then her face went solemn.

"It hit me in the face, their pain and struggle. And how much it took for them to come in and meet me; especially Martha. She was pretty plain, a little awkward, and not too eager to talk. Dave seemed more at ease with the situation, but I had already made peace with what Sam did in his past, so I was only shocked that they had come to see me." Kate sat up on the edge of the swing and looked at Stephen.

"You know it had to be hard for Martha to meet me face to face, but I told them I wished I had known Alison. That girl shortened her own life because of the struggle she had about keeping it all a secret. I really believe she wanted to tell me when she came to my office building and stood there looking up. I wish I'd known that it was her. It's so terribly sad to think she died for nothing, for we all would've taken her in." Kate wiped her eyes.

"I know, angel. The horrible thing about death is that it is final. There's no way to reach her now to let her know that you would've understood, or that Sam did not realize what this secrecy would do to the family if it ever got out."

Stephen held Kate close and they just sat back and watched the fire. Kate silently hoped that this would be the last conversation she had to have about Alison, for it broke her heart and she had such mixed emotions about it all.

Chapter 33

It had been so long since Lauren had known what it was like to feel a part of anything. Every day just seemed the same; the same people, places, and the same routine, she was so desperate for things to change. If her life stayed like this, it was surely going to drive her insane. Working at the city library did help; she loved that she was surrounded by silent intellect, and by the art and intelligence of what a mind could produce. However, there were only so many times you can take a book home for company. Of course, if Lauren were to call and sort things out with Stuart then maybe she wouldn't have to spend so much time reading through the pages and lives of all the great authors. Yes that's what she needed to do; she needed to find a way to move her life forward.

Lauren had always had an inkling in the back of her mind that there had to be a better life out there somewhere for her. She often wondered as a child what it would be like to feel free and to be able to walk in the sun and leave the shadows behind that clouded so much of her childhood. Thank goodness that she had met Stuart. He was working at the bank opposite the college where she studied English literature. They met in the park by chance after he had misplaced his wallet, something he still does today. Lauren smiled to herself just thinking about how absent minded he could be. bBut she knew she loved him; they had been together on and off for five years and he was just about the only person in the world that she trusted, let alone loved. Things had changed recently and Lauren knew that Stuart really didn't understand what was going on in her mind or why she was being so distant of late. In fact, she didn't fully know why herself; only that she had been feeling overwhelmed with the way her life was and that everything about her life right now was confusing her. Memories were creeping in that she had tucked away somewhere in her mind. They haunted her and were making her moods go up and down. So she had told Stuart she needed a little time and space but tried so hard to reassure him that this really had nothing to do with him and everything to do with her. He seemed to take it well but looked so hurt and confused himself. She would call him tonight, when she had finished working at the library. She'd grab a bite to eat, get home as quick as she could, take a shower and then call him. He deserved that at least.

It was getting pretty late by the time Lauren had wrapped up what she needed to and organize the reading circle for the pre-school kids that would be arriving in the morning. She really enjoyed her time with the kids, listening to them laughing and fidgeting on the rug as she prepared to tell them of magical stories of princesses and kings and far away lands. It was certainly a favorite time of hers, where she could lose herself and almost go back to her own childhood and her love of books and writing. It was one rare part of her childhood that was fun to remember.

Coming home when it was so dark, rainy and cold outside was always a treat and this little apartment as small as it was, was home. Everything about it said Lauren; the amateur photographs that covered the walls in the hallway, the pictures of everyday folk going about their day, oblivious to the woman behind the lens capturing their lives on film. There were the towels that had to be in line on the rack in the bathroom, and infantile drawings placed on the refrigerator from her little kids that came twice a week to the reading circle. Everything was so comfortable and safe. She did love living here, and although things had been a little up and down with Stuart, her life was a million miles away from the ghosts that haunted her as a child.

Lauren had just taken a shower and was about to fix something to eat, as she had left so late from work. She had given up on the idea of grabbing something out and just wanted to get home. So when she heard a knock on the door she was a little surprised to see Stuart standing there, soaking wet in the rain.

"Hey can I grab a towel?" Stuart smiled at her in a way that still made her heart miss a beat, for she was sure that she loved him more now than the day they had met.

He had dark hair to his neck a little gray running through places, which only made him more attractive, light olive skin and eyes as blue as the ocean. At five feet ten inches with those broad shoulders and gentle voice, he could melt any woman's heart and not even know. That was a big attraction for Lauren, that he was totally unaware of his own charm and gentleness, let alone his beauty. At thirty four and only four years older than Lauren, they truly were a perfect match.

"I didn't even know it was raining" said Lauren, "Make yourself at home, you know where everything is."

Stuart laughed as he grabbed a towel out of the linen closet. "Yes Ma'am, I only lived here for three years with you." Lauren had loved their time together and even though she was the one who had made the decision that she needed time out, for the most part, she wanted to tell him she needed him. She wanted him to move back in, but she knew deep down in her heart that right now she had to take this time to find herself. However, she was sure that it was only a matter of time before he would be back in her life permanently. Then the world of Lauren Andrews could move forward and begin to be really alive.

Lauren woke to the warmth of the winter sun on her face and to the warmth of the man she loved lying next to her. She turned over and watched Stuart still sleeping; just watching him breathe made her smile and made her feel safe. She sure hoped that this journey she was on would all begin to make sense. Her heart knew what she wanted, but her mind was fixed on trying to work through the shadows and ghosts that had blocked so much of the light from her life.

Lost in thought Lauren forgot all about the six thirty a.m. alarm that she'd set that night. She hit the button so it wouldn't wake up Stuart. She figured that he had a key and would make himself at home before leaving the apartment. She leaned over and gently kissed Stuart on the cheek before getting up to shower and head out for a new day. This was a great morning, cold but bright and pretty warm in the sun, but definitely jacket and scarf weather. Lauren loved the winter, the changing of the seasons around her, the trees and plants, the feeling of being wrapped up with the cool wind on her face. She had always loved the winter even as a child.

"Ok it's quiet time guys", Lauren said to the kids. Circle time was pretty full this morning, eleven kids; that was good news. Lauren had always believed in bringing books and words to children; the younger the better. It wasn't just because it had always been a passion of hers, but because it instilled something that would stay in their souls for eternity. Something visual like TV, just didn't cut it. Circle time went pretty quick. She read two books to the kids, and then they spent the next twenty minutes talking about the story and the characters. Lauren loved this part of her job more than anything. She was so good with children she wondered if she would ever have any of her own.

The morning passed so quickly and before she knew it, Lauren found herself sitting in the staff room eating her lunch. She was lost in thoughts as she ate her peanut butter and jelly sandwich. *Maybe I should've asked Stuart if he wanted to go out this evening; nights are pretty lonely because I still have very few friends.*

Lauren had always been a quiet shy child and that part of her personality never seemed to flourish. She was thankful that Stuart was a big part of her life, as was working here in the City library. One thing that Lauren did love about the job was that now that she had been here for nearly as long as she had known Stuart, they had started letting her do some of the photography for the library advertising and artwork. She lost herself in such projects, always making sure that everything was more than perfect. Lauren had always been a perfectionist and it definitively showed in her work.

That afternoon consisted mostly of stamping the returns and returning all the borrowed books to the correct sections, and tidying up anything that looked out of place. Lauren always took pride in her job, as boring as some of it could be. She certainly was as methodical in the work place as she was at home. Lauren had made a mental note not to forget to contact Stuart that evening, as she needed some fun. Maybe a movie or a bite to eat, but definitely some quality time together was needed. The rest of the day flew by pretty quickly, which was almost a relief as Lauren was looking forward to relaxing and letting her hair down. *Five o'clock couldn't come quick enough,* she thought, smiling.

Lauren decided to walk home this evening; it was cold but at least it was dry. She loved being outside and the walk home was so pretty. The shops were all lit up, and the smell of fresh coffee aroma in the air was refreshing as she walked past The Coffee House. She loved sitting in there on her days off or when she had a long lunch break. She also enjoyed just watching the world go by, sometimes grabbing the camera and clicking away. As she made her way down Main Street she could feel the pocket of her jacket vibrating. As she fumbled to grab her cell it cut off. She checked the screen and saw that she had three missed calls all from Stuart. "Darn, I had better call him back" she thought as she began dialing. He wasn't picking up the phone and as she left a voicemail. "See you at home when you get off work, if that's good for you.! Love you." Lauren smiled as she put her cell back in her pocket and hurried home.

"Well girl this is a turn around, so what's up? Stuart was smiling all the while, sitting on her sofa, all stretched out.

"Well I just thought maybe you'd want to get together, catch up, you know. You do don't you?" asked Lauren, knowing the answer already. She did tease Stuart something rotten at times.

"Of course but you already know that. Now come on girl, we're wasting valuable time here. Let's go eat." Lauren freshened up, changed her clothes and grabbed her purse; the evening was going as planned.

O'Leary's had always been a favorite diner of Lauren and Stuarts. The smell of the fresh bread alone was enough to keep you in your seat, and the atmosphere was so comfortable, almost like a cozy little bistro. Everything matched and was coordinated in light and dark green. The lighting was always gentle and intimate which helped to set the mood for a good night out.

Lauren had been mulling the day over in her mind; the noise of the kids during circle time, and the students that came to look at one of the exhibitions on W.H Auden. She was stopped abruptly by Stuart's comment.

"Are you sure everything's okay? You seem a little distant."

Lauren smiled and gently nodded, "Sure I'm fine, thank you. I want to hear all about your day." With that one sentence Stuart took her hand over the table and began to fill her in on his day at the bank. Lauren sat and listened intently, smiling all the while at the man she truly loved.

Chapter 34

Kate was at her desk, sorting through papers in the files of her patients. She was working on a problem one of the patients had, concerning Post Traumatic Stress Disorder. This had been puzzling her and she wanted to look up some cases that would relate to her patient, even if it was someone who had been to war and was suffering from the same thing. She needed to find a way for this person to cope better than she was coping; up at night, having horrible nightmares and horrific memories of her childhood.

There was a library around the corner from her office that Kate had not been to since her children were young. She put on her jacket, grabbed her purse, and hurried out the door to see if she could find a book on this medical problem. It had started to drizzle so Kate pulled a small umbrella out of her purse; she absolutely hated getting wet when she had to go back to work. *Thank heavens the library is close*, Kate thought. *I'm amazed that I haven't used it much, but I do remember the children loving their times in a group circle there.* Kate walked through the door of the library, and the familiar smell hit her quickly and she smiled. It was almost a sad feeling that she was not expecting at all. It brought back memories of the children laughing and loving to read. Even Seth loved to read. She wanted both kids to love reading, so she made a point of reading stories to them at night, before bed.

She went up to the counter and there was a lovely woman with her back turned to Kate, going through books that had been returned, checking for damages. The woman turned around and saw Kate standing there, and walked over to introduce herself.

"Hi, I'm Lauren Andrews. How can I help you today?" Lauren said, noticing how striking she looked.

"Hello, Lauren. I'm Kate Morrison. I work around the corner as a psychiatrist and needed a reference book on Post Traumatic Stress Disorder. Can you help me?"

"Sure I can, Kate. Just give me a minute and I'll be right with you," Lauren answered.

Lauren was gone a moment and came back around the corner with several books she had pulled out on the subject. "Would these be the type books you are looking for, Kate? We have a whole selection under the Psychology / Psychiatry section, just over there," Lauren smiled and pointed in the direction of the books that Kate needed to take reference from.

"Thank you so much, Lauren. You've been a big help." Kate walked over to a table and sat down, pouring over the books to see if there were cases that she could make reference to that would apply to her patient. She spent about an hour taking notes, never looking up until she was finished. The library was emptying out as Kate stood up to leave, and she took the books up to the counter to be signed back in.

Lauren was standing there talking to someone, and as soon as she finished with her customer, she turned to Kate. "I hope that you found what you were looking for. If I can be of any help, I'm here every day until five o'clock. It was nice meeting you."

Kate smiled and said, "Thank you, Lauren. You've been a huge help to me. I'm sure I'll be back soon. I used to bring my children here when they were young, so this library feels like home to me. It's good to be back."

"Have you been away?" Lauren asked inquisitively

"I've moved to another place her in town recently, Lauren, so my life has been in turmoil for several months with the sale of my home and the purchase of a new home. But things are settling down now, and I'm sure I'll be back often. It was nice to meet you."

Kate walked back to the office and gathered her things, grabbed her purse and called it a day. She was more than ready to head home, light a fire, and give Stephen a call to see how his day had gone. She called Ella on her cell phone on the way home, to touch base and see how she and Michael were doing. There was no answer, so she left a message.

It had been a strange day for Lauren; a lot of thinking. She had to work this thing out in her mind. All the way home she had been thinking about Stuart, and how much she loved him. She didn't want to lose him; she knew that much. *I enjoyed circle time today with the children and also the conversation with Kate,* Lauren thought. *What an attractive woman she was, and how interesting her life seemed, especially working in the mental health field. Maybe she might be someone I need to talk to.* As much as she loved her job she wished she could make more money from what she really loved, photography.

Lauren had invited Stuart back to the apartment. She had decided that she needed to talk to him about how she was feeling. He had been asking what was wrong with her for a while now and it only seemed fair that she at least try to explain a little of what was racing around in her mind. Supper would consist of pasta with fresh bread and a bottle of red wine, she had about an hour to collect her thoughts and go freshen up before Stuart would arrive.

The evening passed smoothly with polite conversation and laughter. Stuart looked so good in his Levi's and t-shirt.

"So Lauren, come on, I know that there's something that you need to tell me. I can feel it" Stuart was right of course, but she really didn't know what or how to explain her recent behavior.

"Do you ever see me as odd?" Lauren asked in a quiet manner.

"Odd? No I don't see you as odd, I see you as special" Stuart always said the right thing at the right time. Lauren decided quickly that she didn't want to pursue this conversation and decided that tonight she would forget her shadows and enjoy the company. "I know I'm avoiding things, but let's not get into it tonight. Is that okay with you?"

'It frustrates me a little, but if that is the way it has to be right now, I will accept it. I do want you to open up to me and let me in before we get too far apart in our relationship. Don't you agree?"

"I do, Stuart. But for some reason it's hard for me to talk about. I promise I will soon."

As Stuart drove home all he could think about was Lauren. He had known from the first time he met her that something was different. Of course he had no idea what it was. Just lately he had noticed a huge change in her. She seemed so distant at times and certainly not herself; she didn't laugh like she used to, almost like the spark had gone. *I just wish she would talk to me. I love her so much and I just want to know what the heck is bothering her.* He thought about her all the way home. He took a deep breath and pulled up into his drive. Another day was over and he was going home alone again.

Chapter 35

After Seth's graduation, he had immediately applied for a job with Barton, Smith and Harrington. No response came from sending his resume. He was disappointed but had another option. So he applied at Holland, Braden & Spencer because he had heard great things about this firm and it wouldn't be a bad second choice for him. He got accepted after several interviews and was given his own office and the news that he would be working under Mr. Braden until he really understood the process. He was very excited for more than one reason; he was ready to marry Lila. It took a few weeks to get his feet wet, but he merged into the mass of paperwork quickly and they gave him more difficult projects to work on.

His desk was covered with books, files, and IRS manuals regarding tax changes, and he was deep into a return for a major corporation. This was his first job that had this high of a responsibility for accuracy, and he didn't want to disappoint Mr. Braden. He knew he could pull this off but he had to keep his mind focused on the job and not his plans for his life. He had never been so excited about anything in his whole life, as he was about a life with Lila. She was everything he ever wanted in a woman; which meant that she was a bit like his mother. He had always thought his mother could do anything she put her mind to, and Lila had that same determination about life.

"Goodmorning Seth. How are things going on the Whitworth & Company account? I know this is a big one for you, but I also think that if you achieve this one, you'll be able to handle anything we hand you!" Mr. Braden laughed as he looked at the piles of files, books and papers strewn all over Seth's desk.

"Oh, I'm going to do this, Mr. Braden. I understand completely about the accuracy and what is at stake with this account. I appreciate your trust in me to do this right." Seth wiped his mouth and sat back in his chair. It felt good to take a break for a moment. He took a sip of his coffee and smiled at Mr. Braden. *No sense in him knowing how nervous I am about this.*

"I'm headed down the street to land a new account, Seth. Would you like to take a break and tag along with me, to see how this is done?" Mike Braden knew how Seth felt being the new kid on the block, so this might be good for him to see the tactics used in winning an account. This would be big money, and the firm could always use a large account like this one.

"Sounds exciting, Mr. Braden. I'll be taking notes!" Seth stood up and shook Mike's hand and they both went out the door talking about the latest football scores on their favorite teams. At least they did agree on who was the best team. That could go a long way for Seth. He knew he had to fit in with these "good old boys."

* * *

Lila and Seth had worked so hard for her to be able to open this new clinic. She was so proud of it and was hoping Lila was working on a client, thinking about using the latest technique to reduce the large pores on her skin. This was one of her best clients and she wanted her to be pleased. The clinic was so very posh, and each client felt pampered and loved their skin by the time they left. Lila was overwhelmed at the amount of appointments she had already gotten, and the clinic had only been opened for such a short time. Not even a year yet. She was proud of what she was doing, and it was great to feel so good about your work. Her job was to make women love that they are; to really enjoy their skin and learn how to take care of themselves. Lila was a dark haired beauty who loved looking her best but also wanted to teach women how to take good care of their skin. She studied endlessly so that she would be at the top of her field. She had a kindness about her that didn't really go with the ruthlessness of her desire to be on top. But it was a nice combination now that she was in business for herself.

When she had a break, she listened to messages on her cell, and found there was a sweet one from Seth. *How did I ever get so lucky as to find this man? He's perfect,* she thought, smiling. *He remembered all the important dates, always remembered her birthday, her favorite color, her favorite singers; there was nothing he let slide. I guess it's his mathematical mind.* She tucked her phone back in her purse and headed to the front of the shop.

I feel like he's going to pop the big question soon, and I'm more than ready. My parents might not be, but I'm old enough to make up my own mind. I'm not their little girl any more.

Getting married was a huge decision; she had watched many of her friends get married and have children. But she had wanted to get her education first before she married.

I'm trying hard to get my business to grow and Seth seems to be happy with his job. It could be that this is the time we both have been waiting for to tie the knot. I'm getting to a place in my life where I hate being without him.....

* * *

Seth sat in a boardroom with Mr. Braden, sipping some hot coffee and looking out a plate glass window across Martin City. It was a lovely view and he was more than ready to learn something today. The room was stately and rows of books lined the massive shelves all around the room. It gave the room a feeling of history and hard work. Very impressive. He took his pen out and wrote down some things that Mr. Braden was saying to the client. He knew this was a big account, and it would be his turn one day to write a contract. So he settled down and paid close attention to the rules of the game. After an hour and a half of conversation on both sides, Jones and Barrett decided to go with Holland, Braden & Spencer for their accounting needs. It was a win/win for both sides, as there wasn't a better accounting firm in Martin City, and this was probably the largest account in the corporate world for Mike Braden to land. The men shook hands and Seth and Mike Braden walked out of the room with smiles.

"Hey, let's get a bite to eat, why don't we?" Mike said to Seth, as they walked to his car.

"Sounds like a great idea, Mr. Braden. My stomach is growling already! I know of that café down the street and around the corner. You know which one I'm talking about?" Seth was starving, like always, and was more than ready to sit and talk with Mike about the firm.

"I know exactly where you're talking about," Mike said, smiling. "I'm hungry too. I didn't think I would make it through that meeting without getting something to drink. But it went better than I had expected. It was good to have you along, Seth. Hope you learned something."

The two men walked into the café and sat down, ordered their meals, and watched the television that was bracketed on the wall in a corner of the café. The place was a little dumpy, but it was packed for lunch. It was noted for the waiters throwing the rolls across the room to the tables. No one seemed to notice the messy floors or dirty finger-printed windows. It was also a bit warm in there, even though ceiling fans were spinning like small tornadoes. There was music playing, and people were talking loudly, but this apparently was the hot spot for lunch downtown.

"So, Mr. Braden, how long have you been with the firm? Or did you establish it with Mr. Holland, and Mr. Spencer?"

"I was there from the beginning, Seth. It was something that took place in Fred Holland's living room one evening. We all were CPA's and were tired of the grind of working for someone else and not making the money. So we decided to get smart and create our own firm; pull together, land some big accounts, and make a good living. It has actually turned out fairly well, seeing as how we didn't really know each other that well when this all came about. I live on the same street as Fred Holland, and John Spencer actually went to church with Fred. So we all came together and it worked." Mike was taking a large bite out of his ham and rye sandwich, and drew a big sip of his coke.

Seth thought for a moment, while they both ate their lunches. "I really appreciate being taken into the firm, Mr. Braden. I know I'm green, but I learn quickly. I'm excited about the return I'm working on for Whitworth & Company, and am eager to tackle more difficult accounts as soon as possible. The more I learn, the more I want to know. The rules keep changing constantly, and I can see that it's going to be a challenge just to keep up with them. I know we're held liable for that knowledge, and there would be no excuse with the IRS for us not knowing."

The men ate in silence for a moment and then Mike interrupted it by saying to Seth, "Hey, Seth, you like fishing?"

"Oh my gosh, yes! I love to fish. I haven't done much of it since college, but I used to go with my father all of the time. Why?" Seth was eager to hear what was next.

"Well, I have a cabin on a lake in Melvin, off in the woods. It's quiet and the best place for fishing I've ever been in my entire life. And I've traveled a lot in my day. I thought you might like to bring your girl friend, and stay for the weekend and fish. I could show you where I go to fish, and then you could use the cabin when it's empty, anytime you wanted. You seem like a nice enough guy, and I want you to feel at home with us here at Holland, Braden & Spencer."

Seth was blown away. To be accepted into this group so warmly was way past what he'd expected when he got the job. He hadn't been there that long, but did work late hours, overtime, and did anything they put in front of him, without complaint. He wasn't playing a game here. This was a serious career move for him, and he didn't want to ever do anything that would jeopardize his position with the firm. The thought of taking Lila to a cabin for a weekend blew Seth's mind. He had a difficult time concentrating on the conversation because he kept thinking about Lila and being on a lake far away from everyone.

"We plan to enlarge our firm slowly, Seth" Mike was saying. "But we'll be very picky about who we bring into the firm. As you know, you had to go through several interviews and took many tests so that we knew you understood Accounting 101. We put you through the mill on questions about taxes and what the new changes were on the IRS filing forms. You came through like a champ, and we couldn't find one reason not to hire you. Not everyone will come through this like you did."

Seth blushed and stood up. He shook Mike's hand and said "Mr. Braden, I'm in this for the long haul. I take my work very seriously even though I'm young. I've been through a lot in my short life and it's made me realize what is important in life, and what isn't ."

When the two men got back into the car, Seth decided to share about the plane crash with Mike Braden. "Mr. Braden, it was unreal. The plane suddenly felt like it was unbalanced and before I knew it, we were headed straight down into the water. The explosion was louder than anything I could have imagined. And the impact blew the plane apart."

"Man! It sounds terrifying! What happened when you crashed?"

"I don't remember hitting the water, but the next thing I knew, I was floating in the water hung up in a seat tangled in the seat belt. Luckily, that ended up saving my life. I was rescued but my sister remained in the water for a much longer time. I began to panic because I wanted to know where she was. It was such a sick feeling."

"I'm amazed at the maturity that you showed. I'm also shocked at how long Ella lived without water and food, with so many broken bones. The rescue she went through would make a great movie! I know you and your family are so thankful she made it through all of this alive. Did you ever meet her rescuer?"

"Yeah. He was the coolest guy! He and Ella hit if off right away, and have not stopped talking since."

The men continued to talk until they pulled up into the parking lot of Holland, Braden & Spencer. Seth got out, thanked Mr. Braden for the wonderful meal and the experience.

"Don't forget about the fishing trip, Seth. I want you to pick a weekend that is good for you and Lila, and let me know. We'll have a great time, I promise you."

"I look forward to it, Mr. Braden. And I'll let you know soon about dates that are good for us. Thank you so much for allowing me into the world of getting new accounts."

Seth went back to work with a vengeance. He knew now that he'd made a great choice coming to this firm. He couldn't wait to share all of this with Lila. Only a few more hours and he could go home.

Chapter 36

K ate sat in her bed, stretching, and sipping her hot tea. It had been a long day and she was ready to sleep, but she wanted to read a few notes in the box before she turned in. She turned her head to look at the box. It was very interesting to think that maybe a young child had put these notes inside the box, trying to find a way to tell someone about her life. Kate was very anxious to find out what this child might have to say. She picked up the box and for a moment she felt a sort of holiness about it. *This might be someone's life in here,* she thought. *I want to be respectful of whatever I find, no matter what it might be.* Her heart raced a little as she opened the lid. She let the lid rest on her knees, and pulled out the first sheet of paper. She was nervous and didn't know why. The first note took her breath away.

the black paper cross is on the door. i am scared to death. i know what is coming. why doesn't somebody help me? he says he loves me but he keeps on hurting me. they see the cross but they do not help me. why doesn't mommy see?

Kate re-read it several times, not wanting to put it down. *What did this mean?* She picked up another note:

mommy is beautiful. she is crying today. i hope it is not my fault. she is always sad. i will try harder. i miss her holding me. what am I doing wrong? she won't look at me anymore. My mouth hurts and I cannot eat but no one sees. they all smile and do not see my tears that fall on my plate.

Kate was sweating. Because of her recent studies, her mind was racing as to what she would find if she kept reading. She decided to read six of them each night. She pulled another note out.

i am invisible. i don't want to tell anyone what is happening. i hate him. but I am confused about love. he says he loves me. i want to die. Everyone sees but no one sees. Invisible. i am dirty. i hate myself.

Now Kate was getting a little angry along with wanting to know what was going on. *This doesn't feel good. It feels black and evil. A paper cross that was black? What is next?*

i am only allowed to play with anna. she is my best friend. she lives down the street with her grandparents. my bedroom is pink and i have flowers on the walls up high with pink gingham curtains on the windows. i sometimes can have a friend over and then i am safe.

Kate pulled the last one out, and breathed out a deep breath.

i dread coming to bed because I can always hear his footsteps coming. in the morning i will still be bleeding but no one will notice. no one hears. the smell makes me sick. i dream i am somewhere else far away, in the flower field where it smells so good. i can disappear and he never notices. I am the saddest one in the family. mommy cries but i don't know why.

Kate closed the box and put it back on her nightstand. She put her hands over her eyes And shook her head. *She was dead sure this was abuse.* It was not going to be good reading the rest of the words in the box, but she knew she would read them because she had to know more about this child. She lay back on her pillow and drifted off thinking about what this child must have gone through in her life. The light on the nightstand stayed on all night, lighting up the box which carried words of darkness.

When Kate awoke, she had a crick in her neck and felt like she hadn't slept at all. She was dying to tell someone about the box and the words she had read. *Stephen will want to know,* she thought. *I'll keep it quiet until I know the whole story. This doesn't need to get out because I don't even know who the person is. What if they are still alive?*

She got up and showered, and went into the kitchen to make some fresh coffee. She came back to her room and sat on the edge of the bed and stared at the box. It had a way of pulling her in. She put her hand on it and knew that years ago a child had touched that same box with secrets that no one wanted to hear. *I wonder if I will ever find out who this child was,* she thought in the silence of her room.

She headed to work and decided not to phone Stephen until later in the day, when they could have more time to talk about what she'd read. She tried to focus on the patients that came in to see her; she really did love her work. But she was haunted by the words she was reading and knew at some point she would probably get the whole picture. She found time to call Susan and Laney in between patients. Laney had been working hard and enjoying her class. Susan was busy but wanted to save a day to eat lunch again and catch up. The day went by uneventfully and Kate left her office, ran by the store to pick a few groceries, and headed home. She called Stephen and asked him if they could eat a bite together at her house, so she could talk to him about last night.

He was thrilled to hear from her. "Of course, baby. I'll be there as soon as I leave work. I'll check out of here in about thirty minutes, if that works for you."

"That's perfect," said Kate. She breathed a heavy sigh , knowing this conversation was going to be emotional for her. Because of all of the cases she had dealt with in the past, and all of her studies on Post Traumatic Stress Disorder, she was very familiar with the signs of abuse. She really didn't have to read any more of the words in the box to diagnose what this child was suffering from.

Stephen knocked on the door and came in. It was so good to see him and Kate ran up and gave him a hug. "I love you so much. I can't wait to share all of this with you! I know you'll understand." She reached up and kissed his cheek and embraced him for a few minutes. It felt so good to be close to him.

"You mentioned a long time ago that you loved how we could talk about anything. Well, I love how you listen one hundred percent and are so good at coming up with a solution to problems quickly. You don't assume anything and it makes me absolutely love talking to Walking around the house was heaven for Kate. Stephen had given her a key and now she could come and go as she pleased. She just stood there and breathed in the smell of the house. It was the layout that drew her in, and the feeling that the house had character. A life of its own. She moved into the kitchen and looked through all the cabinets, the refrigerator, the oven, the microwave. The countertops were granite, and the floor was tiled. She walked into the hearth room and there were windows lining the left side of the house. It let so much light in. Kate decided right then that those windows would remain open.

you." There were only a few people in her world that listened like that.

"Well, I do try, Kate. It's not hard with you, because I want to know what you are thinking and feeling. I'm not sure I do that with the rest of the world!" He chuckled and hugged her close.

"Stephen, please sit down. I've fixed us a light supper so that we could sit here in the hearth room and talk. I have something I'm dying to share with you that we've both been waiting to discover. I read some of the notes in the box last night and they ripped my heart apart. I've only read six of them, and I already know pretty much what the rest are going to be like. However, I may be surprised. I've brought downstairs the six notes that I've read so that you could see them. It's definitely a child's writing and you'll be able to feel her pain just holding the notes."

Looking carefully at the handwriting, Stephen read the notes quietly and handed them back to Kate. He put his hand on her and said "We're looking into a child's life one note at a time, trying to understand what the child is trying to tell us. Something like this is very heavy, very emotional. No one wants to read about a child suffering, especially when other adults are around and do nothing to stop the pain."

Kate moved over towards Stephen and leaned her head on his shoulder. "I'm going to be reading six more notes tonight. I'm worried about what I'll find, but I'm compelled to read them. That box is powerful, for it holds within it words that a child was screaming out. And no adult was hearing. I want to hear, Stephen."

"I know you do, Katie. But be careful with your own emotions. We don't know if we'll ever find out who this person is. Or if they're even alive. Just take it easy, okay? It's not like you haven't had enough in your own life to deal with."

Stephen held Kate for a while, and then they said goodnight. Stephen walked to the door and turned to look at Kate. "Take it slow. I mean it, Kate. This is serious and really has gotten a hold of you."

"I know," Kate said. "But did you ever stop to think that maybe I was meant to find this box? I really don't think there is anything that happens by coincidence in our lives. Maybe there's a purpose in my finding this box and reading the notes inside."

"It could be. I'm worried that you'll get too involved with this. But I also realize this is your area of expertise. Maybe I'm being too protective of you, but man, I've watched you this last year and you've had some huge issues to cope with."

"I agree. I promise to take it slow. I know you're right, but like you said, this is a direction re I feel very comfortable going. Whatever I discover could help me in cases that deal with PTSD in the future. I can't be afraid to dig into this."

Stephen shook his head in agreement. "I'm here if you need me. I'm going to call it a night and head home if that's okay with you, Kate. I love you and want to hear what you find tonight when you read the next six notes."

Stephen kissed her goodnight and left. Kate was alone to her own thoughts. She turned down the lights in the house and walked up the stairs slowly, to her room. The box was waiting on her nightstand, holding within it more suffering with no sound at all.

Chapter 37

Kate brushed her hair and put on her pajamas. It was near midnight and she was getting tired. She went over to the nightstand and turned up the light so she could read easier. She opened the box and pulled out another note.

I am alone in this hell. I want to tell someone but who? I am afraid to talk to anyone about it. They won't believe me. How can I make it stop? He owns my life but he does not know me at all. He does not see my pain. I'm hollow inside. I hate my mother for not seeing what is going on. She has to see. She has to see. She has to see.

Kate shuddered, but she kept on reading the notes one by one, with thoughts of the child who wrote the words.

I sleep with no pillow. I feel like am going to suffocate. I cry some but it feels better to rock back and forth. There is no one to soothe me. Where is my mother? She keeps letting me down. She never sees what is happening. I feel like my father owns every single day of my life. Dinner is at 6 in the evening. I sit at the table and I do not want to go upstairs because he will follow me up, so I drag out my meal. It delays him touching me. Daddy said I could get a new bike today. Mother took me shopping and we got something to eat. He gives me what I want if I keep silent. I cannot leave a glass on the table or anything. I sit quietly at the table and never talk. They do not want to hear what I have to say. I have to play in my room. I misbehave and points are taken away from me. I am never relaxed and I wet myself because I know what is going to happen.

Kate could not read anymore. She was overwhelmed at the struggle this child had, and the fact that no one was aware or refused to believe. *There had to be signs of the abuse. How could they allow this to go on? It's beyond human understanding how anyone could harm a child, or how adults or other family members could turn the other way while someone in their sight was being abused.*

She folded the notes carefully and placed them back in the box. There were a few more to read, but she would save that for another night. *I must talk to Stephen about how to find out where this family is now. Surely there was a way to track this young woman down, if she was even alive.*

Kate turned out the light but was restless for several hours, thinking about what she'd read. *This is hard to get out of my mind. I know better than to allow this to swallow up my emotions, but somehow it's more difficult this time than when I work with patients in my office with abusive backgrounds. Maybe because I found the box in my new house.*

She dozed off unknowingly with thoughts of a child whose youth had been stolen.

Chapter 38

Lauren was busy organizing the after school clubs that would be arriving later on this afternoon, the activities were always fun but educational too. Stuart was working late tonight and then he was going out with some friends from work so tonight she was on her own. As she wandered around trying to find all the literature and stationary for the afternoon, she noticed Kate. This wasn't the first time that Lauren had thought about Kate; for some reason she had been on her mind on and off for a few days. Now Lauren found herself watching Kate as she browsed among the Mental Health section at the far end of the library. *What is it that I find so intriguing? Something is pulling me towards wanting to start a conversation with this woman.* Lauren had never been like this before with a visitor; she didn't even know her but was trying to figure out so much about her. She knew that Kate was a psychiatrist but she really didn't know anything else.

Kate was about to sit down at a table to go through some books on PTSD, when Lauren walked up. "Hi Kate. Good to see you again. How are you?"

Kate was surprised that Lauren remembered her name. "Hello Lauren, I'm doing well. I want to study more in these publications as I'm working on a case. How are you?"

"Doing fine. I'm really enjoying working with the children here twice a week. And I'm now organizing an after school program for the kids to encourage them to read more and to introduce them to the world of authors."

Kate smiled. She was impressed with Lauren's enthusiasm for the kids. And for reading. The library had been a big part of her own children's lives, so it was nice to see someone care about getting children interested early in books.

"I'm impressed with you, Lauren. You could've made this a boring job, but instead you have created a magical place for the children."

"Thanks . It's nice to be recognized for the efforts I've made. I'm trying to step out of the box a little, and it's hard to get the board to agree with some of my ideas."

Kate sat down at the table and smiled at Lauren. "I love people who aren't afraid to push the envelope a little. The problem with most businesses, no matter what type they are, is that the people who work there get stuck in a rut or way of doing things and things get stale. There's no life anymore in what they're trying to do. You're trying to encourage creativity and that is powerful in anyone's life."

Lauren left Kate to her work, and finished putting back the books that had been checked out the day before. *It sure was nice talking to Kate,* Lauren thought. *Maybe we could have lunch one day and share more about our live. Kate is so enthusiastic about life that it pumps me up about what I am doing at my job. No one else seems to care.*

Looking through cases, Kate tried to find things that might apply to one of her clients and also to the child she didn't know much about. She took enough notes to help her client and then allowed herself time to scan through the books. She spent much of Saturday morning looking through publications and books, losing herself and time on a person she didn't even know yet. It was a challenge to Kate to find answers that might stop some of the torture that people suffering from PTSD go through. Her cell phone buzzed in her purse, and brought her back to reality. She looked at her watch, and decided it was about time to go.

Lauren saw Kate gathering her things to leave and walked over to her. "I may be to forward in asking this, Kate, but could we possibly have lunch sometime?"

Kate was pleasantly surprised at the invitation. "Of course, Lauren, I would love to have lunch with you. You pick the day and I'll make sure I'm available."

On her way home, Lauren texted Stuart to meet her at the local sports bar because she wanted to share with him about Kate. Stuart phoned her immediately to say he would be there, but might be a little late. Lauren arrived, ordered the drinks, and sat down in a cozy corner of the bar and waited for him. It gave her time to collect her thoughts about what she would tell him, and also to go over her conversation with Kate.

Stuart turned up a little late, as usual, but cheerful, none the less. He was eyeing Lauren and liking what he saw. *Boy she looks good even after a long day at work. She is amazing.*

They both ordered some light supper and were quiet for a moment.

"How was your day, Stu?" Lauren asked, smiling.

"Yeah, it was cool. We made a lot of loans today, so there was a ton of paper work to go through. Busy, but productive. My kind of day, you know?" Stuart took a bite of the fish sandwich he had ordered.

"I had an interesting day today. A lady came back in the library that I met a few days ago, and she is a psychiatrist. She was doing some research on PTSD," Lauren said, taking a sip of her drink.

"What is PTSD?" Stuart asked.

"It's Post Traumatic Stress Disorder, which a lot of veterans suffer with after a war, you know?"

"Wow. Sounds kind of interesting. So what did she have to say to you?"

"I haven't spoken to her about it much, but I thought it was interesting, and decided it might be a good idea to get together. So were going to lunch soon to get to know each other better." Lauren said with a twinkle in her eye. "She's different, Stu. She's enthusiastic about life and really acted like she cared about what I was doing at the library."

Stuart grinned and did a thumbs up to her. "That's cool, baby. I'm glad to hear you enthusiastic for a change. Let me know how it goes."

They finished their meal, talking about their day and laughing together. He followed her home and they shared a glass of wine before it was time for Stuart to leave.

"I've really enjoyed this little date with you! But I do miss being around you more. I got spoiled living with you. I hope you're getting close to wanting me back into your life in a more serious way.... If I can say that without sounding pushy"

"Oh Stu. I adore you. You know I love you to death. I just needed some time to sort myself out. I promise we'll talk soon about all of it." She kissed him goodnight and closed the door behind him. Lauren sat thinking about her talk with Kate, wondering where it all would end up. *I know the time has come for the past to surface, and Stuart's last statement was a good example. I have been struggling on my own with this for so long. Maybe it was destined that I met Kate at the library. It's time to get this all out in the open.*

Chapter 39

Saturday evening was a time that Kate could kick back and relax totally, away from all the thoughts of her patients, and stress of her work week. She had music on, a glass of Zinfandel in her hand, and she was reading some of W. H. Auden's early work. The house was quiet and peaceful and for the first time in a long while, Kate felt an overwhelming sense of calm in her life. She had dealt with Sam's death and finding out about Alison. Her children were well on their way to having their own lives. It was a great time now for her family to build new memories with each other and put the past behind them. She had fixed a wonderful dinner of grilled fish, wild rice and mushrooms, and grilled asparagus with hollandaise sauce. She always had fresh bread and olive oil with her wine. She had on her pajamas early in the evening, and was stretched out on the sofa in the hearth room. *If I'm so at peace, why can't I leave the box alone?* She fought it for a while, and then put down Auden and walked upstairs. *If I'm going to be honest with myself, I'm absorbed in the life of a child I may never know. How healthy is that?* She began reading the notes, thankful that there weren't many more, or she wouldn't ever get anything else done in her life.

Father would not let me lock the bathroom door. There is an awkward silence between mother and I. Almost like she knows. But she won't do anything to confront him. Even though she is a strong woman, what is she afraid of? I wish I could tell Jake. He was my brother and my best friend. Why did he take his life? I can't believe he killed himself. I need him to be here. He was all I had. I can't wait til I go off to college, then he can't get to me. I almost hate my mother for not stopping him. Daddy lost his job, because of his temper. How will we manage? And will he take it out on me? My life has been hell. I wonder if other families have secrets like this. It is hard to believe no one wants to acknowledge the damage he has done. I have run away once, but there is no where to go. No where to turn. I cannot trust anyone. Ever. I look in their houses as I walk down the street and wonder if they have secrets like we do. I can't be the only one. But it feels like people are staring at me. They have no idea what has been going on in this house.

Dear God, thought Kate. *I only have bits and pieces of this child's life. But I have a feeling it is much worse than what was written down. I must ask Stephen to try to find out when this family moved out of the house.* She looked around, wondering what secrets the walls carried inside. For a moment the house seemed to go cold and she shivered. Even though there was a full moon in the sky, Kate was filled with dread and a deep sadness for a little girl she so wanted to meet. She read the last note reluctantly.

The attic has been my secret place all these years. He will never find this box. No one will. I know one day I'll grow up and move away and he will not own me anymore. He has stolen my childhood and I am not going to give him my life. I hate him more than anything on earth. I despise him. I have lived in this darkness for all these years and not one time did anyone in the family, except my brother, come to rescue me. Or want to know anything. My mother is invisible to me and I am to her. I have no family now that my brother is gone. We have a secret in this family that is as deep as the sea and as dark as the night.

One day I will step out from under the black cross and fly. I will never come back to this family again.

I hope one day to meet someone who will be my real mother. someone who will care what happens to me and hear what I am saying. My mother is made out of stone. She refuses to see. She refuses to speak. I guess he has threatened us all. She lost a son, and one day she is going to lose me. I am sick and tired of feeling guilty and dirty. I have lived my life in a dark dark closet. My bedroom. I hate mirrors because they make me see the eyes he looks at. The face he touches. I hate myself. I hate him. I hate my life. One day . One day . One day.

Kate folded the note and placed it back in the box and closed the lid. Tears were streaming down her face and her mind was racing. She was exhausted but the anger was bigger than the desire to sleep. She lay there for an hour thinking about this last note. *The power in those words was unbelievable. What did this young child go through that would cause such hatred? I have heard many things in my work, but this may top them all.*

She fell asleep finally, but her sleep was interrupted by short dreams of a child crying out for help. Kate got up and went downstairs for something to drink. She sat at her kitchen table thinking about the cases she had studied and how they might apply to this child. Then she suddenly began to laugh. *What in the world am I doing up in the middle of the night worrying about a child I'll never know? Stephen was right, I don't need to take this so seriously.* She got up and put her cup in the sink and walked back upstairs. When she laid her head down on the pillow she was asleep in seconds.

In the morning, the sun was coming through the curtains, and Kate felt a warmth on her face. It was Sunday morning, and she'd decided to call Stephen so that they could go for a walk while the day was warm. Maybe take a picnic lunch to the park. She rang his phone quickly and he answered in his usual good mood.

"Hello Katie, how's my girl this morning?"

"I'm doing fine. Just thinking we should take advantage of this lovely sunny day and have a picnic outside. I'll pack us a lunch, and you pick up some drinks and a bottle of wine. Come by and pick me up when you are ready. How does that sound?"

"Wow. Aren't you adventurous for so early in the morning! It sounds great to me. I have some good news to share with you about the cancer cure that I was talking to you about earlier. So I'll be about an hour, Kate. That good for you?"

"Sounds perfect. See you soon, baby." Kate hung up the phone and smiled. *I'm going to turn around this feeling I'm having about the words in the box, and have a good time with Stephen.* She pulled a picnic basket off the top of the refrigerator and began packing a special lunch for such a sweet man. *I'm missing him suddenly. He brings such stability to my life and I'm grateful for it.*

* * *

Across town, Lauren was lying in bed thinking; staring at the window, wondering what today would bring. She had made up her mind to call Kate on Monday for lunch. She was ready to open up and finally tell her secrets. She sat up in bed and stretched, remembering she had picked today to go to the park with her camera and special lenses to try to catch some photographs of children playing so that she could frame them to hang in the library. She suddenly was full of energy and shot out of bed and showered. She pulled some jeans on and her favorite old hoodie and stuck some munchies in her camera bag. Her car was warming up in the garage when her phone rang. It was Stuart. She made a decision to not take the call. She wanted to be on her own today, to enjoy the trees, and the world around her.

* * *

Stephen and Kate found the perfect tree to sit under. The breeze was blowing slightly and could have made it too chilly to sit out for a picnic, but the sun was warm and bright, so Kate was feeling good in her jacket and jeans. They set up the picnic basket and brought out some wine and cheese and crackers. It was a perfect way to start the day. Stephen was lying back, propping himself up on one arm. *He looks handsome today, with his jeans and white shirt. He is never cold.* Kate tried not to let him see her watching him,

He looked at Kate as she laid out the food. *I want so much for her to be my wife.*

"Hey lady, what in the world did you stick in that basket? It looks like you brought everything in your refrigerator!" Stephen laughed, as he reached to stick his finger in the icing of a cupcake.

"Hey you! Get your hand out of that icing. I just thought it'd be nice to have some choices today. I made you ham and cheese on rye bread and also a turkey club. How does that sound? I have some extra potato salad and pickles too."

Stephen's mouth watered as he grabbed the ham and cheese sandwich. He was starving, and the fresh air made it worse. When he sat up, he felt the bulge in his pocket. A box from a jewelry store that he was going to give to Kate. *I'm a bit nervous about it, but there seems to be no perfect time to ask her the big question, and I'm tired of waiting. I've known for quite some time that I want to spend my life with her. She was distant at first; but my gosh,* thought Stephen, *she'd been through so much that anyone could understand her pulling away. Her emotions were like a roller coaster.*

"I love coming to the park, Stephen." said Kate, squinting as she looked out at all the kids playing on the swings. They were very tall swings so that the kids could go high. She remembered well that feeling of soaring. She also remembered falling out a few times.

"Me too, Kate. We should do this more often. I'm glad you put us near the lake, because I enjoy watching the geese swimming. I imagine they will fly south for the winter pretty soon. I'm surprised they haven't already done so, frankly."

Kate smiled. Then she remembered his cancer cure and interrupted his train of thought. "What about the cancer cure? The rain forest cure you were telling me about? How's that coming along?"

"It's progressing fairly quickly. We got it approved by the FDA after a year of testing, to be used on a trial basis with patients who are terminal. They have to sign up for this program, but Kate, this just might be the first cure that doesn't destroy the bodies own immune system. Do you realize how big this could be?" Stephen was getting so excited and Kate loved to see his enthusiasm.

"Stephen. This is huge. Do you know when this is going to take place?
"Kate was amazed at his brilliance. And his humility.

"Real soon, Kate. They have some red tape to go through but we'll find out in the next few weeks when the trials will be. To be accepted so quickly is unprecedented. All of us working on this took note of that immediately. The FDA just does not approve things without years of testing. I think they are under a lot of pressure to approve some of the drugs that are being tested now that look promising. Too many people are suffering needlessly, especially if this extract does what it seems to be doing in animals."

Kate sat there thinking about the impact this would have on America, let alone other countries. She was suddenly distracted by someone in the distance taking photos and thought how perfect a day it was for that. The girl looked a little familiar, but she was too far away to really tell who it was. As she came closer, Kate realized that it was Lauren so she stood up and waved.

"Stephen, for heavens sake! That's Lauren from the city library. I can't believe she's out here taking photos on the same day we decide to have a picnic!"

Lauren saw Kate waving at her and came running toward her. "Hey Kate! What a wonderful surprise! I'm out here taking photos for the library. Why don't I take a couple of shots of you and your friend?" Lauren smiled at Kate, a little out of breath.

"That sounds like fun," said Kate, laughing. She made Stephen sit up straight and she sat down beside him. Lauren took several shots and then said goodbye. As she left, she told Kate she would let her know about lunch.

Kate waved goodbye and looked at Stephen. "What a nice surprise. I'm sure she will share those photos with us."

Stephen pulled Kate close to him. He whispered in her ear that he had a surprise and that he was waiting to give it to her when they were alone. Kate's stomach went into a knot. She was barely breathing as Stephen pulled out a lovely gift from his pocket in his jacket. It was a small box with a beautiful pink bow. She unwrapped it slowly and was hesitant about lifting the lid of the box.

Stephen looked at her and said "Angel, you don't have to open this if you don't want to. Are you too nervous?"

Kate smiled, took a deep breath and opened the box. Inside was the most beautiful diamond ring she had ever seen in her entire life. She took it out and looked at it, with the sun shining right through it.

Stephen took her hand in his, knelt down and said, "Kate, my precious woman, will you spend the rest of your life with me? I've known for a while that I wanted you in my life permanently, and I waited until things settled down for you a bit. I want you to be my wife. Will you, Kate? Do you love me?"

Stephen was a nervous wreck but did not want to show it. Kate was white as a sheet, but she had a feeling this was probably coming.

"Of course I love you Stephen! I've been through so much in this last year that it's all a blur. I will say I am *nervous* about getting married again; and that is understandable since I was married to the same man for thirty years. But I do know in my heart that you and I entered each other's lives with such ease. I really didn't realize how smooth the transition would be until I looked into your eyes that night in my kitchen when you held me close. You've been so good for me and the kids. I would love to spend my life with you. If you are ready to do this with me, then I'll be your wife. Stephen, *eternity is a long time.*"

Stephen raised her up to her feet and pulled her close to him. He held her in his arms for a few minutes and kissed her several times. "You're the woman I've waited so long for. I can think of no one I would rather grow old with than you. I respect you, Kate. I adore you and your children. And I am willing to do what it takes to make you happy."

Kate smiled and kissed Stephen back. This might turn out to be a one of the few life-altering days that Kate had ever had. She never thought she'd find someone who loved her like Sam loved her. *He understands me so well and we agree on the core values of life,* she thought. *I would be so happy if I married Stephen, and I can't think of a reason not to.* Kate knew in her heart it was the right thing to do. She knew her children would be happy about it. But she needed to sort out her any small feelings about Sam in her heart, quietly, and alone. She kept that thought to herself.

They walked back to the car holding hands. He opened the car door for her and kissed her cheek. They drove out of the park laughing, so glad that they had decided to have a picnic. Stephen walked Kate to the door and kissed her goodbye. "I love you, Katie. I'm thrilled that you want to be with me for the rest of your life. I'll let you set the date, but don't wait too long, okay? I'll call you later."

"I promise, Stephen. I promise I won't make us wait too long. The ring is absolutely breathtaking and I'm overwhelmed with how you love me. Thank you, sweetheart. You are always to gracious to me and so open. I certainly wasn't expecting all this today! I love you with all my heart."

They parted and Kate went inside. The first thing she did was walk to the photo of Sam that was hanging in the hallway.

She looked him straight in the eye and smiled. "Sam, you will always be the love of my life. But I know you'd want me to move on, and to be happy. Stephen is a good man and I have fallen deeply in love with him. In spite of this, I regret that you had that affair, and I hate that Alison had to die. I know that this was not what you wanted to happen. It would have broken your heart if you knew. Even still, I did find out. And she did die. I don't know quite what to think anymore about us, Sam. So I'm going to try to let it all go so I can move on. We had a good life until I found that note. I'm hanging on to the good memories in hopes that I'm reading you right; that you really did love me like you said you did. Goodbye, Sam." She turned and walked away, resisting the urge to look back at his face one more time.

Chapter 40

Lauren woke up with one thing on her mind; to call Kate and have lunch with her. After seeing her at the park yesterday, she could think of nothing else. She got up, showered, caught some of the morning news while she was doing her hair and makeup, and then rushed out the door to the library. On her way in, she picked up a coffee and some donuts for breakfast. She had thrown an apple in her purse so she wouldn't feel so guilty about eating the donuts. Traffic was heavy going to work, and Lauren avoided one wreck after the other, as angry drivers rushed to work. She enjoyed working downtown, but the drive in was always hectic. She pulled into the parking lot, got out, and went straight to her desk in the back. She picked up the phone and dialed Kate's number, thinking of all the things that she would want to talk about, and wondering how she would fit it all in on a lunch hour.

Kate answered on the second ring; her secretary was a little late this morning worrying with a sick child. "Good morning, this is Dr. Morrison, may I help you?" asked Kate.

"Good morning, Kate. This is Lauren! I was calling early, hoping we could have lunch today. If it's not a good time, please let me know. I can be free at around twelve thirty, Kate. How does that sound to you?" Lauren felt nervous just thinking about seeing Kate again.

"I think I can arrange it. If you don't hear from me, then you know I'm able to make it. Let's meet at the park again, as I know a terrific place for us to sit and talk. I'll pick up some lunch for us. Does that sound good to you?"

"It sounds terrific. I'll see you around twelve thirty at the park, then, Kate." Lauren hung up the phone and was so excited that she felt a little sick. *I don't know why I'm feeling this way,* she thought. *But I need to get a grip because I really don't know how this talk is going to turn out.* Lauren took her donut and coffee up to the front counter and began her usual task of sorting through the books that were turned in, making sure they were not damaged, and also signing them back in to the library. She had a large pile of books to be placed back on the shelves and several phone calls to make. It felt good to be at work, and she was so happy at the library. She had read so many books that she was running out of places to put them at home.

* * *

Across town, Ella was finishing up her senior year at the University. She had changed her major to Developmental Education with a minor in Special Education. Her dream was to work with children with learning disabilities and the local middle school was going to let her come in and do some student teaching. She was so excited to get this experience, because it would nail down whether or not she really was cut out for this or not. Michael had encouraged her so much, and really had a great affect on her life. She absolutely adored him, his strength, his determination to help, and his tender heart. He was such a big guy, so strong. But inside, he genuinely cared about people. She was amazed at how many people's lives he had saved. His job was treacherous but he never felt like he was making a choice of his life or the person he was saving. He just said he was doing what was right.

Her nightmares were coming regularly. She had forgotten most of the crash but dreamt about floating on a fragment of the plane out in the middle of the ocean. She dreamt that she fell off the metal piece and just as she was drowning, swallowing lots of water, she woke up every time sweating and screaming. Michael knew about it, but told her that she probably was going to have to go to a therapist to get this one handled. *It was such a traumatic experience that I just can't get over the fear of drowning. I'm glad I decided not to go to my mother as a counselor as it would be too stressful for us both.* Ella made a note to get a referral from her mother so that she could get this under control as soon as possible. *I'm so ready to get past all of this,* she sighed.

Michael rang Ella's cell. There was no answer. He wanted to take her to dinner tonight as it was the anniversary of their first date. He had already ordered flowers and made a reservation. But he'd had so many rescue calls that he wasn't able to call her earlier. *I wonder if she has forgotten,* he thought, frowning. He left a message that it was urgent, hoping she would call right back. He had just got a promotion to leader position in the search and rescue division. That meant he would be the first man down when they were rescuing over water. He loved his job but knew it would be high risk, and he and Ella were getting closer and closer. He was a little worried that it might become a problem if they married and especially if they had children. Of course, there were divers that were married and had children, but they often spoke of how much stress it brought into their relationship at home with their families. He hated to put that on Ella.

Michael tried one more time before going out on another rescue, and Ella picked up. "Hey beautiful! Michael said, smiling. "Where in the world have you been? I have been trying to get in touch with you. Tonight is our anniversary of our first date! Are you surprised that I remembered?"

"Heck no. I know how you are, Mr. I Remember Everything!" Ella smiled and picked her books up from the table and put them into her satchel. "What do you have in mind, Michael?"

"I've made reservations for us at Rondell's and I wanted to pick you up at around six thirty. Is that okay, Ella?"

"Yeah, that's perfect, Michael. I'm so excited that we've made it a year. What a nice surprise. Most of my friends' boyfriends never remember anniversaries. Or anything else, for that matter." They both laughed.

"I'll be ready Michael. I love you so bad. I can't wait to see you tonight. You have made my day!" Ella hung up and grinned. *I'm one lucky girl and I'll never take Michael for granted. He's a little older than me, but I like that. I only wished my Dad could have met Michael. He would've loved him, for sure.*

* * *

Lauren arrived early for their lunch date at the park. She was hoping to beat Kate there so she could think about what she wanted to say to her. She had a lot of questions, of course, about what Kate did. And she was curious about what Kate had read about Post Traumatic Stress Disorder. She sat where she could easily be seen and also where she could see Kate drive up. It was a lovely day; the trees were full of color and some leaves were already falling. There was a crisp smell in the air that made her think of sitting around a fire, cooking hot dogs and eating marshmallows and hot chocolate. The holidays weren't so far away, and this year would be different with Stuart not living with her. Perhaps she should bring him back in. He did love her, and she loved him. But she wanted to sort out some issues of her past before she allowed him back in. Marriage was another matter.

Kate had both arms full of bags of food and drinks. She walked uphill slowly, trying not to spill the drinks or trip on something. She saw Lauren sitting on a park bench under some trees and headed her way.

Lauren soon saw Kate coming and ran to help her with the bags of food. "My gosh, Kate. What did you bring us to eat? It looks like you bought out the deli!" Lauren laughed and grabbed the bags.

"Well, I couldn't make up my mind so I bought a little of everything that looked good. We'll lay it all out and eat what we want and throw away the rest. How's that?" Kate plopped down on the park bench and looked around for a picnic table. She saw one not too far away, near the lake, so they headed in that direction.

"Lauren, I need to know more about you. I feel like I know you in some ways, but we really haven't shared much about ourselves to each other. Let's get settled here and eat our lunch. If you have any questions, please feel free to ask them, ok?" Kate laid all the food out and the two women filled their plates with wonderful food from the best deli in town.

"I can't believe how wonderful this all looks and smells, Kate. I'll have to remember that deli for a quick supper for Stuart and me." Lauren started eating and looked around the park, enjoying the fresh air. They chatted about the library, all the new books coming in, and how much they both enjoyed reading. They began tossing out names of books they had read to see if the other one had read it. They found out quickly that they did love the same authors. Lauren particularly loved Auden. As soon as she said this to Kate, she could tell that Kate was surprised.

"I'm so amazed that you love Auden. I have a book of his in my nightstand that I read before I go to bed." Kate smiled and touched Lauren's hand. "He's a great poet. It goes right to your heart, doesn't it?"

Lauren hesitated and then answered. "I can't tell you how many nights I have sat up reading Auden, allowing the words to sink in and take away the nightmares."

Kate didn't miss the comment, but decided to wait until they were through eating before she answered. As soon as they had cleared up the paper plates and food, Kate threw away the left overs in the nearest garbage can and took Lauren's hand.

"I see a pier down the hill. Let's walk down and go to the end of the pier and sit in those two chairs," Kate said, brushing her hair off her face. Her cell phone rang in her purse, and she stopped to answer it. She had told her secretary not to interrupt this meeting unless it was an emergency with one of her patients. So this call couldn't be a good thing.

"Hello, this is Dr. Morrison," Kate said with some authority in her voice.

"Mom! It's Ella. You have to come over immediately!!" Ella was crying and very upset. Kate could hardly understand her daughter.

"Okay, Ella. I'll be right there. What on earth has happened?"

"It's Michael! He's been hurt. He went on a rescue dive and there was a problem. I don't know what happened. The dispatcher called my house and said I needed to come to the hospital that Michael had been involved in an accident." Ella was over the edge, and Kate knew this was serious.

"I'll be there in five minutes, Ella. Just get your things together so we can head right to the hospital." Kate hung up and walked over to Lauren.

"I'm going to have to cut this visit short. You don't know how sorry I am. But my daughter has called and there seems to have been an accident. Her boyfriend is on the Rescue Squad and has been hurt, I guess. I don't know to what extent. Can we have a rain check on this talk, Lauren?" Kate was getting the tablecloth up and folded. She grabbed her purse and looked at Lauren.

"I totally understand. Go be with your daughter. Let me know how this turns out, will you?" Lauren shook Kate's hand and sat back down on the park bench she was on when Kate arrived at the park. She was struck with a sadness and felt let down, for she had built this meeting up in her mind. It sounded selfish but she was hoping it might be the beginning of her being able to open up to someone. Now she had to sit back and wait again. She was worried about Ella and her boyfriend but the disappointment was huge because of how long she had waited to find someone she could talk to. She sat for a while longer and then got up and drove back to the library. There was plenty of work waiting for her, and it got her mind off the disappointment. She hoped that nothing bad had happened to Ella's boyfriend. *Gosh, life is tough*, she thought, as she got out of her car and headed for the door. *Things always seem to catch us blind sided. If God exists, where is He now?*

Kate ran to her car and pulled out of the parking lot, nearly running a red light before she slowed down and took a deep breath. She had to calm down so Ella would not get hysterical. It took her about five minutes to get to Ella's apartment and she ran up the stairs to the door. It was unlocked, so she went right in. Ella was sitting at her kitchen table, crying, waiting for Kate to get there. She looked up and ran to her mother, sobbing about the phone call and what she was afraid had happened.

"Come on, Ella. Let's get to the hospital. There's no point in us discussing what could have happened. Let's just go find out what really did happen. We can deal with this, Ella. I'm sure it's not as bad as you re dreading." Kate reassured her daughter and they both came down the stairs and got into Kate's car. It began to rain lightly, as some clouds hung over the highway. *It wasn't even supposed to rain today,* thought Kate. *I'll have to go slower. We don't need to get in an accident trying to get to the hospital.*

The hospital parking lot was full and Kate had a difficult time finding a spot to park. She finally saw someone pulling out and raced to take their parking place. Ella was out of the car before Kate had turned the engine off. They both ran into the hospital and asked the information desk about Michael. The clerk looked up the new arrivals and found information on Michael Hayes. He was still in Intensive Care. The desk clerk could not give anymore information out, so Kate and Ella found the elevator and went up two floors to ICU. As soon as Ella got off the elevator she ran to the nurse's station and asked about Michael Hayes. They asked her if she was a relative, and she told the nurse that she was his girl friend. That they were going to be married soon. Kate heard that remark and briefly smiled. She had thought they were getting very close, but didn't know if they had gone so far as to talk about marriage.

"I need to see Michael," Ella told the nurse, frantically.

"You can't see him right now, Ella. But I'll see if the doctor is around so he can share more about what's going on with Michael. Please wait right here." The nurse left the station and went to find a doctor. Ella put her head down in her hands on the counter of the nurse's station. She just couldn't bear it if something happened to Michael. Not now. Not ever.

"Ella, come and sit here. I'm sure it won't take a minute for the nurse to find out something or find a doctor." Kate pulled Ella over to the small sofas that were arranged in the small waiting area. Suddenly the nurse came around the corner with a doctor, who immediately went straight to Ella.

"I'm Dr. Whittington, and I'm the doctor on call today. I have seen Michael and am waiting for his family to arrive. Are you his family?"

"No, Dr. Whittington. But we're going to be married soon. I'm his fiancé, Ella Morrison." Ella held out her hand for the doctor to shake. He took it and held it for a minute.

"Ella, let's sit down. I want to share with you what's happened. Michael was on a diver rescue mission and hit a rock when he went down into the water. He was knocked unconscious and his mouthpiece fell out of his mouth. He took in a lot of water into his lungs and didn't get enough oxygen into his brain. He's in a coma, we have a pulse, but there's no brain activity. He's a strong man, but we have worked on him for hours and we can't get any brain activity. We have taken X-rays and an MRI. He has several broken bones, and a concussion. The main issue is that he wasn't getting any oxygen, and we really don't know how long that was."

Ella was in complete shock. It was like she couldn't take all of this in. *Was the doctor saying that Michael was brain dead? How could that be? She had just talked to him earlier and they* were planning their anniversary dinner?" Ella stood up and pushed the doctor, coming toward him with anger.

"I need to see him. I know he'll come to if I'm there. If he hears my voice." Ella grabbed the doctor's hand and insisted.

"I need to see him, Dr. Whittington. Please, take me to Michael."

"It is highly irregular, but since his family hasn't arrived here yet, I'll let you in for a moment. You must stay calm, Ella. I know this is difficult for you, but we are doing and have done all that we can to help Michael. The brain cannot go without oxygen for very long."

Ella went into the ICU room and there was Michael lying there, with tubes coming out of everywhere, and a breathing machine hooked up to him. He was very pale. He didn't look like himself. Ella walked over to him and laid her hands on his chest. She bent down and kissed his face with tears streaming down her face. *This was her Michael laying here.* The man she wanted to spend the rest of her life with. He saved her life. She couldn't let him go now; there was no way she was going to live without him after what he had done for her. She adored him. She could hardly *breathe.* She called his name and leaned over him to see if he would respond. She yelled his name out, and nothing happened. The doctor stepped over close to the bed and took Ella's arm.

Kate stepped up, with tears coming down her face. "Ella dear, listen to the doctor. I know you are upset. This is a nightmare. But we have to listen to the doctor."

"Ella, listen. Michael is brain dead. He's gone. If I unplug this machine, he is going to die in seconds. In less than a second. His heart will stop, Ella. I hate this for you, but I have to be honest. You need to tell Michael goodbye. I'm waiting now for his family, because they'll be the ones who decide whether or not to pull the breathing machine from Michael."

Ella bent over and kissed Michael one more time. She whispered in his ear that she loved him with all her heart, and that she wanted to be his wife. She told him that she would never love anyone else, that he had to get well. She stood up and moved away from the bed, in total shock and crying. Kate took her arm and led her back to the waiting room. There was nothing but silence for minutes, which seemed like hours to Kate.

NANCY VELDMAN *with Paris Milla*

"Ella, do you want to stay here and wait for his parents to come? Where do they live? Are they out of town?" Kate asked, patting Ella's arm and kissing her cheek.

"Mom, they live in California. They'll be getting a flight as soon as possible, I imagine. I hope they don't tell them the situation until they arrive here. They aren't well, and it could really upset them. I guess we might as well go back home. Can I come to your house tonight, Mom?" *I couldn't bear to be alone tonight. There is no way I am going back to my apartment tonight.*

Kate nodded, and they both got up and walked out of the hospital. Ella was in shock and began to chatter about their anniversary. The dinner. The flowers he had sent to her. How could this have happened to her? This was the man who saved her life and now she was going to lose him. That just didn't happen in real life. It's something you would read in a book, or see on television in a soap opera. This was her husband to be, and he was basically brain dead. He was dying. Before they got back to Ella's apartment to get her clothes and toiletries, Ella lost it. She burst out crying and began to scream his name. She was worn out and had already been through the worst time in her life when the plane crashed. *God gave me a second chance on life and now He is taking away the one He sent to save me.. It just doesn't make any sense. How can I deal with this without losing my mind?*

Kate walked into her apartment with her, and helped her pack. She got some kleenex off the nightstand and told Ella to rinse her face off with cold water. Then they left the apartment and drove to Madison Avenue. Kate walked in and turned on the lights in the hearth room. Ella brought her bags in and chose a room upstairs to sleep in. Kate went into the kitchen and made some tea, pulled out some food that Ella could nibble on, and helped Ella get settled into her room.

"Ella, you need to take a hot shower and put on your pajamas. I know it's not late, but you need to relax. I'll sleep with you tonight. You don't need to be alone at a time like this. I'm sick about this, Ella. I wish we knew more of what happened. I wonder if you called the dispatcher, if he would tell you more details about the accident. It's worth a try, baby." Kate put Ella's clothes up in the closet and took out her folded clothes in the suitcase and placed them in drawers. While Ella was showering, Kate brought up some tea and some crackers and cheese. She'd made a few small finger sandwiches that would go down easy for Ella.

I wonder if tragedy is all we're going to know in this family, thought Kate. *I don't understand all of this suffering, but I'm praying it will end now. Ella cannot take anymore suffering in her short life. She has been through so much that she needs counseling, and now this to deal with. How did this happen to Michael?* She shook her head in disbelief.

Kate was worried about Ella. She talked her into eating some, and pulled down the bed. "I will be back in a moment. I need to turn off lights and get my pajamas on. You sure you want to sleep in this bed, or would you feel better in mine?" Kate asked, touching her daughters face.

"I think I want to be in your bed, Mom. Is that okay with you?" Ella asked, rubbing her swollen eyes.

"That's good for me, angel. My bed is a king size and this one is much smaller. Let's go downstairs and I'll make you some hot chocolate. This coffee may keep you up. Come on. I'll turn on the television in my room so you can relax and get your mind off this for a minute."

The two women walked downstairs to Kate's room, and she turned down her bed. It was cozy and Ella just fell into the bed, crying again. Kate went into the hearth room to cut the lights off, locked the house up and turned one light on in the kitchen. She made some hot chocolate for them both and brought a couple of cookies. She sat the tray down on the bed and held Ella for a minute. As soon as she had settled down, Kate picked up the phone and called Stephen and Seth to let them know what had happened.

"Mom, I'm so worried about Ella. Can I come right over?

"Just wait until morning Seth, because Ella desperately needs a good night's sleep.

Stephen was so loving and gentle that it made Kate tear up. She explained the situation and told him she would call him in the morning.

Kate sat down on the edge of her bed and put her head in her hands. Tears streamed down her face. *I don't think my family can take much more*, she thought. She picked up the framed photo of Sam on her nightstand and looked at him.

Sam! Do you see what has happened to our family? Sam, your daughter can't take anymore. Kate felt the heaviest she had felt since she found out Ella was floating out there on the ocean, unfound.

She turned around and Ella had fallen back on the stack of pillows and was sound asleep from exhaustion. Kate got up and turned off the television, moved the tray to the chair by the bed, and turned off the light. *We'll have to deal with this in the morning. Ella is going to need all the support I can give her.* Kate slept sound but dreamed strange dreams of Sam and Stephen both being in the same room.

In the hospital, even though he was still on a breathing machine, Michael's heart came to a *stop*.

Chapter 41

K ate woke early, tiptoed out of the room, and made her morning coffee. The air outside was brisk, so she wrapped up in blankets and pulled her hood up on her sweatshirt. She grabbed the phone and went outside to sit in the swing. She wouldn't last long outside, but she wanted to talk to Stephen for a minute without Ella hearing anything. She rang his phone and waited. He picked up on the third ring, sounding sleepy.

"Hey baby. What are you doing up so early?" Stephen grabbed his alarm clock and checked the time. 6:30 a.m. He wondered what Kate was doing up this early after such a stressful night.

"Hi honey. Just needed to hear your voice. I'm so tired of this stress, Stephen, that I don t know which way to turn. Ella slept well, but I'm worried about how she'll be when she wakes up. We'll have to call the hospital to check on things and I have a feeling that the news won't be good." Kate sipped her hot coffee to warm her up inside, and the cup felt good to her hands.

"I know, angel. Do you want me to come over early and go with you to the hospital? I can take the day off and spend it with you guys, if it would help." Stephen remembered a meeting later in the day, but he could rearrange his schedule and have the meeting tomorrow or the next day.

"That would be nice. It would make me feel stronger if you were here. I know Ella is going to be a basket case. She's not going to want to accept that Michael is dying. I know her. She is such a fighter, Stephen."

"Well, let's just wait and see what the Doctor has to say, Katie. I'll get showered and eat a bite. Save me some coffee, will you?" He rubbed his face and felt the stubble. He jumped into the shower quickly, shaved and got dressed. He was out the door and on his way to Kate's within the hour.

Kate was waiting for him when he got there. She had showered, pulled her hair back in clasp and dabbed on some makeup. She had so much to talk to Stephen about and this might be her only chance today, since they probably would be at the hospital most of the day. She sat down at the kitchen table and Stephen grabbed a cup of coffee and sat down across from her. He gave her a kiss on her cheek, touched her hand, and said, "Sweetie, I know you are worried about Ella. But let's talk about something else for a moment. You were going to talk to me about the notes in that box you found in the attic. I have read a couple of the notes, but I know you have been upstairs reading more. Tell me what is going on with that now? What else have you discovered about this child?"

Kate smiled for a moment. Stephen was so amazing. He really did care about what was going on and was truly interested along with her about this box she had found. "I've read more, Stephen, and it's overwhelming what this child has been through. She didn't go into detail about what happened in these notes, but she wrote just enough to tell me that it was sexual abuse. I can sort of piece together some of what happened. I wonder where she is now. Can you tell me anything else about this family that lived in the house?"

"I really don't know anymore about this family, Kate. After my parents rented the house to them, all they really cared about was that they got the rent money, you know? My father didn't do a background check on them. He trusted them and just went on his gut feeling that this was a good family. Now I'm getting a sick feeling that maybe things were not what they seemed to be. To think of a child being molested in the house I grew up in, is a bit hard to swallow. You know?" Stephen drank a sip of coffee and rubbed his eyes. He was tired, but he wanted to be here for Kate and Ella. This box was about to drive him nuts. And he could see that Kate was worrying about the child who wrote the words and he didn't like her getting so involved; especially if they were never going to find her. This child had to be a grown woman now.

So your parents wouldn't have any records of where they went after they left this house? I was hoping with a little research I could find this woman. How old do you think she would be now?" Kate sat back in her chair and looked square at Stephen.

"I'm thinking early thirties. But I don't remember the year they moved out. The house has been empty for a few years. There may even have been a short renter in there after that family moved out. I would have to check."

"Don't go to any trouble, Stephen. I may just have to accept that I may never know who this child is. There are a few toys in the box; like maybe some of her favorite things. Kind of sad, you know? It just breaks my heart. One day I would love to meet her and let her know I found the box. That I do understand what she went through. I know it's silly to think I would ever meet her, baby. But I can hope, can't I?" Kate raised an eyebrow and looked at Stephen.

"You can hope for anything you want to. Who knows? Maybe you will find her. Don't get too attached to her, Kate. I know how you are, with your motherly instinct. You don't want to let this one go. Just be careful with your emotions, okay?"

They sat quiet for a few moments. Stephen could hear the clock in the hallway ticking away. "Should we call the hospital now? Or will they not tell us anything? I bet Ella is the one who has to phone. Maybe we should wake her up, you think?"

"No, I'm going to let her sleep as long as she will sleep. There is nothing she can do for Michael now. I'm worried that he will not make it through this. The doctor says he is brain dead so there really is no hope, right?" Kate put her head in her hands.

"That is probably a true statement. If I were the family, I would pull the plug on the breathing machine. Of course, we don't know if the family hasn't already arrived and done just that."

"I know, Stephen. I dread Ella getting up."

Ella appeared in the doorway of the kitchen. Her face was contorted into a look of panic. She held the phone in her hands. "Michael is dead, mother. He is gone."

Kate got up to go towards Ella, and suddenly Ella dropped to the ground. She had fainted. Stephen came and lifted her up and took her to Kate's bedroom. Kate ran and got a cold wash cloth and placed it on Ella's forehead. Then she made a call to their family doctor and told him the situation. He was a close friend of Sam's and told Kate he would come over immediately and give Ella something to calm her nerves. He hadn't seen Kate since Sam's death, but he remembered well how strong she was. Everyone had a breaking point, and he didn't want to find out what Kate's was. Stephen had found a chair in the corner to sit in, and just as he sat down, a hat fell on the floor by the closet. He bent over to pick it up and looked at Kate. She smiled slowly. *Maybe Sam was trying to show me he was around.*

Stephen put the cap back on the hook and smiled at Kate. Ella came to and started crying. Kate tried to console her but could not. She was out of control. Stephen heard the knock on the front door, and went to let the doctor in. He lived a few streets over so it hadn't taken him long to get to Kate's house. He walked in and introduced himself to Stephen.

"Hello, I'm James Sanders. I've known this family for many years. I'm here for Ella."

"Yes, Dr. Sanders. Please come this way. I'm Stephen Jones. Kate is back in the bedroom with Ella."

Stephen led the way to the bedroom, and as they entered the room Dr. Sanders could see how upset Ella was. He went directly to her and calmed her down with his soothing voice. He opened his bag and got out a syringe and filled it with valium and gave Ella a shot in the hip. He pulled some sleeping pills out of his bag and handed them to Kate. She might need these for a few nights, Kate. Just watch her closely and don't let her have these in her room. She has gone through too much and we don't want her to do anything stupid."

Kate nodded, and put the pills in her nightstand. The doctor checked Ella and smiled.

"You'll be ok, little girl. Just do what your mother says; rest and eat lightly. I'll check on you in a day or two."

Ella nodded and lay back on a pillow. She had only been up for an hour, but she was already exhausted. She wanted to go to the hospital to say goodbye to Michael but she had never met his parents. *Would they accept the fact that Michael and her were going to be married? That they had been talking about marriage? I guess it doesn't matter anymore*, she thought. Tears were streaming down her face. The valium was kicking in, and Ella closed her eyes one more time. She dreamed of strong arms holding her close. Of words being whispered in her ear. "I will love you forever, Ella." And then silence.

She was alone.

Stephen walked the doctor out and Kate came behind him.

"Thank you so much for taking the time to see Ella, James. I don't know what I would do without you." Kate hugged his neck and smiled. She always felt better when he was around.

"My pleasure Katie. I've known you for a long time. I'll always be here for you."

The door closed and Kate leaned against it, looking at Stephen. He took her into his arms and held her close. He loved the smell of her hair. She allowed the tension to leave her as they walked back to the hearth room. She lit a fire and they sat on the sofa for a while. The day was just beginning and she was tired.

"Kate, with so much going on in your family, it would be nice if I was here all the time. I'm more than ready to marry you. Don't you think it is time? I'm not pressuring you, but I'm over here so much as it is, and we know we love each other. How do you feel about what I'm saying, Kate? He pulled her close and kissed her.

Kate sighed and pushed away from Stephen. She needed to breathe. "I love you, Stephen. And I need you to be here. But how can we marry with all of this going on? I understand your frustration because it's very frustrating for me too. I miss you when you leave and think about you all the time. Let's get Ella settled down and then we can marry and have the blessings of my two children. What do you think?"

Stephen smiled. "You're right, Kate, I'm just feeling protective of you right now. I hate seeing you go through all of this with your kids. What a year this has been!" He pulled her close and they just sat quiet. The clock was chiming ten o'clock in the hallway; the day had really just begun. Enough had happened this morning to last a lifetime.

Chapter 42

It was a cloudy day, and the church was full. So many members of the rescue squad, fire department, police department were filling the pews, that there was hardly room for family and friends. It looked like the President was being buried but instead it was a hero. Michael had given up his life so that someone else might live. That is the greatest sacrifice any human can give for another person. Ella was dressed in black, and was shaking. This was the first funeral since her father had died, that she had been to in her entire life. And it was the man she loved that was in the casket. *I can't not bear to think about Michael lying in that closed casket. He was so strong and so good in his heart. He has done so much for me without asking for anything in return. I still can't believe he is gone.* She wiped her eyes and shook her head. *She didn't know if she could go on without him, but she had so much life left to live.* She sat down beside Kate, Stephen and Seth and Lila, and grabbed her mother's hand. She needed someone to hold her up.

Kate could feel Ella shaking and put her arm around her. This was going to be a tough thing for all of them to go through, since it brought back memories of Sam. Seth had cried for his sister, and for Michael. It tore him up that Ella was having to bury the man she wanted to spend the rest of her life with. He looked at Lila and his stomach went into a knot. *If anything like that had happened to Lila, I would have died inside. So I know how Ella feels right at this very moment. It would be like the bottom of my world had fallen out from under me; it's not something she will get over very quickly.*

* * *

The day was a blur for Ella. She went through the motions of the funeral and the burial. She shook people's hands that she didn't know, but her face was like stone. She had no emotion left in her. Everyone was so nice and so loving. They adored Michael and would miss him terribly on the rescue squad. All the men were hurting for Ella and Michael's family. His parents had treated her kindly but they didn't know her. She and Michael had moved so quickly into a serious relationship that barely anyone knew. *It was so easy to love him,* she thought as she watched the casket being lowered into the ground. Then she closed her eyes. *I don't want to see the dirt thrown on top of the casket.* She had a rose in her hand that Michael had given to her a long time ago; it was dried. She wanted to lay it on top of his casket. She walked slowly over to the grave and dropped the flower into the hole. Her eyes filled with tears. "Michael, I will love you forever," she whispered.

Kate, Stephen, Ella, Seth and Lila walked away and got into a car. Kate told the driver to take them back to the church where there cars were. It felt good to get away from the cemetery, and Ella breathed a little easier as they turned onto the street where the church was. Kate and Stephen took Ella with them, and they drove home. It was a little chilly outside and Stephen decided to light a fire in the hearth room. "Do you want to lay down on the sofa, Ella?" Kate asked gently.

"No, Mom, I just want to sit up with you and Stephen. So she wrapped a throw around her shoulders and leaned against Kate.

Seth sat down and hugged his sister. He whispered into her ear, "El, you know I'm here for you. *Always.* Anything you need, just say the word and I'll be there for you." Ella started to cry but caught herself. She kissed Seth on the cheek and squeezed his hand. He was such a good brother.

Lila kissed Ella on the cheek and hugged her. She had no words to say. She was so sad that she couldn't speak. She realized that she wouldn't want to live without Seth. Nothing she could say would bring Michael back or make this day any better. She sat down in a chair near the sofa and sipped a Sprite. But she kept her eyes down and wiped them often, because she felt so sad for Ella. Kate turned on the television to help ease the tension in the room. Then everyone went into the kitchen and got something to eat. People had brought a ton of food by, so there was plenty to eat. Kate had requested that no one come by the house because Ella just wanted to be with her family. It was a quiet afternoon for the Morrison household.

Ella sat with her eyes closed, trying to remember Michael's face. His laugh. His smell. *I swear I'll never forget him. As long as I live, I'll love him.* She laid her head back on the sofa, covered her legs up, and fell asleep from exhaustion and great sadness. On her hand was a ring that Michael was going to give to her, but he never got the chance to place it on her hand. She would never take that ring off.

In her other hand was the *feather* Michael had found in the water, after he saved her life. She had wanted to lay the feather on the coffin, but decided to keep it as a remembrance of what he did for her. It also reminded her of her father. The two men in her life that she loved dearly. *Now they were both gone.*

Ella dreamed of her wedding and her white dress. But when she got to the altar, Michael was not there.

Chapter 43

Friday was not a busy day for Kate, so she left early and stopped by the City Library to see if Lauren was in. As soon as she came through the main door, she saw Lauren talking to a young man in the corner of the library. Kate sat down and waited for Lauren to finish her conversation, and then walked towards her to catch her before she went behind the counter.

"Hello, Lauren. I was hoping you would be here today. I wanted to apologize for having to leave our lunch meeting in the park."

"Hi, Kate. I completely understand. How is everything going? I've been thinking about you and Ella."

"Things are not too good right now for Ella. Michael, her fiancé, was killed in a diving accident and it has caused Ella's world to crash. She's having a very difficult time dealing with this. We have been through quite a few rough days." Kate looked down and wiped her eyes.

"Wish I could do something to help. I'll be thinking of her, Kate."

"Thank you, Lauren. That's so sweet. Let's set another date for us to get together. What is good for you, Lauren?"

"That sounds great. Anytime is fine for me, as I know there's a lot going on in your family right now." Lauren smiled and touched Kate's arm.

"Let's see each other on Sunday afternoon. I really did like the idea of walking out on that pier at the park and sitting in those two chairs. It just seemed very peaceful there and I am hoping that it'll be a place where you can maybe open up a little bit and talk to me about your life. Is that good for you?"

"Sounds fabulous to me, Kate. Let's meet at 2:00 pm." Lauren's hands were sweating and she felt a little anxious just thinking about the meeting. *I've waited a long time for this happiness. I hope nothing comes up to ruin this meeting. I'm sick of carrying all of this inside of me..*

"I'll see you on Sunday, Lauren. Hopefully the weather will remain good. Have a great afternoon and I'll see you soon." Kate walked out of the library and got into her car. She had noticed Lauren being nervous and wondered what that was all about. *I guess I'll find out soon enough,* thought Kate.

The traffic was building up and Kate decided to call it a day. She headed home hoping Ella would be in a better frame of mind than when she left her this morning. Maybe if she felt better, they could go out to eat. As Kate walked into the house she heard Ella talking to someone. She walked around the corner to the hearth room and James was sitting on the sofa talking to Ella. She hardly recognized him; he had really cleaned himself up. He had cut his hair and looked totally different. James stood up when Kate walked into the room.

"Hello Mrs. Morrison. I just came by to say hi to Ella. I had heard about Michael from one of her friends."

"That's so nice of you, James. It's good to see you. How have you been?" Kate was very surprised to see James, but decided to leave it all up to Ella.

"I'm fine, just busy. I graduated and am now working at City Bank, in the loan department, and am actually loving it." James looked at Ella and smiled.

"Hey, Ella, I don't want to stay too long. I really just wanted to tell you how sorry I am. If you ever need to talk, I'm here for you. Okay? I mean that." James leaned over and kissed Ella on the forehead and gave her a hug. Ella smiled a little, and got up and walked James to the door.

"Thank you so much, James, for coming by. It really surprised me when I saw you standing at the front door. It's so good to see you. I'll give you a call when things settle down a little, and we can grab something to eat and catch up."

Ella said goodbye and closed the door. *It was nice to see James,* thought Ella. *He really has changed a lot.* She walked into the kitchen and sat down at the table, and put her head in her hands. Kate came over and sat down beside her. She put her arm around Ella and kissed her head.

"I know this is hard on you, Ella. It's pure hell to go through what you've been through. But you have a lot of people around you who love you and understand how difficult this is. What can I get for you?"

"Mom, I'm not even hungry. I know I need to eat, but when I put the fork to my mouth, it makes my stomach feel sick."

"Well, it'll take some time. This was such a shock to you, Ella. It was nice of James to come by. I was surprised to see how mature he was!" Kate poured coffee in her cup and took a bite out of a small sandwich someone had made. They had so much food in the refrigerator that she could hardly close the door. It was time for another family dinner, and she decided right then to call Seth and Stephen to see if they could come over.

"Mom, what are you doing," Ella said, smiling, watching her mother dialing the phone.

"I'm going to fill up this house with our family and light a fire, and make you feel loved." Kate smiled back at Ella.

"It'll feel good to have us all together at the table again. We need some laughter in this house tonight, Ella. You've been through so much and we need to talk and laugh for a little while."

Kate confirmed the dinner with Seth and Stephen and walked down the hall into her bedroom. She lay down on the bed and closed her eyes and felt the quiet. She needed a moment of silence to just not think about anything or anyone. *So much pain and sorrow in this world. Only God knows how to deal with it all.* Kate dozed off and was dreaming. She woke up with a start and Seth was walking into her room.

"Mom! Are you alright?" Seth came up to his mother with a worried look.

"Of course, I was just resting my eyes." Kate yawned and looked at her son with a smile.

"So we're having a family pow wow, huh, mom?" Seth laughed.

"Yes, Ella needs us all here Seth. She is overwhelmed by this death and needs her family around her. Did you bring Lila?"

"Yes. She's coming in her own car. She had a client and it was going to run her a little late. So she'll be here in about thirty minutes. Is Stephen coming?"

"Stephen will come straight from work. Seth, he wants me to marry him. How do you feel about that? Are you okay with that, angel?" Kate tapped the bed and Seth came over and sat down beside her.

"Mom, you are a grown woman with a lot of life left to live. I loved my father more than anything in the world. But I realize that you can't live alone the rest of your life. I don't want you alone. I would worry myself sick all the time, wondering if you were okay. So yes, it's fine with me. Have you guys set a date?"

"No, I wanted to wait until things settled down with Ella. It would be too much right now on the whole family. Stephen is okay with waiting a little bit. It'll happen when the time is right. I do love him, Seth. He is so good to me and I never thought I'd find love again after your father died. I'm still having dreams about Sam. It almost feels like I'm betraying him, even though I know that's silly."

"Mom, that's normal for you to feel that way. I know it is. But Dad would want you to remarry, I'm sure of it. So there! Enough of that talk. Let's go visit with Ella. She's in the hearth room by the fire."

Seth pulled his mother up and they walked into the hearth room and sat down beside Ella on the sofa. Seth wrapped his arms around his sister and held her for a moment.

"Things will be okay, Ella. It seems like your whole world has turned upside down, but you have us around you, and you know you can call me anytime you are lonely or need anything." Seth let her go, and smiled at her. "I'll be your best friend, Ella, if that's what you need me to be. No one can replace Michael; he was such a great guy. I liked him the first time I shook his hand. But Ella, until you are able to find someone else, I'm here for you to lean on."

Seth was always looking out for Ella, and felt responsible for her in a way. Since his father died, he felt like it was his job to see that Ella and his mother were okay. He really didn't worry too much about his mom, but he was afraid Ella was fragile now. That she might not always make the best decisions about her life. He wanted to be there for her in a big way, but not smother her.

Ella turned and winked at Seth. "I love you, Seth. You're the best brother in the whole world. Sometimes you can be a pain in the neck, but you're always there for me. I can't say enough how much I appreciate you. I know Michael loved you too. He couldn't get over how you and I got along. We are lucky, Seth. We always have each other."

An hour later, Stephen walked through the door and Lila came in right behind him. So the whole family gathered around the table, where Kate had laid out so much food that there was hardly room for everyone to find a place to sit. Stephen said grace and everyone started talking at the same time.

I'm so glad that I thought of this gathering. It warms my heart to have the table full and talk in the air. I cherish the time with my children and know they are growing up quickly. Soon I'll have grandchildren walking around the house, leaving fingerprints on everything, Kate thought as she looked around the table at her family... *I can't imagine the love I'll feel towards those children, for my heart can't contain the love I have for Seth and Ella.*

Stephen was watching Kate and read her expressions. I know she feels happy and content tonight. I yearn to make her my own. I want to hold her close and know that I'm not going home to my house anymore. He stretched his long legs under the table and leaned back in his chair.

It would be unreal to move back into a house I grew up in, he pondered. *So much has changed about it, yet it feels the same to me. I hope Kate won't wait too long before she agrees we can marry.* He knew it was the right thing for them both. He felt it in his heart. He would never find a woman like Kate, and he had no desire to look. He smiled at her across the table and she smiled back. There was a connection that Seth and Ella felt as they watched the two of them. Wedding bells were in the air. You could almost smell the love.

Chapter 44

Stephen and Kate were in the hearth room alone at last. The house was quiet; Ella had gone to bed, and Seth and Lila had gone home. It was a wonderful night and Kate was savoring the last few moments with Stephen.

"Baby, I didn't tell you that on Sunday I've set up another meeting with Lauren. She really wants to talk to me. I'm not sure what about; but she seems like such a nice girl, so if I can help her in any way, I'm open to it." Kate brushed her hair out of her face and smiled at Stephen.

"I'm choosing to do this outside of the office, because I don't know what she is going to share with me. I thought it might be nice to be outside if it's not too cold, in a relaxed atmosphere. You know?"

"I agree it might be nice to meet outside. You're so kind hearted to do this, not knowing this woman very long. You met in the library, didn't you?" Stephen had his arm around Kate, loving the closeness he felt. It was hard to keep his mind on what she was saying.

"Yes, we met in the library. But somehow we clicked very fast and I feel an odd connection with her. I don't know what that's all about, but I'll find out on Sunday as long as nothing else happens in my family to stop this meeting!" They both laughed and Stephen took a sip of hot coffee.

"You've not mentioned the box upstairs lately, baby. What's going on with that? Are you through trying to find out who this child is? I know how upset you were after reading the notes."

Kate sighed and laid her head back on Stephen's arm. "No, I haven't forgotten those words in the box. They are haunting me, if you want to know the truth. I've been so side tracked with everything else that I haven't been able to spend any time trying to find out who this child is. I really don't know where to start, Stephen."

Stephen shook his head. This was a puzzle for sure. "I know how you feel, Kate. I wish I had more information about this family, but maybe something will turn up. I can go through my parents' records and didn't find anything."

Kate smiled at him and leaned over for a kiss. She felt so good tonight. Relaxed. Almost like they were already married, but the thought of getting married made her nervous. *I love Stephen enough to marry him, and it feels right. So what was the problem? Maybe it's just normal to feel this way after the relationship Sam and I had. And two children. A lot of history. Even though he betrayed me with Martha and had a child, I still love him. I have to forgive him for it; to keep that anger and hurt inside of me would be fruitless. I have to let it all go so that I can have a life with Stephen with no skeletons in the closet. No dark baggage.*

"Well, Katie, I guess I had better get up and go home. You know I don't want to. Please tell Ella that I'm thinking of her. I'll call you first thing in the morning and we will spend Saturday together. Okay?"

"That sounds like a plan to me, baby." Kate smiled and held Stephen close to her. She loved his smell, his laugh, his heart. "I'll be dreaming of you, dear man. Thank you for always being here for me. One day won't be living in two houses. Won't that be a nice change?"

Stephen smiled. "Yeah, one day I'll be coming back home. For good."

He got up and walked to the door. He turned and winked at Kate, and walked out the door.

Chapter 45

The air was cool but the sun decided to shine after being tucked behind some clouds all morning. Kate walked down the path to the pier and looked behind her to see if Lauren was coming. There was no one around, so she sat down in one of the chairs and looked out across the lake. It was a beautiful afternoon and it felt good to just sit alone for a moment. Kate relaxed and breathed in the air, wondering what this meeting would bring. *I hardly know Lauren at all, but feel a silent connection with her, somehow.* She turned to look over her shoulder and saw Lauren walking down the pier. She called to her and waved.

"Hey Lauren. Come sit down beside me and enjoy this lovely afternoon with me." Kate smiled and pulled her jacket up around her neck.

Lauren was pleased to sit down near Kate, because she had waited a while for this conversation to happen. "You're right, it's a lovely day. And how peaceful is this? So how is Ella?"

"Well, everything has settled down a little since the funeral and Ella is trying to sort things out in her mind. I love having her in my new house, but I wish it was under better circumstances." Kate had brought a thermos of hot chocolate and poured out a cup for her and one for Lauren.

"I'm so glad that Ella is mending a little. I know this has been tough on her." Lauren cleared her throat and looked out across the water. *Might as well get to the point of this meeting.* "Kate, the reason I wanted to meet with you today was because I wanted to talk to you about your studies on Post Traumatic Stress Disorder."

Kate smiled. "Of course Lauren. How does that interest you? I hope you are not suffering from PTSD?"

"Well I'm not sure Kate. My childhood was very difficult and I find your work fascinating. Please tell me more about PTSD." Lauren shifted in her chair, feeling a little nervous.

"Lauren, this disorder can hit people who have suffered a tragedy or a very traumatic experience in their lives, and are not able to cope with it at all. They are haunted by memories of the events that took place, and have no apparent control over when these memories come up in their lives." Lauren was quiet, and Kate let some moments pass before she spoke.

"Do you have something to talk to me about, Lauren?" Kate asked, putting her hand on Lauren's arm.

"I do, but it's hard for me to open up about my past. Can you understand that?"

"Sure Lauren. Just take your time and relax. We can go as slow as you like. I want you to feel safe with me, and that may take some time." Kate took another sip of her hot chocolate and set the cup down.

"We had abuse in my family, and I don't know how to deal with it. I don't even know where to begin. This is first time it has ever left my lips and I feel sick even thinking about it."

Kate looked at Lauren and knew then that this was going to be a very serious conversation. "Please know that whatever you share with me, I'll keep between you and me. I know it is hard to talk about, but it's important to get it out."

Kate paused. "When did this happen in your life, Lauren?"

"I can't remember it not happening. I can remember that I loved the attic where I went to be safe. It was safe not just for me, but for the words I wrote down. Pen and paper were my savior. No one knew about what I wrote, and I couldn't go there often. It was a dark, cool place with a lot of shadows and little color. For some reason I felt safe even though it was so dark there." Lauren was looking out from the pier, like she was looking into her past.

Kate took a deep breath and asked more questions. "Did you have any brothers or sisters?"

"I had a brother who he took his own life. I didn't think I would ever get over his death. He knew all about what was happening. He knew about our father but he could do nothing for me, because my father would threaten him. He threatened me too. It was a nightmare that I had to deal with alone." Lauren was getting emotional and tried to calm herself down. She took a sip of her hot chocolate and stood up and looked away from Kate to the other side of the lake. *I hope I can do this...*

"I see, Lauren. Can you tell me a little more about your family?" Kate was noticing the tension but wanted to help her get it out. Whatever the secrets were, they needed to be told.

"My mother was a nurse and she worked a lot of night shifts. My father was a carpenter and well respected in his line of work. He had a bad temper though. He kept us while mother worked at night He put us to bed and when my brother fell asleep, that is when I would hear the footsteps coming down the hall. My brother was four years older than me, and we were best friends I wanted this to stop and I thought he could save me. As it turned out, it played a big roll in his death. That's hard for me to live with." Kate was trying to put all of this together as Lauren was talking. When she heard that the mother was gone at night that raised a red flag. She waited to hear the rest of the story. She didn't want to rush Lauren, but wanted her to feel safe in telling about the abuse.

"We lived in an old house on Madison Avenue that was perfect for our family. My dad had to ruin everything. I loved my room there and my brother and I had a lot of fun together."

"Wait a minute, Lauren. Are you saying you lived on Madison Avenue when this abuse took place?" Kate's heart was racing. *Surely it's not my house she is talking about. That would be impossible.*

"Yeah, it was the last house on the right at the end of the street. Why are you asking me that, Kate?" Lauren was looking straight at Kate, shaking.

Kate would have fainted if she'd been standing up. She was speechless but tried to pull herself together in hopes that Lauren would open up. "Surely you aren't talking about the house I live in now, Lauren. Tell me that *it's not you* who left a box in the attic." Kate was shaking now, and so overwhelmed she didn't know what to do. She had fallen in love with this child and wanted to so much to meet her, and now she was finding out that Lauren might be this child.

"I left my box in the attic many years ago. Other people have lived in that house since we moved out. Are you telling me that *you* have that box?" Lauren yelled. "My whole life is in that box!"

Kate grabbed Lauren and held her close. She was crying and could not find the words to speak. She could feel Lauren shaking, and pulled back to look at her face. Lauren broke emotionally and fell into Kate's arms and they both cried, but for different reasons.

Kate got her breath and spoke first. "Lauren, I've read out of the box every night until all the notes had been opened. Those words broke my heart and I wanted to find you so badly. I can't *believe* it is you. I've been trying to piece together the life of a child who wrote all of this, and to find out it's you just rips my heart out. I've been dying to find you, and you were so close all this time! To think I was talking to you about nothing important in the library, and you were the child I was reading about every night. That alone is more than I can comprehend."

Lauren was crying so hard, for she had waited so long to speak about the abuse, and to think that Kate had found the box was overwhelming. *I've been drawn to Kate and didn't know why, but now I know..* Kate and Lauren held each other for a while and then sat down to talk.

"My brother knew what was happening to me and he was too young to do anything about it. It drove him insane because he couldn't stop it, and he didn't know what else to do. He didn't feel free to talk to Mother, because she never acknowledged anything. We spoke of it once, but we never spoke of it again. I reassured him that I was fine, that I could handle it. But he knew I was lying. He was one of the most talented people I'll ever know, almost like a child prodigy. His love was unconditional, and he was very gentle and took the back seat a lot. He never cried. The family secret he carried inside tormented him and later he took his life. After he died, I found a poem he had written.

Love is a dolphin
Swimming at sea,
Love is a place
I want to be.
Love is a feeling
Pure and white,
Love is a place
I escape to at night.
Love is a family
Unconditional and real
Love is a place
I have yet to feel.

There were silent tears running down Lauren's face as she stood looking out across the lake. Kate came and stood beside her and put her arm around her waist. They stood quietly, with no words, caught up in the emotion of the moment. "I feel dirty, Kate. I have all my life. Even though I know in my mind it wasn't my fault, somehow he always made me feel like it was. He owned me. The smell that I remember is enough to make me vomit. You read my notes, but I didn't write down anything that happened. Writing it all down would make it real. And I tried to go somewhere else when he was with me. A pretend place. It is a miracle I have my right mind..."

"Lauren, no one would ever believe you had been through such a horrific childhood. You're so poised and self-assured. You do so well with the children in the library. How do you keep this up? You and I need to have long talks about this over a period of time so that you can get all of the self hate out of your heart. It will affect all your relationships. I'm sure you are already finding this out."

"I am so ready. Stuart, my boyfriend, loves me and wants to get close. I've held him at bay because I don't want him to know about all of this. Yet, there is a side of me that wants so badly to tell him. Is that crazy?"

"No, not at all. It is perfectly normal for the situation you are in. Don't ever feel bad about your past. It was not your fault. You're a miracle. The fact that you are alive and functioning is nothing short of a miracle. I'm very proud of you." Kate smiled at her and took her face in her hands.

"Lauren, would you like to come home with me and have a nice supper; I don't feel good about leaving you alone right now. This has been a very traumatic afternoon and we need to take time out to allow all this to soak in, so that we aren't emotionally overloaded. Don't you think that's a good idea?"

"I would love to come with you. It might be good for me to see the house again, under better circumstances. I often wondered who lived there after us, because I did have some good memories there.

Lauren let her hand slip into Kate's and they turned and walked slowly up the pier to the parking lot. Kate made sure Lauren was okay, and they both got into their cars and drove to the house on Madison Street. Lauren noticed as she pulled into the driveway that Kate had named the house Waterstone Manor. .

Lauren teared up again and hugged Kate. They walked into the hearth room together.

Chapter 46

Ella was sitting in her room when she heard her mother come home. She heard voices and walked down the stairway. Her mother was talking to a young woman. *Who could that be?* She walked into the hearth room and her mother was sitting down on the sofa with a woman.

"Hey, Mom" Ella said with a smile. "I heard voices and wanted to see who was here."

Ella walked around the sofa and smiled at the woman sitting next to her mom. Lauren stood up and introduced herself. She looked a mess but wanted to be polite.

"Hi, my name is Lauren Montgomery. I work at the local library. I met your mother there recently, and we just had the most wonderful talk at the park".

Ella noticed that Lauren's eyes were swollen, like she had been crying. Then she looked at her mom and noticed the same thing. *What was going on here?* Ella hugged her mother and then took a seat across the room, near the fireplace. It was getting cooler outside. "Mom, can we light a fire? It's so cold outside."

Kate said yes, and added, "Ella, Lauren used to live in this house! Can you believe that? Her family rented it for years. We were just finding out a lot about each other today." Kate smiled at Lauren, and patted her hand. Ella knew something was up. She wasn't about to ask any questions now, in front of Lauren. She would wait until later, when she and her mother were alone.

"Is Lauren staying for dinner, Mom?" Ella asked, smiling.

"Yes, I'm going in now to fix something for the three of us. Just something easy, so we can sit in here and talk. I'll leave you two girls here while I go into the kitchen to fix something. I'll be right back, Lauren. Make yourself at home." Kate walked into the kitchen and pulled out hamburger buns and ground beef.

She decided to grill hamburgers on the stove and have tomatoes, lettuce and pickles with it. She opened up some chips and dips and took it into the hearth room on a tray. She got drinks for Ella and Lauren, and went back into the kitchen.

I'm dying to call Stephen, but it'll have to wait until Lauren leaves. He's going to die when he finds out that she was the child who wrote those words! I still can't believe it. I'm in shock about what I've heard. Kate yawned. The stress was getting to her. *I'm going to have to go slow with Lauren. I don't want to upset her or trigger bad memories that might stay with her for a long time.*

The three women ate dinner, talking about everything and nothing. Kate turned on the television to a light sitcom and they sat and talked for a couple of hours. Lauren felt relaxed and full. "Kate, may I look around the house before I leave?"

Kate was surprised but tried not to show it. "Of course you can. That's a great idea." She took Lauren to her bedroom first. "It's hard for me to see the bedroom where my mother and father slept. This wasn't the room where the abuse took place, but it does bring back memories of certain times when I slept in the middle of the two of them. My mother never knew that my father was trying to touch me all night." Lauren was shaking but wanted to go through with this journey back into the house.

"I can only imagine what this means to you. I have a hard time understanding why your mother didn't know, or why she avoided talking to talk to you about it." Kate knew this had to be a huge step for Lauren to make.

They moved into the hallway and up the stairs. Kate showed her every bedroom, noticing Lauren tensing as they left one of the bedrooms. *This must have been her bedroom,* Kate thought shaking her head in disbelief. *A dark cross over the doorway. How sick can a person get?* They walked into the game room at the end of the hallway and Lauren stopped. "I see the attic door from here. I would like to walk into the attic if I could, Kate." She started sweating and felt a little sick, but she took a deep breath and looked at Kate with a weak smile.

"Of course, Lauren," Kate said. "Just tell me if it's too much for you, ok?"

Lauren peeked into the attic and was amazed that it hadn't changed that much. *This seems smaller and the roof feels lower than I remember, but other than that, it looks much the same as it did when I was young.*

She saw the blanket in the corner, hidden from sight. *That was where I had put the box the last time I was here. It feels so weird to be here again. I never thought I would ever come back to this attic again.* She took a deep breath. *After all this time of wondering if the box was still there, and worrying about* the *chance of anyone finding it , now I can rest knowing Kate found the box.* **Thank God it was her.** *There was a great possibility that no one else had ever seen the box, for it probably would have been thrown out.* It's a miracle Kate ever found it, Lauren thought, dusting herself off. Suddenly she broke out in a sweat. *I cannot stand the feelings I'm having. All those sick memories are flooding back. I almost feel nauseous.*

She walked back out of the attic, bent over, and came out looking a little pale. "Are you okay? I know how big this is for you. It has to feel pretty strange seeing all of this after so many years." Kate was a little worried about Lauren's emotional state.

"I feel sick inside because of all of the horrible memories. I've wondered how I would feel coming back here, seeing the rooms. Remembering the torture I was put through. But how can I ever thank you for allowing me to share all of this with you. It brings back so many memories that I'd pushed back and ran from for so many years. It kind of feels good to be here again, in a way. I know that may sound strange to you, Kate. I hope not. Because this might just be what I need to get better. To stop those horrible nightmares from ruining my nights."

Kate pulled Lauren close to her and hugged her. Then she smiled and said "It doesn't sound strange at all. I'm so proud of you for doing this. You have no idea how long I've waited to find you. I'm glad we had this talk today, for this is a good beginning for you. Call me anytime and we can talk about all of this. But it's important that you get it out, Lauren. You understand that, don't you?"

"Yes I *do* know that. I've wanted to talk to someone for so long, and when I met you, well, I just *knew* I would be able to trust you and open up. I didn't know I would find this out, though. It's a bit hard to believe, isn't it?"

Kate laughed. "Of course it is. I'm laughing now, but it wasn't funny at all while we were finding all of this out. I know you have to be exhausted, because I am. I could go straight to bed right now! Please be careful going home, and call me soon, and we can get together. I have so many questions I want to ask you."

Lauren blushed and looked away. She saw Ella in the hearth room and waved to her. "It was nice meeting you, Ella. I hope to see you again, soon." Lauren walked to the front door and turned to thank Kate again.

"Lauren, I didn't ask you if you wanted to see the box. Do you? Or would that be too much tonight?"

"No, not tonight. This was just enough, my going through this house. I think seeing the box right now might be too much for me to handle. Thanks for allowing me to do this. I'm still in shock. What are the odds of us ever finding each other?"

The two women hugged one more time and promised that they would get together soon, and Lauren left. When she got to her car, she turned on the engine and just sat there crying and looking at the house. Her heart was about to burst and all she could think about was that Kate had made this house into a lovely home, full of good memories with her family. To Lauren, even though she loved the house and had some good memories, the house was like a dungeon at times; a nightmare that had no end. It was a relief in a way to finally visit it again, but it was hard on her at the same time.

Lauren pulled away from the house and drove home. She wanted to call Stuart and share what had happened, but he didn't know anything about her past. *Would she ever be able to share that with him?* Lauren felt saddened by that unanswered question. *There's really no one she could tell right now about what happened today. That in itself was a little depressing. I still have to keep things a secret.*

She pulled into her driveway and locked up the car. Inside her home, she turned the lights on, the television on for noise, and went into her bedroom. The room was a chocolate brown color and the bedding had blue and brown and cream. It felt warm and comforting to Lauren, but tonight it succeeded in making her feel totally alone. *There isn't one person in my family I could talk to about this, and I haven't made many friends. I'm used to being alone, but right now I feel empty and scared and very sad.*

She took a long hot shower, and put on her pajamas. Right by the bed, the phone rang. She checked the caller ID and it was Stuart. *I should pick it up, but I am so spent emotionally that I have nothing left to give out. I sure don't want to pretend everything is alright. I've done that for too long in my life already.*

Lauren leaned over, turned out the light and lay there looking up at the ceiling watching the car lights flickering across the darkened room. *I don't remember ever feeling so tired as I do right now. I love Kate to death. But I feel alone right now and there is so much to process. So many emotions.*

Closing her eyes, she dozed off slowly, wondering if she would ever allow anyone special in her life that loved her, really loved her. Her thoughts echoed into a silence that was almost unbearable.

Chapter 47

Kate said goodnight to Ella and walked into her bedroom. She knew Ella had questions about Lauren, but she didn't feel like answering them tonight. But she did want to call Stephen before it got too late. She washed her face and put her pajamas on, went to the bed and picked up the phone. Stephen answered on the second ring. "How is my girl tonight," Stephen said, grinning.

"I'm good, baby, how are you?" Kate smiled. He had a voice that grabbed her every time she heard it.

"How was your night, Kate? How was that meeting with Lauren.?" Stephen was very curious about Lauren and what she had wanted to talk to Kate about.

"Well, you're not going to believe this one, Stephen. We had a good talk this afternoon, but shortly into the conversation, I discovered that Lauren used to live in this house! Can you imagine that, Stephen? **She is the child who wrote the box of words!**"

There was silence on the other end of the phone. Stephen was speechless. That was the last thing he expected to hear about Lauren. "What in heaven's name, Kate? Are you telling me she is that child you've been wondering about all this time?" Stephen couldn't believe what he was hearing.

"Yes, Stephen. She's that child! I'm still in shock over it. Lauren and I nearly fainted when we found this out. She was telling me about where she used to live and when she mentioned Madison Avenue I nearly choked on my drink! It's so odd that I would find her this way. I've been to the library several times, spoken with her, and never had aninkling that she was connected in any way to this box. She had no idea where I lived. If I'd told her earlier, then she would have figured it all out, and may not have ever told me anything at all. I'm so thankful it happened the way it did, even though it was gut wrenching."

"Well, I can only imagine the two of you finding this out. Good heavens, Kate. That would be overwhelming for anyone. Is she okay?"

"Yes, I brought her home with me, and we had a light supper with Ella. She looked around the house and went into the attic for the first time since she had left the house as a young girl. It was pretty emotional for her, but good in a way. She needed to come back here and see the house in a different light. I know it'll bother her tonight, but we're planning to get together soon and talk about all of it. "Kate sighed loudly. This had been a tough day for her. She was tired, but her mind didn't want to shut off.

Stephen was sitting on his bed, listening to Kate, trying to put the pieces all together. "I know you'll fill me in later. But this is one heck of a story, Kate. I bet there's more she has not shared with you. That poor girl. She has turned out to be a beautiful young woman. No one would ever know by looking at her, that she had experienced such a difficult childhood. For years she has hidden this ugly family secret, Kate. That's so incredibly sad,"

Kate nodded, even though he couldn't see her. She was feeling so much empathy for Lauren. Her chest almost hurt thinking about what Lauren was going through at home, alone tonight. *I should've asked her to stay and spend the night. But I wasn't sure if Lauren would have wanted to stay a night in this house yet. It might be too quick, after all that has happened.*

"I love you, Katie." He sure wanted to marry this woman. But she wasn't ready for some reason. Ella was better now. She had a ways to go, but she was wanting to move back into her apartment, and that was a good sign.

"I love you, Stephen. I was dying to share this with you. Let's get together so that we can catch up on more of this, okay?" Kate was finally feeling sleepy.

"I'm thinking of you and missing you. You know how I feel, don't you, Kate?'

"I know, Stephen. I love you too. "Kate hung up the phone and sat on the edge of her bed. She got up and walked to her dresser drawer and opened it up. There lay all the notes she had gotten in the past year or so. The thought hit her that she had her own box of words laying there in that drawer. What happened to her since Sam died was in that drawer. Pretty heavy stuff.

She went back to the bed and lay down on her pillow. She closed her eyes and all she could think of was that little child sitting in attic, crying, writing words down for no one to see. Thank God that was over for Lauren. Thank God it was over. Kate fell into a deep sleep brought on by the exhaustion of the day. The last thought before she absolutely passed out was that she was thankful that it had been her that had found the box of words.

Stephen sat on the edge of his bed and wondered if Kate would ever be ready to commit to him. Granted it had been a rough ride since they met. One thing after another. Maybe he was just too anxious to seal the relationship. Maybe he hated being alone more than he realized. He lay back on the bed and thought back to when Betsy was alive and how rich their relationship was. *Kate was nothing like Betsy, but he fell in love with her very quickly. They blended well.*

Chapter 48

Seth was moving up in the offices of Holland, Braden & Spencer. He had overcome some of his shyness about taking on new accounts, had even been given the responsibility of acquiring a new account. He had written his first contract recently and Mr. Holland was very impressed. It was a large corporation located in the middle of town, and they had experienced some accounting issues that hadn't been settled with the firm they were using at the present. It was a perfect time for Seth to call on them. Someone he had met at a bar had given him a lead, and Seth decided to risk embarrassment and step out on this one. It worked beautifully and now he was working on their books to correct some problems that had accumulated over the years.

Now that he was making more money, he really wanted to get married to Lila. She was ready to do it, but they were both trying to set themselves up so that it wouldn't be a struggle when they got married. Lila hadn't come from money; her parents were middle class and hard working people. She wanted a better life for her children and she didn't want to worry month to month about how bills were going to be paid. Seth agreed totally, so they were putting money back in a savings account and had built up quite a sum already. He had picked out a ring, but wanted her to look at it. He would've loved to surprise her, but she had her own taste and he didn't want to ruin the joy of her picking out her own ring.

It was lunch time so he decided to call her. The phone rang and rang. No answer. He wondered if she was with a client, but usually she didn't work through lunch. Just as he set the phone down, she walked up to his desk in a cute dress, heels, and her hair looked fabulous.

"Hey sweet man. Want to take me to lunch?"

Seth turned around and grabbed her quickly and kissed her hard on the mouth. "Hey lovely. Let's go. I was just calling you."

They were eating at their favorite pub down the street from the office, and began talking about their goals and where they were in their plans. Seth decided to be honest and tell Lila that he was ready to marry her. "Baby, I just don't want to keep putting this off. We don't know what tomorrow brings, and I'm ready to have you in my life forever."

"I know, Seth. And I want that too. When were you thinking about?" Lila smiled and blushed a little. He was so darn cute it was hard to resist him. She had known him for quite some time now, and she still wasn't used to how cute he was.

"I was thinking about a Christmas wedding. Nothing is going on special in the family and I think it would be neat to marry at that time of year. It doesn't give us much time to get ready, but we wanted a family wedding anyway."

"Wow. That soon? I was thinking more in the spring, Seth, but I do love that time of the year when it feels cozy and it might even snow. Where do you want to go on our honeymoon?"

"Well we can talk about that later, but be thinking about the Christmas time frame. If we're going to do it, we need to tell everyone now because that's only two months away. Time is flying by, Lila. Gosh, I love you so much, and I just don't want to wait anymore. I wouldn't care if we eloped. You know? All that money spent on a wedding and we could go off and get married and come home and have a party."

"I've always joked about doing that. I've never been that big about a white dress and all the expenses that come with a big wedding, but I do want to marry in a church. That's all I ask, Seth. I want God to bless this marriage, and I know He would no matter where we marry, but I do love a church wedding." Her eyes were as black as night. Her skin was creamy and pure. Seth, at this point, would give her anything she asked for.

"I know, angel. We can have a church wedding; can we keep this down to a small earthquake?" They laughed together and then got serious.

"Ok, Seth. We can keep it small, but that means only family. And the reception could be at your mom's house. I love that house! Don't you think?"

"I know she would love that, Lila. I wish Dad were alive. I know he would think I had hit the jackpot with you. He would love you, Lila. I bet he's looking down on us right now, smiling."

"I bet he is too. You look so much like him, Seth. It is uncanny." Lila looked at her watch and stood up. "I need to run, Seth. I have a client at two o'clock. I love you so much." She bent down and kissed him, and he smiled from ear to ear. He watched her walk away and was pretty much useless the rest of the afternoon.

Before the day was over, Seth picked up the phone and called his mom. "Hello, Seth! What a nice surprise. Is everything good?" Kate smiled warmly.

"I have a bigger surprise, Mom. Lila and I are going to get married in December. Sometime near Christmas!"

Kate dropped her jaw and gasped. "Oh my gosh Seth! Are you serious? I don't know what to say. We have a lot to do. Will you let me know the details soon?"

"Sure Mom. Just wanted to make your day! Now you're going to have another daughter, and she's a beautiful one, Mom."

"I know she is, Seth. You two take your time and plan this like you want it. Just let me know what I can do to help, okay?"

"Sure Mom. I love you. Is Ella doing better, Mom?"

"Yes, Ella is mending pretty well. She wants to go back to her apartment now, so that's a good sign. I may let her go tonight. I'll keep you posted, Seth. Thanks so much for the phone call. What wonderful news!"

Kate hung up and sat at the kitchen table. Her mind was so full of emotion that she didn't know how to feel about this wedding. Her mind was on Lauren at the moment, and she hadn't been able to shake this feeling of dread for some reason. She decided to phone Lauren at the library and see how her day was going. She allowed herself a moment to smile inside and thank God for Seth. He was such a steady young man. She could always count on him to do the right thing.

The phone at the library rang and rang. Finally someone picked up and Kate asked to speak to Lauren. "Lauren took the day off today, can I help you," the voice on the other end of the phone said.

"No, thank you. I'll try to catch her later," said Kate. She put the phone down and sat there thinking. *She isn't a child*, Kate thought, *but something is causing me to feel like I need to go see her. I don't know where she lives. How stupid of me not to ask!*

Kate walked outside and sat in the swing, bundled up with a blanket. She took the phone with her just in case Lauren called. The box of words had been opened up and now the silence had been broken. Nothing will ever be the same for Lauren again.

Chapter 49

Ella decided to spend the night in her mother's house. Before she went to bed, she walked into the kitchen where Kate was washing dishes and sat down at the table. She watched her mother for a moment before she spoke.

"Mother, what was all this about with Lauren. Why would you bring her here to show her the house, and then take her into the attic? Why did she look like she had been crying?"

Kate turned around. She was ready for these questions, as she knew they were coming. "Ella, I met Lauren at the library. Her family used to rent this house when Lauren was a young girl. She had a brother named Jake, and they all lived here until Lauren was in her senior year." Kate paused a moment to consider her words.

"So they lived here, Mom? I don't understand why she was crying." Ella was listening closely, for Lauren was very lovely and she couldn't imagine why she was so upset just walking through the house.

"Ella, Lauren was abused by her father. You know the box on my night stand? It's full of papers that Lauren wrote when she was young. It's a story of her life, in a way. The papers are not dated so you have to sort of piece it all together. After reading them, I knew this child had to have been abused." Kate stopped and waited for Ella to take this in.

Ella felt sick inside. "You mean her father sexually abused her? Mom that's horrible. It's unfathomable. My father would've never touched me. I never even had to think about it. I can't imagine having a father who would do that. Why did no one stop him?"

Kate frowned and went to the refrigerator and pulled out a Sprite. She sat down and shared it with Ella.

"Angel, not everyone has a father like Sam. Lauren was unfortunate in that her father abused her when her mother was gone at night, working as a nurse. Her mother may have suspected, I don't know. We haven't gotten that far into this yet. But at any rate, the abuse kept going until she was around 17 years old. She used the attic as her safe place, and sat up there and wrote notes that went into the box. She left the box there when they moved. Her father wouldn't let her go back to get some things she had left in the attic." Kate took a sip of the Sprite and thought a moment.

"Lauren was worried for a long time about who would find the box. I'm so glad it was me, for someone else might not have ever found Lauren. I believe I can help her, Ella. I think we were meant to meet."

"Oh, I think so too, Mom. You're so good with people, and you know how to get them to open up. I know I could never lie to you!" Ella laughed for a moment. She looked at her mother and smiled.

"You're wonderful, Mom. To take this woman under your wing is so cool. Do you think you can help her, Mom?"

"I know I can help her; I just hope she gives me that opportunity. She's going to call and set up a time for us to talk again. This time we'll have already gotten the worst out on the table. So from this point on, it'll be working through the issues she has, or memories that haunt her."

Kate hugged Ella and before she said goodnight she whispered in Ella's ear, "Seth told me tonight that he and Lila were going to get married around Christmas! Thought you'd want to know."

"Are you kidding me? Oh my gosh! I'm going to get Seth for not calling me and letting me in on this decision. I'm so happy for them. I bet Lila is about to freak out. I'll call Seth tomorrow and get filled in on the details. Thanks, Mom." Ella walked upstairs one more time to sleep in her room. It felt so safe there. Ella turned out the light and dreamed of the water again, the drowning, and the man who saved her life.

Kate turned out the lights and went into her room. She picked up the phone and called Stephen, just to hear his voice. He always settled her down inside. "Hey baby, just wanted to tell you goodnight", Kate said, yawning.

"I was just thinking of you, Katie. I'm laying down looking at the ceiling, wondering why I am here and you are there." Stephen winced, waiting for her reply.

"Well, I'm very close to telling you to drive over here. But it's so late, and we both need our sleep. It's been quite a day, Stephen. Seth just informed me he and Lila are getting married close to Christmas!"

"Are you serious? Wow! Well good for them. He and Lila seem to be a great match, like someone else I know.…..I'm ready for you, Kate. I respect your wishes. So call me in the morning will you? Love you, angel. Glad to hear about Seth." Stephen hung up the phone and laid there thinking about Kate. *What a lovely woman; and she's going to be my wife one day soon. I just hope she doesn't wait until we are too old to enjoy a relationship as powerful as this one.* Stephen smiled to himself. And he fell asleep with that smile on the edge of his mouth.

Kate tossed and turned, thinking of Lauren, Sam, her children, and of Stephen. *I need to stop putting him off. It's time for us to be together. There would always be a reason not to do it, and we're not getting any younger. He's right for me, and I'm good for him. He wasn't Sam, but no one would be like Sam. Of course, I had Sam on a pedestal and he fell royally. He proved that he was human by having a child with another woman Maybe you never really know someone fully. Maybe we all don't know what we are capable of, given certain circumstances. I know that's true by what I've heard in my office; spoken words in a whisper out of the mouths of hurting people.*

Kate stretched, turned over and slept sound. The hat once again fell from its hook near the closet. But this time Kate was asleep, dreaming of Stephen.

Chapter 50

The room was as dark as night, as Lauren lay restless in her bed. Intrusive thoughts came in and she felt like she was ten years old again. Details of the wallpaper were coming to her, the dim lighting, and the sound of his footsteps. The landing always made a noise so she knew he was coming. It was a pre-warning of what was to come. Lauren didn't like to allow herself too much time in this place of remembering, because it was too scary and so real. But tonight, because of Kate finding the box of words, her mind was running rampant. She went over and over the times she was allowed to be alone, and that was when she went to the attic. It was her favorite place in all the world because it was peaceful and safe and she loved the smell of things past that others had forgotten.

In her memory far back in her mind, she could hear his husky voice, deep and demanding. Sometimes he was manipulating, and there was always an element of control. She had to lie there and take it, so she pretended she was somewhere else. She was always in a field and the field was always full of daisies. The grass was long and flowing, and the sun warmed her face. She could hear water but could not see it, and she would always be lying on her back looking up at the sky. It was a good place to be.

Lauren found her glass on the nightstand and drank slowly, trying not to spill any water on the bed. She was sweating, remembering these things. *She always wished she could go to bed and sleep. She dreamed of having a hug without anything expected; a kiss without anything coming after. Bathing without eyes watching.*

Lauren wiped her face with the sheet. *I wondered why her mother could not love her, ever. She had no expectations of her future, except that she wanted the abuse to end.*

Now that Lauren was older and living alone, she wondered what it would've been like to have normal parents in a loving home. She grieved for Jake, her best friend and brother. She grieved for herself, and that part of her that was a child that had no childhood. The secrets that were kept built a wall around the whole family that no one could penetrate. And now the secrets were out.

She turned on the light and went to the kitchen. *I have to find a way to sleep without going through this remembering. It ruins my nights and I dread going to bed. Stuart is wonderful and it helpds having him near me; but soon I'll have to explain it all to him if he's going to be in my life. The reason why I want the room so dark.*

I have to tell him about the box of words, and the years of the black cross on the door. My silence when I'm around Stuart is causing problems in the relationship, and I have to make up my mind if I want him in my life before I open up completely to him.

I have learned somehow to trust Kate quickly and have feelings towards her that I don't even understand. My own mother didn't save me from the darkness in the house, but Kate has cried for me in the night. She wanted to know who the child was who wrote the words.

Lauren took some crackers back into the bedroom, turned on the light by her bed, and dialed Stuart's number. She wouldn't blame him if he didn't answer, after she had backed away from him so many times. The phone rang four times, and on the fifth ring, he picked up.

"Hey young lady! What do I owe this surprise to so late in the night?" Stephen smiled and waited for her answer, puzzled as to why she hadn't called in a while. He missed her terribly but agreed not to push her into a relationship until she was ready.

"Hey Stu. I was just laying here thinking of you. Wondering how you are, and what you're doing." Lauren was making up words to fill the void in her mind. She didn't know how to start to let him in.

"I've been working hard and hoping I would hear from you. I haven't called because I was respecting the distance you have placed between us, baby."

"I know, Stu. I'm sorry. So sorry. I've missed you horribly but just had to sort out some things in my life. I have so much to talk to you about and I hope you'll give me that chance to do it. There is a lot you don't know about me, Stuart, and I'm afraid when you find out, you won't find me lovely." Lauren was crying now. She was about to hang up but Stuart jumped in before she could do it.

"There's nothing you can tell me about you that will make me go away. I want to know you more. We haven't spent this time together just for fun; I really do care about you. I want you to know me too. Give me a chance, will you? I'm not afraid." Stuart was wondering what she had to tell him, but inside he really didn't think it would change anything; especially how he felt about her. What would kill their relationship was her moving him in and out of her life without an explanation. Her moods were sometimes erratic and he couldn't put his finger on why. He would love to know what was behind those green eyes of hers. Her skin was as soft as a feather, and there was something about her presence that drew him in. On a bad day, her laugh could bring you all the way to the moon.

"Okay, Stuart. Let's give it a try. I'll see you tomorrow evening and share my life with you. I just hope when I'm done, you're still standing in front of me with your arms around me. I haven't shared this with another human being except Kate, so this will be a first for me. I do think I'm ready to come out of this darkness. I'll explain more later, Stu." Lauren didn't mean to keep him this late, but she felt like it was time to step over the line drawn in the sand by her own hands. She had limited her chances of ever having a solid relationship with anyone, by holding in the secrets that she'd been told were to be left unspoken. Now that Kate had found the box of notes she'd written, things were different. A *seal had been broken* that had been there for many years, unseen by the eye, but every bit as powerful as it was the first time she heard the words that her life would be gone if she spoke of the abuse.

"Lauren, have a wonderful sleep tonight, and don't worry about anything between us. I'm actually relieved you are opening up to me now. I was beginning to wonder what was wrong with me!" Stuart chuckled and raised his eyebrows. "So let's have a good talk tomorrow night and share about ourselves. This will be new to me, also, but I'm more than ready to do this with you."

Lauren hung up the phone and cried. She cried for all the times she had to hide in the attic, for the secrets held in her heart that caused a sickness in her, and for the craving she had to be loved for who she was, and not hide from what had happened to her. Wiping her face, she laid back down. Somehow she had to break the patterns that had been set when she was young. She had to convince herself and believe in her heart that no one was going to hurt her like that ever again. And maybe Kate and Stuart were two key players in the healing of her heart.

She walked over and opened the window in her bedroom and let the ocean breeze come into the room. It was chilly but it felt refreshing. Somehow she began to feel a slight lifting of the darkness that always held her at bay in the night. She breathed in the air, closed the window and snuggled down in her warm bed. Tonight she wasn't going to have the nightmares that wracked her life. She was going to dream of a life that was normal and pure, and maybe it would be with that handsome, tall, gentle giant she was seeing tomorrow night. For the first time in a long time, she fell asleep with a smile on her face.

For some strange reason that night, the moon came through her window, and gently laid its feathery streams of light across the bed where Lauren lay. The filtered rays of the moon left her face with a dusting of light that was so soft that it was seen only because of the blackness of the room. The streams of light crossed the room and because of the corner near the door, the light refracted and made a cross above the door that was a pale white.

Chapter 51

It was a cold breezy day, even though the sun was shining brightly, and Ella felt very lazy, stretched out in her bed. It felt good to be back in her apartment. She had kept up with her college courses and done most of them on the internet while she was healing from the crash. Now she needed to make sure her major was what she really wanted to do for her career. She was leaning towards Special Education but was't sure what area of that she would work in. It was so hard to know what she wanted to do for the rest of her life. Seth was already on his way to a great career; here she was still mulling over what she wanted to do with her life. She was looking out the window by her bed when someone knocked on her door. *Could it be my mother?* Ella thought to herself. Ella rushed to open the door, looking disheveled and sleepy. When she pulled the door open, there stood Michael's parents.

"Hello Mr. and Mrs. Hayes. Please come in. You'll have to excuse my apartment, as I've been at my mothers since Michael's death. I haven't had the energy or the desire to clean this apartment." Ella was embarrassed but there was nothing she could do about it now...

"Ella, we didn't mean to pop in on you. Forgive us for this unannounced visit! And please call us Phillip and Claire, Ella. I know we don't know each other well, but Michael's death has brought us together in a different way."

"Please sit down Claire, and tell me what brings you to my apartment on this Friday morning?" Ella was puzzled and hoped that nothing was wrong. She sensed something but she couldn't put her finger on it.

"Well, we were going through Michael's things after his death. It wasn't a pleasant task and we decided to get it done now, and not sit around looking at our son's things. It's too painful. Much too painful." Phillip cleared his throat for what he was about to share with Ella. He knew she was going to be very surprised. He and Claire were shocked, actually, and didn't expect to find anything unusual in Michael's papers and belongings.

Ella sat on the edge of her chair, running her fingers through her long brown hair. She felt dirty and was embarrassed that they had come to her apartment to meet her for the first time and she wasn't even dressed decently. She barely knew them, and to have them pop in like this was almost too much for her.

"I might as well get on with it," Phillip said. "We were going through his papers and found an envelope with your and his name on it. We opened it up, and found out that Michael had bought a house for the two of you. Your name is on the deed. This is highly unusual because you were not married yet. It is my understanding that you hadn't even set a date, is that correct?"

Ella was in shock; she could hardly speak. *Michael had purchased a house for us?* She took in a breath and answered Phillip. "No, we hadn't set a date. But he had purchased a ring that I'm wearing now. We really hadn't discussed the details yet, but both of us knew it was going to happen." Ella paused to catch her breath and think.

"So Michael bought a house for us? Where is this house?"

"Exactly. Well, the house is near a lake, right outside of town. He got it for a steal, and nearly paid cash for it. There's a little owed at the bank, but we can take his savings and probably pay the note off. We just wanted to see if you were interested in this house, or if you had other plans that wouldn't allow you to make use of it."

Ella again was speechless. She looked at both of them and then closed her eyes. *Oh my gosh. How am I supposed to make a decision like this so quickly?* "I do want the house, Phillip, but may I see it first before I make that decision? This is all new information to me. I'm stunned, as you would expect me to be. I loved your son with all my heart, and he saved my life. If he bought a house for us, I would definitely want to live in it. We were planning on having a wonderful life together; we got along perfectly. Everything has been on hold since his death, as I haven't wanted to do much of anything. All I think about is Michael, but I know I have to move on." Ella teared up but tried to stay in control of her emotions.

"We know this is a surprise to you, Ella; we were very surprised ourselves. Here it is on paper, and it's legal; your name is on the deed to the house and land. Can we take you there now and show you where it is. We've already been out there, and we feel you might be pleasantly surprised."

"Of course. Just give me a moment to throw on some jeans and I'll be ready to go."

Ella ran into her bedroom and closed the door. For a moment she didn't know what to do. *Why would Michael have bought that house without telling her anything about it? Was he that sure we would marry? I guess he was,* she thought. *He bought me a ring and knew I loved him. But I had no idea he would buy a house. This is all so weird and the timing is unreal.* She ran around, pulling jeans on, a shirt, flip flops, and ran a brush through her hair. She pulled it back with a pony tail holder, hurriedly used some lip gloss, and ran out the door. She grabbed a Sprite in the refrigerator and told them she was ready to go. The three of them walked out to the parking lot and got into the Andrews' lovely BMW; Ella was impressed. She had no idea what Michael's family was like, or whether he came from money or not. That just didn't seem to matter to them in their relationship. The crash had brought her to a new reality in life. Her priorities were different now.

The drive to the lake was peaceful and Ella sat in the back, lost in her own thoughts. Phillip ended up on a road that wound around, heading up-hill towards the outskirts of town. It wasn't far away, but felt like it was in another world. The trees were thick on both sides of the street and it was only a two lane road. There was no development on the road, so it was quiet. The wind was blowing and Ella felt like she was in a dream. *What had Michael done?*

Phillip kept winding around the long narrow road, watching for a turn he had to make. Soon he found the road to turn on; McPherson Road. Ella tried to make a mental note of where she was so she could take Seth back here. They turned down the gravel road and went back deep into the woods. Soon there was a driveway that shot back into the woods even more. But as they came up the driveway, a clearing appeared and there stood the loveliest house Ella had ever seen. She was glad that Phillip and Claire and not told her what to expect; this way it was a complete surprise. She got out of the car, without saying a word to Michael's parents, and walked up to the house. It was surrounded by trees, and there was a dock that went out onto a huge lake. There were birds everywhere, and probably deer in the woods. The house wasn't brand new but still smelled new, as Ella opened the door with the key Clair had given to her. She was overwhelmed with a presence of Michael in the house. There was some furniture already in the house. *He must have wanted to really surprise me,* she thought. She walked through all the rooms, and finally came into the bedroom. Michael had left a note for her. *That was odd. Why did he think to write a note?*

She opened the note and sat down on the bed to read it. Tears were welling up in her eyes so that she had to wipe them in order to read.

Dearest Ella,

I'm not good at this, but I feel I should write you a note just in case something happens to me on my job, before we get married. I know if you see this, you're without me. So I need to explain why I bought this house for us.

For some reason, ever since I saved you from drowning, I knew we were supposed to be together. I had a deep seated peace about it and couldn't shake it. So when I came to see you in the hospital, I knew that I was looking at my wife to be. I don't know how God works, exactly, but I do know He made this really clear to me; He put me there to save your life, and then He made me know we were meant to live out our lives together. That is a *rare* thing, Ella.

I'm hoping that you have come on your own somehow and that I'm not gone. I want to spend my life with you, Ella. This is the home we will have our children in. It's just big enough and I can build on if we need to. Please forgive me for stepping out like this, Ella. But I love you with all my heart and I would die for you. I would give you anything you wanted in this life. But most of all, if I'm gone and you are reading this, then you'll have a safe place to live for the rest of your life. My job is risky, Ella. And every single time I dive, there is a high risk that I may not come back. I didn't want to leave you with nothing. So I made a decision on my own and bought this house, paid mostly cash for it, and put in enough furniture for you to feel comfortable.

I love you, Ella. Please know that for the rest of your life, I will love you. I only hope that nothing has happened to me when you read this note. If it has, remember me, Ella. Remember I loved you as much as any human can love. Please take care of yourself and live a good life without me.

This is my gift to you. You are my girl, Ella. If I am gone, know I'll find a way back to you.

Yours always,
Michael

Ella sat on the bed with tears streaming down her face. She couldn't believe what she was reading. Michael had worried about something happening to him, so he bought this house to protect her. To make sure she had somewhere to live. It was so overwhelming that Ella couldn't contain her emotions. She wanted to scream his name. But his parents were in the other room, and she had to ride home with them. She stood up and took the note and put it in her purse. She looked around the room, touched the pillow where he might have slept, and walked into the living room.

Phillip went to her and hugged her. "Ella, we know this is very difficult for you. I wish there was something more we could do. I want to give you the key and the deed to the property. You can do anything you like with the house, Ella."

Ella stood there, crying; she didn't know what to do. She walked with them back to the car and rode silently back to the apartment. Before she got out of the car, she put her hand on Phillip's shoulder and smiled. "I thank you both so much for coming here this morning and allowing me to see this gift from Michael. I'm speechless, and I'm sure you understand how difficult this is for me. I adore the house! I can't believe he did this for me. How protective could he be? I'm overwhelmed, and want you to know I'm very grateful. You have no idea how much I loved Michael. How close we were. It was meant to be for us to meet. I'll never forget that he saved my life, and brought me back to good health. I owe him beyond measure. Thank you so much for this morning. I love you both."

"Ella, we enjoyed giving you this wonderful surprise, even though it was awkward at first. 'Enjoy the house and let us know if you ever need anything. Stay in touch with us and let us know how you are from time to time."

Ella went into her apartment and fell on the sofa, so overwhelmed and sad. She had so many emotions running through her that there was no way to deal with them all. She was broken, scared and lonely. She had no one in her life right now, except her mother and Seth. She had not felt this lonely for a long, long time. She decided to call Seth and talk to him. He would know what to tell her to do. She missed her father so much right now that she could die. *Why did he have to leave them so early in his life? He will miss so much of our lives.* She could always go to him and he would know exactly what she should do. She thought suddenly of Stephen. *Mother trusts him so much, and he's older than Seth, wiser. Maybe I'll just call him and see what he says.*

Ella made some hot tea, and looked up Stephen's number. She was nervous, but she knew he would be nice to her. The phone rang and Ella felt sick. She had never had so many thoughts running through her mind in her entire life. Ella finally left a message on the answering machine, telling Stephen to call her back at the apartment. She got up and stood in her living room and felt lost. *Michael, Oh Michael. I miss you so much. Why did you have to die? I hate this world! I hate everything.* Ella ran and fell on her bed, sobbing and talking out loud to an empty room. She felt so hopeless and alone. She laid there for what seemed like hours, and then suddenly there was a knock at her door. At first she didn't hear it, and then she pulled herself up and wiped her face quickly. She grabbed a kleenex and blew her nose, opening the door slowly. When she looked up she was surprised to see James standing there.

"Ella, are you ok?" James stepped into the doorway and moved closer to Ella.

"Hi, James. Please come in. I'm sorry. I'm a basket case right now, and may not be too good to be around." Ella moved away from the door and motioned James into her apartment. James sat down on the sofa and looked up at her.

"Ella, I didn't mean to come at a bad time. I guess I was afraid if I called you would say no. I just wanted to see you again. It was so good to see you at your mother's house, but not under those circumstances. I was wondering how you are?"

"It is okay, James. It's really good to see you. I'm just upset. I have just found out something that Michael did before he died, and I'm overwhelmed. I don't know what to do about it. Would you like a soda?"

Ella moved into the kitchen and James followed. He sat on the bar stool and watched Ella getting the drinks. He was sad to see her this way. "Ella, if you care to talk about it, I'm here to listen."

Ella sat at the bar and talked with James for an hour or so. She poured out her feelings and frustrations, and told James about the house. He was so interested and caring that she relaxed and stopped feeling so emotional about it all. In the end, he asked if she would show him the house. Ella was hesitant at first, but then thought *why not?* They got in the car and took the winding, scenic ride to the lake. It actually did Ella good to bring someone else back to the house. It took the eeriness away and allowed her to see the house in its entirety. She now saw a lovely home where she could live, and enjoy nature and the water. They walked outside and stood on the pier overlooking the huge lake. It was so quiet and peaceful there and Ella was amazed at how large the lake was. Michael had chosen this house wisely. It would go up in value, and it would be a place where Ella could raise her children.

James was taken aback by the love Michael had had for Ella. He'd always loved her, but was immature at the time. He'd come a long way in his life in the last year, but he knew he had a ways to go to reach where Michael was. He admired the man even though he'd not ever met him in person. He thanked him silently for saving Ella, because Ella was his first love, and he would always love her in his heart. It was tough to sit there and watch her mourning for Michael. He couldn't help but wish she loved him that way. But he learned early in his young life that you cannot make someone love you. He wouldn't push Ella for a relationship. But he would always love her from afar. *She would be the girl he loved but could not have.*

Chapter 52

Stephen had come in late and found a message from Ella. It surprised him, for she'd never called his number. He had seen Kate at lunch and was headed to her house shortly. Kate had shared with him that Lauren wanted an appointment in her office for some serious work on the issues she was having about being abused. He was glad that the counseling was going to get started, as Kate had shared some of what they'd been talking about, and it sounded pretty heavy. He was amazed she had come through it at all. He dialed Ella's number and at first it seemed like she wasn't going to answer the phone. On the last ring, she picked up and sounded like she had a bad cold.

"Ella, this is Stephen. I came in tonight and found a message from you. Are you ok, Ella?" Stephen couldn't even imagine what she had called him about. He hoped it wasn't anything serious.

"Hello, Stephen, I'm fine. I just have something to talk to you about, and hope you can advise me as to what to do. Do you have a moment to chat with me?" Ella blew her nose again and tried to sit up and not sound so pitiful.

"Yes, Ella. Of course I do. What do you need my advice on, angel?"

"Well, Stephen, I had visitors today. They were Michael's parents, and they had a big surprise for me. They informed me that they were going through Michael's papers and things and discovered that he had purchased a house for us, for when we got married. I didn't know he had made this purchase and I was shocked. They took me there, and it was mind boggling, Stephen. I know I'm running on about it, but I'm feeling a little overwhelmed." Ella stopped to catch her breath. "They gave me the keys and when I walked in I found that it was almost completely furnished. I went back into our bedroom, and there was a note on the pillow."

Stephen was speechless. How could a guy buy a house before he really knew they were getting married? To his knowledge, they hadn't even set a date yet. "So what did the note say, Ella?" He was curious to know what Michael was thinking here.

"Well, he said that he loved me, that he hoped he wasn't dead when I got the note. That his job was very risky and he didn't want to leave me with nothing, He had bought the house because he really felt like we were meant to be together. He hoped I had just come to the house because I found out about it somehow, but he went on to say that if anything happened to him, he knew I would have a wonderful place to live. I don't know, Stephen. It's all just too much for me to comprehend. Do I keep the house? Do I sell it? What do I do with this house?"

Ella was tearing up again. *I wish that Michael was here to help me, to live there with me. It would have been perfect if we were going to have a life together. But could I actually move out there and live alone there? It was sort of in a remote place I might be too far away from people.* She put her head in her hand and held the phone to her ear, crying silently so Stephen did not pick up on it.

"Ella, hold on a minute. So in the note he said the house was yours if something happened to him? And your name is on the deed?"

"Yes, Stephen. I have the deed right here in front of me. Both our names are on it. So legally I get the house because he has died."

"Oh, okay. I get it now. Well, this is very unusual, Ella. He really loved you to do this, you know? He bought a house, knowing he might die early, and he wanted to take care of you. That's commitment if I ever saw it." Stephen thought a moment before speaking.

"Ella, I think you need to go out there and sleep over night and see how you feel in the house. Take a friend with you, or your mother, and see how it feels. You may fall in love with it and want to move right in. Or you may feel like it's too far away from everything you want to do, and it wouldn't be worth it to live there."

"Well, I just feel like it was such a huge gift. It hardly seems right for me to have this house after he is gone. Should I feel that way? That was so kind and generous. Not many men would do that for a woman they weren't married to."

"I agree," said Stephen. "You need to understand that he really felt like you were going to be married. You said he had purchased a ring for you. So I guess he felt like it was a done deal. You mustn't feel guilty at all for taking this gift. He would be offended if he were alive or could see you struggling with this. Just know it's because he loved you so much." Stephen admired this guy had only met a few times at Kate's. He had really been good for Ella in her recovery stage. *It'll be hard to beat that gift,* he laughed to himself. *I hope Kate doesn't expect that from me.*

"Maybe you're right, Stephen. I want you and Mom to come out and see it. Will you do that with me?" Ella was feeling slightly better just talking with Stephen. Now it didn't seem so foolish for her to receive this gift from Michael.

"Of course I will, Ella. I would love to see the house. You tell me when, and I'll bring your mother and we will go for a nice drive to see your new house." Ella hung up and blew out a big breath of air. *Well, I guess I better get used to this idea,* she thought, halfway smiling. Out loud she spoke to Michael. "I love you, baby. No one will ever love me like you do. I'll cherish that house and take care of it like you would want me to. I thank you and will be thanking you the rest of my life, for wanting to take care of me this way."

Ella walked into her bedroom and decided to put on her pajamas and call it a day. She walked over to her bed to sit down and take off her shoes and jeans, and noticed something on her pillow. She reached over and jerked her hand back in amazement. It was her pheasant feather, lying on her pillow. She knew she had put that feather on her desk where she had always kept it and now it was on her pillow. She got up and walked into the living room and looked around. *How in the world did that feather get on my pillow?*

Suddenly she remembered the last line in Michael's note to her. "I will find a way back to you."

Ella wanted to scream his name but stopped herself. "If you are here, Michael, I'll not afraid. God put you in my life at a time when I was drowning. I will love you forever." She spoke the words to the air, hoping somehow he could hear her. A single tear fell from her eyes as she walked to the bathroom to clean her face. She would make him proud of her. She would work hard and make a good life for herself. And somehow Michael would know that she was okay.

Chapter 53

Kate was at work sitting at her desk, thinking over the last few months of her life. She had a full schedule in the afternoon but this morning was set aside for Lauren. So much had happened in her family life that she could not focus. Seth was the only one who seemed settled. He was happy at his job and doing very well, and he was determined to marry Lila. *I really do like Lila, but I've not had a chance to spend that much time around her. I guess Seth knows his own mind, and they seem to get along perfectly.* She turned and looked out the window at the cars going by. *When am I going to settle down in my own life and marry Stephen? He's waiting for me, so I don't need to drag this out much longer.*

A knock on the door brought Lauren in, smiling and carrying some flowers. She felt good about this morning, as this was going to be the first in a long line of sessions to help her rid her life of the nightmares that haunted her in the darkness. Kate was just the person to help her, and she couldn't wait to get started.

"Good morning, Kate. How are you doing this morning?" Lauren smiled big and sat down in front of Kate's desk.

"I'm doing great, Lauren. It's so good to see you again." Kate walked around her desk and hugged Lauren. She really did love her, and wanted so much to help her move forward in her life. After reading those notes that Lauren had written as a child, Kate had fallen in love with this little girl and it was so unbelievable to meet her in person as a grown woman. Kate still had to pinch herself to know that this was really happening. She and Lauren had talked on the phone a lot about each other's lives, and were bonding very quickly. Lauren had shared with her that she'd not spoken with her father or mother since she moved out of the house during her second year in college. There had always been a hole in her life

231

and the relationship between Lauren and her mother was weak or non existent. Kate felt like Lauren's mother had known about the abuse and the guilt kept her from being able to show love to Lauren. It followed a pattern that she'd seen many times over in her work.

"Kate, I'm hoping today that I can get rid of some of the anger I have in my heart, so that I can go forward in my life. Can you help me with this anger?"

"Of course I can, Lauren, now that you're willing to open up." They spent the next two hours talking about where Lauren's anger came from and how to release it. It was going to be a difficult road to forgiveness, but it was for everyone who had ever been hurt in their life.

That pretty much covered mankind, thought Kate. *We all have suffered disappointment or some form of abuse in our lives. Forgiveness is the key to living a whole and happy life, no matter what happened to Lauren.*

When they were finished talking, Kate suggested they go eat something together, which would give them time outside the office to just have fun together. She wanted so much to establish a solid long term relationship with Lauren, so that Lauren would feel like she had a family. Kate made a mental note to ask Lauren and Stuart over some night very soon, with the rest of the family there.

"Well, what a wonderful morning we've had" said Kate, smiling at Lauren, and nibbling on some crème Brule. She never ate sweets but could not turn it down this time.

"Kate, you've been so good to me," Lauren said, wanting so much not to tear up. "I can never thank you enough for what you've done for me."

"Well, I need to give you back the box of words that I found in my attic. I feel funny because I've gotten attached to that box, and now that I've found you, it really needs to be in your house, not mine!" Kate smiled and touched Lauren's hand.

"I would love to have it back, in a way. But it does hold a lot of horrible memories for me. One day soon I need to talk to Stuart about it, Kate. That's going to be scary for me, as he might just turn and walk away."

"I really doubt it, Lauren. Don't be afraid to be honest about your past. If he loves you, he will only love you more for sharing your life with him so openly. It's hard when it feels like you are revealing a family secret you were'nt allowed to tell." Kate squeezed Lauren's hand and smiled at her. Lauren knew she was right, but was still very nervous about it.

"I'm seeing him tonight, Kate. I have told him already that I would talk to him about my life. He knows there is something that has been difficult for me to deal, but he just doesn't know the immensity of it. It was hard enough to talk to you about it, but you'd already seen the notes in that box. Stuart knows nothing." Lauren felt her heart race in her chest.

"Lauren, don't feel so badly about it. It may take some time for you to be able to share the whole thing with him. Just take it slow. Don't put so much pressure on yourself, because you have plenty of time with Stuart to talk to him about your past. Just start it and see how you feel. I don't want you to get upset and go backwards in your ability to deal with the nightmares. It will bring a lot of things back up that you may have forgotten or tucked away in a corner of your mind. Don't be afraid to let it out in the open." Kate really felt sorry for Lauren, and knew her heart ached to be safe and accepted. To know that she was not dirty or guilty.

"I'll try, Kate." Lauren stood up and hugged Kate. They walked out of the café and stood for a moment in the fresh air of the day. Lauren looked at Kate and then hugged her again. "I feel close to you, Kate. You are changing my life by allowing me to be myself, and showing me that I don't have to always feel like I have to hide something."

Kate walked to her car and unlocked it. They got in and drove back to Kate's office. When they arrived, Lauren got into her car and drove home slowly, thinking about what Kate had said. *I will take things slow with Stuart, and not feel like I have to face it all in one conversation. That will make it a lot easier for me to open up to him. He has shown me that he loves me. I just need to accept it and relax. This is all so new to me to allow anyone in completely.*

Kate finished her day with her last patient and cleaned her desk off. She rested for a moment and then walked out and turned out the lights. Her secretary had already left to pick up her child, and the office was quiet. It had been a good day, a productive time with Lauren. It was difficult for Kate to see Lauren as just a client. *What an unusual thing to happen in my life*, she thought as she walked down to her car. It was dark outside and Kate felt a little uneasy as she was the last car in the lot. There was a breeze blowing and Kate pulled her coat around her as she approached her car. Suddenly in the dark she saw a figure move and come closer to her. She stopped and tried to see who it was.

"Hello? Can I help you?" Kate wondered if it was one of her clients who were trying to catch her before she went home.

"Don't be afraid," a man's voice said. "I'm not going to hurt you. I just want to talk to you about something."

Kate almost panicked, but tried to sound calm. "How can I help you, sir?" she backed up a little and tried to see who he was. He came closer to her and stopped, with both hands in the pockets of his coat. He had a hat on and she could not see his face in the darkness.

"I need to talk to you for a minute. Can we walk over to the light here in the parking lot?"

That made Kate feel some better, but she was still nervous about being alone out here in the dark with a strange man. She headed over to the light, watching him all the time she was walking. She stopped and turned to face him, keeping her distance, but didn't recognize his face at all.

"Who are you? What do you want with me?"

"Relax. I don't mean to scare you. I just didn't want to come up in your office because I didn't want anyone to see me. I need to talk to you about Lauren. She is my daughter. I know she is seeing you. I need to ask you something. How can I ever get her to forgive me for what I've done?"

The man fell to his knees and began sobbing. Kate did not know what to do. She was so shocked that she could hardly move. Even with all her training she had never encountered this before.

"Are you saying you are Lauren's father?" Is that what you are saying?"

Kate moved closer to him and waited to hear what he was going to say. He was crying so hard that it was difficult to understand what he was saying. He suddenly stood up and wiped his face with his sleeve

"I'm saying exactly that. I know I've hurt her and that I'm a sick man. How do I get her to forgive me? How do I live with what I've done?"

Just as Kate was about to answer him, he turned and ran. Because it was so dark in the rest of the parking lot, Kate couldn't see where he went. She stood there shaking, not knowing whether to stay or get in her car and get home as fast as she could. *How did he know Lauren was coming to her? Had he been following Lauren for a while?* Kate decided to head to her car and pulled out her cell phone. She dialed Stephen's number and when he picked up she was talking so fast that he could hardly understand her.

"Hold on, Kate. Slow down. Now tell me again what has happened." Stephen was trying to hear her and get what she was saying. Something about a man that approached her in the parking lot in the dark.

"Stephen, you won't believe what just happened! I guess it's not all that strange, now that I think about it. But it was certainly unexpected. I was walking to my car and a man approached me in the darkness. He said not to be afraid, that he wouldn't hurt me. Then he asked me to move under the light pole in the parking lot where we could see each other better. I didn't know him, but he began to talk, asking me how he could get Lauren to forgive him. He started crying very hard and fell to his knees. I was about to ask him more questions when he jumped up and ran off."

Kate took a breath and wiped the sweat from her face. She was nervous and wanted to get home as quickly as she could. She got into her car and drove down the street, watching to make sure she didn't see him following her.

"Kate, get home and I'll meet you there. Are you safe, now?" Stephen was worried that he might follow her home.

"Yes, I think so. I really don't think he would hurt me, Stephen. But then, he was very abusive to Lauren. I don't need to take any chances. I'll be there in five minutes. You can talk to me on your cell while until I get home." Kate hung up and he called her back on his cell as he was starting his car. *I guess we havn't really read the last words in that box, yet,* thought Kate as she pulled up into her driveway.

Chapter 54

Stephen was waiting for Kate when she pulled into her driveway. The only thing on his mind was the thought that this man might have followed Kate home. He obviously was following Lauren.

"Hey Katie. I wanted to be sure and get here before you did, just in case he was around here somewhere. I don't want to overreact but this could be serious. We know he is not a stable man, and I didn't want your life at risk." Stephen hugged her and they both went into the house. Kate was noticeably upset.

"Stephen, you can't imagine how I felt when someone came out of the darkness and started talking to me. After I knew who he was I did relax a little, but then, I didn't have any idea if her father is stable or dangerous. She really hadn't said too much about him yet. I could tell he was broken, Stephen, but I wasn't about to help him in the middle of that parking lot, alone." Kate sat down at the kitchen table and then thought about making some coffee.

"Sit down, Stephen, let's have some coffee. I don't know whether to call Lauren or not. This could set her back if she hasn't seen him in all these years. People who have been abused carry a lot of misplaced guilt and I wouldn't want her to feel so sorry for him that she felt like it might be her fault." Kate poured the coffee noticing that she was handing Sam's old cup to Stephen. Somehow he was still around in her world.

"I agree, totally, Kate. I definitely think you did the right thing by not trying to help him while you are alone. You aren't normally the last person out of your office building. I'm glad that he ran away and you didn't have to talk to him long." Stephen took a sip of coffee and brushed her hair away from her face.

"You've been through a lot, lady. I know you want to help Lauren, but we can't put your life at risk."

"I don't *think* my life is at risk, Stephen, but I know I can't be certain about that. This case is so complicated and I'm dealing with so much emotion that it's difficult to always put things into perspective. I'll have to really think about telling Lauren about this. I sure hope he isn't stalking her house. That makes me think I might need to talk to her about it." Kate sipped her coffee and looked at Stephen. She was thankful, again, that he was in her life..

Changing the subject for a moment, she got up and walked to the sink, turned around and said something he had wanted to hear for a while. "Baby, I think I'm ready to marry you." Kate had a funny look on her face when Stephen looked up at her. Her eyes looked wet like she was about to cry, but she had a tiny smile running across her lips.

He stood up and came to her and held her close. He whispered into her ear, "Katie, my sweet Katie. I didn't think I would ever hear those words. You may be upset tonight. I want you to be sure you mean it." He pulled away from her and tilted her face upward so he could see her eyes.

"Are you sure that you are ready for this?" He didn't smile, but looked intently into her eyes.

"I want you in my life, Kate. I have since the first time you walked into this house. You had me at hello. But I want you to make sure you are not reacting to this event tonight. I know you are worn out, and you've had a long day. Don't feel like you have to say this now, if you're not totally ready."

Stephen was always careful about pushing her. He was so gentle. But for some reason, tonight, Kate was dead sure she was ready. Something just changed in her that very instant that she stood at the sink, and she knew in her heart that is was time. She wanted to lie next to Stephen, to be his wife, and to have him with her all the time. Not just when there was a crisis in her family. A smile flashed across her face. *There seems to be a lot of crisis in my life lately.*

"It's never going to be the right time. And our lives are passing us by every moment. I ran across a poem today at work out of a book that I had read, and it always touched me, especially when Sam was so ill. She pulled the poem out of her purse and handed it to Stephen.

Our lives are on a journey
And we may not pass this way again.
So hold on to the moment,
And do all that you can.
For though grace is sufficient for the day
Moments, like eagles, fly away.

Stephen read the poem and bent down and kissed her mouth. He loved her right at this moment more than breathing. They wrapped their arms around each other and just held each other close for what seemed like an eternity. When they let go and stepped back away from each other, Kate felt like she had moved into a realm of closeness that she hadn't experienced in many years. She smiled at Stephen and they walked into the hearth room and sat down. Kate got up and lit the fire and sat back down, snuggling into Stephen on the sofa. He smelled so wonderful and was always so warm. The night seemed to last forever, watching the flames of the fire, and letting their thoughts drift. For the first time in a long time, probably since Sam's death, Kate had a deep peace in her heart that everything was going to be fine in her life.

Stephen looked at Kate and wondered if she had made a decision about Laura and her father. "So Kate. What have you decided about telling Laura you had an encounter with her father?"

"I guess I have to tell her, Stephen; I would want to know if I were her. I just hope it doesn't not bring up feelings she has not faced in a long time. I have to take that chance, though, because she needs to forgive him somehow so she can heal herself."

The fire was burning low and the room had flickering lights around the ceiling and walls. Kate leaned her head on Stephen's shoulder and let her mind drift. She was tired. *Maybe it's time to think about my own life instead of someone else's.*

She was suddenly ravished and asked Stephen if he wanted to grab a bite to eat. He agreed and they jumped up and got in the car and drove down to a corner café two streets over. It was quiet and they grabbed a table in the back and sat down. She looked across the table and it hit her that she was totally comfortable with the thought that she would spend the rest of her life with this man. It was so good to have finally reached this place where she knew she had completely dealt with Sam's death. No more feelings of guilt for this love she felt for Stephen. At last she could let go of any reservations she kept inside and just enjoy their life together.

Chapter 55

It had been a long day for Stuart, but he wanted this time with Lauren. She had promised him that she would open up to him, and it was long past time for him to know what was eating her alive. He stopped by his apartment and cleaned up, checked his mail, fed his dog, and took him out for a very short walk. He stood in the mirror in the hallway looking at his reflection, preparing himself for what she might say. He turned and eyed the photos of Laura and himself sitting in the park. There were many pictures of her in his house, and he had to admit, this woman had taken his heart several years ago. He smiled and walked out the door to meet Laura at her house. He had loved her from afar, knowing that he was looking at her through a glass that had many colors in it. He had grown to love her laughter, her intelligence, her love of books, and her beautiful spirit. But there was a side to her, a dark side that came out at the oddest of times, and it had often put a chasm between them. He had learned early on not to press her about that darkness, but it didn't stop his wondering. She was so beautiful in a natural way. She could wake up in the morning and not do a thing to herself, yet, when she did add any makeup, it was enough to take your breath away. She had no idea of her beauty; in fact she said she hated herself. She never looked in mirrors, and did not enjoy shopping for clothes. She dressed very tailored and didn't want to call attention to herself. Actually, if he thought about it, it was a miracle that they'd lasted as long as they had.

He reached Lauren's house early and he just sat in the driveway. He didn't want to go in without her being there. She had given him a key, but he chose not to use it tonight. He wanted to earn her complete trust, and not do anything that would make her doubt his motives. This was the woman he wanted to spend his entire life with; sitting on a porch watching the children play, and cooking out with neighbors. This was it for him, but they sure needed to get past this issue she had inside. He was preparing himself for the worst thing he could think of, so that when she shared it with him, his face would not make any expression that would offend her.

Lauren was coming home from work, thinking about what she would tell Stuart. Her stomach was in a knot because she had only spoken this to Kate, and no one else. This had been inside of her for many years, and the idea of letting this all out was so scary to Lauren that felt like she could hardly breathe. What if he thought she was ugly or dirty? That was one of her biggest issues. She felt filthy most of the time. Only when she was with him did she feel better about herself. Alone, her thoughts really went in one direction; guilt and shame. She knew that she had to open up completely or this relationship would never work.

As she pulled up to the house she noticed Stuart was there waiting for her. Her heart jumped in her chest because she was so nervous. She got out of her car and motioned for him to come in. She laid her purse on the table and turned around when she heard Stuart coming through the door. He walked in and hugged her.

"Hey babe. It's so good to see you tonight. I've been thinking about you all day long. How was your day?"

Lauren smiled. "The day seemed to go slow and drag on and on, because I was waiting for this night to get here. I've wanted to talk to you and open up and now that the time is here, I'm a nervous wreck."

Lauren poured a small glass of wine for them both and pulled some chips out, put it on a tray and walked into the living room where Stuart was sitting.

"Lauren, I want to put you at ease. I won't change the way I feel about you, no matter what you tell me. Do you understand that?"

"Well you haven't heard what I have to say yet, and it might change everything."

"I want you to just start to tell me what it is, and take it slow. I assure you, I'm not afraid of what you are going to say." Stuart touched her hand and she began to talk.

"My family had a secret and went to all costs to keep it hidden. My brother and I were abused by our father; my earliest memories are at the age of four years old, but it lasted until I was about sixteen. My mother was working as a nurse in the evenings, and this gave him an opportunity to be alone with us and threaten us. He came into our bedrooms and sometimes put a black cross over the door. Apparently it made him feel like it kept God away. However, I was laying there praying to God to save me." Lauren paused for a minute and took a sip of wine, thinking of the irony of that one thing.

"Baby, I had no idea that you had to go through such a horrendous childhood! Did your mother not know this was going on?" Stuart was feeling sick in his gut. This beautiful woman had survived a living hell and somehow was able to function without anyone ever realizing what she was keeping inside her heart.

"My daily routines were controlled and I wasn't allowed to have a friend over often. When they did come, I felt so safe. I went to the attic as often as I could, to write notes and put them in my box. That was my own private world, where I could write what had happened to me and how I felt about it. I have other diaries that I kept, but no one has ever read them. I saved a few of my favorite things and put them in the box. I never dreamed anyone would ever read those notes. Not one person in my family or extended family ever asked me what was wrong, when they saw me sick or hurting. It seemed like they just turned their head and pretended nothing had happened. I think my father threatened all of us so he could have his way with me. My brother covered for me and cried in his room at night, because he saw something one time. It never left his mind,"

Lauren got up and walked over to the window and looked out at the street. "I used to wonder if I would ever have a normal life. I looked at other families and wondered what went on inside the walls of their house. Did other kids have to hide secrets? Were they threatened like I was? I felt like I was going to suffocate. I could hear him coming because the floor would creak. I would tense up and cry. I was told if I cried I would lose points and if I lost enough points he would kill me. The odd thing is he bought me whatever I wanted so I would keep quiet."

Stuart wanted to do something horrible to this man. It was more than he could stand and he got up and walked to the window to put his arms around Lauren.

"Stuart, my brother Jake was my best friend. We trusted each other because we had no one else to turn to. He wasn't abused as much as me, but it ate him alive. He wanted to tell someone, but he was threatened by my father so he was afraid to speak about it. He ended up taking his own life. I lost my sweet brother because of what my father did. At the funeral, my father fell apart. He knelt by the casket and cried like a man cries, deep and from down inside his body. I had never heard my father cry and it sort of made me feel good inside. I wanted him to hurt. It took me years to get over Jake being gone. If I think of him now, I will cry. His death was a waste, Stuart. He was so talented and had such a good heart. He was like a child prodigy. I feel sick inside because I was too afraid to speak up about this abuse. Even when I was sixteen, I was too scared to tell *anyone*. It's crazy what this does to your mind. I was around so many people at school and other family members when we got together with them, but I never felt like I could let anyone in on this secret. Oddly, they were probably looking back at me, hiding the knowledge of what they thought was happening behind their crooked smiles."

Laura sat back down on the sofa and drank a little more wine. She took a deep sigh and looked at Stuart. "Do you feel like I'm too used up for you?" She began to cry and went to get a tissue. Stuart followed her and wrapped his arms around her.

"Angel, don't say that. You are perfect in my eyes. I love you so much and am so glad you have confided in me. I'm here for you and will remain in your life as long as you want me to. I would like to spend the rest of my life with you, Lauren." Stuart pulled her close to him and kissed her softly. She allowed herself to be pulled in, and relaxed for a moment. She was so tired of feeling like she didn't fit in, like she was odd in a way that people couldn't see. He made her feel safe. For the first time in her life she'd a man in her life that made her feel safe.

Stuart backed away for a moment and said, "Lauren, put your coat on. Let's go for a short walk in the brisk night air. We can talk on our way. I know a wonderful bakery that is open late. Are you up for this? I think it would be good for you to get out for a minute, don't you think?" Lauren smiled and nodded. Maybe the cold air would do her good. She grabbed her coat and neck scarf and they went out the door. Stuart held her close as the walked and talked to her about his life and childhood. He had good memories of playing with his brothers but his father had a bad temper. They laughed and when they got to the bakery, Stuart ordered donuts and coffees. They sat down and ate a couple of doughnuts, and Lauren felt a little lighter in her spirit. This was going better than she had feared and that alone made her relax some. It was fun being out at night with all the signs lit up and cars driving by. It felt like Christmas was in the air and it was only the beginning of November. Winter was coming early this year for Martin City.

The walk home was wonderful and refreshing. Lauren raced Stuart to the house and ran about a block. Of course Stuart beat her, but he allowed her to win at the last minute. They were laughing when they got back inside, and they realized they had not eaten any dinner. For some reason, neither of them cared. Lauren walked up to Stephen and took his coat. She took hers off and folded them both on the chair going into the living room. She lit the fireplace and the room suddenly felt warm and cozy. The two sat close in the sofa, sharing memories of their past. Laura knew she had much to tell him but there was plenty of time now. They had crossed over a big gap that had separated them for a year now.

The phone rang and Lauren ran to get it. "Hello?" Lauren wondered who was calling this time of night.

"Lauren, it's Kate. I apologize for calling you this late, but I was wondering if you and Stuart would come over tomorrow night and have dinner with all the family?"

"Of course we will! Hold on and let me ask Stuart if he is free."

Lauren put her hand over the phone and whispered to Stuart about the invitation to dinner. He nodded agreement and winked at her.

"We're on for tomorrow night. And you would be proud of me tonight. Stuart and I have had the greatest conversation. I'll catch you up on it later."

"Lauren, this sounds promising; like you may have made huge steps with Stuart. I knew you could do it, Lauren. You've taken the first steps; now don't be afraid to go farther. I look forward to seeing you both around 6:30 tomorrow night." Kate smiled and looked at Stephen. He raised his eyebrow, knowing that he and Kate were thinking about the same thing. She was going to have to tell Lauren about her father showing up. And Kate was still struggling with exactly how to do that without making the house of cards fall down.

Chapter 56

Stephen had left late and Kate was tired. She closed up the house and turned most of the lights off. In her room she turned down her bed and looked at the box by her nightstand. Tomorrow night she was going to give it to Lauren. She walked over and put her hand on the lid and lifted it one more time. She could smell something every time she opened the box; *years of sorrow*, thought Kate. *That is what sorrow smells like.* She took the letters out and scanned through them, noticing the change of handwriting as Lauren grew older. She would never forget this box of words, for it had changed her life forever. She'd read about this child who suffered horrendous abuse and had been forced to keep it a secret until she could leave home, and this caused a love to form in her heart that she now felt for Lauren.

I hope that bringing her here to the house, and surrounding her with my family, will start a feeling in her of wholeness and acceptance. I want to meet Stuart and see what he is like. A brave man to take on all of this, but he's also getting a lovely, intelligent woman if he does choose to marry her. Kate closed the box and sat down on the bed, taking her shoes off and laid back on the pillows with her head against the headboard. She thought about the year that had past and what all she had gone through herself. It had been an exhausting year and it was coming to a close soon. Things that her family had suffered could have taken them all down, but somehow they managed to pull through with their faith intact. The thought of Ella drowning to this day caused Kate to feel sick. Yet Seth, with his strong character and watchful eye, had taken good care of Ella and her since Sam had died. Now he had his own love with Lila, and it looked like they were going to be married in December. Her house would be full again, with children and laughter.

As Kate closed her eyes, she thought of how difficult life is and how much suffering people go through to be formed into who they were meant to be. *It is amazing that any of us survive our parents. We somehow grow up and then we go on to be parents ourselves. I hope my children can look back and remember good times with me. I pray they felt loved and secure. I'm so sorry that Sam died early in his life, because he has missed so much already in these last two years.* It was actually closing in on three years since he died and that made Kate very sad. She got up one more time and looked at his photo hanging in the hallway; he was such a handsome man. So much had happened in her life since he died, that she felt a little estranged from him. *I guess that is normal,* she thought. *Life goes on.*

She hoped, as she fell asleep, that life would go on for Lauren. She laid her hand on the box and fell fast asleep.

Chapter 57

Seth walked in the door with Lila, and whistled. Kate was cooking and heard him coming. She smiled to herself, because he was so much like his father. "I'm in here," she yelled. Seth walked in and hugged his mother. She looked so happy and alive.

"Hey Mom! How are you doing?' Seth hadn't seen her in a while and had been so busy he hadn't called much. "It sure does smell good."

"Oh stop. I've missed you so much, Seth." Kate hugged him and took Lila's hand.

"You two look so good to me. I've missed you both and want to hear all about your wedding plans. I'll be out in a minute and we can chat. Seth, make sure there are chairs for everyone around the table."

Stephen came in and helped Kate with the meal. Ella showed up alone and helped set the table. She loved seeing Seth and they did their usual arguing over how things should be. Lila was laughing at the two of them, enjoying a little sibling rivalry.

"Hey Ella! I want to see your new house. I heard it's lovely and right on a lake." Seth said with a wink to Lila.

"Wow." Lila smiled and nodded to Ella. "Wish I could've a man who just went out and bought a house for me!"

Everyone laughed and Kate yelled that dinner was ready. Lauren and Stuart had come in and it seemed like they all were hungry tonight. After everyone was sitting down, Kate asked Stephen to bless the food, and they all held hands for the blessing. While Stephen was praying, Kate looked up and smiled warmly at all the family holding hands. She so wanted Lauren to feel a part. She silently asked God to pull her in so she could feel the closeness that Kate shared with her children. The house was filled with conversation going in all directions, and that was one of the things Kate loved when they all got together. There was no topic left untouched.

"Stephen, let's bring in the dessert, and then we can go into the hearth room and relax." Kate ran in to the kitchen and brought out cookies and wonderful ice cream she had found at the corner Ice Cream Parlor. Everyone was full and happy when they left the table, including Lauren. She was overwhelmed to be included in such a loving family. Someday she wanted a family of her own to bring to Kate's table. She looked over at Kate before they left the table and Kate squeezed her hand. An understanding passed between them that said "forever". Then the moment passed and everyone went into the hearth room.

Kate walked back to her bedroom and picked up the box by her bedside. She was nervous, but knew this had to take place. *Lauren probably is ready for this box to be back in her life*, Kate thought. She leaned down and kissed the top of the box and walked back into the hearth room. Lauren and Stuart were standing by the fireplace laughing at Seth. Kate walked up to Lauren and whispered in her ear. "Hey, Lauren, let's go into the living room so I can talk to you for a moment."

Lauren saw the box in Kate's arms and walked into the living room with a feeling of sadness coming over her. She shook it off and sat down with Kate on the sofa.

"Lauren," Kate started out slowly, "I want you to know first of all that this box caused a change in my life. It drew me in and I was haunted by who you were and where you were. I couldn't stop thinking about your suffering and how you survived it all. I've done enough counseling in my years as a psychiatrist that I knew it was abuse. I didn't have to know the details to determine that. It broke my heart, Lauren. But I wanted to find out more about you and be sure you were okay, because I had grown to love you." Lauren held Kate's hand and wiped tears from her eyes.

"Kate, you've been so good to me; so sweet and loving. My own mother was not this kind to me. She was cold and withdrawn, and I see now that she was probably full of guilt and maybe even jealousy. They slept in separate bedrooms for years and she felt lonely, I'm certain now. I just don't know why she didn't save me. I'll never know that because we don't communicate at all." Lauren paused and cleared her throat.

"I want to thank you, Kate, for all you've done for me, and as I say that I realize we're not through with my counseling just yet. I understand there's a lot of work to do before I stop having nightmares and get to the point where these memories don't control my moods or my life."

Kate wiped her eyes and hugged Lauren. "I've something to tell you, Lauren, and it may upset you. The other night when I left work, it was late and I was the last one to leave the building. Before I got to my car, I saw a shadow coming towards me and it was a man with a long coat on and a hat. I couldn't make out who he was, and I thought it might be a client wanting to talk to me about something."

"He spoke quickly and said he wasn't going to hurt me. He asked me to come over to the one light pole in the parking lot, and I could see him clearer but didn't recognize him. He told me then that he was your father."

Lauren gasped and tried to stand up. She forgot that she had the box in her lap and nearly dropped it on the floor. "Oh Kate, what the heck was he doing in your parking lot? That gives me the creeps. Was he following me? What did he say?" She was shaking and didn't know what to think.

Kate touched her arm and smiled. "Calm down angel. He said that he wanted to know how he could ever get you to forgive him. He fell to his knees crying and sobbing loudly, and then suddenly he got up and ran. I was afraid to go after him because I was alone and saw how upset he was." Kate looked at Lauren intently and wiped her face with a tissue.

"I didn't think he was very stable, Lauren. I called Stephen and he met me at my house, because I didn't know if he had followed me home or not."

Lauren was speechless; she didn't know how to respond. *How in heaven's name did her father find out about Kate? How did he know she went to see Kate?* Her head was spinning with questions and she was aware that Kate didn't have the answers to them.

"Kate, what do we do? What am I supposed to think?"

"I don't know, yet, Lauren. He was noticeably upset and frantic. I don't know what he is going to do now, but I do know he was clearly aware of how he had hurt you. He was screaming for a way to get you to forgive him. I just wanted you to know what he said. Please don't worry, as I'm sure he just wants forgiveness. He didn't seem to want to hurt me, or you, for that matter."

Lauren thought about it for a minute and shook her head. She just couldn't believe he had shown up like that and in the state of mind he was in.

"I never expected him to show up in my life in this way. I don't want to have anything to do with him ever. I guess I hate him for what he did, Kate. That's understandable isn't it? I hate him for what he did to me and to my brother."

"That is normal for you to feel that way, Lauren. But I want you to know that at some point in your life you do need to forgive him. That doesn't take away from the fact that he did hurt you badly and ruin your childhood. All that is real and you have a right to your feelings about it all. But if you can forgive him, it may help you to let go of some of the nightmares and memories that are plaguing you now."

"I'll try, Kate. Someday I'll try. Right now I want to hear what you have to say about the box, okay? I want to tell you that I'm am grateful it was you who found this. I would have always wondered where it ended up, you know? It carries so many memories for me; I hope it's not childish of me to feel this way about a box."

Kate held her hand and laughed. "No, Lauren. It's definitely not childish, it's perfectly normal. That's your childhood in that box. You can share that with Stuart if you choose to marry him. He needs to know what you've been through. Someday you may show it to your children when they get old enough. It would be a powerful way of teaching them strength."

The two women hugged and Kate reassured Lauren that she was officially part of her family now. "I want you to bring Stuart over here anytime you would like, and we'll have more dinners together. You know that Lila and Seth are planning a wedding for December. I'll want you to be a part of that, Lauren. I only hope this makes you happy, and that you're beginning to feel a part of this family."

Lauren hugged Kate and teared up. "Oh yes, Kate. You've been so good to me. I wish I had had a mother like you when I was younger. I'll let you adopt me into your family officially, and I'll try to be a good daughter to you."

The two women hugged and went back into the hearth room with the rest of the family. Lauren walked up to Stuart and whispered that she was ready to leave. They got their coats, thanked Kate for a wonderful evening, and hugged the rest of the family. They left and drove back to Lauren's house slowly, talking about the evening. Lauren saved the part about her father showing up, until they arrived at her house.

"I need to run something by you, Stu. Kate shared something with me tonight that has really upset me." Lauren picked up the box and took it inside. She set it down on the table and told Stuart that she wanted him to put it in the attic before he left tonight.

"My father showed up at Kate's office building two nights ago; he scared her to death. He came out of the darkness in the parking lot and wanted to ask her about how he could get me to forgive him. It was crazy! I'm so upset inside about it. He was following me, Stu. He had to follow me to know I even went to Kate." Lauren was shaking again. It really scared her to think her father was sneaking around her house or following her in his car.

"I can stay tonight if it would make you feel better. I would need to go and let my dog out and come back here. Why don't I do that? If it would make you feel better, I can sleep here on the sofa so that you feel safe."

Lauren kissed his cheek and agreed to the plan. Stuart left and went to his house to let his dog out. He decided to just bring the dog back with him so he didn't have to worry about him. When he arrived back at Lauren's house, she had locked up the house tighter than a drum for fear that her father was watching. Stuart took the leash off and his dog ran around the house smelling everything. He was excited to be in a new place and wanted to check out every room in the house. Lauren reminded Stuart to place the box upstairs so he pulled down the attic stairs and ran the box up the stairs into the small attic. He bent over and found a small alcove in the attic and laid the box down. There was an old blanket there and he covered the box and walked back down the stairs.

"Now, angel, the box is safely up in your attic so you have nothing to worry about. I'm here to protect you and we have my trusty dog to bark if someone should come around." Lauren laughed and felt so much better having Stuart with her. They turned on the television and watched some comedy until they were both tired. Lauren kissed Stuart and walked back into her bedroom and closed the door. She got ready for bed, and went back out to tell him goodnight and found Stuart laying flat on his back sound asleep on the sofa, covered up with a throw. The dog was lying beside the sofa snoring. Lauren made sure the door was dead bolted and went to bed. She lay there thinking about her father, and wondered what he looked like now. What he would say to her if he saw her. And how she could ever wrap her mind around forgiving him for what he had done to her.

Her sleep was broken at first and she tossed and turned. She felt warmed by Stuart's love, and shattered by the thought of her father reappearing in her life again. The moon moved behind a cloud and her room darkened a little, but Lauren didn't notice, for she finally allowed sleep to come.

In the night Stuart's dog was awakened by a slight noise. He got up and walked around the living room, listening. He growled low but didn't see anything unusual. He heard a noise and sat still for a short while looking around, and then he lay down and fell back asleep.

Chapter 58

In the night, when no one was watching, there was a visitor climbing a brick wall of a house in Martin City. He was dressed in black and had a hood over his head to hide his face. He pried open the upstairs window and dropped the crowbar to the ground. He stepped through the window and was inside only a few minutes, and then left the same way he came in. He had a difficult time putting the screen back in the window, so a corner of it was left bent. He hurried down the side of the house on a rope and disappeared into the night.

Lauren awoke feeling refreshed and pulled a robe on, as she walked out of her room. Stuart was stretched out on her sofa, with his feet hanging off in two different directions. His dog was lying on its side under the coffee table, sound asleep. Laura smiled and went into the kitchen to make some coffee and walked outside to get the morning paper. It was still a little hazy as the sun was making its way up the horizon, and it looked like it was going to be a beautiful cold winter day. The air was crisp and it almost smelled like snow, even though it was too early for those flakes to make their way through the atmosphere. She breathed in the cold, fresh air and walked back into the house. Stuart had gotten off the sofa and was stretching as she came into the kitchen.

"Goodmorning baby. How did you sleep?"

"Oh, I tossed and turned for a while, but slept pretty well. How about you?" Lauren poured two cups of coffee and sat down at the table with Stuart.

"I was knocked out, Lauren. For some reason, I was tired last night. I guess partially because of the emotion of our evening. I'm glad I stayed last night, as I would've worried about you and not slept at all." Stephen took a long drink of hot coffee and smiled at her. He would like to wake up every morning and look at her face, but he reminded himself that they had a ways to go before she would agree to marriage.

"Well, I'd better get in the shower and head to the library. I need to call Kate today and thank her for such a wonderful evening. It really sealed my relationship with her and her family. I'll never forget our talk and how much she means to me. She has given me a chance to have a normal, healthy life, and not feel alone." Lauren picked her cup up and put it in the sink.

"Stuart, can you imagine how freeing this is to me? That I can talk to you about my abuse and not cringe? I mean, it's uncomfortable for me, but nothing I can't bear."

"Baby, I've known you had a wall up around yourself for quite some time now. I can see the difference in your face even now. I'm so thankful you can talk about it and work through it with Kate. There's no telling what a difference it's is going to make in your life and ultimately in ours." Stuart hugged her, grabbed his dog, and said a quick goodbye so she could get ready for work.

Lauren stood in the kitchen watching him pull out of the driveway. She was a lucky woman to have him in her life. She hurried to the bedroom, cut the television on and got into the shower. The news was on, but she failed to hear about a man who was found lying in the ocean face down, floating a distance away from the bridge. His body had been brought in by the early morning tide and his name had not yet been released. She dressed and grabbed a breakfast bar and hurried out the door, excited about her next visit with Kate. She was going to work on things more aggressively and get this behind her, because she was ready now more than ever to have a good life.

Kate was up early, watching the news, and reading the morning paper. She was surprised to hear about a man being found in the ocean. It brought back memories of when she found Alison and she shuddered. She felt sorry for the family of this man, but the name hadn't been released yet, so she didn't know who he was. She got dressed and drove to her office, listening to her favorite music on the radio. Suddenly there was a news break and it caught her attention as they were about to release the name of the man found in the water early this morning. *His identification had been verified and his wife had been contacted. The name that was released was Fred Andrews. He was survived by his wife Sarah and a daughter, whose name has not been released, pending notification.*

Kate sat there in total shock. *This is incredible,* she thought. *Lauren doesn't know yet, and she is probably at work now. I can't allow her to find this out without someone there to help her work through it.* Kate called her office and told her secretary that she wouldn't be in for a couple of hours. Laura was wondering how she would rearrange Kate's schedule, but understood by her voice that it was something pretty important. Kate hung up and headed to the library. She phoned Stephen on the way and informed him of what she had heard on the news.

"Stephen, I'm on my way now to the library, and I'll keep you posted on Lauren. I hope this doesn't send her over an edge. I can't believe this has cropped up, and I know it's going to hit her blind sided."

"Take your time, Kate. Morning traffic can be horrendous. I'm here if you need me."

She hung up the phone and noticed that her hands were shaking. She needed to calm down so that Lauren didn't pick up her mood. She pulled into the library parking lot, checked her face in the mirror, put a smile on her face, and walked into the library foyer. She immediately saw Lauren working at the counter, checking books in and talking to another employee. She walked up slowly and Lauren looked up. Somehow, Lauren knew in her gut that something was wrong, even though Kate was smiling.

"Hi Lauren. How are you this morning?" Kate smiled and touched her arm. "I just need to talk to you for a moment. Do you have time?"

"Hey Kate. Sure I have time." She handed her work over to the other employee, and came around the counter. The two of them moved to the back corner of the library and sat down.

"So Kate, what do you need to see me about this morning? I hope nothing is wrong?"

Kate swallowed and took a deep breath. How could she say this without just blurting it out? "Well Lauren, I guess you didn't hear the news this morning. I wanted to be here when you found out, so that you didn't get too upset."

Lauren suddenly got sweaty and her stomach was churning. "What are you talking about, Kate? It's not Stuart, is it?"

"Oh no Lauren! Stuart's fine I'm sure. You know I shared with you that your father came to see me yesterday, right? Well, his body was found in the ocean this morning. It was on the morning news, and at first they didn't release his name. But just a little later there was a news flash and they released his name as Fred Andrews."

Laura gasped. She felt like she was going to throw up. Her emotions were running rampant and she went from feeling relieved to something close to panic. He had been so cruel to her and she had taken things that would have killed most people. But deep inside of her, she had wanted him to love her and be her father. "Oh Kate. No! How did this happen? Do they think it was suicide? Did they say that on the news?"

"No, actually they didn't confirm that it was suicide, although they are leaning that way. I'm sure there will be an investigation. He was found near the bridge. I don't know if he jumped off or if the current took him in that direction. They are trying to contact you to let you know. Can you take the day off?"

"I'll go talk to my supervisor now. Can you wait for me, Kate?" Lauren ran to the back of the library and into the office. She closed the door and sat down and talked to her boss, crying and trying so hard to keep it together. Her boss understood and told her to go. So she grabbed her purse and ran back to Kate, hugging her, and sobbing. They walked arm and arm to Lauren's car and she got in. Kate opened her car door and pulled some kleenex out of the door and gave them to Lauren. "Angel, it's going to be okay. I know you're going to have to work through so many emotions today. But it'll be alright, I promise." Kate tried to soothe her and at the same time understood well what Lauren was thinking and feeling. This was huge in Lauren's life. The man who had abused her and threatened her life for all her young life was dead. It was a freeing time but also a time of great sadness, for she would never get to have a relationship like she should have with her father. Lauren looked at Kate and halfway smiled, but it was more like a sneer. "I wonder what my mother thought, Kate? I wonder if she even thought about how this might affect me. Of course she's not going to try to contact me, I can guarantee that. She's been quiet all these years, why would she be vocal now?"

"I know you're angry, Lauren. You have every right to be. His death has freed your mother, also. So she may come out more now and want to talk to you. It'll be up to you to decide of you want to develop a relationship with her or not." Kate drove to her house and Lauren followed her. They got out and walked into the kitchen. It was beginning to feel like home to Lauren. She felt so safe there and adored Kate. *What would she do without her?*

"Lauren, I want you to relax for a minute and then we need to talk about this and how it feels to you."

The two women spent three hours going over every area of Lauren's life with her father, and all those feelings that had been stored up during the time of abuse, came pouring out. Lauren was full of anger and hatred, and then she was like a little girl wanting to be loved. Kate let her talk for hours so that she could express everything she was feeling. They talked about whether Lauren even wanted to go to the funeral or not. She was afraid to see her mother after all these years, and couldn't make up her mind just yet. At the end of their talk, Lauren got up and wiped her eyes.

"Kate, I guess I need to go home and call Stuart. There are a lot of things I need to decide and it'll take some time for me to digest all that we've talked about. You don't know what it means to me that you came to my work to tell me all of this, instead of letting me find out by the late night news, or someone walking up to me. I would've been horrified if I'd found out that way. You know how to say things so that they can be received easily. I love you for that."

Kate hugged her goodbye and told her to call if she needed anything. As weary as Kate was, she knew she needed to go back to work, so she called in and told Laura that she was on her way. Her waiting room was full and it was difficult to keep her mind on her work. . She had a moment in between patients, to call Stephen. She left him a message to come over after work, because she really needed to have some time with him. He was fast becoming a solid fixture in her life, and for that she was ever grateful.

Lauren entered her house feeling empty and full of mixed emotions; so many thoughts going through her head. She sat on her sofa just looking out the window, thinking; just letting her thought go for a moment. *Her father was gone. No more worrying about whether he would show up or not in her life. A lot of unanswered questions and many unfulfilled dreams.* Lauren knew she had to come to grips with all of this in order to have a life with Stuart. She walked to the phone and called Stuart to see if he would come over for dinner. She didn't want to be alone tonight. Stuart was becoming her soul mate, and she was close to wanting to make that permanent She loved the name of Kate's house; Waterstone Manor. But what it meant was really full of power. Holy water washing over our hearts of stone. Lauren did not want to have a heart of stone; she wanted to feel and love and be able to experience all the emotions life brought.

Stuart answered with a big smile, "Hey sweety! How are you today?" Obviously he hadn't heard the news yet this morning.

"Well, there has been a new event in my life, baby. I guess you didn't catch the news this morning, but a man was found in the ocean near the bridge."

"Really? No I haven't heard that. I'm sorry, did you know this person, Lauren? You sound upset." Stuart looked at his watch and realized she wasn't at work. That was a clue that something must have happened. He listened more attentively to her answer.

"Yes, Stuart. You might say I knew this man. He was my father."

There was dead silence on the other end of the phone. Stuart didn't know what to say. "I can't believe this! I know this is quite a shock to you, Lauren. I have a couple of ends to tie up but I can be at your house in an hour. Would that be soon enough?"

"Don't hurry. I'm fine. Just going through a lot of emotions, that's all. It just seems sometimes that my life is one drama after another. I know the last ten years have been pretty quiet as I've kept my mouth shut about my childhood. No one around me even knew I had any problems at all. Now that I've spoken to Kate and the box of words was found, I feel overwhelmed. Let's just eat in tonight so I can talk to you, okay?" Lauren hung up the phone and cried. She was tired of crying, but she couldn't hold it back. The last thing she wanted was to be alone now, but she would have to occupy her mind until Stuart got there. She had to face the fact that she basically had no family except Kate and her family. She had to put to rest the yearning for a mother, and let Kate step into that role. *I don't know if you ever stop wanting your parents to love you,* she thought. *When do you give up that hope?*

She walked into the kitchen and began preparing a dinner for Stuart. She called Kate and talked to her, letting her know she was okay and that Stuart was coming over later. Oddly, she could feel the box upstairs in the attic. It's presence in the house was definitely obvious to her. All these years she had been without it, and now it was back in her life. *Maybe we can't ever escape our past, but instead, it has to be incorporated into who we become.* She sighed and walked into her bedroom and lay across her bed.

Chapter 59

The dinner Lauren had prepared was in the oven, and the house had a wonderful aroma when Stuart walked in. He put his keys on the counter and walked into the living room. Lauren wasn't there so he went into her bedroom and found her asleep on the bed. He touched her arm and she jumped.

"Oh Stuart! You scared me to death. When did you get here?" Lauren sat up and straightened her blouse. She was disoriented because she had been dreaming about her father lying in the ocean and her heart was racing.

"Hey sweetheart. I know you're upset, and I'm glad I was able to leave a little early today. Let's get you something to drink and we can sit down and talk before dinner. Come on, girl. Get up and go sit on the sofa with me." Stuart didn't really want to hear about her father; he felt so angry at him that he could have killed him. I'm sure Kate felt the same way. It was difficult to have sympathy towards him at all.

"I'm sorry, Stuart. I want you to know that I'm okay; just shaken a little. I wasn't expecting to hear that about my father, even though we hadn't spoken in years. It's sad that a life has to end like that; he must have been riddled with guilt. In a way, I'm glad that he was, because the things he did to me were inhumane. But I wonder how he got that way inside? What made him want to do those things? I never could talk to my mother, Stuart. I never could ask her these questions. And now he's gone, so I'll never know the answers." Lauren sat back on the sofa and teared up. Stuart reached over and held her close, and whispered into her ear.

"Angel, you need to relax. Stop worrying about your father. He is at rest now and you don't have to be afraid anymore. You are safe. I won't let anything happen to you now."

Lauren relaxed a little and smiled. "Are you hungry, Stu? I have a great dinner for us." She wiped her eyes and got up. "I can have it ready in two seconds. Come on, let's eat."

"Okay, angel. I'm ready if you are." He pulled her up and they went into the kitchen and got the dinner ready and on the table. He talked about his day at work and she talked about the library. They avoided anything serious until after the meal. Lauren was relaxing a little and wanted to tell Stuart a little more about her past. She had so much to share with him and now that her father was gone, she wanted to get it all out. She had decided not to go to his funeral, because she didn't want to see her mother there. She was not ready for that reunion yet; she might not ever be. They cleared the table and washed the dishes and put them away. Stuart wanted to walk for a while in the night air again, but Lauren had another idea.

"I want to take you upstairs in the attic so we can read some of my notes that I put in the box. Will you do that with me tonight? I think it's befitting since my father just died. It's a perfect time for you to read them." Lauren looked at Stuart and knew she loved him now enough to marry him. She trusted him completely and wanted to share all of it with him. All of the ugly and the beautiful of her life.

"Sure, baby. Let's go up there right now and look through that box together. It might be good for you to do this." Stuart pulled down the stairs and lowered them to the ground. He went up first and helped her on the last step up. They had to bend down a little to get to the box, but when they got there, they sat down on a board and pulled the box out from under the blanket. Something fell out of the blanket and Lauren picked it up. At first she thought it was a note she had written that fell out of the box. But the handwriting was not hers. She looked at Stuart and raised her eyebrows. "Who could this be from?" he asked frowning.

"I have no idea who this is from. Did it fall out of the box? It's not my handwriting. I don't recognize it. It's not Kate's. It's not yours. How did it get here in my attic?" Lauren opened the note and took a deep breath in. She was shocked. The note was signed by her father. Her hands began to shake. Lauren looked at Stuart and they both looked at the window in the attic. Stuart climbed over to it and noticed that the screen wasn't all the way attached. He opened the window, which wasn't locked, and noticed the rope that was hanging from the outside of the window. Stuart looked at Lauren and frowned.

"Someone has been up here, Lauren. They obviously came in through this window." They looked at each other and sat back down on the board near the box. Lauren opened the note and read it aloud.

Lauren. This will come as a shock to you as I know you weren't expecting to ever hear from me. I've been following you for quite some time, trying to figure out how to talk to you. I approached your psychiatrist the other night and wanted to talk to her, but I was afraid. I knew you'd get very upset if you knew I was around. I didn't know what to do, Lauren. I'm riddled with guilt and I need to talk to you. You have no idea the hell I've been through in my life, knowing I hurt you so badly.

I was raised in abuse. My father abused me and my brothers all our lives. I was afraid of him. He threatened to kill us if we told anyone. I made up my mind that I would not do it to anyone else, but I was so angry that I began to take it out on your mother and then you. Something went wrong inside me, and I couldn't stop what I was doing to you. I can never make it up to you, but I do wish you could find it in your heart to forgive me. It's too late now, I know. I had to try. I'm sorry for trying to break into your life here. Forgive me. Lauren. Somehow.... And don't let what I did to you ruin your life.

I know I'll never see you again, so this is *goodbye*. You were the best daughter a father could ask for. And I ruined every single day of your childhood. *I deserve to die.* I am worthless and there is no way even God will forgive me for what I have done to you.

I am sorry. But I know sorry isn't enough. I will always love you. Goodbye, Lauren. Your Father

They climbed down the stairs and walked into the living room with the box. Lauren took the box from Stuart and put it on the coffee table. Lauren crumpled up the letter, put her head in her hands for a moment. She couldn't believe what she had just read. *So he was abused too. . . . wow. That was an eye opener if there ever was one! That explains a tiny bit why he destroyed my childhood; he never had one himself. Kate had told me that abusers usually were abused themselves. She was correct about this one.*

"I'm actually relieved he left this note, Stu. I needed to read this tonight. Somehow this will help me understand at some point why he did what he did to me. I don't know if I can ever forgive him, but at least I do know some of the reasons why. That has hounded me for years and years. Why did he do this to me? Now I can begin to see why."

Lauren frowned and turned to Stuart. "I have an idea, Stu. Let's take the box downstairs and I'll tell you what I'm thinking about." They walked outside in the back yard where there was a very large fire pit.

"Stuart, it just hit me that I don't need this box anymore. I did when I was a child, but it has no place in my life anymore. The letter from my father was the deciding factor in my getting rid of this box. I'm tired of notes that speak of the hurt and pain I went through. It's time to start a new journal of my life that is filled with joy and the good things that have happened since I left home. Lauren placed the box in the pit and told Stuart to grab a bunch of newspapers in her living room. He brought them outside and laid them around the box. Just before he lit the papers, he looked up at Lauren. "Are you sure this is what you want to do with this box, Lauren?"

"I have never been more certain about anything in my life," Lauren answered with a stronger smile than Stuart had seen in a long time.

"Okay, here goes, Lauren."

The papers lit up and it took a little bit before the box caught fire. It was old so the wood was very dry. Soon one corner of the box caught flame and Lauren stood back and watched all those childhood memories burn. It actually felt good to watch the fire burning all the notes that she had written. Maybe now she could sleep at night, and dream of things to come instead of things of the past.

She grabbed Stuart's hand and they walked toward the house. Lauren looked up at him and smiled. Suddenly she wanted to see Kate, and share what she had just done with the box and tell her about the note from her father. She was yearning to be able to go home, really go home. Now the only home she knew was with Kate. "Stuart. I need you to take me to see Kate." Her eyes were full of tears, but this time there was a joy involved instead of deep sorrow. They got into her car and drove slowly to Kate's house on Madison Avenue; the only place she wanted to call home.

On the way, she tossed the letter from her father out the window. The wind caught the note and it danced in the air, and then took off in another direction over the tree tops. Lauren breathed a sigh of relief and waved goodbye to a man she had never really known. The box of words was for a different time in her life. Not now, not with Stuart. Not ever again.

Epilogue

T he house was quiet as Kate walked through the rooms, thinking about all that had gone on in her life in the last few years, and all the secrets that this house held.... unspoken happiness and sorrow that every house holds within its walls, but in this case, a child's life hidden in a box. She never dreamed that Sam would die, or that her children would suffer so harshly from a deadly plane crash. She didn't expect to ever fall in love again after losing Sam. The box of words was both a treasure in her life and a nightmare in Lauren's. *My life has been rich, thought Kate, for I have loved a wonderful man and had two magnificent children to love. Yet, I have also gained a deeper understanding of the suffering that goes on behind all the lit up houses in the world, where the secrets are hidden behind lovely cars, beautiful clothes, and the empty laughter of children.*

Kate passed the photos on the wall in the hallway, to which she had added several of Lauren, Lila, and Stephen. Just looking at the faces, stories were spoken that somehow words could not express. She loved them all dearly and cherished their presence in her life, yet she still carried a sadness for Sam who hid one of the most precious things a person can hide; his daughter.

For just a moment, before Lauren and Stuart arrived, Kate wanted to go be with Sam beyond the grave. Her heart was so filled with questions that would never be answered in this life. *I wish just once I could have a conversation with you, Sam, to ask you why and how all this happened in your life when I wasn't looking. But I also wish I could dance one more dance with you, and hear you whisper the love words that always stayed between you and me.*

She stopped at the photo of Stephen she had added to the wall, and gazed into his eyes. He had slowly become a soul mate that she did not know could exist. He did not replace Sam in her life, but he brought a new joy to her heart.

The page he wrote in her life was crisp and new, with no shadows that kept her from seeing his heart.

A tear fell as she walked into the front of the house to wait for her new daughter. She would tell Stephen tonight that she was setting a date for their wedding. It was time.

The internet is a marvelous tool of invention that has moved man way beyond what the inventor perhaps envisioned. I was surfing health websites one day and ran up on one in particular that sounded like it would offer support for some health issues I was experiencing at the time. There are millions of people on this site searching for help. The odds of Paris and I finding each other are a million to one. And yet we did discover each other one afternoon a year and a half ago and our lives have not been the same since. It doesn't happen often, but on occasion everything comes together in a universe that God has ordained, and there is no plausible explanation for what happens. I was attracted to Paris's page on the site and decided that I might perhaps be of some help to her. She didn't say too much about her life on the site, but enough to grab my heart. This began conversation between us that was intermittent at first, but later became daily and sometimes hourly. We soon used every source of communication known to man to get to know each other better and this helped me to understand fully what she had gone through in her life. After a time, she trusted me with her story.

This year a book was laid on my heart, called The Box of Words. It came quickly like snow comes in the winter, silently but with much beauty. I knew that the book would be about a woman who had a family and they would move into an old house in which she would discover at some point a box in the attic. I also knew that the box would carry notes of a child who had been abused and that the woman would fall in love with this child. It was not until after I had decided to write the book that I discovered Paris had a box of words in her childhood. And in that box were words written down that no one would ever read. Somehow in this wonderful world we live in, and with the power of two hearts connecting across a vast ocean, I did find out what her box of words said.

So in writing this book, Paris has shared with the world her box of words. We are both amazed and will never get used to the way we met and how much love there is between us. We are alike in many ways in our creativeness, so like mother and daughter, we merge into one beating heart while I write this book with her beside me.

Nancy Veldman

Many astounding things have happened during my lifetime but none so amazing or mystical as my chance meeting with Nancy Veldman nearly two years ago. Like so many others, I was searching for answers and validation that I was going to be okay. Little did I know then that I would meet a woman who would change my life.

Gently, over time, a relationship and a bond began to stem between us, almost silently. When I finally felt comfortable and safe, I began to share my world with her. I expected her to feel and think the worst, but what I got in return was honesty, compassion, and understanding. Because of Nancy's unconditional love I am now on a journey of hope. I have restored faith; I have a life. She has given me more in two years than most have given me in a lifetime.

Being with her is as close to God as it gets. This is a journey that is connected by the vein of love I have gained. Not only a new life, but a natural mother who, though far apart, will create with me many memories and creative work. I thank God for His intervention and for giving me a second chance.

Paris Milla